GOOD INTENTIONS

GOOD
INTENTIONS

JOY FIELDING

C.2

DOUBLEDAY

New York   London   Toronto   Sydney   Auckland

All of the characters in this book are fictitious,
and any resemblance to actual persons, living or dead,
is purely coincidental.

PUBLISHED BY DOUBLEDAY
a division of Bantam Doubleday Dell Publishing Group, Inc.
666 Fifth Avenue, New York, New York 10103

DOUBLEDAY *and the portrayal of an anchor with a dolphin*
are trademarks of Doubleday, a division of
Bantam Doubleday Dell Publishing Group, Inc.

Published in Canada
by Doubleday Canada Limited,
105 Bond Street, Toronto, Ontario,
MSB 1Y3.

Library of Congress Cataloging-in-Publication Data

Fielding, Joy.
Good intentions / by Joy Fielding.—1st ed.
p. cm.
ISBN 0-385-19848-5
I. Title.
PR9199.3.F518G6 1988
813'.54—dc19

Canadian Cataloging-in-Publication Data

Fielding, Joy.
Good intentions

ISBN 0-385-19848-5

I. Title.

PS8561.I44G66 1989   C813'.54   C89-093779-6
PR9199.2.F542G66 1989

BOOK DESIGN BY CLAIRE M. NAYLON

July 1989
First Edition
BG

For Steve and Adeline

GOOD INTENTIONS

1

She knew she was in trouble the minute she saw him.

"Lynn Schuster?" he asked as she slowly opened the front door.

"Marc Cameron?" she asked in return. They both nodded. Good, Lynn thought, stepping back to let him come inside. We know who we are. "Come in," she said, guiding him toward her living room.

He carefully observed all the niceties of the first-time visitor: her home was lovely; it was nice of her to agree to see him, especially under the circumstances; he hoped he wasn't inconveniencing her too much. To which she replied: thank you; no problem; he wasn't inconveniencing her at all. Could he tell she was lying?

"Would you like a cup of coffee?" she asked, not something she had been planning to offer, but he said no, thank you, and then sat down on the green-and-white-striped chair across from the similarly colored floral-print sofa, and stared at her for several seconds without speaking.

Why was he here? Why had she agreed to see him?

"Is something wrong?" she finally asked, carefully avoiding his eyes, which were blue and serious. Seriously blue, she mused, feeling her knees go weak. Like a silly schoolgirl, she thought, and sat down on the sofa, wondering if the attraction she was feeling was mutual, or just obvious.

"I'm sorry," he said, his voice deep, his tone quizzical. "I thought I had it all worked out."

"All what worked out?" she asked, hoping suddenly that he would leave without telling her. His presence upset her in ways she was unprepared to deal with. Of all the reactions she had been preparing herself for since he had phoned and said he was coming over, she was least prepared for this one—to be physically attracted to this man! It just wouldn't do, she thought, looking just past him toward the silver-framed photograph of her with her husband and two children, which sat by the front window.

Marc Cameron was tall, as tall as the man in the photograph, and like Gary's, her husband of fourteen years, his hair was thinning a bit on top. Unlike Gary, however, Marc Cameron's hair was still quite thick, even long, at the sides, where it curved toward his chin and formed a neatly trimmed, reddish-tinged beard. But while Gary was slender, this man was big, almost bulky. He was totally unlike anyone to whom she had ever felt herself even remotely attracted. This was a temporary aberration, surely, she decided, fidgeting, an unwanted, unwarranted visceral reaction to a set of rather peculiar circumstances.

"This is awkward."

"Yes, it is."

Silence. Deep breath. Then another. The first one from him, the next from her.

"You said there were things I should know," Lynn ventured, silently cursing her innate professionalism.

"I guess that sounded pretty melodramatic."

Lynn shrugged, as if to say: What can you do? and waited for him to continue, not trusting her own voice.

"This whole thing has hit me pretty hard," he said finally. "Do you have a drink?"

It was obvious from his pronounced inflection that he wasn't referring to the coffee she had just offered. "There's some beer in the fridge," she began, about to continue when his voice stopped her.

"Beer is great. If you don't mind."

She minded but she said she didn't, and excused herself to go into the kitchen to get it for him. She hoped by doing so to place some distance between them, to use the few seconds to give her back the objectivity she would require to get herself through this conversation, but he was right behind her.

"Who's the artist?" he asked, indicating the many bright-colored sketches that were taped to the refrigerator door.

"Both my children like to draw," Lynn answered, volunteering nothing further.

"You can always separate people who have young children from those who don't by looking at their refrigerator doors." Marc Cameron smiled. "I have two boys. Twins. Jake and Teddy. They're five. They're very heavy into finger painting at the moment. My fridge is similarly covered."

"Is this about them?" Lynn asked abruptly, determining to end this visit as quickly as possible.

"What?"

"Why you're here. What you want to tell me. Does it have anything to do with our children?"

"No." He took the bottle of beer from her outstretched hand.

"Oh, sorry, did you want a glass? Gary never drank beer from a glass." She thought she saw him wince at the sound of her husband's name. "He always preferred it straight from the bottle."

"Then I'd like a glass."

Lynn smiled despite her intense desire not to, and reached into the cupboard to get him one of the tall, curved glasses she'd bought Gary one Father's Day, glasses he hadn't bothered to take with him when he left.

"You're not having one?" he asked.

"I don't like beer."

"I'm not surprised," he said. "Neither does Suzette."

Lynn tried to smile, as she had smiled effortlessly only seconds earlier, but at the sound of his wife's name, she felt her lips gather together in a series of unattractive wrinkles, as if she had just sucked on a lemon. She was trying to appear sophisticated about all this, but he wasn't making it easy.

His phone call had caught her off guard. "This is Marc Cameron," he had announced. "I'd like to come over and talk to you. I think there are some things you should know."

At first she hadn't known who he was or what he was talking about, although he obviously assumed she did. His name meant nothing, although she thought it a handsome name.

"I'm sorry," she began. "I don't know who . . ."

"Suzette's husband," he explained, and then was silent.

Standing alone in the living room of her small, three-bedroom bungalow, Lynn had tried to visualize the man, although they had never met. What exactly did he want to tell her? Experience had taught her that information others felt she should know was usually the last thing in the world she wanted to hear.

"I don't think it would be a very good idea . . ." she had told him, feeling her throat go dry and the words stick to the roof of her mouth.

"It's important."

"I don't see what . . ."

"Please," he had said, adding that it was only a fifteen-minute drive from his apartment in Palm Beach to her home in Delray Beach.

"All right," she had agreed reluctantly, knowing she was probably making a mistake. "In an hour. I'd like to get my children in bed first."

"An hour," he'd repeated. "Oh, and I don't think I'd say anything to anyone about my visit."

"Who would I tell?" she'd asked, then heard the line go dead.

She'd promptly called her lawyer at home. "Renee," she spoke clearly into the receiver, responding with only a hint of impatience to the answering machine, "this is Lynn Schuster, and I'm sorry to bother you at home but I thought this might be important. It's ten minutes after eight, and I just had a rather interesting phone call. If you're back in the next hour, give me a call. Otherwise, I'll speak to you in the morning." Then she'd folded up the reports she'd been working on, large white sheets of paper spread out across the glass top of her dining-room table like a fine linen tablecloth, except that some-one had scribbled all over this one, and stuffed them back into her already well-stuffed leather briefcase. She'd have to get up at least an hour earlier in the morning to finish them off, but she recognized that there was no point in trying to concentrate on work now. Not when, in another hour, a man who referred to himself as "Suzette's husband" would be in her home to tell her some things he thought she should know.

What things? she'd wondered then, as she was wondering now. And how else should he refer to himself if not as Suzette's husband? Wasn't that precisely who he was? At least until the divorce? Was she still not Gary's wife, after all? At least until the divorce?

It was all too confusing, although it was simple enough once you broke it down. Her husband had left her for another woman. A married woman. That woman's husband had called her on the phone approximately one hour ago and asked if he might come over; there were some things he thought she should know.

The hour between his phone call and his arrival had passed in something of a blur. Lynn recalled lingering by the tele-phone for several minutes before suddenly throwing herself into action, scurrying down the long hall to her bedroom, past the bedrooms of her son and her daughter. Seven-year-old Nicholas had already fallen asleep. Lynn had walked to the side of his bed, pulled the covers he had kicked off back up to his shoulders, gently pushed some stray yellow hairs away from his round little face, and kissed his forehead. He hadn't moved. Lynn had stood for a minute and studied her younger child, surprised to find him so still. Even in sleep, Nicholas was usu-ally one of those children who never stopped moving. Lynn found herself bending forward until her face was only inches from his lips so that she could feel the warmth of his breath and reassure herself that he was still breathing, something she hadn't done since he was an infant. He'd suddenly sighed and turned onto his side, almost hitting Lynn's nose with his curled fist. Lynn smiled, kissed him again, and left the room.

Ten-year-old Megan was sitting on her bedroom floor, completely wrapped up in the latest Nancy Drew novel, which Lynn had found strangely comforting. It provided her with a sense of continuity, something lately missing from her life. She had read Nancy Drew herself as a girl and she enjoyed the fact that she had at least *one* thing in common with her older child, who, in every other respect, resembled her father. Like Gary, his daughter was quiet and intense. She had her father's mouth and his same head for figures. (If Lynn has one apple, she'd found herself thinking as she continued down the hall to her room, and Suzette takes that apple, how many apples does Lynn have left?)

She'd reluctantly confronted her image in the mirror across from her unmade queen-size bed, and run a careless brush through her naturally curly shoulder-length brown hair. Then she'd applied a quick smudge of rose-colored lipstick across her full mouth and just a hint of blush to her pale cheeks. Despite her lifelong Florida residency, Lynn was one of those people who were incapable of tanning. She burned bright tomato red within a few minutes of exposure to the sun, unlike Gary and both their children, whose complexions were naturally golden brown. (If Lynn has one tomato and Suzette takes that tomato . . .) The sun isn't good for you anyway, she'd thought, applying a small amount of navy mascara to her eyelashes, remembering her mother's advice that mascara was all the makeup a woman really needed, and wondering why she was going to all this effort for someone she was fully prepared to hate on sight.

"Are you going out?" Megan had asked, suddenly appearing in the doorway, her subtle Southern drawl masking the fear behind the seemingly simple question.

"No, sweetheart," Lynn said to the child, who was, at five feet two, only three inches shorter than herself. "But someone's coming over here."

"Who?"

"A client," Lynn lied, and felt her cheeks flush.

"A man?" Megan pressed, her soft voice hardening, her shoulders stiffening.

"Yes," Lynn replied, trying to keep her voice steady. "He sounded pretty upset on the phone, so if he gets here before you've gone to bed, I'd appreciate it if you'd stay in your room."

"Why can't he come to your office?"

"Because . . . he just can't. Are you ready for bed?"

"Do I look ready?" Megan asked incredulously, her child's body beneath her cotton jumpsuit threatening to burst into full bloom at any moment.

"I suggest you get ready," her mother said, as pleasantly as possible.

Megan, slender, with her blond hair, tawny skin, and gold-flecked brown eyes, fixed her mother with the guilt-inducing stare she had lately turned into something of an art form. Was it Lynn's imagination or did puberty seem to be happening earlier these days?

"Are you wearing perfume?" the child asked accusingly. Then before Lynn could reply: "Are you going to change your clothes?"

Lynn looked down at the white jeans and red-striped jersey she had changed into when she got home from work. "I'm not wearing perfume," she answered steadily, "and what's wrong with what I have on?"

"It's not very businesslike," Megan said succinctly.

"It'll have to do. Have *you* changed yet?" Lynn asked pointedly.

Again the look that reduced cities to rubble. Lynn felt suddenly lost. Why had she agreed to meet this man? Wasn't it bad enough that her husband had left her for another woman? Wasn't it humiliation enough in a small town like Delray Beach that the woman he'd abandoned her for was, from all accounts, neither especially young nor particularly pretty? Did she really have to suffer through the woman's husband as well? Did the fact that their respective spouses had left them for each other mean they were, in some perverse way, related?

She'd made her bed with painstaking care—there were few things she hated more than climbing into an unmade bed—straightened up the living room, and finally tucked a strangely clingy Megan into her four-poster brass bed, completing all these tasks only moments before she heard the front doorbell ring.

"There's someone at the door," Megan called out, chillingly wide awake.

"I know, sweetheart," Lynn said as she passed her room, lowering her voice to emphasize that it was time for the child to be asleep, then proceeded to the front hall, making minor adjustments to her hair along the way and trying to maneuver her lips into a smile. Taking three quick deep breaths, she'd thrown open the front door.

"Lynn Schuster?" the man on the other side had asked.

It wasn't that peculiar, she told herself now, leading him back into her living room, that she should feel such a strong physical attraction for this man. She and Suzette (the name stuck in her throat) obviously shared the same taste in men. Was Marc Cameron a lawyer as well?

"Are you a lawyer?" she asked, resuming her position on the sofa, thinking that by being the one to ask the questions, she retained at least a semblance of control.

Marc Cameron walked to the large front window of the comfortable, predominantly green living room and stared out into the starless night. "You can almost hear the ocean," he said, more to himself than to her, then: "No, I'm a writer."

"Really? What do you write?" She bit down on her lower lip. She had sounded too curious, too interested. Now he would go into a long explanation of the sort of things he wrote and she would be powerless to stop him.

"Books," he said simply, then: "Don't ask me their titles because you won't have read them and my ego's at a low enough ebb as it is." He tried to smile but quickly abandoned the attempt. "I also write the occasional short story for various artsy New York magazines, and lots of silly articles for local publications, profiles of visiting celebrities, that sort of thing. Are you really interested?"

"Well, I . . ." She realized she was, but didn't want to say so.

"I understand you're a social worker."

Lynn nodded. "For twelve years."

"Do you enjoy it?"

"What's not to enjoy? Poverty, violence, neglect, abuse. I've got it all."

"I would think that it might get depressing as a steady diet."

"Well, to be honest"—why was she being honest?— "I'd been thinking about making a switch before all this happened. Now, well . . . I guess one major change at a time is enough." She cleared her throat although she didn't have to, surprised to hear herself continue. "The trick is not to allow yourself to get emotionally involved. You have to divorce yourself . . . Sorry, that was a rather unfortunate choice of words."

"This picture was taken a few years ago," Marc Cameron remarked, changing the subject, as he lifted the small, silver-framed photograph of Lynn's once happy family into his large hands.

"Yes, it was. Three, to be exact. Have I aged so noticeably?" Why had she asked that?

"Not you," he said, returning the picture to its place on the windowsill. "Gary." He pronounced the word carefully, giving it an exaggerated fullness that made it sound vaguely obscene.

"Oh yes," she said, picking at the already chipped white polish of her nails. "I'd forgotten that you've met."

"Met? Why, I introduced them. 'Gary Schuster, I'd like you to meet my wife, Suzette. Suzette, I'd like you to meet Gary Schuster. He's the lawyer who'll be finalizing the deal on our new house.'" He laughed. "A writer's supposed to appreciate irony." He took a long sip of his beer, then looked back out the window. "It's nice to live so close to the ocean," he added incongruously.

"I love to walk along the beach," she confided, finding this a safer topic, momentarily relaxing her guard. "It helps me keep things in perspective."

"Just how *do* you keep this in perspective?"

"I'm not sure what you mean."

"Well, your husband comes home from the office one day and tells you that he's leaving you for another woman. How do you deal with that?"

"Privately," she said, her defenses back on full alert.

He smiled, the creases around his blue eyes deepening. "Sorry. A writer's natural curiosity."

"Sounded more like the curiosity of a spurned husband," Lynn said, then immediately wished she hadn't. What was the point in being cruel? The man had obviously been hurt enough. His question wasn't unnatural or even unexpected. But how could she tell him that even now, almost six full months after her husband had announced that he was leaving her for another woman, had, in fact, packed his bags and his law books—she had known he was serious when he packed his law books—and moved out, the whole thing had a distinct air of unreality? When he told her, straight out, "I've fallen in love with someone else; I'm leaving you," she had experienced the peculiarly insular sensation that none of it was really happening, that she had fallen asleep while reading, comfortably curled up on the living-room sofa, and that this was merely an unpleasant dream. It was only when she spoke, and she had spoken only because he was obviously expecting her to, that she realized she was functioning in all three dimensions, and that her husband of fourteen years, father of her two young children, was actually planning to leave her.

"You're not serious," she had said at the time, although it was perfectly obvious that he was. He had that hangdog look he always got when he thought he was saying something important, and his normally sweet mouth was twitching expectantly, as if he had been formulating his rebuttal even before she spoke.

"I am," he told her slowly, "very serious. You know that we haven't been really happy together in some time . . ."

"What are you talking about?" she broke in, aware that he

hated to be interrupted. "I didn't know that we haven't been happy. *I've* been happy. What are you talking about?"

It was at this point, as he began his painstaking explanation, that she had begun feeling that this was not happening to her, but to someone else. It was as though she were behind her desk at the Delray Department of Social Services, listening to someone else relate this story secondhand. She saw herself sitting where she always sat when sad stories were being related, on the side of the desk that was free of such woes, the professional side, the *safe* side, where she could be moved, sometimes to tears (especially in the early years), but never actually *touched*, and certainly never bruised. She regularly gave ear to stories of severed households, of marriages that had been ripped apart in a flurry of fists, of neglected and beaten children, of emotional blackmail, of souls lost and only occasionally found. It was part of her job to listen, to sympathize, to analyze, to find solutions if possible. And when she was through listening and finding possible solutions, she would write up her reports, trying to force some sense into the madness she had heard. Pain was part of her job as a social worker in the Department of Social Services in Delray Beach, Florida, but it was not part of her life.

And so it was only after her husband of fourteen years had packed his bags and his law books and moved out that the bitter truth began to sink in, and she realized that, like thousands of other women across the country, she had been unceremoniously dumped for another woman. And now that woman's husband was standing in her living room. Why? He still hadn't told her.

"Could we get to the point of your visit, Mr. Cameron?" Lynn heard the impatience in her voice and realized from the way his shoulders slumped that Marc Cameron had heard it too. "Is there one?"

"I'm not sure," he admitted, dropping his large frame back into the green-and-white-striped chair, for which he suddenly seemed too big. "I thought there was when I phoned." He paused, his smile slowly spreading across his face. "My intentions were good. At least I thought they were."

"You said there were things I should know."

He shrugged. "There are things I could tell you, things that might help you with the settlement you're trying to work out with Gary, things, I don't know, just things. But I realized as soon as I walked through the door that none of them would be the truth of why I'm really here." He paused, a flair for the dramatic in the pacing of his words. "The truth is that I was just curious. That word again. The spurned husband was curious," he clarified, "to see what you looked like. You're prettier than she is, you know."

"Am I supposed to say something?" Lynn asked after a long pause during which she desperately tried to think of a witty response.

"I guess I was hoping you'd be as angry as I am, that you'd want to tell me all about it. All the sordid little details—when you found out, what exactly Gary said to you, what *you* said, how you felt, if Gary told you anything about Suzette, if he said anything about *me*. If he said that *she* said anything about me. If I was a lousy husband, a lousy father, God forbid, the worst cut of all—a lousy lover. Details, details. Grist for the writer's mill."

"I'm not a big talker," she told him truthfully, not wishing to find herself dissected in the pages of his next book. "I *am* a good listener, however," she surprised herself by continuing. "If *you'd* like to talk about it . . ."

"The truth is," he said, standing up abruptly, his words gaining speed and conviction, "that I *would* like to talk about it. The truth is that I'd like nothing better than to sit and compare notes with you, match you juicy tidbit for juicy tidbit until we were both too bored to care anymore, and then I'd like to take you to some motel, preferably the same motel they went to the first time, *definitely* the same motel they went to, preferably the same room with the same goddamn bed, and then I'd like to . . ." He stopped abruptly. "Maybe my intentions weren't so good, after all."

There was a long pause during which nobody seemed to breathe.

"That was quite a speech," Lynn said after several moments, trying not to sound shocked or excited, though, in fact, she was both.

"Take that one for a walk on the beach." He finished the last of his beer and deposited the glass roughly on the rattan coffee table between them. "Tell me, social worker, how you put that proposition in its proper perspective."

"You said it yourself—you're a very angry man," she told him, not sure what else to say and feeling shamefully flushed from the heat of his words, hoping her face didn't betray the disturbing emotions he had aroused. She felt seized by the conflicting desires to either order this man out of her house or jump into his arms.

"And you're *not* angry?" he asked as she looked away. "Oh, I forgot. You deal with things privately." He lifted his hands helplessly into the air. "Look, I'm sorry if what I said offended you."

"No, you're not."

"No, I'm not. You're right. It's probably *exactly* what I came over here to say."

"Feel any better?"

"That depends on the answer."

She couldn't help but smile. "The answer is no."

"I still feel better."

"Good, then you can go now."

He nodded, though he didn't move. "I'm feeling a bit stupid at the moment . . ."

"If it makes you feel any better, I don't feel so great myself." She stood up, walking past him to the front door, opening it to the summer night and coming up against an immediate wall of heat. "It's been a rare pleasure meeting you, Mr. Cameron. That's a little further irony for you to appreciate," she couldn't help adding.

"I'd like to see you again," he said. He was standing in the middle of her doorway, preventing her from closing the front door. Lynn felt the warmth of the summer night on her face, the coolness of the air conditioning on her back. "Look, I don't always behave like such a cretin," he was saying. "And I sensed that when I first came in here, well, I *thought* that I sensed a few vibrations. Maybe I was wrong. But the truth is that I like you and that I'd like to see you again. I think that we have a lot in common, aside from the obvious. And"—he hesitated—"maybe I *would* like to talk to you. I'm not coping as well as you seem to be. I guess I don't have the 'proper perspective' on things as yet." She smiled. "Maybe the next time you go for one of your walks along the beach, I could go with you."

"I don't think that would be a very good idea."

"I think I'll call you again anyway."

Lynn shrugged and kept her face resolutely blank as he backed out of her doorway and walked slowly down the front path to where his car was parked on the street. She watched him climb into the compact car, but she closed the front door before he could look back and see her watching. Hearing him drive off, she marched back into her living room, and was surprised to find it all in one piece. She felt as if a hurricane had just swept through. Her hands shaking, she retrieved the empty beer glass from the coffee table and brought it into the kitchen, where she quickly washed it out and returned it to its shelf in the cupboard, all traces of Marc Cameron suddenly gone. She then took a deep breath, and then another, and finally, checking the clock on her microwave oven to make sure the hour wasn't too late, picked up the phone and put in another call to her attorney.

2

There were three messages waiting for Renee Bower when she and her husband, Philip, returned home at just past one in the morning. One was from her sister, Kathryn, in New York, and two were from a client, Lynn Schuster, whose husband had recently left her and who was being offered a fairly generous settlement to end the long-standing marriage.

"I wonder what that's all about," Renee said, sitting at the side of the king-size bed and pulling off the silver shoes which had been pinching her toes all evening. Were her feet getting bigger too? Could toes put on weight?

"You *know* what it's about," her husband told her from somewhere on the other side of the all-white room. "She just needs somebody to talk to."

"I don't mean my sister. I mean Lynn Schuster. I thought we had things pretty much wrapped up. I wonder why she's calling me at home."

"Whatever it is will have to wait until morning. Come to bed," he urged, already undressed and under the covers.

"I don't understand how you can be in bed so fast," Renee

marveled, walking into their large, carefully organized closet and pulling off her black sweater and pants, leaving them on the floor where they fell. She threw a long nightgown over her head and quickly moved across the thick white carpet toward their en suite white-marble bathroom.

"I don't spend twenty minutes on the phone at one in the morning checking my answering machine for messages," he reminded her gently.

"Neither do I." Renee stared at her reflection in the harsh light of the bathroom mirror, thinking her complexion looked sallow even under all her makeup. "Don't blame me because *your* friend decided to throw his wife a surprise party in the middle of the week." She put a large blob of cold cream on each cheek and one on the tip of her short, upturned nose.

"He's not your friend too?"

"I don't have any friends," she joked, then thought this was probably true. All her friends were really his friends, and hers only through osmosis. She had inherited them when she'd married Philip six years ago. All her old friends—some of them friends from childhood—had somehow disappeared, lost to conflicting schedules and only so much time. She rarely thought about them anymore. They belonged to another era, to a world before Philip.

"Will you hurry up and come to bed," he called from the next room, his voice sexy despite his stated fatigue.

Did he want to make love? she wondered, wishing there was a way to speed up her nightly routine, knowing there was not. She needed all the help she could get. She couldn't afford to rush these things. With deliberate slowness, Renee began massaging the cold cream into her skin, taking care not to rub too hard in the area around her eyes, wishing she were naturally more attractive, if not for herself, then for Philip. Though she was only thirty-four, she had noticed at the party tonight that the lines around her eyes seemed more pronounced than those of most of the other women present, including the birthday girl, who was a surprised forty and not very happy about it. Renee pulled a tissue from its marble case and gently began removing the thick cream from her face in a series of soft, steady strokes, studying her pores through tired brown eyes. "Why couldn't I have green eyes like Kathryn?" she asked herself softly, thinking that her sister's voice on her answering tape had sounded even more desperate than usual, desperation being the norm since her husband's sudden death from a heart attack three months before. Still, though the number of phone calls had increased, Kathryn refused to leave New York, even for a short visit.

Renee studied her image in the mirror, trying to find traces of her sister's face in her own. But there were none. Kathryn was the pretty one in the family, Renee reflected again, carefully wiping away the mountain of mascara she had painstakingly applied earlier in the evening. She might have inherited their father's brains, but as their father himself had often pointed out, Kathryn had been the lucky recipient of their mother's deep green eyes and fine, high cheekbones. Whatever cheekbones Renee had once possessed, she thought now, angrily slapping at them with night cream, had long since disappeared into what was at least ten too many pounds, pounds she didn't need but had been carrying around for over a year now, probably closer to two, if she was being honest. Probably closer to fifteen pounds, if she was being *really* honest. She glanced over at the scale—the enemy—she hadn't stepped on in weeks, thinking that, at only five feet three inches, it wasn't her weight that was the problem, but her height.

"You're doing it again," she told herself angrily, amazed that a woman in her position, with everything she had going for her, with everything she had achieved at a relatively youthful age, with all her supposed smarts, was just another obsessive throwback to the days before liberation when it came to her looks and her weight. She was a successful lawyer, she told herself, and a very good one. Her clients all thought her capable and shrewd, even tough. It didn't seem to matter to them that she was a few pounds overweight. What difference did it make how much she weighed? She began to brush her teeth vigorously. When she was with Philip, nobody ever noticed her anyway. How many times had she heard, even tonight, even among their so-called friends, "You're so lucky. He's so gorgeous. How'd you ever manage to land him?" She had stopped being surprised by the insensitivity of such remarks. She'd gotten used to them after almost six years of marriage to a man who was not only handsome, successful, and distinguished-looking but perpetually boyish as well, an interesting combination at age forty-six.

So what if all his friends, all *their* friends, were always telling her how lovely she would be if she would only lose a few pounds? Like that woman at the party tonight, Alicia-call-me-Ali, the slender redhead with the low-cut dress who always seemed to be standing next to Philip, who'd told her that successful dieting was all a matter of willpower. The skinny twit had never had to diet in her life. She counted husbands the way other women counted calories, and if the husbands still had wives attached, so what? A snack was often more satisfying than a full-course meal. "Isn't that right, Renee?" she had queried, in reference to exactly what, Renee couldn't now recall. Had the woman been snacking on Philip?

Reluctantly, Renee felt her mind drift back over the evening's festivities. She had watched as her husband whispered tantalizing tidbits into the ear of an attractive blonde, watched while he danced suggestively with the birthday girl, felt her body bend in time to his as he leaned forward teasingly to confide in the skinny redhead with the low-cut dress. Renee had stood alone in a corner, sipping on her champagne and rooted as firmly to the Mexican tile floor as the potted palm beside her, trying her damnedest not to be jealous, to appear as if she was having a good time. Philip had cautioned her about her jealousy on more than one occasion. She had nothing to be jealous about, he had told her repeatedly, though it sounded more like a warning.

That part of his life was over, he had assured her. She was the only one he wanted, the only one he loved. The others had meant nothing. They were a thing of the past. She knew that. Hadn't she supervised the dissolution of enough marriages over as trivial an issue as a meaningless fling? Did she want to do that to her own marriage? "Don't push me into something I don't want to do," he had told her, and she wondered—though only momentarily—how she came to be responsible for his actions.

Still, there seemed no end to the attractive women he knew, to the *thin* attractive women he knew, most of whom were married to men at least several decades older than themselves. Florida was overrun with beautiful young women married to rich old men, men who fooled themselves into believing that it was their charm, and not their wallets, which was the irresistible force in the relationship. Still, if the marriage fell apart before the husband, the young wife often found herself out in the cold. Florida money had a way of protecting its own, Renee knew, wondering how she would ever survive if Philip were to leave her, how she had managed before they met.

"Renee, for Christ's sake, what are you doing in there?"

For some reason, she thought, marveling at the plump face staring back at her in the mirror, pulling at bits of cold cream which had stuck to the sides of her streaked blond hair, he has chosen me. For some unknown, unfathomable reason, I am the woman he chooses to call his wife. "I am the lucky one," she said aloud, and thought she was.

"What were you doing in there for so long?" he asked as she climbed into bed beside him.

"Should I lose twenty pounds?" she asked, speaking to his back as she carefully adjusted her body around his.

"I wouldn't like you with one leg," he said.

"Thanks a lot."

"Can we go to sleep now?"

"Do you think I should go on that watermelon diet?"

"Why don't you try counting watermelons instead of sheep? It'll probably accomplish the same thing."

"Philip, I'm having a crisis here," she said, only half joking. "You're the psychiatrist. Help me out."

"Office hours are from eight A.M. till four P.M. every weekday."

"Please."

He flipped on his back and then propped himself up on one elbow to face her. "What happened in that bathroom? Who were you talking to in there?"

"Do you think I'm attractive?"

"I think you're just fine."

" 'Just fine' is not exactly what I was hoping to hear."

"Renee," he said, his voice kind although she recognized a hint of impatience at its edges, "you are a bright, capable woman . . ."

"I know that. I know I'm a bright, capable woman."

"You're a lawyer."

"I know I'm a lawyer. You don't have to tell me I'm a lawyer."

"You have a husband who loves you."

"Do I? Do I have a husband who loves me?"

"What do you think?"

"Office hours are from eight to four," she said, throwing his words back at him. "Don't ask me what I think. Save that for your patients. Tell me that you love me. Tell me that you think I'm the most beautiful thing on earth."

"I love you. I think you're the most beautiful thing on earth."

"Why don't I believe you?"

"Because even though you're a bright, capable woman and a very successful attorney, you also happen to be a hysterical female, and if I don't get some sleep soon, I'm going to be a hysterical psychiatrist, which tends to make the patients nervous."

He was about to turn over again when her voice stopped him. "Do you want to make love?"

"Now? It's one o'clock in the morning."

"I didn't ask you what time it was. God knows, I know what time it is. You've told me enough times. I asked you if you wanted to make love."

"You are the most infuriating woman," he began, but he was already pulling her toward him, edging one knee across her ample thigh.

There was a knock on their bedroom door. "Daddy?" the voice called tentatively.

Renee withdrew her arms, which had been about to encircle her husband's still slender waistline. They fell back against her pillow as if there were heavy weights attached to her wrists. She felt Philip immediately pull away, felt him sitting up and straining through the darkness as the pajama-clad figure of Debbie, his teenage daughter, inched toward them.

"Baby?" he asked, his voice so gentle that Renee felt momentarily displaced, as if she'd somehow wandered into the wrong bed. "Is something the matter, darling? Why aren't you asleep?"

"I had a bad dream," the voice quivered, and for an instant Renee was tempted to draw the frightened girl in beside her and hold her and comfort her and tell her that everything would be all right. Until she saw the little half-smirk that the girl was still too much of a child to completely hide, and she froze. Even in the darkness, Renee could make out the fierce determination in her husband's daughter's eyes.

"Do you want to tell me about it?" asked the man who only minutes ago had told Renee that office hours were from eight till four.

"It was a terrible dream," the girl, who was sixteen and looked fourteen, told her father, allowing her shivering frame to be surrounded by his bare arms. "I dreamt that you were in a car accident, you and Renée."

As she always did, Debbie pronounced the double *e* of Renee's name as if it were French. ("It's Renee, rhymes with beanie," Renee corrected her every year when the girl arrived from Boston to spend the summer with them, as she had reminded her when Debbie arrived two weeks before. "Renee, rhymes with beanie—*not* Renée, rhymes with day.")

"You were driving very fast, very recklessly . . ." Debbie continued, unaware of Renee's inner dialogue. "Actually," she continued, "you weren't the one driving. It was Renée."

"Figures," Renee said, almost unheard.

"There were signs all over the road, warnings about dangerous curves," Debbie went on.

"I always ignore signs about dangerous curves," Renee said. "Something about that squiggly design I never liked."

Debbie brought her lips together so that they all but disappeared. "I'm glad that you think this is so amusing," she said stoically, her back stiffening. "I'm sorry if I disturbed you, Re-née. I'll go back to my room."

"Nonsense," Philip said immediately, his arm reaching out again and securing his daughter to him, his eyes fixing Renee with their most withering stare. Even in the darkness, its power was dazzling. "You could never be disturbing us. This is your home."

And this is my nightmare, thought Renee, listening as her husband persuaded his daughter to continue with her description.

"Well," the young girl said, allowing herself to be cajoled, "I saw the danger you were in. I knew that if she didn't slow down"— "she" now, Renee thought, the woman with no name — "she'd drive you both off a cliff and into the ocean . . ."

"And did she?" Renee asked.

"Renee," her husband cautioned.

"I tried to warn you. I called out, 'Renée, Renée' . . ."

"I probably thought you were talking to someone else."

"I guess you couldn't hear me," the child continued, as if Renee hadn't spoken. "The car kept going faster. Finally, it went off the cliff. I watched helplessly as it crashed against the rocks. I screamed."

"My poor baby," her father soothed.

"I got there as fast as I could and pulled you to safety." Renee marveled that there were actually tears in Debbie's eyes. "Renée died," Debbie added, almost as an afterthought.

"Well then, it wasn't such a nightmare, after all," Renee told her cheerfully.

"Really, Renée, I don't know why you're so hostile."

"I'm always hostile after I plunge from a cliff to my death."

"It was just a dream," the girl told her.

"Yes," Renee responded, seeing the young girl as clearly as if she'd just turned on all the lights. "I'm afraid that's all it was."

"Feel better now?" her father asked.

Debbie shrugged and buried her face against her father's hairy chest. "I was so scared for you. There was nothing I could do. I felt so helpless. I tried to warn you. She wouldn't listen." The child was actually crying now.

"Why don't I make us some hot chocolate?" Philip asked energetically, as if it were the middle of the day, and Debbie brightened immediately, lifting her head and smiling just past her father's shoulder to where her wicked stepmother sat motionless and openmouthed. "Remember how when you were a little girl and you'd have a bad dream, we'd go into the kitchen and make some hot chocolate . . ."

"And you'd sit with me while I drank it, till I finished every drop. I remember. I didn't think you did."

"Hey, I remember everything about your childhood. Every bad dream, every sneeze. You'll be all right after you've had a cup of Daddy's special hot chocolate. Now, who's the doctor here? Renee, will you get my robe?"

Renee said nothing, recognizing a no-win situation when she saw one, and moved swiftly to the closet to retrieve her husband's navy-blue silk dressing gown.

"You don't want any hot chocolate, do you?" Debbie asked Renee after Philip had departed for the kitchen, and the two women—one, thirty-four, who knew better than to get involved in this type of power struggle, and the other, sixteen, who knew it all—were left to confront each other. "I mean, you're on a diet, aren't you?"

"Not at the moment. But I'm not thirsty, thank you."

"You look really tired, Renée," Debbie said sweetly. "Have you been feeling well?"

"I'm feeling just fine, thank you. And the name is Renee, rhymes with beanie. Not Renée."

"I prefer Renée," the girl said stubbornly. "Renee sounds like, I don't know, the fat kid in grade school that nobody ever wanted to play with."

Debbie was gone before Renee had the chance to leap out of bed and hurl her from the bedroom window of the sixth-floor oceanfront condominium she had moved into when she married Philip. Not that the child would come to any serious harm, Renee thought, her head falling back against her pillow. The girl was indestructible.

From the kitchen, she heard the sounds of Philip's soothing voice and Debbie's innocent, girlish giggle. How, she wondered, was it possible for the girl to present two such different faces to the world? And how was it possible for a man of Philip's sophistication and intelligence, not to mention his professional training, to be so blind when it came to dealing with his own daughter? How could he allow himself to be so manipulated?

It happened every summer. Debbie would step off the Eastern Airlines flight from Boston and proceed to walk all over the stepmother who initially had been only too willing to be her friend. Renee laughed now when she thought of how eagerly she had awaited the arrival of her husband's only child, how thrilled she had felt when she caught her initial glimpse of the girl who was only ten at the time of their first encounter. Though she was small for her age, Debbie had, even then, carried herself in the controlled manner of someone much older. She had long light brown hair pulled back from her slim oval face into a high ponytail, and her legs were disproportionately long for her height, and very bony, which made her seem all the more fragile. Like a pretty pink flamingo, Renee had thought then. More like a vulture, she had learned, as the girl skillfully avoided her every overture while making it look as though it was always Renee who somehow came up short. "She doesn't like me," Renee had tearfully confided to Philip, who had assured her that the child was only shy, and the victim of conflicting loyalties. It was only natural for his daughter to resent someone else taking her mother's place, especially since their divorce had been far from amicable, he told her, and she had bowed to his superior knowledge in such matters, although instinctively she had known he was wrong. "What can I do to make her love me?" she had asked, and he had told her to be herself. When that hadn't worked—and it soon became obvious even to Philip that it wasn't working—he told her to grin and bear it, that it was only for two months of the year, and surely she could indulge him that much. At first she thought she could. And yet the two months felt longer every year, as the child advanced past adolescence and the subtle maneuvers grew increasingly sophisticated, the barbs better aimed and more skillfully executed.

Philip was no help at all. His guilt at having abandoned his only child to a woman he renounced as unstable made him the easy target of his daughter's manipulations. If he saw through them, and Renee was sure that he did—Christ, even a total idiot could see through them—he was powerless to do anything but respond in the most obvious way. He gave in to all of Debbie's outrageous demands on his time, his money, his psyche. He took her side in every dispute; he understood her position, her fears, her pain. Debbie was afraid of losing him, he told Renee, and didn't seem to understand that she was afraid of exactly the same thing.

"You were very rough on her," he said when he came back into the room, the smell of hot chocolate on his breath. "She's just a kid, you have to remember. She thinks you hate her."

"That's ridiculous, Philip. You know I've tried everything."

"Try harder. Please. For my sake. She was crying just now. She said that maybe she shouldn't spend her summers with us anymore because she can see that you don't like her, and she doesn't want to cause any trouble between us."

"Oh God, Philip," Renee said, feeling totally defeated. "Short of changing my name or driving off a cliff, I really don't know what I can do that will make her happy."

She hoped he would laugh, but he didn't. "You're the adult. She's the child. You have to lead the way. Now, I've got to get some sleep."

"I guess making love is out of the question?" she asked as the phone rang.

"It is now," he said, and she heard the relief in his voice though he tried to disguise it as annoyance.

Renee reached for the phone beside the bed. "It could be for you, you know."

"It isn't," he said, and was right, as he usually was.

"Yes, this is Renee Bower," Renee confirmed to the unfamiliar voice on the other end of the line, feeling a sudden queasiness in the pit of her stomach. "Yes, Kathryn Wright is my sister. Who is this? . . . What? What are you talking about?

Who is this?" She felt Philip sit up in bed beside her, his interest piqued despite his annoyance. Renee listened to the frantic outpouring of words from the woman on the other end, whose name she had already forgotten, at first unable to respond. She rubbed a shaking hand across her forehead. "Oh my God!" she said, and then again "Oh my God!"

3

"This is going to have to be a short meeting, I'm afraid," Renee Bower was saying as Lynn Schuster walked into her office and sat down in the chair across from her desk. "I have to drive into Lauderdale. My sister's arriving on the two o'clock flight from New York." Renee nervously checked her watch. Lynn automatically did the same.

"How is she?" Lynn asked.

Renee looked startled by the question. "Oh, that's right, I keep forgetting you went to school together. She's not so good," Renee said without further elaboration. "Now, what can I do for you? You said it was important."

"I don't know if it's important," Lynn immediately qualified, and Renee looked confused. "I had a visitor last night. Marc Cameron, Suzette Cameron's husband."

"Interesting," Renee said, though Lynn could read nothing from her expression. "And?"

"And?" Lynn thought quickly back over the events of the previous night, lowering her head to her lap and chipping away at whatever remained of the white polish on her nails. "And . . . he wants to see me again."

"I seem to be missing something," Renee Bower said evenly. "Is there something you're leaving out?"

"Not really," Lynn told her. "He called, said he wanted to come over, that there were some things he felt I should know."

"Such as?"

"Well, I don't think he actually got around to mentioning them."

"I see. What exactly *did* he get around to mentioning?"

Lynn shook her head. "It's all very confusing."

"I can see that. Lynn, what exactly did the man say?"

"He said that he was curious about me, that he wanted to see what I looked like. He said that I'm prettier than Suzette. He said that he was having a hard time dealing with what had happened. He said that he thought we had a lot in common. He said that he'd like to see me again."

"And what did you say?"

"I said no."

"Good."

"Why 'good'? Why do you say that?"

"What do you mean, 'why do I say that?' What else would I say? Why would you *want* to see him again?"

"I don't know."

Renee folded her hands on top of her desk. "Lynn, what's going on here?"

"I don't know," Lynn confessed, feeling infinitely foolish. Why was she here? This whole scene was beginning to assume a dreamlike—almost nightmarish—quality. She was becoming disoriented.

"Excuse me a minute," Renee was saying, rising and walking toward her secretary, a young brunette who had just stuck her elaborately coiffed head through the open door. "I'll be back in a minute," Renee said after conferring with the young woman, and then shut the door behind her as she excused herself from the room.

Lynn looked around the small office, the windows of which looked south onto the inner courtyard of Atlantic Plaza, a relatively new, bright pink shopping mall located on the city's main thoroughfare, Atlantic Avenue, between Seventh and Eighth streets. She found herself staring at the immense ficus tree which dominated the open central courtyard, its branches hovering over the empty benches that dotted the pink brick patio. As far as Lynn could see, there was no one in the mall at all except those who were paid to be, the weary sales help in the empty stores and the bored waiters in the small, dark restaurants. It was summer in Delray Beach.

Summer in Delray was a quiet time of year. Like most beachside resort communities, Delray really came alive only in the winter months, when the "snowbirds," as the seasonal residents were called by those who lived here year-round, and the "snowflakes," short-term tourists only, flocked to the beaches and filled up the shops. In the "season," Atlantic Avenue was a different street entirely. Then the cars stretched bumper to bumper from turnpike to ocean at all hours and the city vibrated from the hum of their motors.

Now the silence, combined with the stillness, was almost frightening in its intensity. Lynn had always been especially wary of summer in Florida. The temperature often climbed as high as one hundred windless degrees, and for those not fortunate enough to work in air-conditioned premises and live in air-conditioned homes, it was unbearable. Fuses were short and tempers long. Lynn had too often seen the results of the summer heat on the battered faces of already battered psyches. Too often people stood in front of her desk with their broken bones and broken dreams and she was supposed to fix them up with a few well-chosen phrases. ("Please don't beat your wife again, Mr. Smith, or we'll be forced to take action.") Lynn hated the summer.

The only place to be in these months was at the ocean, where there was usually a breeze. Normally, Lynn would be there now. It was her lunch hour, and she usually headed straight for the sprawling, cabana-lined public beach, parking her car along the empty ocean highway, removing her panty hose and sandals, and walking barefoot along the ocean, watching the teenagers with their surfboards waiting for the perfect wave, as oblivious to her presence as they were to their own mortality.

Megan and Nicholas were happily ensconced in day camp. The bus picked them up every weekday morning at eight o'clock and deposited them back home at five. In between they played tennis, enjoyed arts and crafts, and swam in one of three Olympic-size pools. Lynn always made sure to take them to the ocean on weekends. Before the separation, she had occasionally been able to corral Gary away from his work and the family would have a Saturday-afternoon picnic at the beach. Now Gary picked the kids up on Saturday morning and disappeared with them for most of the day. He rarely took them to the beach. The ocean had never meant the same thing to Gary as it did to Lynn, something she had never really thought about till now.

In the summer, the ocean was as warm as bath water, and the breeze that blew off it was welcome and soothing. "Whenever you're feeling like the world has got you by the tail," her father had once advised as they walked hand in hand by the water's edge, not long after her mother's death, "take a look at this." And his hand had swept across the stunning, brilliant blue panorama of surf and sky. That had been nine years ago, she realized with a start, snapping back into the present and casually absorbing what she knew would be described in one of her reports as a "well-appointed" room.

The walls of Renee's office were pale gray trimmed with a white high-gloss border, and the furniture was shades of delicate peach. The only thing that provided a discordant note was the mess of papers that looked as if it had been heaved across the top of Renee's desk. Somewhere in that mess, Lynn thought, are the remains of my marriage.

Lynn closed her eyes and buried her face in her hands. What was she doing here? Why hadn't she simply told Marc Cameron to take his good intentions and go to hell, where such intentions invariably led? Why had she agreed to meet with him in the first place?

She wasn't used to behaving in such a reckless, ill-conceived fashion. Throughout those first few months after her husband had walked out, Lynn Schuster had done nothing rash, conducting herself in a thoroughly professional, levelheaded manner, her composure never breaking. Her colleagues at work had all expressed admiration for the superb way in which she was dealing with everything, and she had missed not a single appointment on her busy schedule. Similarly, she went about the business of being a working mother with her usual calm, making the final arrangements for the children's day camp and disbursing the necessary checks, not bothering to ask Gary for the money. When Gary called to discuss their children, when he came by to see them or take them out on Saturdays, she was unfailingly pleasant. Only once, when she first learned that the woman her husband had left her for was not some mindless twenty-two-year-old but a married woman almost her own age, had she come close to collapsing.

Were these the kinds of details Marc Cameron had been after? "Tell me all about it," he had said. "Tell me exactly what Gary said to you, when you found out, how you felt. Details, details. Grist for the writer's mill."

How could I possibly tell you what I felt? she wondered now, sitting on the wrong side of the untidy desk, the side where pain was more than something to listen to, when I was feeling so many things, when the cumulative effect of all those emotions was to make me feel numb. And why had she not cried until someone—she couldn't remember who, she must have blocked it out—had told her that she'd seen the two of them together—her husband and this woman he'd left her for —in some little art gallery on Worth Avenue, and that they were kissing, kissing in public beside a piece of overgrown modern sculpture, and that the woman was neither particularly attractive nor scandalously young? Why had it taken this knowledge to bring forth the rush of sudden bitter tears, shed only in the privacy of her own home, locked inside her bathroom, her angry sobs muffled (so that her children wouldn't hear) by a large yellow beach towel?

It was this fact that puzzled her the most, although she was loath to admit it, and she would certainly never have discussed it with anyone, not even her lawyer. Somehow she felt that the whole situation would be easier to digest—that she would be somehow less to blame—if the woman her husband, a quiet, thoughtful, attractive man of forty, had left her for had been a big-bosomed, empty-headed Lolita. Youth and stupidity she could understand, even tolerate. There was something very attractive about both these qualities at the end of a busy day. To come home to someone who was as uncomplicated as she was unlined, this was an aphrodisiac she could sympathize with, if not condone. She had seen examples of it often enough: a man divorced his wife of many years for a woman who looked exactly like his wife's old photographs. Often even the names of the women were similar. Caroline became a Carol; Joanne was replaced by a Joanna. And if that was what Gary wanted, then there was nothing she could have done differently to prevent him from leaving. But this woman, this Suzette (whose name was nothing like her own name), was reportedly no great beauty—even the woman's own husband had told Lynn that she was the prettier of the two—and was, at age thirty-seven, only two years younger than herself. Why then had Gary left her?

They had shared fourteen (fifteen, if you counted their courtship) relatively strife-free years, years that had produced two children and two successful careers. For fourteen years, Lynn and Gary had shared similar tastes and interests, and had made a point of being mutually supportive of the other's work and needs. Their marriage had been markedly free of serious problems. Both were healthy and well-paid professionals, although his income easily outdistanced her own. Still, they never argued about money. Nor had they ever argued about politics, religion, in-laws, or sex. In fact, they almost never argued about anything. As far as the outside world was concerned—as far as Lynn herself was concerned—theirs had been as close to perfection as most modern-day marriages come. Lynn and Gary, Gary and Lynn. They fit together as easily as their names. Lynn had thought that there was nothing about her marriage that she would change. Gary had obviously disagreed. Why hadn't he told her his feelings before their differences became what the law defined as irreconcilable? Why had he waited until the words that came out of his mouth were "I've fallen in love with someone else. I'm leaving you"?

In the beginning, she thought he would come back. In a few days, she thought, then, in a few weeks. Her lawyer advised no sudden moves, which was fine with Lynn, who rarely moved suddenly. A typical mid-life crisis, she decided, straight out of the textbooks. If she were advising a client, she would say to forgive and forget when the affair ran its course, as affairs of this kind usually did. But after the first week became a month, and then two, then three, and now six, with no signs of abating, in fact signs quite to the contrary, Lynn was forced to conclude that her husband might, in fact, be serious in his newly stated intention to actually get a divorce so that he might marry this other woman.

He was proposing a fair settlement. She could have their tidy bungalow on Crestwood Drive, he offered through their respective lawyers, and all the furnishings, with the exception of a Queen Anne chair which had always been in his family and which, in truth, she had never particularly liked. He wanted half the art they had collected over their years together and all of his vast collection of vintage rock-and-roll records. He offered no alimony but generous child support, and he agreed to continue paying the mortgage for another five years. Renee Bower had told Lynn that she thought she could persuade him to extend this period for another few years, and she quibbled with a few of the minor points, but it was generally agreed that Lynn and Gary Schuster were on the path toward a fair, amicable dissolution of their marriage. She was to be congratulated. She was behaving in the manner of a mature, responsible adult. "Consider yourself lucky," Renee had told her when the first offer of settlement reached her desk. "He's obviously marrying money."

Somehow that knowledge provided scant comfort. Gary had never been a man to let the almighty dollar govern either his life or his libido. He was a busy lawyer with a thriving, well-respected firm, and had recently been made a partner. He made a good living. He liked what he did. He had never aspired to the heights of the Social Register. Lynn understood that the fact that this woman had money was only incidental to whatever other qualities had attracted Gary to her in the first place. Whenever Lynn tried to picture what those qualities might be, her eyes filled with tears and her breath became uncomfortably short, and so she had willed herself to stop thinking, concentrating instead on her job and her children. And then Marc Cameron had phoned and come over and upset her with his unexpected words and his interesting face and his overgrown, teddy-bear body, and now she was thinking about these things again, all these things she didn't want to think about.

"So, you still haven't told me," Renee Bower was saying, and Lynn realized her lawyer had reentered the room, "why on earth you'd want to see Marc Cameron again."

"I'm curious," Lynn heard herself say, the same word Marc had used the night before.

"About what? About how far you can go to really mess up your life?"

Lynn said nothing for several seconds, staring down into the deep rose color of her pleated skirt. "About his wife," she said softly. "I guess if I'm being honest, I'd have to admit that I'm as curious about her as Marc Cameron was about me."

"And you think he'll tell you what you want to know?"

"I think he's eager to."

"Why?"

"I don't know. To get it off his chest maybe."

"No, not why does *he* want to talk about *her*, why do *you* want to know?"

"Wouldn't you?"

Lynn saw a look of indecision flicker across Renee's soft brown eyes. "I don't know. Maybe. I don't think so. No," Renee pronounced finally. "What good would it do?"

Lynn shrugged. "It might clear up some things for me."

"More likely it'll just confuse the hell out of you. What else? You're not telling me everything."

Lynn looked around the room, pretending to study the delicate painting of two ballerinas to the left of Renee's head. "I find him very attractive," she said finally, in a voice so soft it was barely audible.

Renee lowered her hands into her lap and sat back in her chair. "Finally," she said, "a reason that makes sense."

Lynn's eyes shot directly to those of her attorney.

"What exactly happened last night, Lynn?" Renee asked carefully.

"Nothing," Lynn told her quickly. "Honestly. Absolutely nothing. But there was this . . . chemistry, if you will . . ."

"You won't."

"I beg your pardon?"

"You won't," Renee repeated. "This chemistry. You won't start . . . experimenting."

"Isn't that what chemistry's for?" Lynn tried to smile but she could see how serious Renee was. "Why not? What would be so wrong?"

"What would be right? For God's sake, Lynn, you know what would be wrong or you wouldn't be here. You don't need my permission to have an affair. You're a big girl. You came here, you called me at home—*twice*, I might add—because you know that getting involved with this man would be a big mistake and you wanted confirmation. So I'm giving it to you, and it's costing you over two hundred dollars an hour to get it, so here it is again, as clear as I can say it: don't go out with this man; don't sleep with him; don't talk to him; don't even think about him."

"I still don't understand why I shouldn't . . ."

"Because he's the husband of the woman your husband ran off with. That's just for starters. On a more practical note, think of the effect it might have on your children. Think about the fact that this is a small town and people will talk, especially about something as juicy as this, so you better think about your professional reputation and your career. But mostly think about your settlement, which is a good one and which you could blow right through the roof if you do something to make Gary really angry before we get it signed, sealed, and delivered."

"Why would my seeing Marc make Gary angry?"

"Think about it, Lynn. Take a few days—a few months—and think about it. The territorial imperative, or whatever it's called. If the situations were reversed, how do you think you'd feel? At the very least, Gary might suspect your motives. And he'd be right." Lynn opened her mouth to object, but Renee ignored her. "Lynn, Marc Cameron is hurt. He's confused. Frankly, he sounds like a kook. What man in his position actually picks up a phone and calls the wife of the man his wife ran off with? *Why* does he want to see you again? Think about it. He's been screwed. And what better fantasy fulfillment than to get back at the man who screwed him by quite literally screwing that man's wife? Lynn," she said, lowering her voice and taking a deep breath, "he's a very angry man. He may not even realize on a conscious level what he's doing. He may not be deliberately setting out to hurt you, but what difference does it make if he hurts you nonetheless? Do you need this?"

"You don't think that there's an outside chance that Marc . . . that this man just finds me attractive?"

"I think there's *every* chance that he finds you attractive. Why wouldn't he? You're a lovely, bright woman, and he'd have to be blind not to find you attractive. But, Lynn, *you* don't really have anything to do with this." Renee pushed her chair back, then walked around to Lynn's side of the desk. Lynn thought in that moment how pretty her lawyer would be if only she'd lose a few pounds. "Lynn," Renee began, not allowing Lynn's eyes to wander from her own, "one day you'll meet a man who will find you attractive for all the right reasons. But not this one." Renee Bower carefully studied her client's clear gray eyes. "You're not going to listen to me, are you?" There was an equal mixture of incredulity and resignation in Renee's voice.

"I don't know," Lynn replied honestly after a silence.

"Can you at least wait to see him again until after we get the separation agreement signed?"

"I'll try."

"Try hard." Renee paused and Lynn realized that she wasn't quite off the hook yet.

"What?" Lynn asked.

"I think you should talk to someone."

"Someone? What do you mean?"

"Someone professional."

"I am talking to someone professional. I'm talking to you."

"To a psychiatrist," Renee said plainly. "And don't tell me I'm overreacting," she continued, just as Lynn was about to. "Lynn, you've handled this whole divorce thing up to now very well, maybe even too well. There are a lot of pent-up emotions in you. What harm could it do to talk everything over with someone?"

"Your husband needs the business, does he?"

"My concern at the moment is not with Philip. He's doing very well, thank you. How about someone in your own office?"

"Don't you have to get to the airport?" Lynn asked, then checked her watch. Renee Bower did the same, understanding the subject was closed.

"Jesus, yes, I better run." She didn't move.

"Is something wrong?"

Renee threw her hands up in the air. "What the hell. You don't have the corner on craziness. My sister tried to kill herself last night."

"What? Oh my God!"

"Yes, that's what I said." For several moments, Renee stood absolutely still. "Kathryn always did know how to get my attention."

4

Renee studied the disembarking passengers as they pushed through the swinging doors into the arrival area at the Fort Lauderdale airport, wondering if Kathryn would be among them. The woman who called last night—Renee still couldn't remember her name—had promised to drive Kathryn to the airport and make sure she got on the plane, but what could she have done had Kathryn simply refused to go?

Renee followed the slow gait of a middle-aged man as he greeted his anxious-looking wife with a distracted hug, and found herself smiling as a teenage girl flew into the arms of her eager grandparents. Renee liked watching people, guessing the nature of their relationships. She projected that the distracted middle-aged man was returning from a convention in New York, to which he'd also brought his girlfriend, the woman who had marched through the swinging doors just ahead of him and never once bothered to look back. Now the man was smiling wanly at his wife who was peppering him with questions about his trip, as eager as her husband to maintain the charade of their marriage. Renee wondered how long it would be before they ended up in an office like hers, possibly even across from her desk. Would she recognize them if they did?

As for the teenage girl giggling inside the protective grasp of her grandparents, Renee surmised that she was the product of a broken home. Her grandparents, probably on her father's side, hadn't seen her in several years. Her mother had finally given her reluctant consent to the reunion, and the girl and her grandparents were almost beside themselves with joy.

Renee realized she was staring and looked away, thinking that Philip was probably right when he said that her profession was starting to color her attitude to life. When he first made this observation, Renee had been defensive, even hurt. "Isn't yours?" she had asked, peevishly.

But maybe he was right, Renee thought now. It was true that in her world everyone was either on the verge of or recovering from a divorce. Even in her fantasies, she thought, watching the middle-aged couple push past the teenager and her grandparents and disappear down the hall. Why couldn't life be simple? Why couldn't we all just live happily ever after, the way the storybooks promised? Who needed reality when reality was usually so damned unpleasant?

Not my reality, she assured herself quickly. I married the handsome prince. I'm living my fantasy. Give or take a few pounds.

Three more people burst through the doors into the arrival area, two women and a young, sulky-looking boy, not more than ten years old. Sisters, Renee quickly deduced. One never married, the other newly separated, bringing her reluctant son to Florida for a brief holiday before the custody battles began. Possibly a bribe. 'See, sweetie, isn't Florida beautiful? Stay with Mommy and we'll take lots of trips like this.' Renee turned away. Philip was definitely right.

She wondered what Philip was doing. He had told her this morning that he would try to accompany her to the airport, that she should phone when she was ready to leave. But when she called, his secretary informed her, in clipped British vowels, that Dr. Bower was tied up with a patient and could she please call back in five minutes. Renee had waited, called again, been given the same message, and then waited until she would be late for her sister's plane if she waited any longer, dialing her husband's number one final time only to find it busy. Then she left. She was almost twenty minutes late getting to the airport, but luckily so was Kathryn's flight. Renee looked at the row of telephones against the far wall and thought of calling Philip yet again, hoping he wouldn't be angry that she hadn't waited. It occurred to her briefly that it was she who had reason to be angry, but she quickly dismissed this thought from her mind.

Renee looked back at the swinging doors and saw a woman several years older and several inches taller than herself step through them and stop. The woman was very pale, the color and consistency of skim milk. Her thin blonde hair hung lifelessly around the sides of her hollow face. This woman has suffered a recent tragedy, Renee thought, walking closer. She's been married for almost two decades to a man she loved very much, a man who had recently abandoned her, not through divorce but through death. She has no children (having suffered at least three miscarriages), no career (her husband having been her career) and now, as she can see it, no reason for living. And so, last night, she telephoned her sister and a few friends to say goodbye—her friends assumed she was going to Florida to visit her sister; her sister assumed she could call her in the morning—and then she settled inside a nice hot bath and calmly slit her wrists. Her friends found her at just before midnight and rushed her to the hospital where she was bandaged, scolded, and released. The wounds weren't very deep, the doctor told her matter-of-factly. He said she was depressed, and prescribed Valium and sent her home.

Renee studied the bandages on the woman's slender wrists and fought the sudden urge to throw up.

"Kathryn," she said softly, and drew her older sister gently into her arms.

Renee felt as if she were hugging an apparition. There was no weight to the person she held in her arms. There was no substance. Kathryn pulled back slowly and looked deeply into her sister's frightened face. Renee said nothing, watching as tears formed in her sister's still startling green eyes, realizing that she was crying as well.

"You're so thin," Renee said, her voice breaking as her sister tried to smile, a tear curling around her upper lip and disappearing into her mouth. "How was your flight?" she asked, not wanting to probe too deep too fast.

"We ran into some turbulence," Kathryn whispered, obviously an effort to speak. "I'm still a little shaky."

"You'll lie down as soon as we get home." Renee took Kathryn by the elbow, hoping to maneuver her toward the baggage claim area, but Kathryn's body refused to move. Her eyes stared blankly at some vague point in the distance.

Renee studied her sister's delicate face, not sure how to proceed. Kathryn's green eyes were still her best, most prominent feature, although they were temporarily rimmed with red, and her high cheekbones were still model-perfect, all the more pronounced because of her obvious weight loss. But even without any makeup, even in her distracted state, Kathryn was undeniably beautiful. Arnie's death had been a terrible shock. Again, Renee's eyes traveled the length of her sister's frail arms to her gauze-covered wrists. Why? she wanted to ask, but said only, "Kathryn, we have to get your luggage." Then transferring her own queasiness to her sister: "Are you all right? Are you going to be sick?"

Kathryn's eyes focused on Renee with an intensity that caused Renee to pull back, bring her arm to her side. "You didn't tell Mom and Dad, did you?"

Renee shook her head. "No. I thought you could call them later . . ."

"No!"

"After you're settled."

"No!"

"Just to let them know you're here."

"I don't want them to know I'm here. I don't want them to know what happened."

"Kathryn, they're our parents."

"Please." Kathryn's voice was verging on hysteria. Renee noticed several people in the vicinity turn in their direction.

"Okay. Okay," Renee agreed. "Whatever you want."

"I don't want them to know. You know how upset Mother will be. You know how it will disappoint Daddy."

Renee nodded, guiding her sister to the baggage area, thinking that their mother would be upset only so far as Kathryn's attempted suicide might upset their father, and that their father's disappointment would be summed up in a silent stare, as if he'd known all along it would come to this, as if her depression was a personal affront, as if . . . as if . . . That silent stare had spoken volumes throughout their childhood. It projected disappointment of almost biblical proportions. Renee understood Kathryn's reluctance to confront it even as she understood that Kathryn would have to confront it sooner or later.

"What color is your suitcase?" Renee asked, watching the luggage as it paraded past her on the turnstyle.

Kathryn looked perplexed, then blank. "I can't remember," she said finally. "I didn't pack. Marsha packed everything. She's the one who phoned you, the one who took me to the airport. I don't remember what color my suitcase is," Kathryn said again, bringing her bandaged wrists in front of her eyes to hide the tears.

"It's all right. We'll find it."

Kathryn wiped at her eyes. "The doctor wasn't very impressed with my wounds," she said, almost casually. "He said he didn't think I really wanted to die."

"Thank God for that." Renee took her eyes off her sister only long enough to scan the bags that were tumbling onto the moving ramp. "Is that it?" Renee directed her sister toward an old navy-and-brown canvas suitcase that looked vaguely familiar. "Kathryn, is that your suitcase?" she asked again, before reaching over and pulling it off the ramp. She checked the name. Kathryn Metcalfe Wright, the tag read. "Are there any more? Do you remember how many suitcases your friend packed?"

Kathryn shook her head. "I think just one."

Renee half carried, half rolled the heavy bag out of the terminal, her other arm tightly wrapped around her sister's waist.

Reaching her white Mercedes—a gift from Philip on their last anniversary—she threw the bag into the trunk and led Kathryn to the passenger door. "Get in," she said gently.

Renee pulled the car out of the airport terminal and onto the road leading to I-95. She patted the top of her sister's hand gently, as if she were touching a fragile piece of china, and watched as her sister's eyes closed. A few minutes later, she heard Kathryn's soft, steady breathing and was relieved to discover that she had fallen asleep.

"Hello? Is anybody home?" Renee called as she guided her sister into the mirrored foyer of her condominium. She saw Kathryn wince at the sight of her own reflection, and quickly ushered her sister down the hall into the living room. The ocean sprang into immediate view. "I guess Debbie went to the beach," Renee said, seating her sister on the white sofa facing the floor-to-ceiling window, hoping her voice didn't betray the relief she felt at finding the apartment empty.

"This was a terrible time to do this to you," Kathryn said.

"What are you talking about?"

"You already have Debbie staying with you. The last thing you needed was your crazy sister."

"Didn't anybody ever tell you that's what condominiums in Florida are for? Hey, that was a joke. You're supposed to laugh."

Kathryn managed a wan smile. "I could really go for a glass of water."

"Don't move. I'll get it." Renee went immediately to the kitchen, poured Kathryn a large glass of water, then opened the fridge door and peered inside. "Do you want anything to eat?"

"No, thanks. Water is great."

Renee fumbled with a bag of miniature 3 Musketeers chocolate bars at the back of the refrigerator, popping one quickly into her mouth before returning to the living room. "You should eat," she told her sister. "You have to keep your strength up."

"I'm not hungry. Maybe later." Kathryn's eyes drifted

around the room. "Do you realize that I've never been to your apartment before?"

"That's because you never leave New York."

"Arnie doesn't like to travel."

"So, what do you think?" Renee asked, ignoring her sister's reference to her husband as if he were still alive. "Like it?"

For a moment, Kathryn said nothing. Renee wondered whether she had heard the question and was about to repeat it when Kathryn spoke. "It doesn't look like you," she remarked, as if she were examining a photograph.

"Well, it isn't. I mean, it is, but it isn't," Renee stammered, feeling foolish. "It was Philip's apartment, but it's so perfect, we didn't see any reason to move. It's right on the ocean and it's certainly big enough for our needs. There are three bedrooms. It's perfect," she repeated.

"It's so white."

Renee tried seeing the apartment through Kathryn's eyes, trying to remember what her first reaction had been when Philip brought her here some six and a half years ago. "Philip doesn't like clutter. He says he sees enough of it at the office every day without having to come home to it at night. He likes things neat and clean."

"And what do you like?"

"What do you mean?"

Kathryn said nothing.

Renee watched her sip gingerly at her water. "I like things exactly the way they are." She followed Kathryn's eyes as they swept across the walls of the living room, taking in the museumlike display of modern abstract art. "White surroundings accentuate the art better."

"You're happy?" Kathryn asked.

"Very."

"I'm glad."

Renee sat down beside her sister, afraid to ask the next question, knowing she had no choice.

"Why did you do it, Kathy? I know how much you loved Arnie but . . ."

"You don't know," Kathryn said, her voice flat.

"What do you mean?" It was the second time she had asked that.

A look of alarm raced through Kathryn's eyes. "You don't know how much I loved him," she said, recovering quickly. "He was my whole life."

"He was a large part of your life, but he wasn't everything."

"He *was* everything," Kathryn corrected. "I was barely eighteen years old when I married Arnie. I was a kid. He was almost old enough to be my father. Do you remember how furious Daddy was?"

Renee nodded. Their father's fury was not easily forgotten.

"Arnie was my whole life. He did everything for me. He took care of everything. I never had to make a decision. I never had to make arrangements. Arnie always made sure that everything was taken care of. And we did everything together. For almost twenty years. Twenty years! And then one night, he got up from the dinner table. I'd made this spicy meat loaf. Arnie didn't like it because he didn't like spicy food, but I thought this recipe sounded pretty safe, and so I tried it. And he didn't like it all that much, but he ate it. And then he stood up, and he suddenly keeled over. That was it. He just dropped to the floor. I screamed. I rushed over to him. At first I thought he was joking, you know, kidding around, because I made the meat loaf too spicy, but then I turned him over and saw his face, and I knew right away that he was dead."

"Kathy, that was three months ago. We've been through all this. I'm not sure it's good for you to keep dwelling on it."

"What am I supposed to do, Renee? What else is there for me to do with my life?"

"You have to get on with it. You're young; you're beautiful. Life can be so wonderful. You have to give it another chance. It's what Arnie would have wanted."

"Arnie would want me with him."

"No," Renee said vehemently, grabbing her sister's hands and watching her wince. "I'm sorry," she said quickly, releasing Kathryn's hands and feeling them tremble. "But Arnie would not want this. He would want you to be happy and to get as much out of the rest of your life as you can . . ."

"No." Kathryn shook her head and closed her eyes.

Renee felt momentarily as she had earlier in the afternoon when talking to Lynn Schuster, as if there were parts of the conversation missing, key facts being withheld. "Kathryn," she said slowly, "is there something you're not telling me?"

Kathryn opened her eyes, a look of fear passing quickly through them. "No, of course not."

"Why are you badgering her?" came a voice from behind them. Kathryn's body snapped to immediate attention, turning toward the sound. Renee remained slumped forward on the sofa. She didn't have to turn around to know who it was.

"Kathryn," she said quietly, "this is Philip's daughter, Debbie. Debbie, my sister, Kathryn."

"We won't shake hands," Debbie said, walking into the center of the room and motioning toward Kathryn's bandages.

"I didn't think anybody was home. I called out when we came in. I guess you didn't hear me."

"I heard you. I didn't realize it was a summons."

"Of course it wasn't a summons," Renee began, then stopped. What was the point?

"So, how does it feel to slit your wrists?" Debbie asked.

"Debbie!"

"No, that's all right," Kathryn said quickly. "I don't mind talking about it."

"She wants to talk about it," Debbie said defiantly, dropping down into the middle of the white carpet between the white sofa and the white chair, and folding her legs under her. "How did it feel?"

"It hurt." Kathryn stared at the bandages as if she could see through them. "It hurt a lot. That's probably why I didn't cut very deep."

"Was there a lot of blood?"

"Oh, for God's sake . . ."

"Yes," Kathryn answered, ignoring her sister's exclamation. "I looked like I was taking a bath in tomato juice."

Debbie giggled, and surprisingly Kathryn joined her.

"Which way did you make the cuts?" Debbie asked, leaning forward.

"Like this." Kathryn ran a trembling finger across the short width of her wrist.

"If you want to kill yourself, you're supposed to slice lengthwise," Debbie explained dispassionately. "I saw that in a movie once. They said that if you only want to go to the hospital, you cut widthwise. If you really want to die, you cut the same way your vein runs. That way nobody can sew you up again. Of course, the fastest way is probably with a gun. My dad has a gun. He keeps it in the night table beside his bed."

"Can we please talk about something else?" Renee begged, her queasiness returning.

"I think this is interesting," Debbie told her stepmother.

"That was not a request," Renee informed her curtly, deciding to move the gun elsewhere at the earliest opportunity. She'd always objected to its presence, in any event. Why had Debbie even mentioned it? Did the girl have no sense at all?

Debbie's hand formed a brisk salute. "Aye, aye, Captain."

Renee turned toward her sister. "I just think that we could find something else to talk about."

"My mother tried to kill herself once," Debbie announced. "Did you know that, Renée?"

"No, I didn't," Renee admitted, too stunned to say anything else.

"She was a mess after my father left. Of course, I was just a kid at the time but I guess she must have felt a lot like you feel now." Debbie smiled at Kathryn, who was watching her intently. "She started drinking and taking sleeping pills to get her through the night. One night she had too many drinks and too many pills. We rushed her to the hospital. They had to pump her stomach. It was pretty gross."

"Excuse me." Renee hurried into the kitchen and poured herself a glass of water, drinking it quickly before reaching into the fridge and tearing another chocolate bar out of its plastic bag, swallowing it in three quick bites. In the living room, she heard Debbie rattling on about her mother, telling Kathryn how beautiful she was, how thin she was, very much like Kathryn, she was saying. Nothing at all like Renée.

It was true. Renee had seen pictures of Philip's former wife,

Wendy. She *was* beautiful. And thin. And unbalanced as all get-out. Renee couldn't think of Debbie's mother without recalling the story that Philip had confided in her early in their relationship. Apparently, she'd once provoked a fight while they were getting ready for bed, and when Philip had insisted that he would spend the night in a hotel rather than listen to any more of her ravings, she had actually run down the street after his car, totally naked. Running after his car like a dog, he had said tearfully, then confessed that he'd never told that story to another living soul, he'd been so ashamed.

"I think that Kathryn should probably lie down now," Renee said, reentering the living room to find Debbie on the sofa next to her sister, Kathryn wrapped gently in Debbie's arms, her eyes closed in sleep.

"Don't worry about Kathryn," Debbie said sweetly. "I'll take care of her."

"That's very nice of you, Debbie," Renee said, softening, feeling grateful all of a sudden for her stepdaughter's presence.

"And then I'll take care of you," Debbie said, and turned to stare serenely out at the ocean.

5

The phone had been ringing all morning. Lynn Schuster glanced up from her paper-strewn desk at the well-groomed young woman who stood in the doorway to her small, tidy office. "For you. Line one," her secretary said, her hands buried beneath a neat stack of files. "I'm going to run these reports down the hall."

Lynn nodded and picked up the phone, thinking that she hated Fridays. They were always the worst. People seemed to be most desperate just before the weekend, something she had never really understood until Gary left her. Until then, Friday was always a day to look forward to because it meant that—in theory anyway—the family could spend the next two days relaxing and being together. In practice, Gary was more often working than not, the kids were somewhere playing with friends or home fighting with each other, and she was struggling to finish off work which never seemed to meet its deadline. Still, the illusion was there. The possibilities existed. When Gary walked out six months ago, he had taken the possibilities with him. Lynn no longer looked forward to the weekends, which only served to underline the unhappy statistic she had become. "Lynn Schuster," she announced into the phone.

"Marc Cameron," came the immediate reply. "And before you hang up on me," he continued—in fact, the thought had not occurred to her— "I'd like to apologize for my behavior the other night."

"Apology accepted," Lynn replied briskly. "Thank you for calling."

"Don't hang up," he said again, this time as she was about to.

Lynn glanced nervously toward her office door. Her secretary was down the hall delivering files. That was good for at least a couple of minutes. "What can I do for you, Mr. Cameron?"

"For starters, you can call me Marc. Then you can have dinner with me tonight."

Lynn took a deep breath, slowly expelling the air in her lungs and inadvertently blowing several sheets of paper off the top of her desk. "I don't think that would be a very good idea," she said, watching the papers float toward the beige carpet at her feet.

"Why not?" His voice was stubborn, provocative.

"I would think that's obvious."

"Because of what I said?"

"Because of what you are."

"A writer?"

She laughed. "Suzette's husband."

"Can't we just forget who we are? Correction," he said immediately. "Who we *were.*"

Lynn's fingers moved nervously to the thick gold band on the fourth finger of her left hand. "I think that might prove difficult."

"Not if we don't let it."

"I'm busy tonight," she said, then continued when he said nothing. "My father and his wife are coming over for dinner. Really."

"Tomorrow night?"

"I can't."

"Your father again?"

"My better judgment. I'm sorry. I just don't think it would be a very good idea."

"So you've said."

"I'm really sorry that we had to meet under these circumstances . . ."

"Sounds like something you say at a funeral." He laughed. "Hell, I'm a writer. I'm used to rejection. Look, will you do me a favor?"

"If I can."

"Get a piece of paper," he instructed. Lynn reached for her notebook as her secretary reappeared in the doorway. "Write this down." He dictated a number and Lynn dutifully copied it, repeating it aloud when he asked her to. "My phone number," he explained. "I'm renting an apartment until all this is settled. If you change your mind about seeing me again, as I sincerely hope you will, give me a call."

"I'll do that," Lynn said, motioning for her secretary to come in and sit down. "Thank you for calling."

"A pleasure, as always," he said, and was gone. Lynn replaced the receiver, smiling perhaps a little too hard at the blond, ponytailed young woman who sat before her.

"Something wrong?" her secretary asked, bending forward to indicate her willingness to listen. "You look like you're in pain," she continued, and Lynn forced her mouth to relax. Her secretary, whose name was Arlene and who was somewhere in her late twenties, lifted a slim file folder from her lap and reached it across the top of the desk toward Lynn.

"What's this?" Lynn pushed Marc Cameron into the back corners of her mind, concentrating on the file her secretary dropped into her hands.

"It's from McVee," Arlene said, standing up, about to return to her own desk just outside Lynn's office door. "Suspected child abuse. He wants it handled very carefully. All files are to be kept in his office. Strictly confidential. Apparently we might be treading on some very big toes. Check out the address."

Lynn opened the folder and glanced at the few lines typed across the first and only page. By the time her investigation was concluded, she knew, there would be many such pages. Too many. Keith and Patty Foster, she read, not recognizing the names; daughter, Ashleigh, age seven.

Lynn's eyes shot automatically to the framed photographs of her own two children, which were all but hidden by the stacks of paper on her desk. Impatiently, she shuffled the papers around until they afforded her a clear view of the two smiling figures which when last seen boarding their bus for day camp that morning, were glaring in barely concealed fury at each other's recent transgressions. Megan, who had been nine years old at the time her picture was taken, looked shy and quietly beautiful, the woman already visible behind the child's delicate features, whereas Nicholas's photo, taken last January on his seventh birthday, was one big, toothless record of self-congratulation.

Lynn closed the file folder and rested her chin against the palms of her hands. She didn't want to read about seven-year-old children who were the possible victims of parental abuse. In her twelve years of front-line work for the Department of Social Services in Delray Beach, this was the one aspect of her job to which she had never grown accustomed. Reluctantly, she reopened the file, checking out the address as her secretary had suggested. Harborside Villas, she read, then shook her head. Not the usual address for this sort of thing, but then she had learned long ago that money and social standing had little bearing on matters such as these, although they obviously had a great deal to do with the careful way this case was being handled.

The suspected abuse had been reported by a neighbor, she read, a Mrs. Davia Messenger, who lived in the town house next to the one owned by the Fosters. Lynn understood that she would have to drive out to the Harborside Villas to interview the woman as soon as possible. She looked around for her appointment book, and saw only the notepad with Marc Cameron's phone number scrawled boldly across it. "Arlene, what's my schedule like today?"

"You have a meeting at two o'clock."

"And this morning?"

"Nothing that can't wait."

A few minutes later, Lynn was in her car heading south on Federal Highway toward the Harborside Villas, a Mrs. Davia Messenger, and a story she didn't want to hear.

The Harborside Villas were part of a horseshoe-shaped complex situated on the Inland Waterway, boasting a private marina, two large swimming pools, and four tennis courts. Prices started at a quarter of a million dollars for a one-bedroom apartment, and went up from there, the most expensive units being the row of eight identical, white, two-story town houses that ran parallel to the main building and directly overlooked the Inland Waterway.

Davia Messenger lived in the second-to-last house next to the corner unit owned by the Fosters. Lynn walked steadily across the curving sidewalk of interlocking red bricks, her eyes casually perusing the luxury that was everywhere around her, to the Messengers' front door. She barely had time to lift the bronze dolphin-shaped knocker before the door was opened by a tall, thin, slightly stooped woman whose sharp, irregular features had long ago cemented themselves into a look of anxiety.

"She didn't see you come in, did she?" the woman greeted Lynn nervously in the entranceway of her designer-perfect town house. Lynn made a mental note of the woman's age— late fifties—and flaming red, geometrically shaped hair. She said nothing as the woman shut the front door behind her and ushered her inside the spotless living room, awash in shades of glistening yellow and gray. Lynn walked carefully toward the matching pale yellow love seats situated in the middle of the large room, which afforded a most spectacular view of the Inland Waterway. She had the distinct feeling that this was not a room that was used to visitors.

"I'm sorry I'm a bit late. I got stuck in traffic. You have a beautiful home," Lynn remarked almost in one breath, seeing

Mrs. Messenger wince as she sat down and took out her note-book and pen.

"You will be careful," the woman stated, more than asked, "with that pen."

"Of course," Lynn told her, and tried to look reassuring, although she felt as she imagined her children must feel when told to get their crayons out of the living room. "How long have you lived here, Mrs. Messenger?"

"Six years," came the rapidly delivered reply. "We're the original owners. We bought when the units were still under construction. We knew how beautiful they were going to be. We have an eye for beauty, my husband and I." She tried to smile but the corners of her lips only twitched, and so she abandoned the attempt. "I don't enjoy doing this, you know," she said. "You will keep my name out of it, won't you? The man I spoke to, he assured me that my name would be kept out of it."

"Your identity will be kept strictly confidential, Mrs. Messenger." Lynn watched as the woman made repeated circles around the second love seat, picking up imaginary pieces of lint from the obviously expensive material.

"They're important people, the Fosters. He's with Data Base International. Quite the big shot." Davia Messenger's eyes darted nervously around the room. She reached down and swept up a suspected speck of dirt from the pale Drury rug at Lynn's feet. Lynn obligingly lifted her heels off the floor, lowering them only after the woman's attention had been diverted elsewhere.

Lynn made a quick note describing the woman's highly agitated state, which she suspected was aggravated, but not defined, by her visit. The woman was starting to make her nervous as well.

"Why don't you tell me what prompted you to call our agency, Mrs. Messenger."

Davia Messenger seemed surprised by the question. "Well, the little girl of course. Ashleigh. She's why I called. So many Ashleighs these days, don't you think?"

"You suspect her parents are abusing her?"

"Not suspect. *Know.*" Davia Messenger swooped hawklike toward Lynn, her long fingers outstretched and shaking. "How else do you explain why that poor little thing is always covered with bruises? Last week she had a black eye. A few weeks before that it was a broken arm."

"Children have accidents, Mrs. Messenger." Lynn felt Davia Messenger's gaze shift from her face to the area just to the left of her cheek above her shoulder. Before she had time to wonder what exactly Davia Messenger was staring at, the woman reached over and snapped up a stray hair which had been dangling from the side of Lynn's head, and which had obviously offended her strict aesthetic sense.

"No accidents. Patty Foster is abusing her daughter."

"Have you actually witnessed this abuse?" Lynn was finding it increasingly difficult to concentrate. She wished Davia Messenger would sit the hell down.

"I've witnessed the results. I've heard the child crying at all hours of the day and night."

"But you've never personally witnessed Patty Foster physically mistreating Ashleigh?"

"I've already answered that," the woman snapped.

"What specifically prompted your phone call, Mrs. Messenger?"

"I don't understand. I told you . . ."

"You indicated that this has been going on for a number of months, yet you waited until now to phone us. Did something happen last night?"

"If you'd heard that child crying, you wouldn't have to ask. I just couldn't take listening to it anymore."

"Did your husband hear the crying as well?"

"Well, of course."

"Could I speak to him?"

"Oh no, no, no," Mrs. Messenger trilled, her hands fluttering wildly in front of her. "Leave him out of this. He doesn't want to get involved. He told me not to call you. He said that nobody would believe me. That Mr. Foster is an important man in the community. No, no, no. Leave my husband out of this."

Lynn lowered her pen to her lap, aware that Mrs. Messenger seemed to be holding her breath. "What makes you so sure that it's *Mrs.* Foster who's abusing her daughter, and not Mr. Foster?"

"Oh no, no, no," the woman said again, this time with conviction rounding out the vowels. "Mr. Foster is a gentleman. He would never do anything to hurt a child. It's his wife. She's much younger than he is. Young enough to be his daughter. His granddaughter, even. Pretty enough, I suppose. She doesn't do much. Sits around the pool all day in her bikini. Don't know why she had children. They're not allowed, you know. At least that was my impression when we bought the place, bought it while it was still under construction. We have a real eye for beauty, my husband and I. Decorated it ourselves. Please be careful with that pen."

Lynn put the cap back on the black felt pen, closed her notebook, and returned both to her briefcase. It was obvious she had already received whatever worthwhile information she was going to get from Mrs. Davia Messenger, and she was afraid that if she stayed any longer, the woman might break into hives. "Thank you, Mrs. Messenger. I think I'll talk to the Fosters now."

"You can't do that."

"I beg your pardon?"

"Don't you see? She'll see you came from my house, and she'll know I was the one who reported her. She's a very vindictive person."

Lynn Schuster stared deeply into the eyes of the woman who was squinting in her direction, watching them narrow further to emphasize her point, aware that she was not the most credible of witnesses, but aware also that each report of suspected child abuse had to be investigated fully.

"I assure you your identity will be kept confidential."

"She'll try to fool you, of course. She can be very persuasive. You mustn't underestimate her," Mrs. Messenger continued as she followed Lynn to the front door, then hid behind it as Lynn stepped outside into the hot sunshine.

Davia Messenger was an unpleasant, possibly even unbalanced woman, Lynn was thinking as she cut across the narrow strip of lawn to the house next door. She would make a most unreliable witness in court. With that in mind, Lynn knocked tentatively on the Fosters' door, and was relieved to discover that no one was home.

A few minutes later, she was sitting in her car in the middle of a monstrous traffic jam. It was extremely hot, and already cars on the busy highway were starting to overheat. Motorists who were stranded on the side of the road, their faces polished in sweat, their mouths distorted with agitation, stood beside raised hoods, steam shooting from overheated engines. Lynn observed them dispassionately, reaching over and flicking off her own air conditioning to spare herself the same fate, lowering her window instead, feeling the immediate attack of hot air as it quickly clambered in through the open window, as if it too was looking for a place to escape. Lynn rested her elbow on the car door, withdrawing it almost instantly, feeling her flesh burn as if she had pressed it against a lit torch.

She peered out her front window, trying to make out what was causing the delay, but a large yellow van with bright flowers painted across its back window blocked her view. In the car to her right, a man and a woman were fighting. She couldn't hear what they were saying but she could tell by the way their narrow faces were distorted that they were blaming one another for the futility of their current situation. "I told you not to come this way," she understood the man was saying, "but no, you knew better."

Lynn looked across the highway divider, caught the sardonic smile of a young man in a sports car as he continued unimpeded in the opposite direction. He reminded her of Marc Cameron, she realized, wondering for a minute if it had, in fact been him. But no, Marc Cameron had a beard, she remembered. The man in the sports car had been clean-shaven. And he was at least ten years younger than the man who had visited her home earlier in the week. He didn't look anything like

Marc Cameron at all. What was the matter with her? What was she thinking about?

She heard the car behind her honk, and noticed that the van ahead of her had inched forward almost imperceptively. Grateful for the diversion, she traveled the requisite several inches, then stopped, putting the car into neutral. She couldn't afford to waste valuable time thinking about men like Marc Cameron. So what if she found him appealing? So what if he was the first man since Gary had walked out—the first man since Gary, period—who had stirred these kinds of feelings inside her? She hadn't had sex in over six months. She needed these kinds of feelings like a hole in the head. Who needed feelings like these, feelings that made you squirm and fidget and lose sleep? Especially when she wasn't prepared to act on them. *Was* she prepared to act on them? She had his phone number. All she had to do when she got back to the office was pick up the phone and dial. "Hello, Marc Cameron? This is Lynn Schuster. I know this great motel for dinner."

"Don't be silly," she said out loud. You're already having dinner. With your father and his charming wife, Barbara, the one he married three years ago, the one who's given him back his youth, that new lease on life and all those other glorious clichés she never gets tired of trotting out. Life is what you make it; when God hands you a lemon, make lemonade; it's always darkest before the dawn. The woman was a walking encyclopedia of superficial words to the wise. Lynn had never understood how her father, an intelligent, well-read man, had allowed himself to get involved with such a woman. Not that there was anything wrong with her. Barbara was attractive and well-mannered, but her reading consisted solely of self-help tomes and diet books, and her conversation began with quotes from Leo Buscaglia and ended with the words of Rollo May. In between was advice from everyone from Richard Simmons to Dr. Ruth. Lynn doubted that the woman had ever had an original thought in her life. And yet her father seemed to hang on every silly syllable. Even after three years, he continued to smile benignly at his wife's pronouncements, adding a few well-chosen observations of his own, commenting lovingly on

Barbara's latest accomplishments. It was always "Barbara this" and "Barbara that" and "Did you see Barbara's name in the paper the other day? She's running that new charity drive." "Charity begins at home," Barbara would say. Home is where the heart is. Anywhere I hang my hat is home. Home, home on the range.

Her mother would have choked at the very idea of such a woman. Not that she would have objected to her husband marrying again—not that Lynn objected to her father marrying again—but surely he could have found someone more suitable, if not to *his* taste, well, then, to *hers*.

Was that what bothered her so much about the woman? That her father, who had relied on her so heavily in the year immediately following his wife's death, hadn't consulted her at all when he found a new wife? That he had presented her proudly to his only child as a fait accompli? And the woman, short, dark, and nothing at all like her mother, had pressed her hand warmly and said how delighted she was to be part of the family. You're not losing a father, you're gaining a friend. Anytime you need me, I'll be there. Love is where you find it. All you need is love. She loves you, yea, yea, yea.

The list was endless. Her mother would have gagged.

Lynn arched her back and pushed her hair away from her face, feeling guilty for the meanness of her thoughts. That was one thing you could say about Barbara: the woman didn't have a mean bone in her body. She had loved them all away with her collection of uplifting aphorisms. Mean bones didn't stand a chance in such a relentlessly perky environment. They begged for mercy and cracked under the pressure of all that good cheer. And her father lapped it up. He hadn't looked better in years. Probably due to the new low-fat, no-salt, no-sugar diet Barbara had him on. No fat, no salt, no sugar, no negative vibrations. It didn't make for a very interesting dinner party. And she had passed up an evening of potentially sordid sex for dinner with Miss Congeniality?

It wouldn't be the first time she had chosen safety and security over high risk, despite the potential of a greater return on one's investment. The fact was that she wasn't a gambler. She stayed where she knew she belonged. She didn't take unnecessary chances. It was probably just as well she had decided not to accept the job she had been offered with the Palm Beach County Board of Education. Even though it was definitely a step up, even though she would have been virtually running the Social Services Department of the Board of Education for the entire county, it also meant a retreat from the front-line work she knew so well and an increase in responsibility she wasn't sure she was capable of assuming at this time in her life. She'd had enough upheavals in the last six months. She didn't need a new job. She didn't need a new man. She certainly didn't need Marc Cameron. Or sex. Or even thoughts of sex. What she needed was to get out of this traffic and back to her office. What she needed was a cup of coffee. What she needed was an idea for what to serve for dinner.

Again the car behind her sounded his horn. This time it wasn't one honk, but several, like hiccups or a persistent cough. Lynn quickly focused on the line of traffic in front of her and realized it was moving. She threw her car into gear, glancing into her rearview mirror in time to see the man in the car behind her lift the middle finger of his right hand angrily in her direction. Just what I needed, she thought. The image of her father's wife, Barbara, immediately appeared before her eyes. Have a nice day, it said.

6

In Renee's dream, she was sitting at her kitchen table, wearing the luxurious new white Pratesi bathrobe Philip bought her at Christmas, working on the New York *Times* crossword puzzle and drinking her eighth cup of morning coffee. She knew it was her eighth cup because she had arranged the other cups in a large circle on the table so as to resemble the face of a clock. The phone was ringing, as it had been ringing all morning. Renee looked lazily in its direction, trying to decide whether or not to answer it.

Ultimately, its persistent ring persuaded her. Renee reached over, not moving from her seat at the kitchen table, and lifted the white phone to her ear. Even before she could say hello, a voice was speaking. "This is Marsha, from the Cross Your Heart and Hope to Die Dating Service," the woman said, in harsh New York tones. "We're calling to tell you about our fabulous celebration."

A face suddenly appeared to go with the voice. Marsha, of the Cross Your Heart and Hope to Die Dating Service, appeared, raven-haired and grossly overweight, the Cheshire cat behind the frightening smile.

"As you know, the Cross Your Heart and Hope to Die Dating Service has been bringing people together, people like you and your husband, for the last ten years."

"No," Renee started to tell her, reality intruding into her dream, trying to make its presence felt. She and Philip had been introduced to each other in a restaurant by a mutual acquaintance, who was surprised, even startled, by their marriage a scant five months later. No dating service had been required. "You must have the wrong number."

"So the party we're having," the woman continued, oblivious to the interruption, "is half *our* celebration and half *yours*. We're bringing all our happy couples together for a great big anniversary bash, and since you and your husband are one of our major success stories, we're sure that you'd like to attend the festivities. Have you got a pencil to write down all the information?"

The woman metamorphosed from fat and dark-haired to blond and petite. Her wrists were heavily bandaged.

The pencils sat in a glass jam jar on the other side of the phone, and in order to retrieve one, Renee had to step over the body of her husband, which was lying on the white tile floor in front of her, a wooden-stemmed butcher knife plunged rather neatly through his heart. Of course, technically speaking, Renee was aware she shouldn't be able to see the knife from this angle, but she saw it nonetheless.

Philip was lying on his stomach, and except for a rather large pool of blood, he looked remarkably undisturbed, as if he merely decided to have a quick nap on the kitchen floor. He had done crazier things, Renee thought, stepping over him and grabbing a pencil from the glass jar. She informed the woman that she was ready, and listened as the woman dictated the time and place of the upcoming festivities, dutifully writing it all down, interrupting only long enough to ask the proper spelling of the designated street.

The police suddenly appeared, and waited patiently for her to take down all this useless information. She told them that she was a good girl, that she'd always been a good girl. They slapped handcuffs on her wrists and a gag into her mouth. Despite the gag, Renee informed them that she knew her rights and demanded to see her lawyer. They reminded her she *was* a lawyer. The corpse on the floor turned over and smiled. Its hand reached out and grabbed her ankle. "Got you," he said.

Renee bolted upright in bed, her breath coming in short, angry bursts.

"What's the matter?" Philip asked, sitting up beside her, obviously disoriented. "What happened?"

Renee brought her legs up to her chest, hugging her shins, resting her forehead against her knees. "I had a terrible dream."

"Oh, Christ," Philip said, and lay back down, collapsing against the pillow as if he had been pushed. "You scared me half to death."

"Sorry." She tried ridding her mind of the image of Philip lying dead on the kitchen floor. "It was a horrible dream."

Philip said nothing.

"Do you want to hear about it?"

"No."

Renee felt a short stab of resentment in approximately the same spot she had pictured the knife through Philip's chest. You listened to Debbie's dream without complaint, she wanted to say, but didn't because she knew how childish it would sound, how childish it *was*. "I dreamt you were dead," she told him anyway.

Philip turned on his side away from her. "That's only natural under the circumstances."

"It is? What circumstances?"

"Your sister's husband died three months ago. Your sister is staying with us. You feel empathy for your sister. Simple transference."

"I dreamt *I* killed you. I dreamt I stuck a knife through your heart."

"Nice person."

"It was awful. I feel terrible."

"So you should. Come on, Renee. We can get another ten minutes sleep here."

Renee looked through the darkness at the luminous face of the clock, recalling the final seconds of her dream, and seeing Philip's ghoulish smile reflected on the clock's surface. "What time is it?" she asked, her voice rising in alarm. "Does that say ten minutes to seven?"

"She reads too," Philip said, covering his head with his pillow.

"I have to get up. I'm going to be late." Renee threw off the covers, about to jump out of bed when Philip's hand stopped her.

"What's going on?" he asked patiently.

"I have a partners' meeting in one hour! I'll never be ready in time. I don't understand what happened. I set the alarm for six-thirty."

"I reset it for seven," Philip said calmly.

"What?"

"I reset it for seven," he repeated. "I thought it must be a mistake. Stop worrying—there's no reason you can't be ready in an hour."

"Philip, you know how long it takes me to get ready. I have to shower and do my hair and put on my makeup . . ."

"And kiss your husband . . ."

Renee leaned forward, intending to kiss Philip on the side of his mouth, surprised when he quickly turned his head so that she was kissing him directly on the lips, even more surprised when the kiss grew into a passionate embrace. She pulled gently, reluctantly, out of his arms. "Philip, I have to go."

"Can't you spare a few minutes to tell your husband that you love him?"

Renee smiled. "I love you."

"Can't hear you."

"I love you," Renee repeated a little louder, giggling, feeling like a schoolgirl.

"Prove it."

"Philip, I can't. I have to go."

"I love you," he said, kissing her again, this time the kiss even more insistent.

Renee felt his tongue in her mouth, felt his hands slide gracefully up her arms to her shoulders, his fingers lowering the straps of her nightgown. "This isn't fair."

"What isn't fair?"

"I'm late," she whispered, feeling the nightgown drop to her waist, his hands at her breasts, his mouth buried against the side of her neck.

Renee pulled away, pulled up her nightgown, readjusting the straps. "I should have been up half an hour ago."

"So, you overslept."

"I didn't oversleep. You reset the alarm clock. You shouldn't have done that."

"All right, so I made a mistake. But, frankly, you could use the extra sleep. You've been looking a little tired lately. You can't tell me that your sister being here isn't a strain. The extra sleep would do more for your appearance than a ton of make-up. Come on, Renee, you've still got lots of time to get ready. Indulge me. Make love to your husband."

Renee was about to object when his fingers on her lips stopped her.

"We hardly have time to make love anymore. I remember when we first got married. You couldn't wait for me to make love to you."

"I still feel that way."

"Do you?"

Renee felt Philip's hands return to her shoulders, his breath slide close against her face.

"Tell me what you want, Renee," he was saying. "I'm not going to do anything that you don't really want me to. If this meeting is really so important to you, then I'll understand."

"Nothing's more important to me than you are."

"What do you want?" he asked again, his lips on the side of her neck. "Tell me what you want me to do. Do you want me to back off? Do you want me to leave you alone? Let you get ready?"

"I want you to make love to me," Renee heard herself say.

"Do you?"

Renee nodded, her breath coming faster.

"Is this what you want?"

Renee felt his fingers teasing the front of her nightgown.

"Is it? Tell me."

"Yes."

"What else do you want?"

"Philip . . ."

"I won't do anything that you don't tell me to do."

"Please . . ."

"Please what? This?" She felt his hands lifting the skirt of her nightgown, felt him push her back on the bed, lift the nightgown up to her waist. "Tell me what you want me to do."

"I can't. I'm embarrassed." She felt his hand between her legs.

"Do you want me to touch you?"

"Yes."

"Then say it."

"I want you to touch me."

"Where?"

"Oh God, please . . ."

"Where do you want me to touch you? Here?"

Renee groaned.

"Do you want me to use my mouth?"

"Philip . . ."

"Say it."

"I want you to use your mouth."

"I'll do whatever you want me to do," he was saying.

Renee closed her eyes, clutching at the pillow beside her head, feeling her husband's tongue between her legs, hearing her own gasps through her open lips, feeling dangerously close to tears, frightened and not sure why.

"What do you want me to do now?" he was asking hoarsely.

"Whatever you want," she said, not wishing to speak. "Do whatever you want."

"No, we're going to do what you want. Do you want me inside you?"

Renee tried to answer but no sound came.

"Say it," Philip said, from somewhere above her. "Tell me you want me inside you."

"Please . . . I want you inside me."

She felt his hands lifting her buttocks, felt him plunge inside her roughly, repeatedly. She opened her eyes and saw him staring down at her. He was smiling.

When it was over, Philip sat up in bed and asked for some tissues. "Sorry I took so long," he said with a nod toward the clock. "But it was your fault. You inspired me."

Renee patted her perspiration-soaked hair. "I should call the office. Tell them I won't be able to make the meeting."

"Fuck 'em." He smiled. "I guess we already did that."

"Philip," Renee began slowly, not sure this was the right time to bring the subject up but unable to think of a better one. "Have you thought anymore about what we talked about a few weeks ago?"

"What was that?"

"About having a baby," Renee said quietly, still feeling Philip inside her.

"I don't think it's a good idea," he said gently, resting his hand on her shoulder before walking into the closet and reemerging with his robe across his shoulders, monitoring himself in the mirror across from their bed.

"Why not?"

"I'm just trying to be realistic, honey. How many things can one person do and do well? You're already overloaded." He looked from Renee to the clock beside their bed and back again. "You don't have time to take a shower, for Pete's sake. When are you going to find time to have a baby?"

"I'd make time."

"As much time as you make for Debbie?"

"That's not fair."

"No, what's not fair would be bringing another child into this already overcrowded world when you're not fully prepared to look after it properly. I don't want some housekeeper who doesn't even speak English bringing up my child."

"Philip, lots of women work and have children."

"You're not lots of women. You're you. And right now the most important thing in your life is your career." He laughed. "I almost have to make an appointment to make love to my wife."

"I'd slow things down."

Philip walked over to her side of the bed and leaned over to kiss her forehead. "You can't slow down. Your mind is totally focused on your work. Even when we were making love, you were worried about what time it was. Weren't you? Don't try to tell me otherwise. I always know what you're feeling." He gave her a look of bemused resignation. "I'd love some bacon and eggs for breakfast," he said on his way to the bathroom.

Renee sat for a few minutes on the side of the bed, then reached over and lifted the phone from its carriage. She dialed quickly, ignoring the fact her hands were shaking. "Hi, Dan. It's Renee. I won't be able to make the meeting. I haven't been feeling so hot this morning. No, I think it was just something I ate. I'll try to be in by nine o'clock. Thanks. I'm really sorry."

Renee replaced the receiver and approached her image in the mirror. "Oh God," she said, shuddering at the sight of her naked body. "How can he bear to look at you?" She turned, focusing on the pink welt that cut across her left buttock.

Philip had lately taken to punctuating their lovemaking with two sharp slaps to her backside. It had started several months ago, maybe longer, she thought now, trying to recall the exact occasion. She remembered them coming home from a party one night and making love in pretty much the usual way, when Philip had suddenly flipped her over onto her stomach and slapped her twice, hard, across the buttocks. The first slap had been like a rebuke—stinging, fast, sharp. The second had been more pronounced. It stayed, left a mark.

Renee studied the fading streak of color slashed across her pale flesh, realizing that this was a habit she didn't think she liked. Still, she hesitated about mentioning it to Philip. He might accuse her of being uninventive, of not wanting to try new things. Renee dropped her gaze to the floor, careful not to look back in the mirror.

She found her nightgown in the middle of the mess of bed-sheets, pushed it over her head and retrieved her terrycloth white robe—the same new white Pratesi robe of her dream—from the closet, pushing her arms through its sleeves, hearing Philip singing in the shower as she walked past the bathroom door.

Debbie was in the kitchen, standing by the sink and drinking a glass of orange juice.

Renee took a deep breath. "You're up early."

"You're late," Debbie answered, looking at her strangely. "Love your hair."

Renee blushed and turned away, smoothing her hair behind her ears self-consciously.

"Kathryn still asleep?"

"She usually sleeps till around ten."

Renee reached into the refrigerator and pulled out a carton of eggs and a package of bacon.

"They say breakfast is the most important meal of the day," Debbie said, not even trying to keep the disdain from her voice.

"It's for your father."

Debbie nodded, saying nothing while Renee arranged the bacon in the frying pan.

"I want to thank you for being so sweet to Kathryn all week," Renee told Debbie, surprised she could legitimately apply the word "sweet" to her stepdaughter. "I think it's been good for her, having somebody around."

Debbie shrugged. "You don't have to thank me. I like her."

"Well, it was nice of you to take the time . . ."

"Somebody should," Debbie said pointedly. Renee wondered if the girl and her father had been communicating in their sleep.

"Something smells nice in here," Philip said a few minutes later, stopping in the doorway to the kitchen.

"It's all ready," Renee told him, holding up the plate for his approval.

"Looks wonderful, but I really should get going. I didn't

realize how late it was." He put his fingers to his mouth and blew his wife and daughter a kiss. "See you later."

Renee stood for a moment with the plate of bacon and eggs in her hands. She watched Debbie deposit her empty glass into the sink without bothering to rinse it out.

"Excuse me," Debbie said, slipping past her stepmother into the hall before disappearing into her room.

Renee carried the plate of bacon and eggs to the kitchen table and sat down, seeing the dream-image of her husband sprawled across the white tile floor, feeling his cold hand surround her ankle. She stuffed a piece of bacon into her mouth. "Got you," she said.

7

Lynn sat alone at her kitchen table, frowning at the half-eaten bowls of cereal and still full glasses of juice. Nicholas had arranged the leftover crust from his toast into what looked like a face, its tongue protruding, mocking her. Megan's four-minute egg sat uncracked in its cup. "Megan," she called to her daughter, "you didn't touch your egg."

"I'm in the bathroom," came the reply from down the hall.

Lynn checked the clock on her microwave oven. It was after nine o'clock. Gary was late. Usually he arrived to pick the kids up first thing on Saturday morning. Today he was already fifteen minutes late. Just as well, Lynn thought, knowing how long Megan could take in the bathroom. She started clearing the dishes from the table, deciding that it was pointless to try forcing them to eat more. They ate little on Saturday mornings since the separation. Lynn assumed they were nervous and excited about seeing their father. Today they were especially anxious. Their father was taking them for the whole weekend. Lynn had heard Megan get up to go to the bathroom three times during the night. The child's overnight bag, packed so tightly its zipper wouldn't close, had been sitting in front of her bedroom door for two days.

"Where do you think Daddy's going to take us?" Nicholas asked, returning to the kitchen and watching his mother stack the dishes in the dishwasher.

"I don't know, sweetheart." Your father doesn't discuss these things with me anymore, Lynn added silently.

"Do you think he'll take us to Disney World?"

"We were just *at* Disney World," Lynn reminded him. Two months before your father left, she thought.

"I know. But we didn't get to go on all the rides. And Daddy said we could go again."

"Well, that's something you'll have to talk over with Daddy." Would she ever get over this strange sensation of being excluded from her children's lives whenever the subject of their father came up?

"I bet he's taking us to Disney World," Nicholas said confidently.

"Well, don't get your hopes up, honey. But I'm sure that wherever Daddy takes you, you'll have a good time." Why did she say that? She wasn't sure of any such thing.

The doorbell rang.

"Daddy!"

"Why don't you answer the door," Lynn began, but Nicholas was already running toward the front hall. "I'll just wait here in the kitchen with the rest of the servants," Lynn muttered, hearing her husband's voice, seeing him in her mind as he bent down to scoop up their young son. She pictured the dimples that creased his handsome face, and her hand groped toward the kitchen counter for support. "When does this feeling stop?" she asked, catching her reflection in the smoky glass of the microwave oven.

Nicholas came bounding back into the room. "Daddy wants to talk to you."

Lynn forced a smile onto her lips. "Why don't you make sure you have everything ready to go," she suggested. Again Nicholas was gone before she could complete her sentence.

Gary was standing in the living room, staring out the large

picture window that faced toward the ocean, in much the same position Marc Cameron had assumed the week before. He was wearing a new sports jacket, a sure sign, Lynn decided, that Disney World was not on the day's agenda.

"Hi, Gary." Lynn cleared her throat self-consciously, making sure she was still smiling.

"Lynn," he said warmly, turning toward her without moving. "You look great."

"Thank you. How are you?"

"Good. Great," he corrected, unnecessary emphasis on the final word. "You?"

"Pretty good. The kids are really excited about this weekend."

A look of guilt laced with unexpected defiance cut across Gary's face, his lips wavering between a smile and a frown. "That's what I wanted to talk to you about," he said slowly. "Something's come up. I'm afraid I won't be able to take the kids for the whole weekend the way we planned."

"What are you talking about? We decided weeks ago. It was your idea." The sentences tumbled out before Lynn could stop them.

"I know that, and I'm sorry."

"You're sorry." Lynn pictured Megan's overnight bag sitting expectantly in front of her bedroom door. "The kids have been counting on . . ."

"I know that. Look, what is this in aid of? Are you trying to make me feel guilty?"

"I'm trying to understand," she answered.

"What's there to understand? It's simple. I can't take the kids for the weekend. I'll take them next time. I'm not saying I can't take them for the day. I just won't be able to keep them overnight, that's all."

That's all, Lynn repeated silently. "What about *my* plans?" she asked, wondering why she was persisting in a conversation that was so obviously futile.

Gary seemed genuinely surprised that she might have any. "Well, I'll pay for a sitter, of course, if you have plans to go out."

"And if I have plans to go away for the weekend?"

"Do you?" His face became soft, curious.

That word again, she thought, then admitted after a pause, "No, I'll be here this weekend."

Gary lifted his hands into the air as if to ask what then all the fuss was about. "Would you tell them?" he asked.

Lynn thought of all the things she could say, the stinging remarks she could administer, the arrows she could fling, then decided there was no point to any of them. Ultimately she would only be hurting herself. "Is there anything in particular you'd like me to say?" she asked, managing to keep the sarcasm out of her voice.

"Tell them I'm taking them somewhere special for lunch. Tell them to dress up nicely."

They'll be thrilled, Lynn thought, but said nothing.

She found Megan in her room sitting on the edge of her bed, her overnight bag unpacked, her nightclothes strewn about the floor. "You heard?" Lynn asked, though the question was unnecessary. She sat down beside her daughter and put her arm around her shoulder.

"It doesn't matter," Megan said, brushing her mother's arm aside.

"There'll be other weekends."

"It doesn't matter," Megan repeated, staring straight ahead, refusing to look at her mother.

"I love you," Lynn offered.

"So does Daddy," Megan said quickly.

"Of course he does," Lynn told her, though she drew the line at defending his actions.

Nicholas popped his head in the doorway. "Let's go," he said. "Daddy's waiting." He looked around the room, his eyes resting on Megan's overturned overnight bag. "What's the matter?"

"Daddy can't take you for the whole weekend. He's going to take you somewhere special for lunch instead. He wants you to change and get all spiffy," Lynn said in a gulp, watching Nicholas's face drop and his eyes fill with tears. "He says there'll be lots of other weekends," she continued as Nicholas walked slowly from the room. Lynn thought in that instant that she hated her husband.

"Goddamn you, Gary Schuster," she said out loud after he had left with her children and she was returning Megan's clothes to their proper drawers. "Goddamn you to hell."

The doorbell rang.

"What? Lunch over so soon?" She checked her watch. Half an hour had passed since her family's departure. Lynn walked briskly to the front door and opened it without asking who it was. Marc Cameron stood smiling on the other side.

"I thought you might like to go for a walk on the beach," he said.

"It's a very strange feeling," Lynn was musing as she walked beside Marc Cameron along the crowded ocean strip, "to come into your kitchen and find your soon to be ex-husband leafing through your mail, helping himself to something from the fridge, checking things out as if it were still his home." She tried to smile. "I guess as long as he's paying the mortgage, that's how he thinks of it. Not much I can do."

"You can tell him to go to hell."

"Not if I want him to keep on paying the mortgage, I can't," Lynn replied honestly, wondering what she was doing walking along a public beach with this man.

"It's probably my fault about tonight," Marc said.

"What? What do you mean?"

"This guy, a wrestler that I interviewed a couple of days ago, sent over some tickets to the match at the Auditorium tonight, and told me to bring my boys. I called Suzette after I got the tickets and asked if it would be all right for me to take them. She said okay. Therefore, Suzette is free tonight. Suzette doesn't like to spend her Saturday nights alone."

Lynn swallowed a sudden rush of renewed anger. "Where are your boys now?"

"They're at a birthday party. A day at Lion Country Safari. I'm picking them up at four o'clock."

Lynn became aware he was staring at her but she refused to look back.

"So you had to cancel your plans for tonight?" he asked.

"It was just a movie with a girlfriend." It doesn't matter, she heard Megan say.

"It's not fair," Marc said simply, sidestepping a big blue man-of-war that was lying in his path.

"Maybe not, but that's the way it is."

"You get all the headaches and he gets . . . what?"

"He gets to be in love," Lynn said, hearing her voice shake.

"Watch out," Marc Cameron warned, pushing Lynn roughly aside before she stepped on another man-of-war washed up by the tide. "A big juicy one too," he said, grabbing Lynn's arm to steady her. "Sorry, I didn't mean to push you so hard. Are you all right?"

Lynn took a quick glance at the sand beneath her feet. "I'm still standing," she remarked, then found herself staring directly into his eyes. And then suddenly he was kissing her. She didn't know how it happened, and even later was unable to recall exactly what had led to what. There'd been no telltale tilt of his head, no slow angling toward her face, nothing to indicate he was intending to kiss her. His mouth was simply suddenly on top of hers, his arms around her waist, the softness of his beard pressing against her chin. She realized she had never kissed a man with a beard before, then realized that she was kissing him back. She pulled away immediately, catching her attorney's horrified expression on the face of a woman bather who was walking past. "That was not a good idea."

"Sorry," he said quickly.

"No, you're not."

"No, I'm not. Are you?"

"It can't happen again," Lynn said, avoiding his question, looking around self-consciously, feeling all eyes watching, waiting for Marc's next move.

It seemed as though every resident in town was beachside, although, in truth, their kiss had attracted little attention. Farther down the beach, closer to the water's edge, teenagers hurled Frisbees across the bodies of sunbathers. More prudent visitors retreated to the shade of colorful cabanas. Some buried sunburned noses in books, while others watched over restless toddlers who periodically broke into impromptu runs for freedom. BATHERS TO THE RIGHT, SURFERS TO THE LEFT, a large wooden sign proclaimed from the foot of the lifeguard's tower, but there were few surfers out today, and fewer waves. Lynn realized with relief that if anyone had seen the kiss, it was already a forgotten memory.

Her hand touched her chin where his beard had rubbed. She found herself wishing that he would kiss her again and started walking faster in an effort to clear her head. What was she doing out for a Saturday-morning stroll with the one man common sense—not to mention her lawyer—dictated she should have nothing to do with?

"So you've lived in Florida all your life?" Marc was asking, running to keep up with her.

"All my life," she answered curtly, not slowing her pace.

"Your parents still live here?"

"My father does. My mother died nine years ago." She stopped abruptly. "Is this small talk? Are we engaging in small talk?"

"Would you rather I kissed you again?"

"Small talk it is," Lynn said, resuming her brisk pace. It was several miles back to where they had started. She might as well make the best of it, although the beach wasn't great for walking this morning. The sand was too soft and wet, and her feet kept sinking into it.

"What does your father do?" Marc asked, having hit his stride and having no trouble keeping up with her.

"He's retired. He was in waterproofing, but he sold the business after my mother died."

"What does he do now?"

"Plays golf mostly. He got married again a few years ago."

"You don't like her," Marc stated, and Lynn stopped again, turning to him in surprise.

"How do you know that?"

"Just the way you said he got married again. What's the matter with her?"

"Nothing. She's a perfectly nice lady."

"Then why don't you like her?"

Lynn was about to deliver a flip answer, but the sincerity in his blue eyes stopped her. He must be a first-rate interviewer, she thought, wishing she had a good answer to his question.

"I don't know. She's a perfectly nice woman. She's polite, she's a good cook, and she can spend all day talking about her living-room furniture. God knows, she's cheerful enough. I really don't know why I don't like her. I just wouldn't have picked her, that's all."

"Nobody asked you to."

"Maybe that's the problem." They resumed walking, but at a much slower pace. "She's not my mother," Lynn continued, after a pause. "That's probably the most truthful answer I can give you, and I know it's not fair for me to dislike her for that reason but . . ."

"That's the way it is," Marc said, using Lynn's earlier words. "Tell me about your mother."

Lynn felt the push of tears behind her eyes. Even now, she thought, after nine years, the tears were only a few well-chosen words away. "She was a remarkable woman. Very much her own person. She was a housewife all her life, but when she was fifty, she went back to university and got her bachelor of arts degree. In medieval history, of all things. She was always reading. Every time I think of my mother, I picture her with a book in her hands."

"I like her already."

Lynn smiled. "She was the one who insisted I go to college, have a career, make something of my life. She told me not to wait for anyone else to do things for me."

"How did she die?"

"Alzheimer's disease," Lynn said, a wayward tear betraying the sudden flatness of her voice. "She just kept losing bits of herself until there was nothing left. In the end, she had no control over anything. Not her bodily functions. Not her mind. She didn't even know who I was."

"That must have been very hard on you."

Lynn shrugged. "That's the way it goes," she said, unmistakably ending the conversation.

"How did you meet Gary?" Marc asked after they had walked for a stretch in silence.

"Is this an interview?"

"Just trying to find out more about you."

"And what have you found out so far?"

"That you're beautiful," he began, "sensitive, caring. That you like to be in control. That you walk fast," he said, and she laughed despite herself. "That you're a good kisser."

"I met Gary right here on the beach," Lynn said quickly, pushing his words away with her own. "I'd come with some girlfriends. He was also with friends. Somehow these friends all disappeared and Gary and I ended up sharing the same blanket." Lynn tried to make it sound very casual, but even now she could feel the soft breezes that had been blowing that afternoon against her skin, and see the assorted stains that dotted the bright orange-and-yellow beach blanket they had sat on. Her mind reached out to touch the dimples that had creased Gary's cheeks around his mouth, and she recalled the bitter taste of the beer he had offered her as he confidently transferred the bottle from his lips to her own. "There was something so calm about him. He didn't push. He was a good listener, which I liked, because in those days, I thought I had a lot to say. I'd just gotten my master's degree and I was very eager to show everyone how much I knew. I really thought I had met the man I was going to spend the rest of my life with." Again, she felt the presence of unwanted tears. How could she reconcile what she was feeling for Gary now with the feelings he had aroused in her so few hours ago? "I think I'm all talked out," Lynn said, and was grateful when Marc asked no further questions. They walked the rest of the way in silence.

As they left the beach and headed up the street to her house, Lynn wondered what she would do if he asked to come inside, if he tried to kiss her, if he suggested they see each other again. She recalled the things that Renee had told her, the reasons why any thought of a relationship with this man was out of the question. She also thought of how angry she'd been at Gary, how powerless he'd made her feel, how nice Marc's kiss had felt, how excited by it she'd been. Would he try to kiss her again? Would he repeat his suggestion of taking their relationship to the nearest motel?

They reached his car. "You have my number," he said.

8

"We'd like to settle this thing with as little fuss as possible," the lawyer on the other side of the round conference table was saying, giving Renee a carefully constructed smile.

Renee returned Herbert Tarnower's grin, glancing from the small, rotund attorney to his tall, voluptuous client. Penny Linkletter was twenty-five years old, six feet tall, and looked as if she had just stepped off the stage of a Las Vegas nightclub. All that was missing was the sequins, Renee thought, turning her smile toward the young woman's elderly husband. Why was the size of a man's wallet, she wondered, so often inversely proportionate to the size of his brain? Why didn't people get smarter, and not just older?

"We don't think that what Mrs. Linkletter is seeking by way of a settlement is in any way out of line," her attorney further explained, about to say more when Renee stopped him.

"You don't think that a lump sum of two million dollars plus twenty thousand dollars a month in alimony isn't just a tad excessive?" Renee made no attempt to hide the sarcasm in her voice.

"Mr. Linkletter is a very wealthy man. His wife is entitled to a share of his earnings."

"Mrs. Linkletter has been Mrs. Linkletter for a total of sixteen months . . ."

"During which time she has been an exemplary wife to Mr. Linkletter."

"During which time she has slept with apparently half of Dade County," Renee interrupted, pushing a folder across the conference table, watching it slide to a halt at the tips of the opposing attorney's well-manicured fingernails. "You'll find sworn statements from a variety of men and women, ranging from the Japanese gardener to the Cuban maid. Mrs. Linkletter was nothing if not an equal-opportunity employer." She smiled at Penny Linkletter, who, strangely enough, smiled back. "We also have photographs," Renee added.

"Can I see them?" Penny Linkletter asked, then backed away under her attorney's hostile gaze. She adjusted the shoulder pads of her cotton-knit white sweater, pulled at the hem of her short skirt, and said nothing further.

Herbert Tarnower paused a moment to try to reconstruct his former expression. "Obviously, we're prepared to negotiate," he said.

"But *we're* not," Renee told him directly. "We think that the settlement Mr. Linkletter has suggested is more than fair."

"Fifty thousand dollars? Why, last year alone the man made over five million."

"Maybe you should take a look at these photographs, Mr. Tarnower," Renee reminded him.

"Look," Herbert Tarnower said quickly, his voice moving from indignation to gentle concern, "we have no interest in going to court. And I'm sure that Mr. Linkletter feels the same way. Revelations of this nature can only prove embarrassing to both parties, and to a man of Mr. Linkletter's age and stature . . ."

"Mr. Linkletter is seventy-eight years old and has been married and divorced a total of five times. His last three wives have all been tall blondes in their twenties, two of whom took Mr. Linkletter to court and came away with nothing. I suggest to you, Mr. Tarnower, that if Mr. Linkletter were a man who embarrassed easily, he would never have married your client in the first place." Renee walked to the door of the conference room and opened it, signaling that the meeting was over. "Think about it," she advised Penny Linkletter and her attorney before helping a silent but smiling Mr. Linkletter out of his chair and ushering him out the door, "and let me know what you decide."

"Your line has been frantic all morning," her secretary advised her when she got back to her office.

"Did Philip return my call?"

"Not yet. Do you want me to try him again?"

"No, I'll do it."

"Fiona Stapleton has called three times."

Renee made a face indicating displeasure. "All right. I'd better speak to her. Give me a minute to call Philip and then get her on the line."

Renee walked briskly into her office, hitting her hip against the sharp corner of her desk as she reached toward the bottom drawer to retrieve a miniature chocolate bar. "Serves me right," she said, quickly unwrapping the bar and eating it as she dialed her husband's office. She waited for Philip's secretary—an anorexic woman with an equally thin voice—to come on the line. The woman, whose name was Samantha, had spent a summer in England some years before and had affected a slight British accent ever since. Philip thought it cute; Renee found it insufferable. "Is my husband free?" Renee asked as soon as she heard the woman's tinny greeting.

"Hasn't he returned your call?" Samantha asked, knowing full well he hadn't. "Well, he's been frightfully busy all morning. Is it urgent?"

"No, nothing that can't wait." Renee reached inside her bottom drawer for another candy bar. Philip had mentioned the possibility that they might meet for lunch, so she had held off making plans of her own, but as it was almost noon now, there seemed little chance they'd be getting together. "I'll speak to him later. Thank you," she added, though she wasn't sure why. She quickly ate the second candy bar, then closed the drawer before she could be tempted by a third.

Her phone buzzed.

"I have Mrs. Stapleton on line one," her secretary told her.

"Thanks." Renee pushed the appropriate button.

"You haven't been returning my phone calls," the woman on the other end said, her voice angry.

"We've been through this," Renee explained patiently. "I've already told you that I can't proceed any further with your divorce action until you bring your account up to date."

"Where am I supposed to get five thousand dollars?"

"Mrs. Stapleton, I sympathize with you. I really do," she added over the woman's harsh laugh. "But you knew my rates when you contacted me, and you agreed to the schedule of payments. This is a complicated case: I've spent a great many hours on it, and you can't expect me to work for nothing. Now, I've already given you several extensions, but as I explained, it was decided at our last partners' meeting that we really couldn't continue with your case until all previous bills have been brought up to date. I'm sorry, but that's just the way it is." She heard the phone go dead. "And thank you for calling," she added, dropping the phone back into its receiver.

The door to Renee's office suddenly opened and Debbie strode confidently inside, her arms full of shopping bags, followed closely by Kathryn, smiling meekly and similarly encumbered, with Renee's frantic secretary trailing behind them. "Your sister is here," Debbie announced as Renee's secretary was about to. "And your wicked stepdaughter." Debbie laughed, throwing her parcels on one of the chairs across from Renee's desk and motioning for Kathryn to do the same.

"It's all right, Marilyn," Renee told the somewhat dazed young woman whose hairdo added at least three inches to her height. "I don't think you've met my sister, Kathryn. She's visiting from New York. And this is my husband's daughter, Debbie. She's with us for the summer."

"From Boston," Debbie said sweetly. "I live there with my mother."

"To what do I owe the honor of this visit?" Renee asked, viewing the many shopping bags with awe, as her secretary excused herself from the room.

"Debbie took me to the Boca Town Center," Kathryn explained quietly.

"Bloomie's," Debbie said, her smile growing wicked. "I charged everything to Dad's account."

"I'll pay him back," Kathryn added quickly. "Debbie said it would be all right."

"I talked Kathryn into the sexiest bathing suit. Dad'll go crazy when he sees it. Kathryn has a beautiful figure, don't you think, Renée?"

"What are you doing here?" Renee asked, trying to pull her jacket over her spreading hips, and anxious to get Debbie out of her office.

"We came to take you for lunch," Kathryn said, looking to Debbie for confirmation. While Renee was grateful to Debbie for getting Kathryn out of the apartment and pleased that the girl had actually persuaded Kathryn to go shopping, she was skeptical of her motives. It wasn't in Debbie's character to help people when they were down.

"I don't think so . . ." Renee stammered, wishing she had been able to get hold of Philip.

"You have to eat," her sister told her, her voice a gentle plea. "Come on, Renee. It'll be good for you. Just like going shopping all morning with Debbie was good for me."

"We'll go to the Troubadour," Debbie chimed in.

"The Troubadour? That's pretty pricey, Debbie."

"So what? Dad's treat." She reached into her canvas bag and pulled out a glistening gold credit card. "I heard Dad say the Troubadour is the best restaurant in Delray."

"Come on," Kathryn urged, a small smile creeping into the corners of her mouth. "You know you're going to give in eventually."

"Why don't we just go to Erny's?"

"The Troubadour," Debbie told her stepmother adamantly, returning the credit card to her purse. "Come on, Renée, let me do something nice for you."

. . .

They were ushered inside the dark restaurant and given a round, linen-covered table near the far corner of the elegant, pink-and-plum-colored room, where they were immediately offered a basketful of rolls and a wine list. Waiters hovered nearby with helpful suggestions and a list of the day's specials. They ordered quickly, Renee vetoing Debbie's expressed wish for a bottle of champagne, and ordering three glasses of grapefruit juice instead.

"You're a spoilsport," Debbie told her.

"You're underage," Renee reminded her, thinking it was about time someone did, "and I'm working."

"Busy morning?" her sister asked.

"Very."

"You didn't look very busy when we came in," Debbie said, her eyes casually perusing the room.

"That's the trick," Renee said pleasantly. "To be busy but look relaxed."

"I didn't say you looked relaxed. Just not busy."

Renee reached for a roll.

"So who's getting divorced today? Anyone we know?" Kathryn asked, her eyes moving warily back and forth between her companions.

Renee shook her head, and bit into a chewy roll, which, she was surprised to discover, was warm.

"Renée can't discuss her cases," Debbie said knowingly. "I've asked her a few times," she continued, sounding hurt, "but she won't."

"It's privileged information, Debbie," Renee said, trying to sound patient. "You understand that. Your father has the same problem."

"My father doesn't have any problems."

"Situation, then. He can't discuss his patients."

"He does, though," Debbie said, managing to sound both knowing and innocent. "With me."

Renee said nothing, letting her eyes adjust to the dimly lit room. "I've never been here before. It's lovely."

"Dad's been here," Debbie said, her eyes straining through the dimness toward the far corners of the restaurant. "I heard him talking about it on the telephone. He said it's his favorite spot."

"Really?" Renee heard herself ask, then wished she hadn't.

"You should see the white dress Kathryn bought," Debbie continued, changing topics with ease. "Very sexy. No back."

"I still can't believe I bought it. It's so unlike anything I've ever owned."

"It looks great on you."

"Debbie's quite the salesgirl."

"I'm sure she is."

"Kathryn has such a beautiful body," Debbie reiterated. "I think she should show it off." Her eyes traveled from Kathryn to Renee. "It's so hard to believe she's your older sister."

"Almost five years older," Kathryn established.

"You'd swear it was the other way around." Debbie smiled sweetly. Renee gripped the underside of her chair.

"*Bon appétit,*" Debbie said, when lunch was delivered some twenty minutes later. She took a long, hard look at Renee's plate. "Should you be eating all those french fries, Renee? What's the matter? Didn't I pronounce your name right that time?"

Renee began eating her steak and french fried potatoes in small, steady bites, speaking only when she had no other choice, deliberately finishing everything on her plate, and then making a point of asking for dessert, which the others declined. "Might as well do it right," she said. She added a spoonful of sugar and a dollop of whipped cream to her coffee, then had a second cup.

"Isn't that my father?" Debbie suddenly asked, straining her head toward the far right corner of the room. Renee had noticed Debbie looking in that direction several times during the course of the meal, but she had thought better of turning around. Now, her head spun in the direction of Debbie's eyes. "It *is* him. Who's he with?" Renee could see only the back of the woman's head, but even in the soft darkness and from a distance of some forty feet, she could recognize the familiar red locks of the woman who had once introduced herself as Alicia-call-me-Ali Henderson. "Do you know her, Renée? I don't think she's anyone I've ever met. Daddy!" Debbie called out suddenly, jumping out of her chair and waving wildly across the room.

Renee turned back toward the table just as Alicia-call-me-Ali swiveled around in her chair. She caught reluctant sight of the woman's regal profile and ample bosom before bringing her eyes tightly closed. She didn't have to see Philip to know that he was already getting out of his chair, that he was even now on his way over. She didn't have to hear his words to know what he would say, just as she now understood that her being in this restaurant was no accident, that this chance meeting was no coincidence, that this was Debbie's way of "doing something nice" for her. Debbie had probably overheard Philip on the phone making his plans. Philip was as careless as his daughter was meticulous.

"Renee," Philip was saying jovially as he bent forward to kiss her cheek. "What a wonderful surprise. Hello, Kathryn," he continued, "how are you feeling today?"

"Much better." Kathryn smiled, unconsciously touching her wrists, oblivious to the drama she was witnessing.

"I'm sorry I didn't get a chance to return your calls. You know how time can just get away from you. Was it anything important?"

Renee shook her head. He'd obviously forgotten their tentative arrangements. There was certainly no point in bringing the matter up now. "Just calling to say hello."

He smiled pleasantly. "How was your meal?" he asked. "The food here is wonderful. If I'd seen you earlier, I'd have recommended the swordfish. In fact, any of the fish or pasta dishes are first-rate."

"I had pasta," Debbie said proudly. "Kathryn had the red snapper. Renée," she added flatly, "had steak and french fries."

"Oh, that's too bad," Philip told them. "Steak is steak."

"Next time, I'll know," Renee said, and wondered what exactly she meant by that.

"Who are you with, Dad?" Debbie asked.

"You remember Alicia Henderson from Bennett's party," Philip whispered, leaning close to Renee's ear. "She's having a few problems with her husband. Says he schizophrenic, but he refuses to get help, and she doesn't know what to do about him anymore. She wanted some advice, and she didn't want to be seen coming into my office, so I agreed to meet her here. She's a little embarrassed, so she doesn't want to come over, although she said to give you her regards."

Renee nodded without speaking, and reached up with her lips to kiss those of her husband.

"I'll see you later." Philip gave his daughter a big hug. "It was great seeing you," he said, and managed to sound as though he meant it. "It's nice to see my girls out together having a good time."

"She's gorgeous," Debbie said after Philip had returned to his table. "All that beautiful red hair, and what a figure." Renee looked toward the waiter and signaled for the check, wondering how long it would take her to dismember Debbie's body, and thinking of appropriate places where she could hide all the pieces.

"Lynn Schuster on line two," Renee's secretary announced over the intercom late that afternoon.

"Lynn, I've been thinking about you lately." Renee forced a note of cheeriness into her voice although cheery was far from the way she actually felt. Her lunch—both the food itself and the accompanying events—had been repeating on her all afternoon. She hoped she hadn't let Debbie see how upset she was. She'd simply gritted her teeth and smiled, following her husband's lead, and told the girl how much she'd enjoyed their outing, all the while fighting growing feelings of acute anxiety. It had never been easy for her to lie. She wondered how Philip could do it so effortlessly. But then, maybe he wasn't lying, she tried to convince herself. Maybe the lunch with Alicia Henderson was every bit as spontaneous and innocent as he claimed. And maybe she would be appointed a Supreme Court Justice. And maybe the moon really was made of cheese.

What was she doing wrong? What was it about her that drove Philip into the arms of all the Alicia-call-me-Alis of this world? What was missing? Renee looked down at the bulging buttons of her blouse. It wasn't what was missing, she told herself. It was the opposite. There was simply too much. She had to start another diet. She had to get her weight under control. "I'm sorry," she stammered when she realized that she hadn't heard a word Lynn had been saying and that Lynn sounded very upset. "What? Say that again. . . . He what? Sent you flowers? Who sent you flowers? . . . I don't believe it. . . . All right, all right. Calm down. Throw the flowers in the garbage, if it makes you feel better, which I suspect it will, and then go fix yourself a good stiff drink. Lynn, are you listening to me? . . . Good. I haven't had such a great day myself. I'll tell you about it some other time. But right now, chuck the flowers, have a drink, and try to relax." They exchanged good-byes, and Renee replaced the receiver, shaking her head. "Men," she repeated until the word lost all meaning.

9

The flowers had arrived just minutes after Lynn walked through her front door at the end of a frustrating day. She had spent hours at work on the phone getting nowhere and several more hours going in a similar direction with a family whose lives had been torn apart by their son's drug use. To top it off, she'd had to endure a lengthy lecture by a lawyer named Stephen Hendrix, who represented an angry Keith Foster, father of the allegedly abused child, and who had told her plainly to stop harassing his client or he would have no alternative but to take legal action against her. Her *personally*, the lawyer stressed.

"We've received a complaint regarding a possible case of child abuse," Lynn had told him, trying to keep her voice even, "and as I'm sure you're well aware, Mr. Hendrix, all such complaints have to be investigated fully. I've tried to contact both Mr. and Mrs. Foster repeatedly to set up an appointment, and have met with the utmost resistance. The last time I drove out to the Harborside Villas, Patty Foster refused to open the door. I am not harassing your clients. I simply want to interview them, and their daughter, Ashleigh. I not only have that right, but that responsibility. If need be," she had continued, looking up into the eyes of the man, who was a good foot taller than herself, and refusing to be intimidated, "I will bring along members of the Delray Beach police force on my next visit. You can sue them too. The choice is up to your clients."

"I intend to be there," Stephen Hendrix had announced at that point, capitulating, though he made it sound as if he still maintained the upper hand, "to monitor the conversation."

"As you wish." She had her secretary make the appointment for the following week. The Fosters were out of town and would be unavailable until then. Mr. Foster was a very busy, very important man, Stephen Hendrix had explained, not for the first time.

"We're all busy," she had told him plainly. "The child is who's important here."

Much as Lynn hated to admit it, such scenes took a lot out of her. She hated confrontations, voices raised in anger. Boy, did you get into the wrong line of work, she told herself as she pushed through her front door at the end of the day, heading straight into the kitchen to pour herself a glass of freshly squeezed orange juice from the oranges that grew in her back yard. Megan and Nicholas would be home soon. She had just enough time to crawl into a nice, soothing bath. And then there was the knock at her front door, and a young delivery boy all but hidden behind a large box of flowers.

"Lynn Schuster?" he asked, quickly shoving the flowers at her before she had time to confirm or deny her identity. She watched him leave in something of a daze, the flowers balanced precariously in her arms, her eyes staring blankly ahead. It couldn't be, she thought. He wouldn't.

Slowly, not moving the rest of her body, she extended her right foot forward and kicked the front door gently closed. No, she thought, once again standing resolutely still, he wouldn't.

She didn't know how long she remained there, barefoot in her front hallway with a long rectangular box of flowers in her outstretched hands, but she gradually became aware of the box's weight. She marched determinedly into the living room and sat down on the sofa, tearing open the box, temporarily ignoring the card. He wouldn't, she thought again, staring at the dozen beautiful, long-stemmed yellow roses.

She left the roses lying in the box, watching her reluctant fingers stretch toward the small envelope, momentarily debating whether or not to open it or simply throw it out. "Oh, look, kids, someone sent us flowers," she rehearsed, hearing in her mind the barrage of questions that would undoubtedly follow, ultimately tearing open the envelope and pulling the card free.

"Thank you for so many wonderful years," she read out loud, her eyes clouding over. "Here's hoping we can remain friends for many more." She dropped the card on the rattan coffee table in front of her. "Love, Gary." In the next minute, she was trying to hurl the top of the flower box across the room, but it was still partly secured to its lower half with a strip of adhesive tape, and so it merely bounced into the air and then dangled over the edge of the table threateningly. "God damn you to hell, Gary Schuster," she cried, bursting into a flood of bitter tears.

She had been avoiding the reality of today since she had first opened her eyes that morning. July 16. Her wedding anniversary. She had ignored the calendar, skipped over the date on her appointment book. She had thrown herself into the mountain of work on her desk, dealing with her phone calls and clients, and confronting the Fosters' unpleasant lawyer head-on, working right through lunch, avoiding, doing, until it was time to go home. Somehow she had managed to make it through most of the day.

And then the flowers had arrived. Were they Gary's idea of a joke? Or had the flowers been Suzette's idea? She stared into the box, amazed as she always was by the natural perfection of roses. Yellow roses were her favorite. Gary knew that, just as *she* knew that it had been Gary's idea to send the flowers, not Suzette's. The woman probably wasn't even aware he had done so, would have been properly horrified at the thought, just as Lynn was horrified at having received them.

She knew Gary well enough to know that he had not intended to be cruel, that he genuinely believed he was doing something nice. The sensitive male of the eighties. Is this really what modern women wanted? Flowers from their exes on what would have been their anniversaries?

Absently, she reached down and fingered the card, which she read again. "Thank you for so many wonderful years," she repeated aloud, incredulously. She brought her fist down angrily on the table and watched the flowers jump. "If they were so damn wonderful, why did you leave? And who the hell wants to be friends?" She shoved the box roughly to the green carpet, watching the roses spill out in attractive abandon, and then bent over to scoop them up. "Dammit," she cried, carrying the box into the kitchen and dumping it into the sink. "What were you thinking of?" she asked, seeing Gary's smiling face in front of her. "What on earth could have possessed you to send me these?"

And yet, deep down in the part of herself she had been hiding from all day, she had to admit she wasn't all that surprised. Somewhere in the back of her mind, she had suspected he might do something like this, although for a second before she looked at the card, she had entertained the possibility that the flowers might have come from Marc Cameron.

What was she supposed to do now? Was Gary expecting her to call and thank him? Should she, for God's sake? What was the proper etiquette in a situation like this?

The hell with him, she thought, reaching for the phone, calling her lawyer instead. "Hello, Renee? It's Lynn. Gary just sent me flowers. Can you believe it? It would have been our fifteenth wedding anniversary today, and the lunatic just sent me a dozen long-stemmed yellow roses. I'm shaking, I'm so upset. And I have to calm down before the children get home, but I keep looking at the flowers and reading that stupid card. Can you believe it? He hopes we can be friends for many years," she continued in one frantic outpouring, vaguely aware that the woman on the other end didn't seem to be giving her her full attention. And then Renee had snapped into action and told her to throw the flowers in the garbage and to make herself a good stiff drink. Somehow she had managed to pull herself together. Had she really carried on that way on the telephone? And what had made her call Renee Bower of all people?

This wasn't a legal problem. She had other, closer friends whom she could call. And yet, since her separation, she had felt curiously removed from all her old friends, most of whom had always viewed her as one half of a happily married pair. No one, least of all herself, quite knew what to make of her new status. Lynn reached into the sink, pulled out the box, and dumped the beautiful flowers into the trash can under the sink. She was pouring herself the good stiff drink Renee had recommended when she heard the camp bus pull up in front of her house.

"How was camp?" she asked her children as they scrambled past her toward the kitchen.

"Thirsty. I'm so thirsty," Nicholas growled, clutching at his throat and knocking his plump little knees together, as Lynn reached into the refrigerator and poured both children a large glass of milk. "First taste," Nicholas said, quickly taking a sip before Megan had a chance to lift the glass to her lips. "It was great," he answered when his glass was empty.

"It was all right," Megan said quietly, not even bothering to compete for the first loud gulp of milk.

"Something wrong, sweetie?"

Megan shook her head, finished her drink, and wiped her mouth with a napkin, about to discard it into the trash can under the sink when she saw the flowers. "What are these doing in here?" Megan pulled the yellow roses gingerly from their unorthodox vase. "Mom, why are these flowers in the garbage?" Lynn only shrugged, unable to come up with a suitable response. "Who sent them?"

"Your father," Lynn said truthfully, then immediately wished she hadn't. There had been no need to involve Megan in her misery.

"Oh."

Lynn expected her daughter to react with furious indignation, and watched in amazement as Megan simply returned the flowers to the trash can and shut the cupboard door. "Megan?" she called after her as the girl fled the room in tears. Lynn turned toward Nicholas, who stood watching the scene with eyes like saucers. "All right, what happened?"

"Nothing," Nicholas answered, averting his gaze to the floor and shifting his weight from one foot to the other. "Camp was great . . ."

"I don't mean at camp. I mean on Saturday. At the lunch with Daddy. Neither one of you has said a word about it, and Megan's been especially quiet ever since."

"Nothing happened."

"Nicky . . ."

"Can I have another glass of milk, please?"

"Did Daddy say something that upset Megan?"

"Not Daddy," Nicholas answered, and then literally held his breath.

"What do you mean?" Lynn realized she was holding her own breath as well. "Was there someone else at the lunch with you and Daddy?"

Nicholas shrugged. "Sort of."

"Sort of?"

"There was sort of this woman there."

"Do you remember this sort of woman's name?"

Nicholas nodded. "Suzette," he said finally, as Lynn had known he would.

Lynn reached over and drew her young son into her arms. "Thank you, sweetheart. I'm sorry you felt you had to keep that inside you."

"Daddy said he thought it would be better if we didn't tell you."

Lynn nodded. I'll bet he did, she thought, remembering that Gary had agreed not to introduce Suzette into his children's lives until a few more months had passed. Let them deal with one thing at a time, Lynn had urged, and he had agreed. What had changed his mind? What was going on in that handsome head of his? She pictured the flowers behind the closed cupboard door. "You said you wanted another glass of milk?" she asked her son, surprised, as she always was, by how much he looked the way she herself had as a child. It was ironic, she thought, the word immediately conjuring up the image of Marc Cameron, that sons so often resembled their mothers whereas girls more often looked like their dads. Lynn poured

Nicholas a second glass of milk before the boy had time to reply, then excused herself to check on Megan.

Megan was lying on the bedspread of her four-poster brass bed, staring blankly at the ceiling. Her long legs, which were caked with dirt around her bony knees, were stretched out across the soft white of the bedspread, the bottoms of her frayed sneakers making dark creases in the quilted fabric. Lynn approached her daughter slowly, arranging herself at the foot of her bed. "Nicholas told me that Daddy brought a friend to your lunch on Saturday."

"It doesn't matter," Megan whispered, her answer for everything these days.

"Do you want to talk about it, sweetheart?"

Megan stubbornly shook her head.

Lynn knew all the proper things to say at moments like this, soothing phrases neatly laid out in her textbooks, things she would probably say if this were not *her* child, if this weren't happening to *her*. Instead she simply patted Megan's knees and said nothing.

Megan suddenly burst into tears, the bed shaking with her heart-wrenching cries. "I don't want to be a lawyer anymore, Mommy. Do I have to be a lawyer?"

Lynn felt her own eyes once more spilling over. Today is obviously a day for tears, she thought, reaching over to gather the sobbing youngster in her arms. "No, darling, of course not. You can be anything you want to be."

"I don't want to be a lawyer."

"You have lots of time to decide."

"I want to do what you do."

"Whatever you want," Lynn told her, patting her back.

Megan suddenly pulled back, so that Lynn's arms had to stretch to hold on to her. "And I don't want to take any more ballet lessons."

"You've always loved ballet," Lynn said, trying to keep up with the abrupt twists in the conversation.

"I don't want to take ballet anymore," Megan insisted.

"Okay. You don't have to. Maybe you'll change your mind," she said as Megan snuggled back into her arms. The sobs, which had momentarily subsided, picked up again with re-newed vehemence.

"Why did she have to be there?" Megan demanded angrily. "Why did Daddy have to bring her?"

"Don't cry, baby. It'll be all right."

"I hate her, Mommy. I hate her for taking Daddy away from us."

"I know, sweetie. I'm not so crazy about her myself."

Lynn heard footsteps, and turned her head to see Nicholas tiptoeing—as only he could tiptoe—toward them. Soon the three Schusters were curved into a tight little ball, all arms and legs and tears, swaying rhythmically against the almost unbear-able sense of loss that each was separately experiencing.

"I'm glad you called," he was saying. Lynn lifted her fresh strawberry daiquiri into the air in a silent toast. "I wasn't sure you would. Why did you? Not that I'm objecting, mind you. Just curious."

"A writer's curiosity?" Lynn asked, and Marc Cameron smiled. "It's my wedding anniversary."

"Curiouser and curiouser."

"I thought you'd appreciate the irony."

His smile grew wider. "So I'm a convenient substitute?"

"I'm not sure what you are, to be honest." She paused, look-ing around the small, empty Italian restaurant in Lake Worth where she had suggested they meet. "I was angry and de-pressed. I just needed to get out of the house for a while. My neighbor said she'd stay with the kids. I probably should apolo-gize in advance. I don't think I'll be very good company."

"You're doing fine so far. Are you ready to order yet?"

She shook her head. "I'm not very hungry." She finished the last of her daiquiri in two quick gulps. "I wouldn't mind another one of these, however."

Marc Cameron immediately signaled the waiter to bring them each another drink.

"So, tell me about your writing," Lynn asked, careful to

avoid his watchful blue eyes. "Are you working on anything now?"

"I have an idea for a novel I'm tossing around in my head."

She laughed. "I'll bet you do. It wouldn't by any chance be about a recently separated man who gets involved with the wife of the man his own wife left him for, would it?"

"That depends."

Lynn looked directly into Marc Cameron's eyes. "On what?"

"Are we involved?"

"Figure of speech," Lynn said, and cleared her throat. She was relieved when the waiter returned with her second drink. "I don't much relish the idea of finding myself in the pages of your next book."

"Most people are thrilled to find themselves immortalized in print."

"Even the unflattering portraits?"

"Even those. Of course, you have to remember that the bad guys rarely recognize themselves. Besides, what makes you think you'd come off badly?"

Lynn lifted her glass to her mouth and was surprised to see that when she put it down it was half empty. "Women who are dumped tend to be whiners at best, pitiful creatures at worst. I'm not crazy about either of those prospects."

"Suggest an alternative."

Lynn pondered the question. In truth, she already knew what her answer would be. "Oh, I guess I'd like to be . . . oh, what the hell . . . heroic." Marc Cameron laughed at her choice of words and she lifted her glass in another silent toast, though she didn't take a drink. "Shouldn't heroines be heroic?"

"What makes you think you'd be the heroine?" He smiled, his mouth a crooked grin, his eyes teasing hers, as if he knew all about her, as if he understood all her secrets, which buttons to push to get the desired results.

"I read *Small Potatoes*," she said after a slight pause, referring to his last book, and was pleased when she saw the tease in his eyes change to surprise.

"You did? When?"

"I went to the library after our walk on the beach and took it out. I tried to find it in the bookstores, but nobody had it."

He laughed sadly. "Figures. So?"

"So . . . I liked it. You're a man of complicated thoughts."

This time he laughed out loud, throwing his head back, obviously enjoying her appraisal. "It's never been put quite that way before. I think I'm flattered."

"I got the impression that it was very autobiographical, though in a very different way from your first book, *Awkward Pauses*."

"Now I really *am* flattered. Do you realize that you may be the only person in the state—hell, forget that, in the *country*—who has read both my novels? I don't think even Suzette got through *Awkward Pauses*."

"It wasn't as well thought out as your second book," Lynn said, and watched him frown. "I thought *Small Potatoes* was the better of the two. You don't agree?" The waiter hovered nearby, but Lynn shook her head at the prospect of another drink, and he retreated.

"I agree, but I still don't like to hear it. No matter what you may hear about writers appreciating constructive criticism, it's all a pile of baloney. We don't like criticism of any kind, constructive or otherwise. We want only good reviews, especially from our friends and lovers." He stared forcefully into Lynn's eyes. Lynn immediately pictured the two of them rolling across the top of her queen-size bed. Instantly, she brought her glass to her mouth and took a long swallow, finishing what was left. For a minute, she debated calling the waiter back, having another drink, hell, maybe another two or three, then she thought better of it.

"And which one am I?" Lynn asked, then wished she hadn't, seeing the two of them locked together at the hip, disappearing underneath black satin sheets. What was she doing here? What was she doing, period?

"I leave that up to you."

Lynn lowered her glass far enough away from her lips to be able to speak. "Which would be more interesting in the pages of your next novel? Which would make me the heroine?"

"The lover, unquestionably," he answered without hesitation.

Lynn lowered her empty glass to the table, without releasing it. What was she getting herself into? "I thought your ambivalence about your father was very well observed in your second book," Lynn sidestepped, hearing her words echo somewhere in her head, feeling Marc's invisible hands on her breasts, moving down her body. She cleared her throat. "You seemed less angry than in your first book. You seemed to accept him more." She tried focusing on his mouth as he spoke.

"My father left my mother when I was very young. Younger than my boys are now. He moved to Florida from Buffalo, which is where I grew up, and I really didn't see him again until I was in my teens. Suddenly, he was writing letters, showing up at my high school and college graduations, stuff like that." Lynn nodded, trying to concentrate on what he was saying, remembering these details from the pages of his books. "I was still so angry, I didn't want much to do with him. But after my mother got married again, I didn't feel quite the need to hate him as much as I had before, although God knows, the child in me still hasn't forgiven him for abandoning me when I was four years old, and probably never will entirely. But about a dozen years ago, he invited me down to Palm Beach to visit him, and I accepted, and I decided I liked the idea of not having to shovel a mountain of snow off my car every morning six months of the year, and so I decided to look around, see if I could get any work free-lancing. I mean, hell, a writer can work anywhere. So I went back home and packed a few bathing suits and my Selectrix typewriter, and set up shop. I sold a few pieces pretty fast, and soon I was asked to do a story on the plethora of little ballet studios which seemed to be springing up everywhere in Palm Beach at the time, a pretty unusual thing when you consider that the average age of the Palm Beach citizen is ninety-seven."

Lynn laughed. The waiter appeared again, this time impatiently standing beside their table with his pad prominently displayed, ready to take their order whether or not they were ready to give it.

"The special?" Marc asked, looking at Lynn.

Lynn checked the menu, noted that the special was blackened snapper, and nodded, listening as Marc gave their order to the waiter, who looked vaguely put out by their choice.

"And that's when you met Suzette?" she asked, suddenly aware of the source of Megan's aversion to ballet.

"Her parents had financed this little studio for her. She'd studied to be a ballerina, but it hadn't worked out. Believe it or not, she'd been kicked out of school for having an affair with her very married head instructor when she was all of sixteen. Anyway, she eventually ran off with some would-be actor and spent a few drug-filled years in Hollywood before coming home to Mommy and Daddy and letting them set her up in a little ballet studio. I went out to interview her as part of the story I was doing, and I guess I liked what I saw. She has one of those interesting, almost Egyptian-like faces, all sharp angles and prominent features. Anyway, we moved in together not long after, over her parents' vociferous objections, I might add. I mean, their poor baby had already been defiled by two nogood artists and they hardly welcomed a third, if I can include myself in the category of artist. They decided to ignore me and my relationship with their daughter. But then Suzette got pregnant, and when you're pregnant with twins, you're kind of hard to ignore, so they casually suggested it might be time for us to get married, which, of course, we did, and the rest, as they say, should be good for a few more novels. What are you looking at?"

Lynn had tried focusing her eyes on Marc Cameron's mouth during his long speech, but his beard kept getting in the way. Normally, Lynn watched people's eyes when they spoke, but Marc Cameron had the disconcerting habit of watching right back, sending her signals she was unprepared to deal with, so she had tried to concentrate on his mouth instead. She wasn't used to men with beards, she thought, immediately recalling the feel of his beard on her face, feeling her skin start to tingle. She always thought she preferred her men clean-shaven. Lynn almost laughed. Her men! What men? Gary had been the only man in her life for the last fifteen years. They had discovered this stupid little restaurant, with its surly, impatient help, together. Why had she come here? What was she doing with this bearded man who was not her husband on the night of her fifteenth anniversary?

"Is everything all right?" Marc Cameron was asking.

Lynn shook her head, unable to speak.

He reached across the table and lifted her chin so that her eyes were forced to confront his. Immediately, they filled with tears. Marc Cameron became an unfocused blur.

"Do you want to leave?" he asked.

"What about the food?"

"We'll come back for it another time." Marc Cameron quickly deposited a couple of twenty-dollar bills on the table and then was at her side, helping Lynn out of the low-backed wooden chair. "Come on. Let's get some fresh air."

Lynn allowed herself to be led gingerly from the restaurant, soon finding herself on the sidewalk outside. Moving from the cool air conditioning of the restaurant into the outside heat, she felt like she had stepped into a sauna. The tears refused to dry despite the dark intensity of the night heat. If anything, they increased. She could barely see past them to walk. Marc Cameron led her down the street and stopped her in front of his small red Toyota. "Where are we going?"

"Just get in the car," he said gently, and she did as she was told.

She could barely make out where he was driving her, and realized that they were near the beach only when she heard the familiar, comforting roar of the ocean. She walked haltingly beside Marc, his hand on her elbow, guiding her across the concrete of the large parking lot until they came to the Lake Worth pier, still crowded with young people coming out of John G's, a popular night spot in the area. Still holding on to her arm, Marc Cameron led Lynn down onto the darkened beach and sat her gently by the water's edge. In the next instant, Lynn was aware of a handkerchief against her cheek, and she pressed it under her eyes, feeling it soak up her tears like a blotter. "I always knew these things would come in handy for something," Marc was saying. "Feel any better?"

"I feel like an idiot," Lynn said, blowing her nose noisily into the wet handkerchief, aware that he was tugging at her shoes, rolling up her pant legs. "Should I ask what you're doing?"

"I thought you might feel better if you got your feet wet. Don't ask me why."

"Are you going to take advantage of my depressed and vulnerable state?" She realized that the question was only partly facetious.

"Call me old-fashioned, but the idea of making love to a woman drowning in tears doesn't exactly turn me on."

"My God," she wailed, hating the sound, "I can't stop! What's the matter with me? Where are all these tears coming from? They're getting on my nerves." He laughed softly as she buried her head in her knees. She heard him moving away. Was he going to just leave her here, crying in the sand? Not that she could blame him. This wasn't exactly the fun evening he might have been expecting. Where was he going?

She felt his hands at the back of her neck, kneading the tense muscles at the top of her spine. "That feels so good," she whispered after a few minutes, hoping he wouldn't stop.

He didn't. His hands pressed firmly into the muscles of her shoulders, his fingers disappearing into her hair to massage her head, then moving slowly down the length of her back. She thought she should probably tell him that was enough, but the truth was it wasn't enough, not nearly enough. As his hands moved back up toward her shoulders, Lynn suddenly spun around and pushed herself into his arms with such force she knocked him over, pressing her mouth against his as they fell. His arms immediately wrapped around her waist, and once again the soft bristles of his beard tickled her face as they rolled over in the sand. Not quite the black satin sheets she had envisioned earlier, but infinitely more satisfying in the flesh than in her fantasies. She felt his tongue inside her mouth, his hands moving down to grip her backside. What on earth was she doing? As suddenly and forcefully as she had pushed him over, Lynn now pushed herself out of Marc's arms and sat up, looking at the ocean as if searching for a satisfactory explanation for her behavior.

"I thought you said that the idea of making love to a woman drowning in tears didn't exactly turn you on," Lynn said when none was forthcoming.

"I guess I'm kinkier than I thought."

"This will make a wonderful chapter in your new book."

"I'll be kind."

Lynn stumbled to her feet and started brushing the sand from her clothes. "I'm sorry."

"No, you're not."

"No, I'm not." She stopped shaking the sand from her clothes and smiled. "But I should be."

"Why?"

"I ruined your dinner, for one thing. You had to put out all that money for food you didn't even get to see."

"I wasn't hungry."

"And then I did nothing but cry."

"You warned me you wouldn't be very good company."

"And then I attacked you."

"Things were definitely starting to look up."

"And then I stopped."

"A woman of mercurial temperament."

Lynn looked around helplessly. "I really should go home now . . ."

"But . . . ?"

"But I'm starving," she said, and suddenly they were both laughing. "I don't believe it but I'm famished." She looked toward the restaurant up by the road. "Do you want to give dinner another try? My treat this time."

He said nothing, only nodded and guided her up the sand to the restaurant.

"You're a nice man," she said as they pushed through the door into the noisy, crowded restaurant. His lips moved in reply but Lynn couldn't hear what he was saying.

It was only after they'd been seated at a small table by the wall and the waiter approached to take their order that she realized what he had said: "Not always."

10

Renee sat watching her sister. Kathryn lay, stretched out like a cat in the sun, on the large balcony of Renee's sixth-floor oceanfront condominium. The balcony, which was covered with squares of freshly washed white tile, curved around the side of the corner unit, so that it always faced directly toward the ocean. Kathryn had positioned her chaise longue on that part of the balcony which ran perpendicular to the ocean and parallel to the large pool, which was deserted despite the heat of the late afternoon. The building, known as the Delray Oasis, was more than half empty at this time of year, and those residents who lived here year-round rarely sat out in the sun. Those nasty liver spots might prove to be something nastier still, the dreaded brown markings of an incipient carcinoma. That is, if their pacemakers didn't give out first. Two of the building's more elderly residents had died over the winter, and another was in the hospital and not expected to return.

Renee watched as Kathryn flipped over onto her stomach, carefully avoiding putting any pressure on her wrists. She had removed the bandages, revealing a series of ugly-looking, if superficial, cuts, and now twisted the insides of her palms outward for the sun to get at them. Kathryn had always loved the sun. It was ironic, Renee thought, that Kathryn had been the one to leave Florida for New York, a city in which she herself had always wanted to live. She'd had several offers from important law firms up North, but had chosen to return to Florida to go into practice with a respectable, if not spectacular, firm. Why? Florida was a living tomb, she used to tell anyone who'd listen, an old-age home in the shape of a state, God's little waiting room, as she was fond of quoting. Philip was always throwing statistics her way showing that Florida was America's fastest-growing state, its population getting younger every year, people screaming to get in. They could have it, Renee thought but never said anymore, knowing that Philip loved Florida, that he would never consider leaving. Renee tried to get comfortable, feeling the buttons from the lounge's extended white cushion poking into the backs of her thighs. She should have changed when she got home from work—early, for a change—but the thought of putting on a bathing suit only depressed her, another reason to hate Florida.

People screaming to get in. Renee shook her head, recalling Philip's words with amazement. From as early as she could remember, Renee had wanted nothing but to get out. She had never especially liked the ocean, never appreciated the unrelenting sunshine. She hated the humidity and the lack of seasonal change. Florida was for people who liked things as pretty and as flat as a postcard, with no shadows on the horizon. Florida was for people, like her parents, who were too self-centered to notice the population was as lifeless as the air, or for people, like Philip, who'd always been larger than their surroundings. Florida was merely a sunny backdrop for the force of Philip's personality. But not her own. For some reason, Renee had never felt she belonged here. She'd managed to get out, briefly, when she attended Columbia Law School, but something had drawn her back. What? she wondered now. And why?

Renee adjusted her legs so that the chair's buttons were no longer making holes in her thighs. She glanced toward the living room, where Consuela, the maid who came three times a week to clean the three-bedroom apartment and prepare meals, was vacuuming the white carpet in the center of the room. "It's very white," Kathryn had said, and there was certainly no arguing about that. Renee found herself remembering the bright clutter of the room she and her sister had shared as children, hearing their mother plead with them to put away their toys and keep things neat. She and Kathryn always ignored her until their father intervened. Renee remembered one occasion when their father had angrily ripped several prized posters off the wall and into shreds because he had warned them not to tack them up with Scotch tape. Several small squares of paint came off along with the tape, and he told the sobbing youngsters, surveying the wreckage of their once happy room, that they'd brought it on themselves. Renee had immediately filled in the ragged white spaces on the wall with bright colors from her set of Magic Markers, and had been spanked soundly for her efforts.

Now she surveyed the stark whiteness of her living room and wondered how she came to feel at home in a place which, objectively speaking, resembled nothing so much as the lobby of an exclusive hotel. Even her office was more personal and warm. Renee turned her head back toward the pool area. There was certainly no warmth in the frozen perfection of her apartment.

Still, as Renee had told her sister, she wouldn't have it any other way. When Philip was happy, she was happy, and there was no question but that Philip was in his element—Philip, a man of sweeping gestures and well-chosen words, words which, when delivered in his deep, confident voice, focused all attention in his direction. When Philip entered a room, he brought with him all the color the room required. Perhaps he had planned it that way.

Renee found her eyes starting to grow heavy in the sun's harsh glare. It was just past four o'clock, and though her time in the office had been relatively short, she'd worked very hard. She'd come home early to find her sister sleeping on the balcony, and had quietly pulled over another lounge chair to join her. Kathryn hadn't said anything further about why she had tried suicide. Maybe now was a good time to try to get her to talk. Consuela would be leaving soon. Debbie had announced plans that morning to spend the day on Singer Island with friends. Philip wouldn't be home for another hour.

Renee found it a pleasant switch to be the first one home. Usually she didn't get back until at least six, and often much later. She would rush in, all apologies and soothing phrases, hurrying to get whatever dinner Consuela had prepared on the table, asking Philip about his day, trying to give him the attention he needed, the attention he deserved. Philip dominated the conversation as he dominated everything else in his home. Renee occasionally realized that he rarely asked her questions in return, that he seemed unconcerned about the mechanics of her day, and that he often disappeared from the table after dinner without so much as an appreciative glance in her direction. She would clear the table with no help from either her husband or her husband's daughter, who she had overheard confide to her father that she thought Renee had the personality of a doormat. "She makes you want to step all over her," Debbie had giggled, eliciting only mild objections from Philip. Since when could anyone refer to her as a doormat? Renee wondered, smarting less from the term than from Philip's half-hearted defense on her behalf.

Her father had used words in the same way, as weapons, using them to ridicule and to wound. When she had been small, a large black snake had curled itself around her ankle while she was playing outside, and her screams had disturbed her father's Sunday afternoon nap. He had called her a cry-baby and a selfish little girl and told her it served her right for playing where she shouldn't. "Cry-baby, selfish little girl," echoed inside her head long after the snake had been frightened away. She could hear them even now, still feel the pain they had caused her.

Perhaps that was why she had chosen law, so that she could fight back. "You're too good with words," Philip occasionally accused her now. Had she gone too far in the opposite direction? Could someone be too good with words?

Maybe her father had been attempting to toughen her up, to force his sensitive younger child to be strong. She had to admit that if such was his plan, it had worked. She had a reputation for toughness. And her life had turned out better than even she could have hoped. She certainly had everything she could possibly want: a rich husband, a fancy apartment, a successful career. Everything but children, Renee acknowledged, and maybe Philip was right. Maybe children would be too much for her to handle.

"You make me sorry I ever had children," she remembered her father saying, and she had understood, even as a small child, *especially* as a small child, that she was the reason for her father's coldness, the source of her mother's unhappiness. She was unloved because she was unlovable. They had told her that often enough, though perhaps more by what they didn't say than what they did.

Renee suddenly saw herself as a six-year-old child running toward her mother's waiting car. Her mother was sitting there, her back rigid, the car engine running, and she was looking straight ahead, her lower lip trembling, her hands twisting nervously on the steering wheel as Renee crawled onto the seat beside her. "I'm sorry I'm late."

"All the other children were out ten minutes ago. You know how your father hates it when I'm late. You know how he always likes me to be there when he gets home."

"I couldn't get my ballet shoes untied. They were all in knots."

"The other children had no trouble."

"They didn't have knots."

"It's always something, isn't it, Renee?" She blinked rapidly, trying to stop several tears from falling down her cheek and streaking her makeup. She succeeded only partially, and grabbed a tissue from her purse, dabbing furtively at her lashes.

"Are you mad?"

"No, of course I'm not angry," her mother corrected, her voice so low Renee had to strain to hear her.

"I'm sorry."

"I know you are. But 'sorry' isn't going to get us home any faster."

"Why do we have to get home before Daddy does?"

"Because that's the way he likes it," Helen Metcalfe said, checking her reflection in the rearview mirror, reapplying the mascara her tears had dislodged. "Your daddy works very hard to make sure we have a nice life. He doesn't ask for a lot in return," she continued, speaking as if she were reading from a prepared text. Renee watched her mother return the mascara to her handbag and pull out another familiar container. She observed her mother open the small, flat box and take out a worn brush, which she used to painstakingly add color to her cheeks. Renee realized she had never seen her mother's face in its unadorned state. Even first thing in the morning, even at the beach, her mother's face was always fully made up. Renee wondered what was so wrong with her mother's face that she worked so hard to cover it up.

"Why do you put all that stuff on your face?"

"Because your father likes it," her mother answered, as Renee had known she would. Helen Metcalfe returned the blush to her purse and snapped the handbag shut. She turned to her daughter for the first time since Renee had entered the car. "Do I look all right?"

"You look pretty."

Helen Metcalfe permitted herself a brief smile. "Maybe your father will be late. Maybe if we hurry we can get home before he does."

He wasn't, and they didn't. He was already pacing across the living-room floor when they got home. Her mother immediately abandoned Renee's side, hurrying over to kiss her father's cheek, running to mix him the gin and tonic for some reason only she could fix, explaining Renee's class had gone late, trying to soothe his ruffled feathers, explaining, soothing, trying vainly to keep the peace, siding with her husband when Renee tried to intervene on her behalf.

"I don't have to take ballet lessons," Renee had offered, hating her mother's abandonment of her, hearing only her mother's words and not the fear behind them as she tried in vain to placate her father. "I don't even want to take ballet lessons."

"Well, you'll take them, young lady, and you'll learn to appreciate them." Her father stared at her with barely concealed fury. "Honestly, Renee, you make me sorry I ever had children."

Renee looked away from the image of her father's face toward Kathryn, and envied her sleep. She hoped it was dreamless. "You shouldn't upset your father," she heard her mother say, dragging her back into the past with this familiar refrain. No one ever asked how her lessons had gone. Except Kathryn, she remembered, who had sat with her that night, patiently showing her how to tie her shoe ribbons so that they wouldn't knot, begging her not to argue with their father, to accept what he said in silence and let it roll off her back.

But it didn't roll off her back. It rolled over her head like a dangerous wave, pulling her under, ultimately robbing her of air, submerging her, drowning her. Perhaps that was why she disliked the ocean, Renee thought now, closing her eyes and listening to its protesting roar.

She wasn't sure when she realized that someone was standing on the other side of the sliding glass of the kitchen door. Instinct told her to keep her eyes closed. She heard the door slide open, and tilted her head to the side as if lost in sleep. If it was Philip, and Renee was convinced it was—she thought she might have heard him saying goodbye to Consuela—perhaps he would choose to wake her up with a kiss, the handsome prince her just reward at the end of a trying day.

Renee heard further movement and lifted her lids a fraction so that she could see what was going on while retaining the appearance of sleep.

She saw Kathryn stretch and turn over, sitting back on her chair, unaware for the moment that she wasn't alone. Kathryn turned her head, saw Philip and jumped, her hand moving to her mouth to stifle a scream.

Philip was immediately at her side, his fingers on his lips urging her silence. "I'm sorry," he whispered. "I didn't mean to startle you." He motioned to his left. "Renee's asleep."

"My God, I must have been really out. I didn't even know she was here. How long have you been standing there?"

"Just a few minutes."

Kathryn checked her watch. "Everybody's home so early."

"Cancellation. I can't speak for Renee."

He walked to the railing and leaned over its side, looking with great intensity at nothing in particular. "I was just about to make myself a drink. Would you like something?"

"That would be nice."

"Gin and tonic?"

"Perfect."

"I'll just change my clothes first, if you don't mind."

Renee was about to open her eyes fully and announce she'd also like a drink, but Philip had already gone back inside the apartment. Why the charade? Why hadn't she simply opened her eyes and told them she wasn't asleep? Why didn't she do it now?

Something stopped her. Maybe it was better this way, she decided. She'd been hoping that Kathryn would get a chance to talk to Philip alone. But he'd been so busy, or there was always someone around. Now maybe they could talk. Maybe Kathryn would open up. Maybe Philip could help her. Renee would have preferred not to be there at all, but if she tried to excuse herself now, Kathryn would only insist that she stay. Renee felt she was a reluctant eavesdropper. She also felt she had no other choice. One lie invariably led to others. The road to hell was paved with good intentions.

"Here you go," Philip said minutes later, coming back onto the balcony and depositing a tall cold drink in Kathryn's waiting palm. "One gin and tonic for the pretty lady." He pulled up another chair, not a chaise longue, one with a straight back, and sat down easily, his legs wide apart on either side of the chair's legs, holding his extra-dry martini in his lap. Philip always drank extra-dry martinis, which he made himself, something for which Renee was still, even after six years of marriage, disproportionately grateful. Renee noted through half-closed lids the white pants and expensive black-and-white short-sleeved silk jersey and wondered absently how much money Philip spent on clothes in any given year. Certainly more than she did. Her clothes, while new with each season, had the look and feel of yesterday's castoffs. "Classic" was the word Renee used most often to describe her wardrobe, but "matronly" was the better descriptive term. Loose-fitting shifts in navy or olive green, solid-color suits in fabrics that never wrinkled or distinguished themselves in any way, save for perhaps their plainness. Lots of black pants and long sweaters. Anything to disguise her bulk. How could she have let herself get this way? How could her fierce determination in most matters have so far eluded her when it came to controlling her diet? She'd never been such a big eater before. While it was true that her father had a tendency to put on a few extra pounds, that was usually when he'd been drinking more than usual. Renee rarely drank more than the occasional glass of wine at dinner.

Philip, on the other hand, usually enjoyed a few drinks before dinner, just as her father had always done. Renee's lips curled into a wry smile, as if she were having a pleasant, if disconcerting, dream. How long had she been aware of her husband's similarity to her father, at least on a superficial level? When had she recognized the way each looked just past you when you spoke, the casual arrogance that was at once so infuriating and so appealing, the almost childlike self-absorption that only men as handsome as Philip and her father were able to get away with? Even physically, they were remarkably alike, although Philip was unquestionably the more massive of the two, probably a good three inches taller than her father's six feet, with broader shoulders and a wider frame. A football player's body, she thought, recalling that Philip had played the game in college before deciding on medicine as a career, the same career as her father, although the specialty was different. Ian Metcalfe was an internist, now retired. His wife was a former nurse. They had met in a hospital cafeteria and fallen in love. It was funny how both men had chosen women almost a foot shorter than they were. Renee pictured her mother standing primly beside her father, the image immediately superimposed on that of herself standing next to Philip, as if they were designs on a piece of paper, waiting to be traced. Such strange-looking couples, she decided, discarding the image. She had never accepted the notion that women married men like their fathers. Her own father was a taciturn, unpleasant man. Philip was neither. He was gregarious and charming. He had swept her off her feet when she was still light enough to lift. He had rescued her from a life of longing and loneliness, filling her head with words she had been desperate to hear at a time when she was most desperate to hear them. "You're beautiful; you're worth ten women; I love you because you're lovable. I love you. I love you. You mean everything to me." If the words came less frequently these days, if there was any trouble in their marriage—no, not trouble; surely trouble was too strong a word—it was less his fault than hers. Not his fault at all. If there was trouble—no, not trouble; problems—then the problems—problems could be solved—were of her making, and hers to correct.

"What are you thinking about?" Philip asked, and for a second Renee had been about to answer. Then she realized he was talking to her sister.

Kathryn appeared startled by the question and her hand jumped, spilling part of her drink onto the freshly washed tiles.

"Oh, damn. She just cleaned." Kathryn was almost on her feet when Philip's hand on her arm stopped her. Both Renee and Kathryn watched him dramatically pull a tissue from his pants pocket—as if he were a magician and this his best trick—and bend over to wipe away the few drops of liquid that had spilled close to his feet. Renee noticed that he was wearing Gucci loafers and no socks, remembering that this was a look he had adopted long before it became popular to do so. "Sorry," Kathryn apologized. "My mind was . . ."

"A hundred miles away. That's why I asked. You look like you have very deep thoughts."

Kathryn laughed. "First time anybody's ever accused me of that."

"So, are you going to tell me?"

"I'm trying to think of something suitably profound so you won't be disappointed."

He said nothing, obviously waiting.

"I was thinking about my mother," she said finally, and

Renee found it curious their thoughts had been vaguely connected.

"You've come to the right place," he said, laughing.

"I guess you hear a lot of that."

"Not as much as I used to. It's not as fashionable as it once was to blame Mommy for everything."

"Renee thinks I should call her. Tell my parents I'm in town. Tell them what I tried to do."

"And you? What do you think?"

"I think I'm just not ready to face them."

"Then don't."

"I can't keep running away."

"What's the matter with running away?"

Kathryn laughed, and Renee had to turn her head to hide her grin.

"We all need to run away sometimes," Philip continued.

"I've been doing it all my life."

"I don't think that's true."

Kathryn stared at her sister and for a moment Renee thought Kathryn might have realized she wasn't asleep. "I'm a mess," she said at length.

"You look pretty good to me."

Kathryn rubbed the tops of her bare legs. She was wearing the new bathing suit she had purchased at Debbie's insistence. Renee had to admit it was the perfect choice for her beautiful figure. She felt a stab of jealousy, and immediately felt ashamed.

"I don't know," Kathryn said, shaking her head. "I don't know what I'm so afraid of all the time."

"I can understand your fears," Philip said, his voice a magnet, drawing both women's eyes toward him, although he concentrated his full attention on Kathryn.

"Can you?"

"I like to think so. Understanding," he said, and he smiled shyly, "is what I do for a living." Renee listened to them both laugh, wishing she could join in. "Come on, Kathryn, indulge me. My last patient canceled. I'm feeling lonely and insecure."

Kathryn laughed again, this time more boldly. "How can I help you, Doctor?"

"Talk to me. Tell me what goes on in that pretty head."

"Not much," Kathryn said, shaking off the compliment with a toss of her hair. Was she even aware of it? Renee tried to remember the last time Philip had paid her even so casual a compliment.

"Tell me," Philip urged gently.

"It's so trite."

"Feelings are never trite."

"I never felt loved as a child," she began, then laughed self-consciously. "I'm sure Renee has told you the same thing."

"She has," Philip concurred. "But we're not talking about Renee now. We're talking about you."

Renee listened as her sister spoke out loud her own thoughts of only a minute ago.

"Arnie was the first person, the first man, to make me feel loved. Of course, what did I know of men? I was eighteen years old when I married Arnie Wright." Kathryn's eyes clouded over. "But he was so good to me. He was so kind, so thoughtful. I didn't deserve him."

"You didn't deserve to feel loved? To feel cherished?"

"I wasn't good enough for him."

"Did he tell you that?"

"Arnie?" Kathryn laughed. "Of course not. Arnie told me he loved me every day of our married life. He thought I was the most wonderful thing on earth."

"But you didn't believe him."

"How could I? You see me. I'm nothing. I don't do anything. I don't have anything. My whole life was Arnie. I don't exist without him. And after he died, whatever I had been died with him. Except here was this body still walking around, and it needed to be fed and clothed and taken care of. And I just don't have the strength."

"You have lots of strength, Kathryn. You just need to locate it."

"And if I can't? If I don't want to?"

"You would have made the cuts deeper," he reminded her, taking her hands and gently turning them palm-up to expose her damaged wrists. Slowly, deliberately, Philip brought her wrists to his lips and kissed each one in turn. "You just need someone to kiss them and make them better."

"Oh God, Philip, I'm so afraid."

"Don't be afraid, Kathy."

Renee was as surprised at Philip's use of the diminutive of her sister's name as she had been by his earlier gesture of kissing Kathryn's wrists. No wonder all his patients loved him, she thought, wishing she were anywhere else, feeling dirty for her deceit.

And suddenly Kathryn was in Philip's arms, crying against his shoulder. "I've made such a mess of my life," she sobbed, burying her head into his chest.

"We all mess up from time to time."

"Not like me."

"Just like you." Philip pulled back, out of their embrace, although one hand remained in hers. "We all do stupid things from time to time. Sometimes we spend years doing stupid things." He shook his head, his black hair falling across his forehead. "We all mess up." Both women waited eagerly for him to continue. "My first marriage was a complete disaster," he confided. "I'm sure that Debbie has told you her mother is beautiful. Well, she is. Also very bright and loving. At least that's how she was in the beginning, when we first got married. Oh, she was insecure, but I told myself that was endearing. It's funny how very beautiful women are often the most insecure. I guess I thought it was something she'd outgrow, but if anything, it got worse the longer we were married. She was insanely jealous. She'd call me at the office when I was busy with patients, demand to be put through. A couple of times, she actually stormed into my office in the middle of a session. One night, we were having an argument as we were getting ready for bed. I was too tired to fight anymore. She'd been screaming accusations at me all day. I just wanted to go to sleep, and I told her so, but she wouldn't let up. She was shouting at me, and I thought, if I don't get some sleep, I'm not going to be able to function in the morning, and I told her that if she didn't stop yelling, I was going to spend the night in a hotel. When she didn't stop, I put my clothes back on and walked out the door. And do you know what she did? She came running down the street after me, screaming at the top of her lungs, stark naked. My wife, the psychiatrist's wife, chasing her husband's car down the street like a yapping dog, and she's absolutely naked. I knew then that I had to get out of that marriage or she would destroy me. My career, my practice, everything I'd worked so hard to achieve. Not to mention my sanity, my self-respect. I knew that if I didn't leave, I was a dead man." He shook his head, finishing off the last of his drink. "Leaving Debbie was the hardest thing I've ever done. She was just a little kid. I'm sure she didn't understand. I know how unhappy the divorce made her." He looked back at Kathryn. "We all mess up," he said.

"Debbie loves you. She thinks the world of you."

"Yes, but will she ever really forgive me?" He lowered his head. "I'm sorry."

"What for?"

"I'm the psychiatrist. I'm supposed to be listening to you. Not the other way around." He looked toward Renee. "I've never told that story to anyone. Not even Renee. Thank you." Kathryn looked as puzzled as Renee felt. "For hearing me out," he explained.

"My pleasure," Kathryn said. "You made me feel needed. I should thank you."

They fell silent. Why had Philip told Kathryn he'd never told that story to anyone? Not even to Renee, he had said. He'd told her that story almost verbatim soon after they'd started dating. Had he forgotten? Or had he used the story—exposed his own vulnerability—as a way of getting Kathryn to understand that she was not alone?

Renee smiled and opened her eyes, suddenly overwhelmed with gratitude for the love and concern her husband had shown her sister. Philip acknowledged her awakening with a nod of his head. Kathryn was sitting back in her chair, looking relaxed and even happy. Renee watched Philip take his hand from Kathryn's, slowly, casually, as if he hadn't realized it was there.

11

"We'll have the blackened snapper," Marc Cameron told the waiter as Lynn suppressed a smile. "It got interesting results the last time." He winked and Lynn covered her eyes with her hands, partly from embarrassment, more because she was afraid of what they might reveal. They were sitting across from each other in a quiet corner of a casually elegant restaurant in Pompano Beach. "So, tell me about your week."

"Is it my imagination," Lynn asked, "or is it just because I know you're a writer, that you always look like you're about to take notes?"

"I am taking notes." He pointed to his head.

"I was afraid of that."

"Any new and interesting cases?"

Lynn fought the strong urge to reach across the table and put her hand in his. There was something in the way he asked even the most innocuous of questions that made her want to tell him everything, something about the way he looked at her that said she was the only woman in the room, that she mattered in a way others did not, that any man would be a fool not to pay close attention to her, that he was no such fool. "I spent most of the morning counseling a couple of newlyweds. It seems they spent the better part of their honeymoon beating each other up. They came in wearing matching black eyes to go with their matching wedding rings."

"And what did you tell them?"

"I explained that this was not appropriate adult behavior," Lynn said, fighting off the image of herself and Marc Cameron rolling through the sand. "I said there were better ways to work out their problems, that there was such a thing as self-control." Lynn felt her breath become shallow and she turned away, pretending to be looking around the restaurant. She noticed for the first time since joining Marc at the back of the large room that it was almost full, and becoming increasingly crowded. She checked her watch. It was after eight o'clock. "It's pretty busy for a weeknight."

"Popular place."

"Not too popular, I hope."

"You said you wanted out of the way. You didn't say anything about unpopular."

"Have you been here before?"

"Once, a few years ago. The food was excellent. I just never came back because it was kind of . . ."

"Out of the way?"

"Out of the way." They laughed.

"I shouldn't be here," she said.

"Why shouldn't you be here?"

"My lawyer would kill me."

"Don't tell him."

"Her," Lynn corrected. "And it's too late. I already did."

Marc Cameron's eyes widened only slightly, revealing nothing.

"Her name is Renee Bower. Have you heard of her?" Marc shook his head. "I went to school with her sister. Anyway, I like her a lot. She's smart and shrewd. And nice. Very nice. She's married to a psychiatrist. Philip Bower. Have you heard of *him?*" Again, Marc Cameron shook his head, although this time he smiled. "Apparently he's very well known."

"Not to me."

"Renee thinks I should talk to him. At least that's what she said. What I think she really means is that I should have my head examined."

"For seeing me?"

Lynn nodded.

"And what do you think?"

"That she's probably right." Lynn looked directly into Marc's eyes. "I mean, what am I doing here, Marc?"

"I don't know. What *are* you doing here?"

"I don't know."

"How about this?" He stretched across the table and kissed her.

Lynn pulled back instantly, trying to figure out exactly how all this had happened, how she came to be sitting in the corner of a crowded restaurant in Pompano Beach kissing the husband of the woman her husband had run away with.

"I'm sorry," he said.

"No, you're not."

"No, I'm not. Are you?"

"No," she said, surprising herself yet again because she had meant to say yes. "But we have to stop this. We really do. We can't keep grabbing at each other like a couple of teenagers."

"Why not?"

"Because it's not . . ."

"Right?"

"Smart. It's not smart."

"What's so great about being smart?"

"It generally gets better results than being stupid."

Marc reached across the table and took her hands in his, unwilling to release them even when she tried to pull away. "I like you, Lynn. You like me. What's so stupid about two people who really like each other having a relationship?"

"Why?" she asked. "Why do you like me?"

He looked confused. "Why does anyone like anybody? What can I say? You're lovely, you're bright, you're interesting . . ."

"I'm Gary's wife."

There was a moment's silence before he spoke.

"Was that who kissed me just now? Gary's wife? Or was it simply Lynn Schuster, the woman I'm having dinner with?"

"They're the same person."

"They don't have to be."

"You wouldn't want me any other way," she told him plainly, and felt his hands withdraw. Immediately she brought her hands into her lap, hiding them under the table. "Face it, Marc, you wouldn't even be here if I wasn't Gary's wife."

There was silence as Lynn scanned the faces of the other diners at the nearby tables, none of whom seemed to be looking their way. Had any of them seen the kiss? she wondered, as she had wondered on the beach during their last such encounter. She recognized no one, although for a fleeting second she wished she did. Anyone, she thought, so that she could jump up from the table and shout hello, make a few minutes of polite, inconsequential conversation, break the spell this man seemed to have over her, this man she shouldn't be seen talking to, let alone kissing. In public. Just like someone had reported seeing Gary and Suzette. Was that why she was here? Tit for tat? Two wrongs struggling to make a right? What was wrong with her?

The woman at the table closest to theirs turned toward Lynn and smiled, fidgeting in her seat, making Lynn aware she had been staring. Lynn looked away from the woman, careful at the same time to keep her eyes away from Marc's, pretending to peruse the posters of old-time movie stars lining the walls. The restaurant, which looked like a small house from the outside, was surprisingly large inside. In fact, this restaurant was full of surprises, Lynn thought, knowing she would have to look at Marc sooner or later, wondering again how she had gotten herself into this mess when she had spent her whole life avoiding messes, being cautious, always weighing the consequences of every decision before taking action.

"This is so unlike me," she said finally, forcing her gaze back to his. "I don't do things like this . . ."

"You haven't done anything."

"I feel so confused. I feel like such an idiot." She heard her voice rising, and lowered it immediately. "I've always been in total control of what I do."

"Is being in control so important?"

"I think so, yes."

"Why?"

"Because there's nothing worse than feeling powerless," Lynn stated. "You're a man. You can't possibly understand. You're naturally in control. Women have to fight for it all the time. When we go into a relationship with a man, it's a constant juggling act. We're always trying to balance how much of ourselves we need to keep with how much we have to give away. Most women give away too much. Then when the relationship ends, they're left with nothing."

"So you think that because I'm a man, I'm always in control?" Marc asked, not waiting for an answer. "You think I'm *naturally* in control. Isn't that what you said?"

Lynn nodded.

"How much control do you think I had when my wife announced she was leaving me? I mean, here I am, forty years old, reasonably well established for a writer, all things considered. I think I have my whole life more or less arranged, all my ducks neatly lined up in the pond. And then she comes along and blows them all out of the water. In a matter of minutes, my life is irreversibly altered. I lose my wife, my house, my sons. Suddenly I get to see my boys all of twice a week, not to mention every other weekend. Do you honestly believe that I wouldn't choose to do things differently if I had any control whatsoever over my life?" He laughed, but the laugh was bitter, hollow. "I think if I've learned anything from all this, it's how little control any of us really *does* have. What is control anyway? I'll tell you what it is—it's a joke. We think we have power, but we don't. So, Ms. Schuster, you might as well give up some of that precious control because you don't really have it anyway."

The image of her mother in the final stages of Alzheimer's flashed before Lynn's eyes. "Tell me about Suzette," she said softly, eager to displace the image.

"What do you want to know?"

"Everything."

He smiled and she felt grateful.

"What's she like?"

"Artistic," he answered quickly. "Willful. Charming. Needy. Suzette," he continued, and this time he was the one who was careful not to look in Lynn's direction, "is a woman of many needs."

"And Gary is a man who likes to feel needed."

"Bingo."

Lynn looked at her empty glass, feeling a definite thirst.

"Gary isn't the first man Suzette's been involved with since our marriage," Marc said after a pause. Lynn felt her mouth drop open in surprise and quickly closed it. "Since her parents died a few years ago—they were killed in a car accident . . ."

"Oh, my God."

"Yes, it was pretty terrible. Suzette took it very hard, which, of course, is perfectly understandable. She had a lot of guilt. I was part of that guilt. Suddenly the whole idea of the starving artist didn't seem as appealing as it had originally. The rebellious daughter loses something of her edge when she has no one to rebel against. Anyway, that's when the affairs started. Not that there were that many of them. Only a few. I never said anything because, quite frankly, I didn't know what to say. I wasn't interested in ending my marriage. I loved my wife. I was trying to understand what she was going through. I didn't want to break up my family, to leave my sons, the way I felt my father had deserted me when I was a kid. My boys mean more to me than anything in the world. I'd do anything to keep from hurting them."

"I'm so sorry, Marc."

He waved away her concern. "It's funny how things work out, isn't it? Here's a woman whose whole rationale for leaving me is that she wants some stability in her life, that she wants someone who's settled and who knows where he's going, someone she can look up to and feel secure with because she knows he'll take good care of her, like her father always took care of her. And what does she do? In her search for stability, she disrupts the lives of everyone around her. My life, our sons' lives. Yours. Your children's. It's ironic. I know"—he shrugged — "I'm supposed to appreciate irony."

"Maybe her relationship with Gary will just run its course, the way the others have."

"Maybe. I don't think so. Do you?"

"I thought so in the beginning. I was sure Gary would come back."

"Would you take him back now if he did?"

"Probably," she answered, thinking this was the truth. "Would you take Suzette back?"

"No," he answered forcefully. "Too much water under the bridge. How's that for an original expression?" He tried to laugh. "So, tell me about Gary."

Again, Lynn found herself searching the poster-lined walls of the restaurant. "What can I say? He's intelligent, soft-spoken, gentle. I always assumed he was faithful to me, and I think he had been until he met Suzette. But there are a lot of things about Gary that I obviously don't know about or understand. I thought he was happy. It wasn't until he told me he was leaving that I learned otherwise. You can imagine how that made me feel. I mean, aside from the obvious, the abandoned wife and all, I'm a social worker. I'm supposed to be trained to recognize when people are in pain. You'd think that after fourteen years of marriage I might have had some inkling that my husband was unhappy. I always thought," she continued, aware that she was rambling but too wound up now to stop, "that one of the things he liked about me was my independence, the fact that I had my own career, my own interests, my own life. That I was with him because I *wanted* to be with him, not because I *needed* to be with him. But the night he told me he was leaving, and he was standing there with one foot out the door, and I asked him to tell me why, he said that he had met a woman who needed him, really needed him. I said I needed him too, that our children needed him, and he said it wasn't the same thing, and that it would be better for all of us if he left. I said I didn't want him to go, and he said I'd be all right, that I always was. I think he really believed—believes—that he's doing the right thing. I know it was never his intention to hurt me or the kids."

"He hurt you anyway."

Lynn smiled, throwing her head back and staring at the ceiling fan directly overhead. "You sound like Renee."

"Renee?"

"My lawyer, remember? When I told her about you, she said to be careful, that you might not mean to hurt me, but what difference would it make if you hurt me anyway?"

"Who else have you discussed me with?"

Lynn shook her head. "No one."

"Not even your father?"

"Especially not my father. He's basically a simple man. I don't think he's ready for any of this. *I* don't think I'm ready for any of this."

"How about my father?"

"What?"

"Think you're ready for him?"

"I don't understand."

"I'm going to visit him this Saturday. He's in a place called Halcyon Days." He chuckled. "An ironic name for a nursing home."

"It's a lovely place," Lynn told him reassuringly. "The best."

"He had a stroke a few years back. It made it hard for him to look after himself. I still feel guilty as hell about having put him there."

"Don't feel guilty. What other choice did you have?"

"Are you saying I wasn't in total control of the situation?" he asked, a sly smile curving across his lips.

The waiter approached the table and cautiously deposited their dinners on the place mats in front of them. "Be careful," he said, almost as an afterthought, "the plates are hot."

"Wine?" Marc asked, still smiling, lifting the bottle from its Plexiglas cooler and filling her glass before she could answer. "So what about Saturday? Gary has the kids, doesn't he?"

"Marc, I . . ."

"You'd like my father. He's kind of a crazy old guy. Bought

himself a baby-blue Lincoln convertible a couple of weeks ago. Of course, he doesn't have a driver's license anymore, so he's not allowed to drive it, and the damn thing, which cost over thirty-five thousand dollars, just sits there in the parking lot gathering dust. He had a phone put in it too. Bought it outright. None of this renting nonsense for him."

"The car just sits there?"

"Sometimes he lends it to one of the nurses. That is, when he's not sending them on expensive holidays to Rome or Greece."

"Does he have that kind of money?"

"I guess he did." Marc Cameron cut into the large piece of the blackened snapper on his plate. "Apparently he's been storing it away for years, like a squirrel. From what I can understand, he's got bank accounts in virtually every bank in Florida. I just found out about all this a few weeks ago when one of the banks called me about honoring the check he wrote for the car. They said he didn't have enough money in his current account but that they could take the money from one of his term deposits. I didn't know what they were talking about. Anyway, I thought I'd better find out. That's one of the reasons I'm going to see him this weekend. I'd be grateful for the support, if you'd care to come along."

"I don't think I should."

"I could use your professional guidance."

Lynn raised a large piece of fish to her lips, but was unable to put it in her mouth. "Can I think about it?" Why didn't she just say no?

"Did you ever think that maybe you think too much?"

Lynn nodded. "Good chance of that."

"I can be very patient," he told her, "as well as persistent."

There was a long pause during which they both sat with forks poised and neither made a move. For an instant, Lynn was tempted to shove the fish into her mouth as Nicholas would no doubt do, and yell triumphantly, "First taste!" Instead she said, "There have to be some ground rules."

"Name them."

"No more kisses across the table. No more clinches on the beach. No more rolls through the sand."

"How about in the back seat of my father's new baby-blue Lincoln convertible?"

Lynn said nothing. The image of the two of them groping at each other in the back seat of a car pressed itself teasingly against her eyes, lingering, refusing to leave. She chewed the blackened snapper with grim determination, refusing to acknowledge that her mouth was on fire from the heavy layer of pepper.

"Hey, I'm just joking. No back seat, honestly. No sudden lunges across the dinner table. No frolicking by the ocean. Lips sealed," he said, grimacing, and she laughed, lunging for her glass of water.

"I don't mean to sound like a prude," she found herself explaining, abandoning the water for her glass of wine. "It's not like sex hasn't been on my mind lately. I mean, it's been over six months. I'm not interested in celibacy as a way of life. But I just don't want to rush into something I'll end up regretting."

"I won't rush you."

"I think it's important to keep our relationship platonic. At least for now," she added, then bit down hard on her tongue. Why had she added that? Why couldn't she stop when she was ahead?

Marc Cameron lifted his wineglass into the space between them. Lynn quickly raised her glass to his, listening to the delicate click of their touch. "For now," he said.

12

     His hands were cold on the back of her neck. "Your hands are cold," Renee told him, feeling Philip's fingers slide gently away from the base of her throat, where he had been doing up the clasp of her wide gold necklace. Renee rarely wore the necklace, a gift from Philip on her last birthday, because she was slightly uncomfortable with its weight, more uncomfortable with the unwanted attention it brought to her overly round cheeks. She thought about the last time she had worn it, the surprise birthday party of a number of weeks ago when her husband had spent much of the night engrossed in conversation with Alicia-call-me-Ali Henderson. Thoughts of Alicia Henderson led to thoughts of the unpleasant surprise that Debbie had arranged for her in the restaurant the previous week. She hadn't said anything further to Philip about that afternoon, and, of course, he hadn't mentioned it, each pretending the incident was as innocent as he claimed. There were times she'd been tempted to bring it up, but Philip always seemed to have one foot out the door, or there was Debbie or Kathryn to contend with, and when they finally found themselves alone together in bed at the end of the evening, Philip would plead exhaustion and roll over and be asleep within minutes. Renee patted the heavy gold links at the base of her throat. A man of grand gestures, she thought. And casual infidelities. "How do I look?" she asked.

"It looks great."

"Not *it*," she corrected, wondering if he had been aware of his choice of words. "Me. How do I look?" She dropped her hands to her sides, feeling naked despite the fact she was fully dressed, waiting nervously for his assessment.

"Terrific," he said, staring at his own image in the mirror across from their bed, smoothing his hair carefully at each side.

"You don't think it draws too much attention to my double chin?"

"What double chin?" He moved behind her and cupped her full breasts inside his large hands. "Who even notices your double chin when they have these glorious doubles staring them in the face?"

"Thanks a lot." Renee leaned her body back against his, welcoming the feel of his touch despite his words, not caring that her freshly done hair was being mussed or that her new black silk lounging outfit was being crushed between his careless fingers. It felt like an eternity since he had touched her this way. She suddenly didn't care that they were already late for dinner with several of her partners; she was unconcerned that neither Debbie nor her sister had returned home from their afternoon outing. She wanted Philip's hands on her body. She needed to feel close to him; she needed this reassurance.

He pulled away. "You look great," he said, appraising himself again in the mirror. "I think I'll change my shirt."

"Now? Philip, we're already running late."

"And whose fault is that?"

"I'm not saying it's anybody's fault. It's just that we're already half an hour late, and the shirt you're wearing looks great."

"It's the wrong shirt for this suit, but fine, if it's going to create problems for you to be a few minutes late, I'll wear it. At least one of us will look good."

"You look terrific," Renee told him, her voice a gentle plea. How could he think he looked otherwise?

"Whatever you say."

"No, no," Renee said, giving in. "You have to feel comfortable. If you're not comfortable . . ."

"It's the wrong shirt," he explained, an endearing half-grin on his face.

"Which shirt do you think will be better?"

"I don't know," he said, moving to the closet. "What do you think?" He returned to the side of the bed with two blue-striped shirts. "I think the stripe is more interesting than the plain," he said, referring to the shirt he had on. "Which one do you like better?"

"They both look the same."

"God, Renee, you're so unobservant. This one has a much wider stripe."

Renee looked harder but still couldn't see the difference. "The one in your right hand," she said finally.

"Really? I prefer the one in the left."

"That's fine."

"Your enthusiasm is overwhelming."

"I'm sorry, Philip. Really, it just doesn't matter to me."

"That's obvious. Now, if it concerned what *you* were wearing, that would be different."

"Don't be ridiculous."

"Oh, so now I'm being ridiculous. What other names are you going to call me?"

"I'm not calling you any names."

"Oh, I'm sorry. I could have sworn you called me ridiculous."

"This whole conversation is ridiculous," Renee said flatly. "Look, let's not argue. I'm sorry for what I said and I'm sorry if I sounded disinterested about what shirt you should wear." She checked her watch. "I guess I'm just a little nervous."

Philip's voice became soft, concerned.

"Why, for heaven's sake?"

"I guess because we're already late, and these are my partners. I don't know. I can't help it."

"Yes, you can. You decide whether or not you want to be nervous."

It was at times like this that Renee wished she had married a plumber and not a psychiatrist. Did he always have to be so damned analytical? Did he always have to be pointing out that she had a choice in most matters and that she usually opted for the wrong one?

"Renee," he was saying, a hint of impatience in the way he said her name, as if it were a burden of great weight, "you have to decide what's important to you."

"You're important to me."

"Not as important as being on time for dinner."

Renee said nothing. How many times could they cover the same ground? She watched him return both shirts to the closet. "Aren't you going to change?"

"It's not worth it. Your partners are so boring, I doubt they'll notice what I'm wearing anyway."

"I don't think they're boring."

"They're lawyers," Philip said, as if the word was all the explanation necessary. "Is Debbie home yet?"

"She and Kathryn went to the beach this afternoon."

"It's after eight o'clock," Philip said. "They wouldn't still be at the beach now."

"They said they might go to a movie and for a bite to eat."

"Christ," Philip muttered, shaking his head.

"What? What is it?"

He continued shaking his head. "Well, you really don't give a shit, do you? Debbie is sixteen years old. Your sister is seriously depressed. They've disappeared, and all you care about is getting to your stupid dinner party on time."

"That's not fair, and it's not true," Renee said, hearing her voice rise and struggling to steady it. "They haven't disappeared. They went to the beach and probably to dinner and a movie afterward. Kathryn has been feeling much better lately and Debbie is quite capable of taking care of herself. I'm not worried because there's nothing to be worried about. Philip, what's going on here?" She closed her eyes, wishing his hands were back on her breasts, that he would surround her with his large arms and tell her he was sorry, that he was acting like an idiot, that he loved her more than anything in the world, and let's get out of here now before it gets any later. Instead he stayed where he was, on the other side of the room, clearly angry with the conversation, and with her. What was wrong with her? Why did she always rise to the bait? Why couldn't she just go along with him occasionally? Why did everything have to be such a big deal?

"You tell me," he said, his voice cold.

"I don't understand."

"You've been so distant lately," he said, sounding very much like a small child.

"What?"

"I don't even think you've realized how distant you've become. I'm not trying to blame you, Renee. I understand how busy you are at work, how preoccupied you are. And I know you've always been busy, but you used to be able to handle it better. You used to have time for me. But think about it. You're always working. In the last couple of months, we haven't had much time to be together, and I guess I miss it, that's all."

"I'm not always working," Renee whispered, hearing her voice trail off and disappear, caught off guard by his words.

"What time did you get home last night?" he asked.

"Around seven."

"And the night before?"

"I'm not sure. Probably the same."

"Try closer to seven-thirty."

"I was home early the day before that."

"Congratulations."

"Philip, what is this? You've never complained about my working late before."

"What good would it have done?"

"Well, I . . ."

"Would it have made any difference?"

"If I'd known you were unhappy . . ."

"I didn't say I was unhappy."

"I don't understand. What are we arguing about?"

"I was merely pointing out why we haven't been spending

much time together recently. You're too busy with your work. And if it's not work, it's work-related, like tonight."

Renee looked helplessly around the room. "I'm sorry," she stammered, and she was, though she wasn't sure why. "I didn't realize . . . I guess it's hard to find time between both our busy schedules and my sister being here, and Debbie . . ."

"So it's Debbie's fault we haven't had any time together?"

"That's not what I said."

"You don't spend two minutes with Debbie. The kid comes to visit for two months, and you're too busy with your damn practice to spend two minutes with her."

"That's not fair, Philip. I've tried with Debbie. You know I've tried. She doesn't want to be with me."

"If you really wanted to win Debbie over, Renee, you would. You're a good lawyer. You know how to win."

"Wait a minute. How did we get onto Debbie?" Renee asked in frustration. "Why are we talking about this?"

Philip paced angrily back and forth in front of the bedroom door. "Oh, I see. We only talk about what you want to talk about. Is that it?"

"No, of course not. Nobody said . . ."

"What is it *you* want to talk about, Renee? The weather? Politics? My practice? *Your* practice? All of the above? None of the above. You want to ask me about my lunch with Alicia Henderson, isn't that it, Renee? Isn't that what all this is about?"

Renee tried to form the words to protest. It was true she had been thinking about the woman earlier but . . . Did he know her so well?

"You're nervous about tonight, and you're worried about your sister, and so you have to take it out on someone, and Debbie's not here to pick on, so it might as well be me. Go on, Renee, fire away. It's been eating you up for days, so you might as well spit it out."

Renee stared at her bloated image in the mirror across from their bed, holding her breath to try to keep the budding tears at bay. She didn't want to cry. Philip hated it when she cried. Besides, if she cried, her eyelids would puff up, make her look more bloated than she already was. Did she really have to ask herself why he turned to other women? Couldn't she see the answer staring her in the face?

"I was wondering how long it would take until you found some excuse to mention that lunch," he was saying. "I actually had hopes that maybe you'd grown up enough not to bother bringing it up at all."

Renee wanted to stop him, to remind him that, in fact, she hadn't been the one to mention his lunch with Alicia Henderson, that she never would have been the one to bring it up, that he was the one who had brought this woman into the conversation, into their lives. But she said nothing because, after all, what difference did it make who had been the first to say her name out loud? The woman had been in her thoughts, and Philip had seen her there. There was no point in denying his accusations when they were true in essence. He could read her mind. He had once told her that and looked surprised, even indignant, when she had laughed.

"Go on, Renee. Say what you have to say. Do your damage."

"That's not fair, Philip." Renee groaned under the weight of his accusations, feeling like a child. That's not fair, Daddy, that's not fair.

"No, what's not fair is what you're about to say."

"I don't want to say anything."

"Who are you kidding? You have to say it. You'll burst a blood vessel if you don't. You can't withdraw now. It's time to escalate. That's a favorite lawyer's trick, isn't it? Let's see what kind of real damage you can do here. Let's see how you can turn a perfectly innocent little lunch into something I should feel guilty for."

"I'm not trying to make you feel guilty."

"No? What are you trying to do?"

"Nothing," Renee yelled.

"Please don't raise your voice to me again," he said calmly. "I won't stand here and be yelled at."

"I'm sorry. I didn't mean to lose my temper."

"I get enough pressure at the office, Renee. I don't need this kind of hysterics at home."

Renee felt a wave of nausea sweep across her body. She felt suddenly exhausted. "I don't want to argue."

"So you've said. Why do you suppose, then, that's what we're doing?"

"I don't know. Let's just drop the whole thing."

"No, let's finish what you started. What is it you want from me, Renee? You want details of my romance with Alicia Henderson? Fine, I'll give you details."

"I don't want details."

"Alicia Henderson and I have been carrying on a mad, passionate affair every lunch hour now for several months. We do it everywhere we can, the more public the place, the better we like it. The Troubadour is one of our favorite spots, as a matter of fact. We do it between courses, under the table, on the table, in the washroom . . ."

"Philip . . ."

"More details? Well, let's see. Some days we don't even bother with lunch. I eat her instead. Are these details steamy enough for you, Renee? Or too much like the kind of stuff you hear every day?"

"I don't want details," Renee cried out bitterly. "I want denials!" She felt her eyes well over with the tears she had thus far managed to hold back, knowing she would streak her makeup and that she would have to redo the whole damn thing after she'd taken so long with it the first time, gotten it almost perfect. She backed up until she felt the baseboard of the bed hit the back of her knees, and she sat down, letting her head fall forward, feeling the cold metal of her necklace tightening across her throat. She stared into her lap, catching the tears with the back of her hand before they could stain the silk of her new clothes, and didn't look up until she felt Philip standing directly in front of her, his knees touching hers.

"Hey," he was saying, his voice suddenly gentle, "denials are easy." He bent forward and kissed her gently on the forehead, his anger gone, as if it had never existed, as if it were something she had only imagined. "There was nothing to it,

Renee. I swear it," he said, kissing her closed eyes. "I'm not sleeping with Ali Henderson. I have no desire to sleep with her. And the only thing I ate that day," he continued, as she felt his boyish smile grow wide against her skin, "was lunch." His lips skipped lightly down her face. Renee immediately lifted her mouth to his, her arms reaching up to wrap themselves around his neck, her body responding to him the way it always did.

Everything would be all right now. He had forgiven her. He was tender again and caring, the way he used to be, the way he had been in the beginning, when their relationship was new, before she had allowed herself to be consumed by petty jealousies and her own insecurities. Before she had allowed her weight to balloon and her work load to overtake so much of her life. No wonder he was resentful and defensive. She hadn't realized how strongly he objected to her late hours, how willfully she was neglecting his daughter. She'd make it up to him.

She felt him fussing with the zipper on his pants, felt his lips moving away from hers and his hands pushing her head gently forward. In the next instant, he was in her mouth and his hands were clutching at the sides of her hair, manipulating her head back and forth in slow, deliberate strokes. He grew quickly inside her mouth as he determinedly and repeatedly thrust himself inside her, guiding her hands between his legs, showing her exactly what he wanted her to do.

She thought of Debbie, pictured the girl suddenly barging in on them, then quickly dismissed the unwanted image. Her jaw was starting to ache with the strain of her prolonged ministrations. Good, she thought. It was what she deserved for the scene she had caused. If she wasn't careful, she would drive him away, as his first wife, Wendy, had done with her jealous accusations. How many times had he told her that Wendy's insecurities had driven a permanent wedge between them? That awful story of Wendy, naked, chasing his car down the street as he drove off into the night! Is that what she wanted for her own marriage? To send him driving off into the night into the arms of someone like Alicia Henderson? Alicia-call-me-Ali, she thought then. He had called her Ali.

His hands at the sides of her head grew more insistent, commanding her silently to pick up her pace, that he was almost ready. Renee closed her eyes tightly as his body shuddered to a climax, his hands immediately relaxing, loosening their grip on her hair. Renee swallowed quickly as he pulled away. "Get me a tissue," he said, his voice hoarse, and Renee moved to the box of tissues by the side of the bed. "Go rinse your mouth," he said, taking the tissue from her hand, turning away from her quickly.

Renee stared at her disheveled image in the bathroom mirror. She looked awful. There was no other word. Her eyes were puffy and red from crying, and her mascara was caked and smeared, although it was supposed to be waterproof and smudgeproof. Her lipstick, a bright cherry red when first applied, had been rubbed into invisibility, and her mouth appeared wayward, as if it had been slapped on the bottom of her face without much thought or care.

Renee patted the gold necklace at her throat and began the business of carefully reapplying her makeup, touching up the dark circles under her eyes—the one area of her body that the extra pounds seemed to have avoided—brushing on an extra layer of blush, starting high on her cheeks in the space between her eyes and ears, drawing a diagonal line halfway down the center of her cheeks, hoping to give her face more definition, the way she had read in *Vogue* that models often do. She chose a different shade of lipstick from the one she originally had on, this one a burnt shade of orange, and she carefully applied a fresh layer of navy mascara to her lashes, wishing they were longer and naturally curly, like Debbie's.

Renee came out of the bathroom to find Philip sprawled on top of their king-size bed, his eyes closed in sleep. "Philip?" she whispered.

He opened one eye. "I'm so tired," he said. "Do we have to go tonight?"

"They're expecting us."

"We're already late. Do you really think they'd miss us?"

"Philip, I . . ."

"I'm sorry, honey. It's just that arguing with you takes a lot out of me. I know it works for you in court, but it's hell on husbands." He smiled. "And then you made things worse. You went and got me all excited. And now all I want to do is lie down, maybe watch a little television, have my wife whip up some scrambled eggs. God, Renee, that would mean so much to me. A nice quiet evening at home. In bed early for a change. Is this dinner really so important?" he asked.

Renee sat down on the bed. "No," she said, "it's not so important."

13

"Mr. Foster, I'm Lynn Schuster from the Delray Department of Social Services, and I'm afraid you're going to have
to talk to me whether it's convenient or not."

Lynn stood outside the by now familiar town house at the
Harborside Villas and hoped that the tall, impeccably dressed
gentleman who had answered her knock would let her in.
Keith Foster was in his late fifties or early sixties, approximately six feet tall, with very black hair (which she suspected
he dyed), dark eyes, and a nose that dominated his face. The
nose, straight, long, and somehow too narrow for the rest of his
wide face, kept him from being described as handsome. It was
simultaneously too much and not enough. Like a lot of things,
Lynn thought as he ushered her inside.

The layout of the Foster town house was identical to that of
Davia Messenger's, except that where Davia Messenger's home
had been a cool and careful mix of yellows and grays, the Foster house was like stepping into the warm underbelly of a soft
pink cloud. The pale pink tile of the foyer gave way to the thick
rose-colored broadloom of the living room, where a deeper-

hued rose sofa sat comfortably across from two pink-and-plum-flowered wing chairs. The pink lacquered coffee table in front of the sofa boasted a beautiful mauve china vase filled with pink roses, and everywhere Lynn turned, there were more pink flowers. The walls were the same delicate shade, trimmed with white. Another large vase of pink flowers sat in the middle of the long, glass-top dining-room table, lined on either side by a row of pink-cushioned, straight-backed chairs.

"You have a beautiful home," Lynn said, and meant it, sitting on the sofa, feeling herself sink down into the soft cushions, feeling warm and comfortable. Keith Foster positioned himself across from her on the edge of one of the wing chairs, looking oddly out of place in his own living room. He was the weed in the delicate garden, Lynn thought, the dark streak of oil on a pastel canvas. He didn't belong. This was a woman's home, she decided, not surprised that a man of Keith Foster's physical stature would look ill at ease here, only surprised that he would allow it to be so. Even Gary—who had granted her pretty much free rein when it came to decorating their home—had balked at her suggestion of a pale pink bedroom.

"What can I do for you?" he asked, his voice congenial, as Lynn unzipped the black leather folder in her lap and brought out her notebook and pen, mindful of Davia Messenger's warning to keep it away from the sofa.

"Is Mrs. Foster at home?" Lynn asked, looking around the quiet room.

"She took Ashleigh out for a walk," Keith Foster told her pleasantly, as if eight o'clock in the morning was a usual time for a mother-and-daughter stroll. Lynn had deliberately selected the early hour in hopes of catching everybody at home. She'd hurried her own children through breakfast and enlisted the help of her neighbor so that she could get to the Fosters' town house by eight o'clock.

"Will they be back soon?" Lynn asked, trying to keep the annoyance out of her voice.

"I couldn't say. That's something beyond my control."

Control, Lynn thought, recalling her conversation with Marc. Is being in control so important? he had asked. "I'm sure your lawyer has advised you it would be in your best interests to cooperate with me, Mr. Foster."

"It's been my experience that government agencies rarely have my best interests at heart."

"Will you settle for the best interests of your child?"

"I have no wish to antagonize you, Mrs. Schuster," Keith Foster said carefully, smiling. "Or your department. Believe me, my wish is to be as cooperative as I can in every way in order to settle this nasty little matter as quickly as possible. Do you sail?" he asked unexpectedly, walking to the large window overlooking the Inland Waterway. Lynn found herself drawn to the sight of sailboats sparkling white against the blue sky just beyond where she was sitting. She shook her head. "Someday you must be our guest," he said, one of those things that people say.

"Mr. Foster, we have been given to understand that your daughter is often seen covered with bruises . . ."

"Ashleigh is accident-prone," he answered quickly, cutting her off. "She has been ever since she was a baby. She's always falling off something, running into something else. When she was eight months old, she fell out of her crib and broke her collarbone. A month or so ago, she fell off a swing at school and broke her arm."

"She broke her arm at school?"

"Yes."

"What school does Ashleigh attend, Mr. Foster?"

"Gulfstream Private School."

"What grade is she in?"

"Uh, do you know, I'm not altogether sure." He laughed. "Just a minute. The first grade, is it? Or second? Sorry, it's been a long time since I had to deal with things like this. Grade two," he said finally. "Yes, she just finished grade two. She'll start third grade in the fall."

"May I have the name of her teacher, please?"

"Her teacher? Why?"

"I'll have to check out the accident, Mr. Foster. Find out the exact circumstances with regard to Ashleigh's broken arm."

"I just told you the circumstances. She fell off a swing in the playground."

"I'll need confirmation of that."

"I resent that."

"I'm sure you do, and I can appreciate that . . ."

"Can you?"

"Yes."

"Do you have children, Mrs. Schuster?"

"Yes."

"How would you feel if some stranger barged into your house and accused you of abusing them, especially on the word of a crazed neighbor?"

"Which neighbor would that be?" Lynn asked cautiously, ignoring his question.

"Please don't play games with me, Mrs. Schuster. *You* know, and *I* know, who I'm talking about. Davia Messenger, patron saint of dust balls and little children." Lynn had to hold her breath to keep from smiling. "She's a fruitcake, you know that. You talked to the woman. She spends her days and nights cleaning her house and spying on her neighbors. She's the scourge of these villas. Ask anyone. Ask her husband, if you can find him. He ran out on her about three months ago. She's been nuttier than ever since he left. If that's possible."

"Why would your neighbor report you to our department, Mr. Foster?"

"Because she's crazy! She has nothing better to do with her time. How many times can you clean the floors in one day? Plus, she's very jealous of Patty."

Lynn said nothing, waiting for Keith Foster to continue.

"My wife is very young and very pretty. Mrs. Messenger appreciates neither."

Mrs. Messenger has an eye for beauty, Lynn thought. "I'll still need the name of Ashleigh's teacher," she said.

Keith Foster stopped his pacing and stared at Lynn with suddenly cold eyes. "I believe it's a Miss Templeton," he said finally. "I also believe she's away traveling for the summer. I *also* believe," he continued, underlining the word as if it were of special significance, "that the school is closed for the summer months."

Lynn thought he was probably right but was reluctant to say so. "It has been reported that Ashleigh cries at all hours of the day and night."

"It's simply not true."

Lynn jotted down his denial, noting that he made no attempt to explain why it should have been reported otherwise. This was something in his favor, she recognized. Guilty people often felt compelled to search for outside explanations, to provide answers, anything to throw others off their track. Keith Foster offered no such explanations. "It's simply not true" was all he said. "Do you mind my asking how old you are, Mr. Foster?" Lynn asked, hoping that Mrs. Foster would appear soon with Ashleigh, and that everything would be as Keith Foster said it was, as lovely and picture-perfect as their home.

"Fifty-nine," he answered easily, obviously quite comfortable with his age. He moved swiftly back to the wing chair and sat down, although he kept the bottoms of both feet on the floor, ready to leap into immediate action. "I'll be sixty in August."

"I'll be forty in August," Lynn admitted, testing the sound. "How old is your wife?"

"Thirty-one."

"I take it this is your second marriage?" Lynn indicated the many photographs on the coffee table, several of which showed Keith Foster flanked by two young men who were his duplicate in every respect save age.

"Actually, it's my third. Those are my sons from my second marriage." He reached across the table and picked up one of the expensively framed photographs. "Jonathan and David. Handsome boys." He lowered the picture and picked up another, this one of himself and another young man, who looked nothing like him at all. "This is my son from my first marriage. Actually"—he laughed—"Keith Jr. is the same age now as Patty."

"So Ashleigh is your only daughter?"

"The light of my life." He smiled and his smile was warm

and genuine. He reached across the table and picked up a pink enamel framed photograph of a young girl with light brown hair, braided and festooned with bright red ribbons, her smile shy, her eyes large and teasing, looking just past the photographer, refusing to acknowledge the lens.

"Does Mrs. Foster have other children?"

"No. She was only twenty years old when we married. I am her first and only husband. Eleven years. An enviable record in today's world, wouldn't you say?"

Lynn smiled self-consciously, and wrote the information down, aware that her hand was shaking slightly and hoping he didn't notice. "Who does the disciplining in this house, Mr. Foster?"

Keith Foster brought his eyebrows together, his eyes all but disappearing. "I'm afraid that neither one of us is very big on discipline," he said finally, as if it were something of which to be ashamed. "I know we've probably spoiled Ashleigh, but I just can't bring myself to deny her anything she really wants. Patty's the same way. That's why this whole thing is so outrageous. And so upsetting. The last thing in the world either of us would ever do is hurt Ashleigh. Can I get you a cup of coffee? Patty left some brewing in the kitchen before she went out."

"That would be terrific," Lynn told him gratefully, having left her house without any breakfast, and hoping to stick around as long as she could.

"How do you take it?"

"Black, thank you."

Keith Foster excused himself and went into the kitchen. Lynn read over the few remarks she had scribbled down, then let her eyes travel the width of the beautiful living room, trying to reconcile Davia Messenger's accusations with the reality of what she saw, which was a home decorated with warmth and love, and an obviously doting, if understandably defensive, father, who was not altogether at ease here. Maybe it was just her presence. How *would* she feel if a stranger barged into her house and accused her of abusing her children? How would she react to a stranger assuming control of her life?

Davia Messenger had lied to her about her husband. She'd made no mention of the fact that he had left her. Lynn tapped her pen nervously against her notepad, seeing Gary's face in the reflection of the large back window overlooking the water. Perhaps that omission was understandable as well, she thought. Just as it was understandable that Keith Foster could not immediately recall what grade his daughter was in at school. Would Gary have been able to answer that question immediately? Gary had enough trouble remembering his children's birthdays. He never got Megan's right, and remembered Nicky's only because it was so close to his own. Lynn reached for the enamel framed photograph of Ashleigh Foster. She certainly looked happy in this picture.

From the kitchen she heard something fall and shatter, a low curse, and some quick shuffling. Lynn walked swiftly toward the kitchen, finding Mr. Foster on his hands and knees in the middle of the room, retrieving bits of fine pink-and-white china from the ceramic tile floor.

"It slipped out of my hand," he said sheepishly.

"Here's a piece." Lynn picked up a small crescent of china peeking out from under the large, gleaming white refrigerator.

"Patty won't be happy about that. It was her grandmother's. Been in her family for generations."

Lynn examined the delicate hand-painted sliver of china in her hand. "It's lovely. Maybe it can be glued back together."

"Maybe." He quickly poured her another cup. "Black, you said?"

"Thank you." Lynn took the cup from his outstretched hand, following Keith Foster out of the glistening kitchen. She'd thought kitchens only looked that good in the pages of *Better Homes and Gardens.* It dismayed her, in some vague way, that real people with real children could have kitchens that looked as tidy as this one. When was the last time her stove top had been free of dirty fingerprints? When was the last time her fridge door had glistened so white as this one? Come to think of it, when was the last time she had actually seen her refrigerator door? It had been covered with her children's artwork for as long as she could remember. What was it Marc had said? Something about always being able to spot people with young children by the outside of their refrigerator doors? His own fridge was similarly covered, he had told her.

There was no artwork adorning the Foster refrigerator.

"Are there any other children in this complex, Mr. Foster?" Lynn asked as they returned to the living room.

"None Ashleigh's age. We've been thinking of moving because of that."

"Does Mrs. Foster work outside the home?"

"She prefers being a full-time mother."

"It must be quite a strain for her, spending so much time at home with a child, especially when there are no other children in the vicinity."

"I think I resent the implications of that statement."

Lynn moved into the center of the room and deposited her cup on the low oblong table. "Could I see Ashleigh's room, please?"

Keith Foster said nothing. He moved purposefully to his right, to one of the two closed doors on the south wall of the living room, and opened it.

Ashleigh's room was more soft pinks and flowers, with a myriad of dolls in every assorted shape and size lining the walls and bookshelves, as well as covering the top of the small pink bed which stood in the middle of the room. There was a large dollhouse, a small desk, two toy boxes, which doubled as benches underneath the window, and a child-size plastic kangaroo whose pouch doubled as a laundry basket. The room—like all the others—was neat, but not uncomfortably so. There were a few toys in the middle of the floor, some papers spread across the top of the desk, a couple of crayons left out of their box. A child's room, Lynn thought, grateful that there was nothing here to arouse suspicions. It looked like the room of a privileged, happy little girl.

Lynn approached the desk and casually perused the drawings Ashleigh had left lying across it, surprised by what she saw. Despite the many brightly colored crayons which were everywhere in evidence, Ashleigh's drawings were almost entirely sketched in black. In one, a large stick figure loomed menacingly over a smaller one. The larger stick figure, which could have been either a woman or a man, was all eyes and hands; the smaller figure had no hands. In another picture, a group of children were playing on the beach. None of the children had any arms.

"I'm afraid I really can't spare you any more time, Mrs. Schuster," Keith Foster said as Lynn checked her watch. "I have to get to work." He began walking to the front door, and stopped only when he realized Lynn wasn't right behind him.

"Is that your bedroom?" Lynn indicated the other closed door. Keith Foster nodded. "Can I see it?"

"Not without a search warrant."

"Mr. Foster, I thought you understood the importance of cooperating with my department. It is absolutely essential that I talk to your wife and daughter. If they're in there, you're not doing anybody any favors by hiding them."

Keith Foster walked quickly to the front door and opened it. He waited impatiently for Lynn to join him, then surprised her by extending his hand for an amicable farewell.

How big his hands are, Lynn thought as his fingers wrapped around hers. (Why, Grandma, what big hands you have! The better to beat you with, my child!) Lynn pulled her hand away. Was it possible Davia Messenger had simply misplaced her accusations?

"I'll have my wife call you later and make an appointment to bring Ashleigh in to see you," Keith Foster said pleasantly, as if it were his idea. "Now, if you'll excuse me, I really have to get to work."

After lunch and a brief stroll along the beach, Lynn found herself window-shopping along Atlantic Avenue, not anxious to return to her office. She'd had an altercation with her boss, Carl McVee, over her handling of the Foster inquiry. Keith Foster's lawyer had called and given him an earful. Why were they harassing his client on the word of a crazy neighbor? Patty Foster had generously consented to bring Ashleigh in the following week for an interview and a doctor's examination. In the meantime, Lynn had been told sharply by her boss: Lay off.

Lynn brushed the image of Carl McVee aside, momentarily seeing him as Ashleigh Foster might have sketched him, and stared absently at each of the store windows, thinking she could probably use a few new things. She had never been much of a shopper, and her job demanded a certain amount of necessary understatement as far as her wardrobe was concerned. Gary, she realized suddenly, peering in one window at a dizzying array of feather boas and floor-length gowns of the sort Lynn had never seen anyone actually wear, had made something of a habit of buying her designer clothes at every gift-giving occasion, but she had never felt comfortable in clothes with other people's initials all over them, and these items had generally found their way back to the stores.

Lynn heard the sudden trill of women's laughter behind her and she glanced over her shoulder at two women fumbling with shopping bags and a car door. "I can't get it open," the shorter of the two women squealed.

"Put them in the trunk. I'm not finished yet anyway."

Something in the second woman's voice—low, seductive, imperial—made Lynn turn away even before she heard the woman's name. "Suzette," the first woman squealed again, "you've done enough damage. How many outfits do you need?"

"Shush," the woman whose name was Suzette said, still laughing, "I finally found a man who appreciates good clothes. I'm going to enjoy it."

Lynn lowered her head so deep into her chest she thought her neck would crack, as the two women threw their shopping bags into the trunk of the car and hurried by her into the store. Her heart was racing but her feet seemed glued to the sidewalk, as if the soles of her shoes were mired in tar. Even if she had wanted to, Lynn couldn't have moved. Not that she wanted to. Not that she knew what she wanted.

Even as she tried to convince herself that the woman she had just seen, in truth had *barely* seen, was not Suzette Cameron, she knew it was. How many Suzettes could there be in a small town like Delray Beach? And even as she told herself that the odds were unlikely that both she and her husband's new love would show up in front of the same store at the same time, she also knew that it was far from impossible. People ran into each other every day. What was even more surprising was that they had managed to avoid running into one another up until now.

Go back to work, she said to herself, forcing her legs to move. Go back to work. Instead, she pushed open the door to the small shop and walked inside.

The interior of the store was bright and well laid out, making optimum use of its small space: dresses and evening wear to one side; more casual clothes to the other. Lynn's eyes took in the entire store in one glance, though she kept her head low. She quickly located Suzette Cameron and her friend behind a long rack of dresses. Lynn could hear them giggling, and wondered if they were giggling about her.

Don't be silly, she chastised herself, taking several small steps in their direction, her eyes on her toes. Why would they be giggling about you? They don't even know you're here.

Don't they? a little voice asked. You knew her, even without hearing her name or getting a good look at her face, you knew it was she. The radar that soon to be ex-wives possess about the women who are poised to replace them. Lynn edged closer, pretending to be studying the dresses. What was she doing here? Did she intend to confront this woman? If so, what in God's name did she intend to say?

"What do you think of this one?" she heard Suzette's companion ask.

"Too plain," came the immediate reply. "I'd like something a little sexier."

Lynn buried her fingers into the jersey fabric of one of the dresses on the rack, making an involuntary fist and absently pulling on the material. Keeping her head down, she edged in front of a nearby mirror to get closer to the two women. Just a look, she told herself. I just want to see what she looks like.

"Now this is more like it," Lynn heard Suzette exclaim as she skipped around the end of the rack to where Lynn was standing and held the dress against her. She positioned herself in front of the mirror and Lynn realized with something of a jolt that she was standing directly in Suzette's line of vision. "Excuse me," Suzette Cameron said, smiling at Lynn, the kind of smile people give you when they want you to get out of their way. Lynn obligingly backed away from the mirror, relieved not to be recognized, aware she was staring but unable to stop. Still, despite the undisguised intensity of her gaze, her mind seemed incapable of grasping the details of this woman's physiognomy. Even forcing herself to concentrate, Lynn was unable to say initially whether Suzette Cameron's hair was blond or brown (it was dark brown) or whether she was short or tall (the answer was: very tall). It was only after she directed her eyes to small, seemingly insignificant details, as she had trained herself to do at work—Suzette's ears were pierced, her nails were freshly manicured—that Lynn was able to digest the woman in her entirety.

Suzette Cameron was tall and thin and surprisingly muscular, or maybe not so surprising since she had trained as a dancer. Her legs were long, her calves their focus, calves which protruded like bowling pins from under her fashionably short skirt. Still, they were not unattractive legs, Lynn grudgingly admitted, glancing down past the hem of her own too long skirt, aware that days spent walking along the sand had given her legs their own kind of musculature. She wondered if Suzette's thighs were as sculpted as her calves, and found herself hoping they were flabby, knowing they would be anything but.

Suzette Cameron was a woman of odd and interesting angles. Her stomach, even after the birth of twin boys, looked flat, and her bosom was more ample than Lynn would have imagined for a dancer (correction, teacher) of ballet. Her hands were long and sinewy—she would have made an elegant dying swan, Lynn thought, wishing she could help her along. Her hair, which was so dark it looked black, though naturally black, not like Keith Foster's vaingloriously dyed locks, was thick and shiny and shorter than her own. It hovered around her chin, which Lynn was gratified to see ended in an unattractive point, as if an artist painting a portrait had grown bored and simply drawn the two sides of her face together in order to be done with it. Her nose was the same narrow shape, although her cheeks were full, and her eyes, though large, were strangely nondescript, somewhere between green and blue without the sharpness of either. While the woman was hardly ugly, she was far from pretty. Lynn was surprised to find that she agreed with everyone's previous assessment—that she herself was easily the prettier of the two.

Lynn studied the woman studying herself in the mirror, the dress, a low-cut frilly orange thing of no discernible shape, pressed against her. She tried to picture Gary standing beside the woman, and then Marc. Neither seemed to fit, in much the same way that Lynn decided that the dress Suzette was considering would not suit her. It wouldn't suit me either, Lynn thought. She quickly found another dress like the one Suzette was admiring, wondering with a sense of perversity that was new to her whether or not she should try it on, as Suzette Cameron and her friend disappeared into the first of the two fitting rooms at the far end of the store.

"Can I help you?" a voice said from somewhere behind Lynn and she jumped.

"I'm just looking," Lynn told the startled salesgirl, who had jumped when Lynn did. "On second thought, I will try this on," she said, grabbing the orange dress off its hanger without thought to its size and carrying it into the second dressing room.

"What do you think?" she could hear Suzette ask her friend, as Lynn pulled her own skirt and blouse off and quickly pulled the dress over her head. Lynn stared at herself in the mirror. The dress was at least two sizes too large. She looked like a giant pumpkin.

"Look what time it is already," she heard Suzette say. "You never told me it was so late. I'm supposed to meet Gary at Boston's in five minutes for lunch."

Lynn stood paralyzed in the middle of the tiny dressing stall. She stared at her orange reflection in the mirror. Woman as Giant Pumpkin, she thought, then Woman as Large Orange Fool. What was she doing playing cat and mouse, cat and mouse and *cheese*, she thought, looking at herself again, when she should be at the office? She had to get out of here. She had to get out of here before Suzette recognized her; she had to run to her car before she ran into Gary. If she moved fast enough, she could get out of the store before anyone even realized she'd been here. But she had to move fast.

She was out of the dressing room and almost at the front door before she realized she was still wearing the orange dress, the same dress that Suzette was now modeling in front of the mirror in the middle of the store, the same one that the salesgirl was hollering at her about— "Where are you going with that?" —when Gary pushed open the door to the store and froze in his tracks.

He must think he's wandered into a nightmare, Lynn thought, watching as first the smile and then the color faded from his face. Here were his abandoned wife and the woman he had abandoned her for standing within ten feet of each other, both wearing the same god-awful orange dress, and orange was his least favorite color. At least Suzette's dress was the right size, Lynn thought, and almost cried, realizing that the dress suited Suzette quite nicely, that it hugged the curves of her body provocatively while Lynn's hid the fact that she had any curves at all.

"Gary, how did you find me?" she heard Suzette ask before the woman realized anything was amiss.

"I saw your car," he started to answer, his words drifting to a halt, his eyes staring blankly into the space between the two women, not sure where to look.

"Where are you going with that dress?" the salesgirl asked again.

And then nobody spoke, and everybody looked at everybody else until everyone, including the poor confused salesgirl, had figured out exactly who everyone was and what kind of situation they had here, and Suzette's friend gasped.

"This dress is just not me," Lynn told the stunned gathering. Then she disappeared inside her tiny dressing stall and didn't come out again until she was sure that everybody else had left.

14

Renee sat on the large white sofa in the middle of her large white living room and stared at her husband's latest acquisition, a bright paint-splattered explosion by a Florida artist named Clarence Maesele. Abstract illusionism, Philip had called it, and Renee thought that as good a description as any. She liked the painting. It was colorful and dynamic and it *moved.* Unlike much of the artwork that lined the walls of Philip's apartment (when had she started referring to it, even in her own mind, as Philip's apartment?), consisting of static, flat lines of color, Maesele's painting was three-dimensional, its multitude of colors leaping off the canvas in bold, erratic layers. Normally, just looking at the painting made her happy. When Philip had first brought it home a few months before, and announced that he had bought it that afternoon (when had he stopped consulting her about major purchases? had he *ever* consulted her?), Renee had been excited and glad. (And a touch anxious. Come on, Renee, admit it. He didn't even stop to ask your opinion, whether you thought he'd paid too much, gotten a steal, where you thought he should hang it, whether or not you even liked it.) She had run to get him a pencil and a ruler so that he could measure and mark the spot where he would hammer in the nail, then she had helped him hang the large painting, mindful not to scratch the wall. Then she had sat back and studied the painting, letting him tell her all about it, formulating a few observations of her own but keeping them to herself, afraid to risk his censure or ridicule. Philip was the authority on art. There was a time when she knew a little something about it, but lately, she had let that knowledge slide. Maybe she *had* let her practice overtake her life. Maybe she had lost sight of her priorities.

Renee turned away from the painting. While it normally made her happy, tonight it made her nervous, even a touch sad. It jumped out at her, pointing colorfully accusing fingers in her direction, although she had lost sight of what exactly she was being accused of. She turned toward Philip, who stood in the middle of the room, trying to concentrate on his words, not wishing to be accused of not listening.

"I'm sorry, Philip," she said, trying to remember what she should be sorry for, deciding that it didn't matter. She didn't care.

"You're interrupting."

"I'm sorry."

Interrupting again. Sorry again.

What were they arguing about this time? When had all these arguments started?

There had been a time when they didn't fight, when his words had been soothing and soft and reassuring and loving, not harsh and nasty and mean and relentless, God, so relentless. I'm the one who's supposed to be so good with words, she thought. I'm the legal eagle, the courtroom wizard. I'm the one with the bagful of lawyer's tricks. Isn't that what he tells me? About my ability to twist everything he says? Face it, Renee, you thrive on confrontations. Isn't that what he's always saying? That I'm not happy unless I'm making someone else miserable?

And yet there had been a time, in the beginning, when they didn't fight.

"Tell me everything about your day," he had said when they were making love one night early in their courtship. "Every detail. I want to know everything."

"I took some bastard into court," she told him, feeling his mouth on her neck, his hands at her breasts.

"Did he have any balls when he walked out?"

"Oh, I let him keep those." She laughed. "I just took his money."

"I love what you do," he had said, sitting her on top of him, maneuvering himself inside her.

"You do? Why?"

"It's very sexy."

"Sexy?" She laughed again, feeling him thrust deep within her. "Why? How is it sexy?"

"It just is."

When had it stopped being sexy? When had her work stopped turning him on and started turning him off?

"You should have seen me in court today, Philip. If I do say so myself, I was fucking brilliant."

"Do you have to use profanity?"

"What?"

"Do you have to swear? Can't you just be brilliant without having to be *fucking* brilliant?"

"I'm sorry. I was just crowing a bit, I guess."

"A *bit?* You *guess?*"

"All right, a *lot*. I *know*. But, Philip, I nailed that sucker. He was up there on that stand, lying his fool head off. 'I never laid a hand on her,' he was saying. 'I never touched her.' And I'm sitting there with a fistful of sworn affidavits from relatives and neighbors who saw him beat his wife on numerous occasions. 'I have no assets,' he whines, and I know all the details of this little trust fund that he uses to keep his money out of his name but inside his pockets. And this bastard, I'm sorry, this *schnook* has the nerve to sit there on the stand, under oath, the man is under oath, and he swears that he's never hit his wife and that he's on the verge of bankruptcy. And he's good. The man is good. Very convincing. He should consider acting as a career. And do you know when I knew I had him nailed? I asked him a seemingly innocuous question about how his trust fund was set up and administered, and he hesitated. Just for a second, it was only a second, but I saw this look cross his eyes, and I *knew* that he was going to lie, that all I had to do was push him a little and he'd fall straight into hell."

"So, you pushed."

"I sure did."

"And you're elated because you tricked some poor schnook, as you call him, into lying . . ."

"I didn't trick him."

"You waited for the look and then you pushed. That's what you said."

"Yes, but . . ."

"And the poor schnook didn't have a chance. You nailed him."

"Damn right."

He smiled, indulgently, "I find it interesting that you can be so sure you're right. As a psychiatrist, I've learned that things are rarely as one-sided as you make them seem."

"I'm being paid to represent my client . . ."

"The truth be damned?"

"The truth will out."

He turned away. "You have an answer for everything, don't you?"

But she hadn't had an answer then, and she didn't have one now. Just a lot of nagging questions. Why did every discussion turn into a disagreement? Why did everything she do feel wrong, as if, when presented with two alternatives, she automatically chose the wrong one? What had happened to their relationship? When had the balance of power shifted so dramatically in his direction?

In the beginning, he'd been proud of her work, proud of the way she looked. But she'd put on so much weight in the last few years, he couldn't help but be frustrated by her appearance. Perhaps it came out as criticism of her work instead. But even as these thoughts were forming, something inside Renee said it wasn't so, that his barbed critiques had started before she took to eating Snickers bars for breakfast and 3 Musketeers for lunch.

Their problem had evolved slowly, sneaking up on them like a giant wave, building in power as it grew, pushing them out above their heads, knocking them down. Overwhelming them. Or at least her. Philip didn't seem too overwhelmed. He was still standing. He looked better all the time.

No doubt about it, she had the handsomest man in Florida on her arm and in her bed. He was bright and beautiful and successful, and out of all the women he could have had, he had chosen her. He loved her, and for a time, he loved her success. And then the balance had shifted. Subtly at first, then more forcefully. His praise became less lavish, then guarded, then laced with venom. Finally the venom had taken the place of the praise altogether. Why? What had she done?

Renee sat in the all-white living room and watched her husband pace back and forth in front of the large window overlooking the dark ocean below. She wanted to stop him, throw her arms around him, and tell him that whatever she had said or done, whatever he was so upset about, she was sorry, she would take it back. Let's go into the bedroom, she wanted to say, and make love the way we used to, but she said nothing because she was afraid of interrupting him.

Interrupting again. Sorry again.

The light beside her illuminated her face, and Renee became aware of her reflection in the floor-to-ceiling window. She saw her normally straight posture perverted, her body hunched forward, her knees twisted in on one another, her face half hidden by her hands.

In the beginning, it was so good, the reflection in the glass explained, talking to Renee as if they were two distinct people.

Explain further, said the lawyer on the sofa.

We made love all the time, responded the witness clearly from her glass booth. He was always so gentle. Not like now. I thought everything he did was wonderful. Of course, I'd just about given up on finding a husband.

Come on, the lawyer on the sofa broke in impatiently, rearranging her knees, balancing her elbows on her thighs.

You're a product of the liberated generation. Women can do anything. We don't need a man to define us. We don't need a man to make us happy. You have a brain!

Yes, but I'm not pretty. And brains or not, pretty was all I ever really wanted to be.

There's nothing wrong with the way you look.

Maybe not, but I'd grown up believing that Kathryn was the pretty one in the family, that I'd always have to work harder for what would come naturally to her, that Kathryn had inherited our mother's eyes and cheekbones. And she had. No question, Kathryn was the pretty one. And looks were what counted when it came to getting a husband, according to my mother, who firmly believed it. Looks, not brains. Brains'll only get you into trouble, she used to say. None of this liberated nonsense for her. And me, the smart one, the "fem-libber," as my father calls me, I bought it all. No matter what fancy words I used, what modern-day rhetoric I spouted, it still came down to two things: I was nothing without a man, and I would never get a man because I was too smart and too plain.

But somehow you did it, the lawyer on the sofa reminded her reflection. You got Philip to love you, and you got him to marry you. What did I get? A law degree? Let me tell you, law degrees make lousy lovers. Shall I tell you about my graduation from law school? The one that everyone but Kathryn was too busy to attend?

You can't blame them, her reflection admonished with just a hint of sarcasm. It was in New York. It was too far to come, too expensive a trip. Dad was busy with his practice; Mom couldn't leave him all alone.

Hey, don't get me wrong. I'm not blaming them. I've learned to accept my parents for what they are.

Is that why you rarely see them?

We have nothing in common.

They're your parents.

They're cold people who never should have had children. God only knows why they did except that everybody else in those days was having them. So they had Kathryn and then they had me, and then they left us with a succession of housekeepers until we were old enough to basically raise ourselves. I accept all of that. It happened. It's over. Besides, how badly did things turn out? I'm a lawyer, aren't I? I never would have gone to law school except for my father. I thought it might make him proud of me. I wanted him to be so proud of me he could burst. I stood third! Third in the entire graduating year. At Columbia! But he couldn't take the time to come to my graduation. Well, if the mountain won't come to Mohammed, Mohammed will go to the mountain. So I came back and got a job with the best law firm in Delray. I could have gone to New York. I've always wanted to live in New York. I had a wonderful offer. But I came back home instead.

And I met Philip, and I married him, the voice in the glass took over. The man of my dreams. Except that the dream is becoming a nightmare. And I don't understand why. I married the most wonderful man in the world. We were on our way to living happily ever after. And then things changed. At first, I told myself: Don't be silly. Who's happy one hundred percent of the time? What's wrong with being happy eighty percent, or even sixty? And then, one day I woke up to find the percentages were reversed. Our lovemaking changed. We always seemed to be fighting. There were other women. And the bright, happy woman he married had turned into an insecure, overweight, jealous combination of everything I've always despised. Look at me. I hate what's happened to me. But I still don't understand how it happened. And I think: Renee, what's the matter with you? You might not have the looks, but you *have* the brains. What the hell happened to your life? And then I look at Philip, and I remember what my mother told me. She said I'd have to work hard to keep him, that's what she said, and I feel I'm losing him, so I know I'm not working hard enough. I know that I'm to blame for what's happened. I'm not good enough. I'm not understanding enough. I'm too smart for my own good. I'm too selfish. I'm too preoccupied. I'm too concerned with winning. I always have to be right. I don't know how to give. I'm always saying things to upset him, to make him feel guilty, when I'm the one who should feel guilty.

You *are* guilty, said the lawyer on the sofa, now the judge and jury as well. Guilty as charged.

Philip suddenly positioned himself between Renee and her reflection.

"Did you hear a word I said?" he was demanding.

"I'm sorry, I . . ."

"You think that by saying you're sorry that makes everything all right?"

"I don't know what else to say."

"You're the one who started this whole thing, and then you think that a simple apology is going to set things right again."

"Aren't you the one who's always telling me that we choose our emotions?" she asked, immediately wishing she hadn't. "You can choose to be upset or you can choose to accept my apology," she continued, thinking: What the hell, I might as well go all the way. Philip shifted his position, resumed his angry pacing.

"You have a very convenient memory. Tell me, why is it you're always able to quote me when it suits your purposes?"

"Can't we just drop it?" Renee pleaded, the beginnings of the argument crowding back into her brain.

"I come home from work after one hell of a day to be accused of deliberately missing dinner with you for sex with a client. And I'm not supposed to get upset?"

"I didn't accuse you of anything."

"No? What did you say exactly?"

"I don't remember *exactly*." Renee tried to look past him to her reflection, as if the figure in the window might be able to come up with a better response, but Philip was in her way. She thought of Kathryn and Debbie, and hoped they were both sound asleep. "I thought I asked you where you'd been all night. It's almost eleven o'clock. We were supposed to have dinner with Mike Drake and his wife at seven. I was concerned when you didn't show up."

"I've already explained that I got tied up with a patient."

"I called your office at five o'clock and again at six, six-thirty, seven, and every half hour after that. I called before I left my office and when I got to the restaurant. I called between courses, and again after coffee."

"And you think that's the sign of a healthy woman? Of a healthy marriage?"

Oh, please, don't call the marriage into question, Renee thought. Instead, she kept her voice steady and said, "It's the sign of a concerned wife. Of a wife whose husband was supposed to meet her for dinner at seven o'clock and never showed up. I was afraid that something might have happened to you, that maybe you'd been in an accident . . ."

"That I'd driven off a cliff?" he asked, sarcastically. "I think you were afraid I was with someone."

"Were you?"

"Yes. I've already told you that."

"A patient."

"Yes. A suicidal patient."

"A woman?"

"They usually are."

Renee was almost too upset to be angered by the insensitivity of his remark, but not quite. Despite her good intentions, she found her voice rising in anger. Don't bite, she tried to say. When you rise to the bait, you always lose. "Philip, that dinner was important to me. We've already missed a number of important dinners with my partners and Mike Drake has done a lot over the years to help build up my practice. You knew how important it was to me . . ."

"More important than my patient's life?"

"No, of course not more important than someone's life." Renee tried to peer past him to the woman who would be reflected in the glass (surely she would be calm), but Philip remained stubbornly in her path. "But you could have at least called me, warned me that you might be late, that you might not show up . . ."

"What was I supposed to say? 'Excuse me, lady, please don't jump until I get back—I have to call my wife and tell her that I might be late for dinner'? How about 'Look, lady, if you're going to jump, would you do it soon because my wife has an important dinner engagement tonight and she doesn't want me to be late'? How about either of those?"

Renee knew she should stop now, not allow herself to be sucked in further, and she determined not to answer, so she was surprised to hear a voice (my God, her voice! idiot!) breaking into the stillness. "If it were the first time," the voice started, the sound of tears not far off. "But, Philip, it seems that whenever we have somewhere to go that relates to me, we never make it."

"I'm a doctor, Renee. I can't always predict my timetable."

"You don't seem to have a problem with your schedule when the function relates to you."

"Are you saying that I deliberately missed dinner tonight?"

"No, I'm not saying that."

"Then what are you saying?"

"That it's not the first time."

"No, and it probably won't be the last. Jesus, Renee, I'm talking about a patient's life, and you're upset because I missed dinner. Can you really be so selfish? What's happened to you?"

"I just think that . . ."

"You don't think, Renee. That's your problem. You're worried about your sister or you're angry at Debbie for some unknown reason, or you're worried about your practice or impressing your partners, so you take it out on me. As usual. You don't care how the things you say might upset me. *My* feelings aren't important to you."

"That's not true. Your feelings are everything to me." Renee brought her hand to her head. She was becoming dizzy. Was there any truth to what he was saying? She didn't know anymore.

He was suddenly sitting on the cushion next to her, his hands touching hers, his voice soft and conciliatory. "You've changed, Renee," he was telling her. "You take on too much. You can't handle it all. Look at you. You're exhausted. You look like hell." He said all this kindly, as if he were thinking only of her own good. "You have no compassion," he was telling her compassionately. "What happened to the girl I married?"

Renee felt a sharp stab to her chest. Was he threatening to

leave her? Was he saying that unless she shaped up, he would ship out?

"You've been fighting in the dirt for too long," he continued, as she struggled through her panic to pay attention. "When you fight in the dirt long enough, you can't help but get dirty. You're too good at what you do, Renee. You're not happy unless you're in an adversarial position. You relish discord. I strive for harmony. I don't know. Maybe we've just been fooling ourselves."

Renee snapped back to attention, her whole body alert. "What are you saying?"

He stared into her eyes and his eyes were alive and clear despite his proclaimed fatigue. "I love you, Renee," he said slowly, "but I don't know if I can live with what I see happening to you."

There was a long pause, during which Renee tried to think of what she could say to make things right again. Tell me, she thought. I'll say it. I'll say whatever you want. Just don't leave me. I'm nothing without you. You're my life. There is no life without you.

"I love you, Philip," she whispered as he took her head in his hands and began kissing the sides of her hair. She looked awful, she knew. He had told her so. How could he bear to kiss her? How could he bear to look at her?

He bent his head toward hers, kissing the sides of her lips, licking at her tears with his tongue. "You have to decide what your priorities are," she heard him say just before his mouth covered hers.

From out of the corner of her eye, Renee caught sight of Philip's image in the window as he bent over to kiss her. The thought crossed her mind that he looked like a Mafia chieftain bestowing the kiss of death on a doomed member of the clan. Renee felt his lips pressing down tightly on hers, and banished the unpleasant observation from her mind.

15

Lynn leaned her head back against the car's black leather interior and closed her eyes. "Are we there yet?" she asked.

Marc Cameron laughed quietly. "You sound like my boys. Just another few minutes."

She kept her eyes closed, opening them again briefly when they stopped for a red light at Military Trail. They were heading west, away from the ocean, and Lynn thought that the scenery in her mind was probably a good deal more interesting than anything she could see outside her window. It wasn't until she saw Gary staring back at her from behind her closed lids that she forced her eyes open wide and kept them that way for the remainder of the ride.

Would she ever forget the look on Gary's face when he walked into that tiny store to find himself confronted by his once and future wives dressed in identical outfits? She glanced at Marc, who looked back at her and smiled. She hadn't told him. Maybe she would one day, when the pain wasn't so fresh in her mind. And her heart. When she could see the humor behind the humiliation, then maybe she would tell him. Right now, it was still too awful to think about, let alone voice out loud. Even Gary had refrained from mentioning it when he came by early that morning to pick up the kids. He hadn't even come inside, just stood fidgeting in the doorway until Megan and Nicholas were ready to go, his eyes looking past Lynn as he told her he would have the children home again by five o'clock. It was half past nine when Lynn watched his car pull away from the curb. An hour later, Marc Cameron pulled up in her driveway, and now they were on their way to see his father in a place called Halcyon Days. Lynn wondered what she was doing here, realizing how often lately she asked herself that question. She decided the answer was irrelevant—if this was where she was, it must be where she wanted to be.

"Does your father know you're bringing a visitor?" she asked as they turned south off the main thoroughfare down a long, twisting, unpaved road lined on either side with ancient royal palm trees.

"I thought I'd surprise him." Marc Cameron shook his head. "I have a few surprises for him, I'm afraid."

"Oh?"

"I saw a lawyer this week about getting a power of attorney over my father's finances. Then I consolidated all his accounts in one bank, so I can keep track of them, and I had a long talk with the bank manager. As of now, my father is on a strict allowance. No more Lincoln convertibles, no more trips to Greece for the nurses. He's not going to like it."

"You did the right thing."

"Yeah? Then why do I feel like such a shit?"

"It's hard when you have to start being a parent to your parents. It's not a role we're prepared for." The image of her mother in the last months of her life, diapered and unable to feed herself, forced itself on Lynn's consciousness as Marc pulled into the newly resurfaced parking lot in front of the large four-story pink building that was known as Halcyon Days. He pointed across the lot to where a long blue car with a white canvas top sat glistening in the bright sunlight. "There's the famous baby-blue convertible."

Lynn glanced gratefully in its direction, the image of her mother gradually receding. "It's hard to miss."

"Check out the license plates," he said as they approached the automobile.

"PEACHES?" Lynn tried not to laugh.

"Custom plates no less. Apparently Peaches is the pet name some of the nurses have for him. He's not going to like having his popularity curtailed."

"You did the right thing," Lynn assured him again. "You just couldn't sit back and let him throw his money away."

"Why not?" he asked, and Lynn understood he'd already had this discussion with his conscience many times. "It's *his* money. What right do I have to tell him how to spend it?"

They stood in the parking lot outside the pink stucco building. "You have a responsibility to see that your father is protected in his old age, that he has enough money to look after himself. And you have a responsibility to yourself to make sure that he doesn't become a financial burden on you. Marc, you've told me yourself, writing isn't the most secure profession. You have enough pressures on you as it is without having to worry about supporting your father, especially when he has more than enough money to take care of himself. You can't let him squander it all away. You're doing the right thing," she said again.

She knew he was going to kiss her even before he started moving toward her. What surprised her was the speed and passion with which she responded. "You promised me you wouldn't do that anymore," she said, breaking out of the embrace.

"I lied." He took her arm and guided her inside the building.

Marc's father was sitting on an old green vinyl armchair looking out his window at the parking lot below. Lynn realized he must have seen them arrive, and consequently couldn't have missed their rather public display. But the senior

Cameron made no acknowledgment of their presence as Marc and Lynn approached his chair.

"Keeping an eye on your new car?" Marc asked, his voice deceptively light.

"Who's that with you?" Ralph Cameron asked, his words slurred and difficult to understand (whozatwityou?), the result of his stroke.

"This is a friend of mine, Dad. Lynn Schuster." Marc motioned for Lynn to move closer, and Lynn placed herself directly in front of Ralph Cameron's line of vision, not quite as embarrassed as she thought she should be.

The old man lifted his graying head slowly, and with obvious difficulty, toward Lynn, allowing a smile to come into his eyes. "Schuster?" he repeated. "Are you any relation to the comedian Schuster?"

The words all ran together (areyanylationtothecomedianschuster?) and it took Lynn a few seconds to replay the question so that she understood it. She shook her head. "I don't think so."

"Used to be on the Ed Sullivan show a lot. Had a partner. They did a skit about Julius Caesar. I remember . . ."

"No, no relation," Lynn said.

"How are the boys?" Marc's father asked (haretheboys?), and for the first time since entering the small private room, Lynn allowed her eyes to wander. She saw the photographs of Jake and Teddy on the end table beside the single bed, and thought them an interesting combination of both their parents, as Marc was undoubtedly an interesting combination of both his mother and the old man who sat before her, his face now cruelly twisted but attractive nonetheless, traces of his youth not entirely banished. When he talked, he gestured sporadically with his right arm, his left arm remaining stiff and still on his lap. But though his movements were slow and awkward, and his words difficult to follow, there seemed nothing wrong with his faculties. While his speech made his thoughts appear random and strange, Lynn understood that his mind was still sharp. His eyes were the same shade of blue as his son's, and standing he would be almost as tall as Marc, although the stroke had robbed him of his bulk, rendered him delicate and thin. "Why didn't you bring them to see me today?" the old man was asking.

"They're with their mother," Marc answered. "I'll bring them next time. There were some things I wanted to talk over with you today."

"Such as?" The words came out "Sshush us?" and Lynn felt Marc's body stiffen beside hers.

"How are they treating you here, Dad?" Marc asked, not ready to plunge right in. Ralph Cameron shrugged with half his body. "Nurses still can't keep their hands off you?"

"It's a terrible state of affairs," the senior Cameron said, and once again his eyes smiled.

"So you're happy? No complaints?"

"None at the moment," Marc's father said, eyeing his son skeptically, as if he knew that was going to change. He winked at Lynn, and Lynn responded to the gesture with a wide smile. There was definitely nothing slow about the old man's mind. For a moment, Lynn wondered which was preferable—a failing mind, like her mother's had been, lost inside a reasonably healthy body, or a healthy mind, such as Marc's father obviously had, imprisoned in a body that had failed him.

Marc Cameron sat down on the bed facing his father and took the old man's hands in his.

"Do you want me to wait outside?" Lynn asked.

"Please stay," Marc whispered softly, and then proceeded to explain to his father the steps he had taken with regard to the senior Cameron's finances. Lynn listened as Marc patiently, and with as much tact and gentleness as was possible, told his father that he now had power of attorney over his money, that there were to be no more trips for the nurses, no more baby-blue Lincoln convertibles, that he would be put on a weekly allowance.

"And watched like a child," his father said, refusing to look at his son as tears fell unimpeded down the length of his cheek. He made no effort to wipe them away.

"No, Dad, not like . . ."

"I guess I might as well die now," Ralph Cameron said, and for the first time that afternoon, his words were slow and clear. Lynn felt her breath catch in her throat.

"Mr. Cameron . . ." Lynn began, but Ralph Cameron raised his good arm, telling her to be quiet.

"Please go," he said.

"It's for your own good, Dad," Marc Cameron pleaded. "I can't just sit back and watch you throw your money away on cars you can't drive and trips for the nursing staff. You worked too hard all your life for me to let you do that."

Ralph Cameron lifted his head and stared directly into his son's sad eyes. "Bastard," he said.

Lynn saw Marc's body sway, as if he might topple over. She felt his pain and wished there was something she could do to ease it, knowing there was nothing. She watched him turn from his father and walk quickly out of the room. Slowly, carefully, Lynn approached Marc's father and knelt down before him. "Your son loves you very much, Mr. Cameron. This was very hard for him." The senior Cameron said nothing, his gaze directed resolutely out the window toward his convertible. "Goodbye," Lynn whispered when she could think of nothing further to say. Sometimes it was best to leave bad enough alone.

She caught up with Marc in the hall. He was staring at the closed elevator doors with the same intensity as his father had been staring out his bedroom window. Lynn knew better than to speak at such a time. She stood beside him quietly, letting him know that she was there without saying anything.

There were already two people in the elevator when Lynn followed Marc inside, the tags on their white coats identifying them as doctors. Lynn smiled hello. Marc said nothing, seemingly oblivious to their presence. His eyes followed the numbers of the floors as they descended from three to one.

"Excuse me, Mr. Cameron?" one of the doctors asked. He was about the same age as Marc, short, stocky, with the beginnings of a mustache sprouting under his small, bulbous nose. Marc turned toward him as if in a trance. "Dr. Turgov," the doctor continued, extending his hand. "We met last time you were here. You're the writer, right? Your father is the one who sent Nancy Petruck to Greece to see her grandmother." He laughed. "That car of his is something else. He let me take it for a spin the other day. Great car. How's the writing coming?" He said all this in one sweeping mouthful, apparently unaware of Marc's almost palpable hostility. "You know, I always thought that when I retired, I'd take up writing."

"Isn't that a coincidence?" Marc said in return, the sarcasm clinging to each word like honey on a knife. "I always thought that when *I* retired, I'd take up medicine."

The elevator door opened as if on cue, and Marc exited before Dr. Turgov had time to understand he'd been insulted.

"It's amazing the things people will say to writers." Marc was still fuming as they waited for the bridge that connected West Palm Beach to Palm Beach to lower. "Can you imagine saying to a lawyer, 'I think I'll take up law when I retire'? Or to a dentist, 'I'll take up dentistry'? But everybody thinks they have a book in them. And maybe they do; maybe they've lived particularly interesting lives, and have exceptionally sharp insights. But that still doesn't mean that they're capable of recording them coherently or entertainingly enough to make anyone want to read about them. 'I have great ideas,' people are always saying to me. 'I could be a writer.' Well, they couldn't. Because while they may have ideas, even *great* ideas, what they don't have is the discipline that it takes to sit down and write every day, to face that blank piece of paper every morning and turn it into a mirror of their souls so that the readers see their own reflections in it. Writing's like any other skill. Not everybody can just sit down in front of a typewriter and do it, and yet everybody thinks that when they retire, they'll just write a little book. 'If you can do it, I can do it.' Do you know how many times I've heard that one? From friends too, not just casual acquaintances. Like people who look at a Picasso masterpiece and say, 'My kid can do that.' Well, I'd like to see that kid try. Christ," he said, banging his fist against the steering wheel, "this bridge is taking a long time."

Lynn strained her head to see around the lineup of cars in front of them. "I think the last boat is going under now," she said, watching the mast of a large sailboat as it passed between the raised sides of the large bridge. She watched as the two halves of the bridge began their slow descent, joining at the middle as they came together and then lying flat, the cars once again free to cross over. "What else do writers hear?" she asked, grateful for the doctor's insensitivity because it had allowed Marc the opportunity to blow off necessary steam without brooding about his father.

Marc warmed to his subject. "I'm asked a lot where I get my ideas."

"Where *do* you get your ideas?"

"Impossible question to answer." He laughed, relaxing his grip on the steering wheel. "But people never believe that. They like things neat and tidy. So you tell them that you get your ideas from newspapers, from what's happening in your own life and that of your friends, that sort of thing. The truth is that you don't know where you get your ideas any more than anybody else does. I guess it has something to do with the way writers look at the world. You and I may overhear the same argument at a dinner table, and you'll come away wondering what you could do to help, and I'll come away with a scene for a book. Writers use everything. Use it, change it, pervert it. Everything is stimulus. Nothing is sacred."

"Nothing?"

"Nothing."

Lynn squirmed in her seat, uncomfortable with the conversation for the first time. "Where are we going?" she asked absently, thinking it was probably a good time to change the subject.

"I thought we'd have some lunch."

"Good idea. I'm famished."

"I thought we'd have it at my place," he said, and she said nothing.

. . .

"A lady was by to see you earlier," the doorman announced as Marc led Lynn through the front doors of the lobby of his apartment building.

"Did she leave her name?"

"No, sir," the elderly gentleman replied, sweating beneath his too tight uniform. "No name, no message. I asked her, but she said she'd try to reach you herself later."

Marc shrugged, seemingly unconcerned, and he guided Lynn toward the elevators in the back of the building.

"It's a nice apartment," Lynn lied once they were inside the small foyer of the dark two-bedroom apartment.

"It's a lousy apartment," he corrected her. "And you're a lousier liar. Brown, for God's sake," he exclaimed as they entered the cramped living room, furnished entirely in shades of brown and mustard yellow. "I'm not saying that everyone has to do blues and greens, but come on, even a little beige would have been welcome." Lynn followed Marc into the tiny galley kitchen, the cupboards of which were a depressing imitation wood. "But what the hell, it was furnished, cheap, and it was available, and until I know for sure what's happening, it'll do just fine. Now, what can I get you to drink?"

"I'd love a Coke."

"A Coke for the lady," he announced, the hint of a laugh in his voice as he handed her a cold tin from the fridge, immediately followed by a glass. Lynn's eyes fell across his sons' recent finger paintings, which were taped to the fridge door. "And a beer for her would-be suitor."

Lynn pretended she hadn't heard the last remark, as they returned to the living room. She was thinking that she shouldn't have agreed to come here, and was alarmed to discover she couldn't wait to see what was going to happen next.

"I have a wonderful crabmeat salad in the refrigerator for later. Made it myself this morning."

"I'm impressed."

"Good. I did it to impress you." He winked, and she understood the gesture was inherited.

"Where do you write?"

"I have a desk set up in my bedroom. Care to have a look?"

"No," Lynn said quickly. She should never have agreed to come here. He could rape her and no jury in the world would convict him. "I thought it was what she wanted," she could hear him tell a crowded courtroom. "Why else would she go to my apartment? She knew my intentions were less than honorable." How many times had she advised young women not to put themselves into positions like this? Where were her brains? More importantly, where was her self-control?

"What are you thinking about?" he asked.

"That this is really a depressing place," Lynn answered, taking a quick look around. "Why don't we get out of here? I'm not really very hungry."

"You said you were famished."

"Actually I was just thirsty." She held up her Coke, taking a long sip for emphasis.

"What about my crabmeat salad?"

"What about a picnic on the beach?"

"Sounds great. Can I finish my beer first?"

"Oh. Oh, sure. Of course."

"Would you like to sit down?"

"No. No. I'm very comfortable standing."

"You don't look very comfortable."

Lynn took another sip of her drink, wishing he would do the same with his. "What do your boys think of the place?"

He laughed. "They think it's great."

Lynn looked at the unadorned mustard-colored wall across from where she stood, realizing she had never even seen the house in Gulfstream that Gary had temporarily rented.

"Of course, it's quite a switch from where they're used to living."

"Must be quite a switch for you too." Lynn tried to picture how Gary must have felt upon abandoning their house on Crestwood Drive, how he must feel each time he returned to it. Of course, Gary had chosen to leave. Marc had been given no such choice.

"You get used to everything," he told her. "Besides,

Suzette's home was never my home. For years I tried to pretend it was, but the truth is that I was always just a visitor there, a boarder with special privileges, if you will. Suzette's parents bought and paid for that house, the same way they bought and paid for everything their daughter wanted. The princess is supposed to live happily ever after, remember?" He shrugged, and took a long sip of his beer. "After her parents were killed, she wanted no part of the house. Said it had too many memories. So we started looking for a new house." He laughed. "We found a little more than I bargained for." Lynn watched his free hand form a fist. "Come on, let me show you my etchings."

Lynn had no time to object. Marc's arm was at the back of her elbow, half guiding, half pushing her down the narrow hall. "Is this where the boys sleep?" Lynn asked, braking to a halt outside a small brown-and-yellow room whose twin beds were all but hidden by stuffed dinosaurs and model airplanes. Lynn walked inside the room, pretending to study the collection of Hardy Boy mysteries that lined the small bookshelf along one wall. "They're a little young for these, aren't they?"

"They were mine," Marc confessed, a bit sheepishly. "I saved them, actually brought them with me when I moved down from Buffalo. I used to love the Hardy boys."

"I'm a Nancy Drew fan myself," Lynn told him, and laughed. "Megan is reading them now."

"And they ask what makes a classic."

He was moving closer. "What's that?" Lynn asked.

"What's what?"

Lynn pointed to what looked like a large fish tank, something long and black lining its bottom. "That." She edged closer, out of arm's reach.

"Oh, that. That's Henry."

"Henry?" Lynn was almost on top of it when she saw it move, and she realized that Henry was a snake. "Oh my God."

"You don't like snakes?"

"I like things that jump," Lynn said, feeling squeamish, not sure which way to turn. "Snakes don't jump." She pushed quickly past him into the hall, then turned right, finding herself in the master bedroom. "Wrong turn," she said, aware that he was behind her, his large frame blocking the doorway. He began moving closer.

"Marc, I don't think this is a good idea."

"You want me to take a blood test?" He smiled and so did she.

"That's not the point."

"What is the point?"

"The point is I shouldn't even be here."

"I know, your lawyer advises against it."

"I'm too old for games, Marc."

"I'm not playing games. How much more straightforward can I be, Lynn? I want to make love to you. I think you want to make love to me. Am I wrong?"

"It's not as simple as that."

"Why isn't it?" He took another step forward; she took an immediate step back. "Hey," he said, stopping, standing absolutely still, his hands in the air as if a gun were at his back. "I'm not about to do anything you don't want me to do."

"I don't know what I want you to do," Lynn admitted honestly.

"You have to make up your mind. You have to tell me what you want."

Lynn closed her eyes, wishing she knew. Even with her eyes closed, she could feel the intensity of his gaze, the strength of his desire for her. Her body ached to respond. It had been so long since anyone had desired her. She saw herself lying beside Marc in the back seat of his father's car, felt him removing her blouse, his lips at her breasts. Her body swayed toward him. A loud noise filled the apartment. Lynn opened her eyes. "What's that?" she asked, pulling her shoulders back, straightening her spine.

"The front door," Marc explained as the telephone began to ring. "And the telephone." He smiled. "Must be what they mean by 'saved by the bell.' I'll get the phone if you'll answer the door."

Lynn walked purposefully toward the front door as Marc headed for the phone in the kitchen. "She is? Now?" she heard him say, her hand on the doorknob. "It's the doorman," Marc called to her. "He says that the woman who was here earlier is on her way up."

Lynn pulled open the door. Suzette Cameron stood, stunned and openmouthed, on the other side.

16

Renee stared at her reflection in the mirror and thought she looked pretty damn good. She'd spent the morning at the hairdresser's and she thought her new shorter hair well suited her round face. It hugged the sides of her cheeks, ending just below her ears, and Renee thought it flattering and youthful. Similarly, her new emerald-green lounging outfit was slimming and understated. Understatedly overpriced, she thought, pulling in her stomach, grateful that her new clothes made a concerted effort to disguise what needed to be hidden while accentuating her more positive attributes. The top of the outfit allowed for an admirable display of cleavage, and the fabric drew down from her bosom in lines that made her waist appear small and girlish. It was worth all the money she'd paid for it, she thought, checking the clock next to her bed, wondering whether Kathryn would be dressed by the time Philip was out of the shower and ready to go, wondering whether it had really been a good idea on Philip's part to insist that Kathryn come with them to the party.

Kathryn wouldn't know anyone, and she had confided to Renee a nagging feeling of guilt. It was too early after Arnie's death to be going to parties, she had told Renee adamantly when Renee first suggested Kathryn accompany them. So Renee had been very surprised when Philip had been able to change her mind. Not that she should be surprised, she thought. She knew how persuasive Philip could be. Still, she sensed Kathryn's unease and determined to stay close to her all night to make sure she had a good time. The only problem with staying at Kathryn's side, however, was that it left Philip's side dangerously empty. There would be too many women at tonight's party willing to fill that space.

Renee fastened her heavy gold necklace around her throat, feeling it cold against her warm skin. She had to banish such thoughts. She had to learn to trust her husband or, as he had told her, there was surely no hope for their relationship. Tonight would mark a new beginning. She would show Philip that she could be everything he wanted, everything he needed. And she would show him this by leaving him alone, letting him wander, letting him engage in the mindless, meaningless flirtations that this kind of party inevitably encouraged. She would go her way and let him go his. When they met together at the end of the evening, it would be without the usual jealousies and recriminations she always inflicted on them. Tonight, she decided, she would fasten her energies on Kathryn.

There was a small knock on the bedroom door. "Kathryn?" Renee asked, knowing it could only be her sister, since Debbie was already out for the evening with friends.

"I can't get the back of this thing done up," Kathryn said, tiptoeing into the room on her bare feet and swiveling around to reveal a large, exposed triangle of skin in the middle of her dress.

"What back?" Renee asked good-naturedly.

"There. At the top." Kathryn's hand reached up behind her shoulders, but her fingers failed to reach the clasp. Renee quickly slipped the tiny loop around the appropriate button. "What do you think?" Kathryn executed a delicate spin, her hands holding out the sides of the calf-length white dress to better show off its full skirt.

"Pretty daring," Renee said, taking note of how revealing the dress actually was, while appearing initially, especially from the front, to be quite modest and conservative. It was white, almost virginal, with its high neck and long skirt. It was only when Kathryn turned that one saw the deep plunge underneath each arm, revealing an exposed curve of breast, and the back of the dress was virtually nonexistent, except for the small clasp at the top of the spine. It dipped so low under the waist that Renee wondered momentarily whether Kathryn was wearing panties, but she thought better than to ask. Kathryn was self-conscious enough without adding to her worries.

In truth, the dress was lovely, and Renee realized that Kathryn could effortlessly afford to expose what she herself went to great lengths to hide. She also realized she was more than a touch envious, and she frowned.

"Not appropriate?"

"It's lovely," Renee told her truthfully. "Is it new?"

"I bought it with Debbie that day we all went to lunch. Remember?"

Renee nodded vaguely. She preferred not to think about that day. She stared into the mirror, saw Alicia Henderson flutter her fingers in her direction. Would she be at the party tonight?

"Listen," Kathryn was saying, her voice so low it was almost a whisper, "I've been thinking again that maybe I shouldn't go to this party tonight. I won't know anyone, and I'll only hold you and Philip back, keep you from having a good time."

"Don't be silly. After two minutes, you'll know everyone as well as I do. Trust me," she said, wondering why she was using that expression, "you'll have a good time."

"I don't want to be an imposition."

"You won't be."

"I've been enough of an inconvenience to you already."

"Says who?"

"Nobody has to say anything. You're all much too nice for

that. That's your problem. You end up getting stuck with people like me. But I've been here over a month, and you have your own lives to get on with."

"Please don't talk about leaving. Don't even think about it. I want you to stay as long as *you* want to stay." Renee was only now starting to realize how good it felt to have her sister around. Kathryn supplied a warmth that had been missing from her life for too long. Despite the added stress of Kathryn's presence, Renee didn't want her sister to leave.

"Wow!" came the masculine voice from the small hallway that joined the bedroom to its ensuite bathroom. Philip entered the bedroom wearing nothing but a large white towel wrapped expertly around his lower torso, rubbing another towel through his wet, dark hair. Both women turned expectantly toward him. "That's quite a dress, Kathryn. Turn around and let me see." Kathryn did a quick spin, her cheeks slightly flushed. "Great dress," he said, looking toward Renee. Renee pushed back her shoulders, eagerly waiting her turn to be praised. "Renee, don't you have a pair of earrings that would go great with Kathryn's dress?" Renee looked toward the dresser, where she kept her jewelry box. "You know, the ivory-and-silver ones with the big loops. I think they'd be the perfect touch. Your ears are pierced, aren't they?" He moved to Kathryn's side and brushed her long hair away from her ears.

Renee opened the top dresser drawer, seeing Philip's gun beside the jewelry case, quickly covering it with some silk scarves. She had moved the gun there after Debbie had revealed its former location. Had Kathryn seen it? she wondered, aware of her sister's eyes on her hands as she opened the jewelry box and retrieved the earrings.

"Yes, sure, these will be perfect." Philip took the earrings from Renee's outstretched hand. "Here, try these on." He handed them to Kathryn, then stood back and watched Kathryn fit them through her ears. "What did I tell you? Absolutely perfect."

"What do you think, Renee?" Kathryn asked.

"They're perfect," Renee agreed, thinking that they were. "Philip is right again."

"You don't mind if I wear them?"

"Of course she doesn't mind," Philip answered for her.

"I really love them." Kathryn studied her reflection carefully in the mirror, obviously delighted by what she saw.

"Now, we'll just have to find something for you," Philip said, smiling at Renee.

"What's wrong with the ones I have on?" Renee fingered the heart-shaped pearl-and-gold earrings she had earlier selected.

"No pizzazz. Too conservative. How about these?" He reached into Renee's jewel box and pulled out a dangling pair of black onyx and rhinestones.

"I thought that with the gold necklace . . ." Renee began.

"Take off the necklace. It's not right with that outfit anyway. It makes you look too much like a dowager empress. You need a little bit of fun in your wardrobe, Renee. You're turning into an old lady." He said all this sprightly, with a lilt of good humor, his smile never leaving his face. Then he turned back to Kathryn. "What shoes are you going to wear?"

"I thought a pair of white flats."

"Perfect. And what's that perfume you have on?" He lifted her hair away from her ear for the second time and buried his nose in her neck.

"I can't remember the name." Kathryn blushed. "It was a free sample."

"It's great. You should loan some to Renee."

"I'm already wearing perfume," Renee said before her sister could offer, hoping her voice didn't betray the tears she felt hovering close by.

She had really thought she had chosen well this time, selecting an outfit she was sure Philip would like, trying to see herself through his eyes as she preened and fussed before the fitting-room mirror. She should have asked him to come with her. She knew what wonderful taste he had. He was always telling her he knew how to put her together better than she did, and it was true. Philip was the one in the family with the artistic eye. He knew instantly what would go well with what. He loved going into stores, watching her try things on. He enjoyed having a say in what she bought, helping her choose.

How many women had told her how lucky she was to have a husband who was interested in such things? What I wouldn't give! they all said. She should have taken him along when she bought this outfit. Then he would have advised her against it before it was too late, before she purchased something that made her look like a dowager empress, that turned her into an old lady. "Do you think I should change?" she asked him after Kathryn had returned to her own room.

"Too late now," he said, and disappeared into the walk-in closet to get ready for the party.

"Your sister is so beautiful," someone was saying as Renee reached across the long buffet table for a second kiwi tart. "And so thin," the voice continued as Renee popped the small tart into her mouth in its entirety. "I guess you have to be thin to wear a dress like that."

Renee fought the urge to help herself to yet another dessert, feeling Philip's disapproving eyes on her even though he was on the other side of the room and, when last she looked, totally absorbed in a conversation with her sister. She turned to face the woman who was speaking, recognizing her as her hostess, Melissa Lawless, a woman of approximately sixty years of age, whose husband was a respected cardiologist. "Yes, she is beautiful," Renee agreed, locating her sister as she was about to step out onto the patio, Philip still at her side.

"I always wanted to be thin like that," Melissa Lawless continued. "Thin but round, if you know what I mean. I could never understand how girls as thin as your sister got to have such full bosoms. I had the full bosom," she said, taking note of Renee's similar attribute, "but I was just as full everywhere else, if you know what I mean."

"You have a beautiful house," Renee told her, wishing to leave the full-figured discussions to Jane Russell.

"We like it," came the automatic reply. "I'm so glad you

were able to talk your sister into joining us tonight. I understand she's had some recent tragedy in her life."

Renee was caught off guard by the woman's assertion. Who had told her anything about Kathryn's problems? Surely not Philip, she thought, knowing it could hardly have been anyone else. "Yes," Renee answered, formulating her words carefully. "Her husband died." Of course her hostess must be referring to Arnie's death.

"I understood that she tried to kill herself," Melissa Lawless continued as pleasantly as if she had just said that she understood it was going to be sunny the next day.

Renee felt her breath catch in her throat. Her voice, when it finally emerged, was constricted and strange, as if it belonged to someone else. "Yes," she said. "Her husband's death was an awful shock. It took her a while to start seeing things clearly again. She's fine now." How could Philip have confided anything so personal to this woman? And why had he found it necessary to say anything at all? Surely, he simply could have asked if he could bring his wife's sister to the party without providing his hosts with a résumé of her past? Why would Philip, who was trained, even obligated, to keep confidences, have betrayed her sister's so easily?

Renee took a deep breath, slowly releasing the air in her lungs as if she were exhaling smoke from a cigarette, and reminded herself that Kathryn was not Philip's patient, that he was not bound by professional ethics to keep her secret. Not that it *was* a secret, she further reminded herself. Still, she felt hurt by Philip's careless gossip, for how else could she describe it?

"I'm surprised Philip told you all this," Renee surprised herself by saying.

"Oh, he didn't say a word to me. Alicia Henderson is the one who told me. I happened to mention to her the other day that Philip would be bringing his sister-in-law to the party tonight . . ."

Renee was aware that the woman was still talking even after she stopped listening. When had Philip aired the family laundry in front of Ali Henderson? The afternoon they had all run into him at lunch? The lunch in which poor Mrs. Henderson was supposedly so distraught over her husband's incipient schizophrenia that she couldn't bring herself to go to Philip's office? "Don't worry, Ali," she could almost hear Philip saying. "There's a little craziness in everybody's family. My wife's sister, for example. Her husband died and three months later she tried to slit her wrists." Or maybe not at lunch at all. Maybe at dinner. The dinner he had missed with her because he was busy saving a potential suicide. My, my, but the world was conveniently full of people who were eager to do themselves in. "Did I tell you about my wife's sister?" she heard Philip ask again, this time picturing him, not in the darkness of a public restaurant, but in the warm confines of Alicia Henderson's private bedroom. Why had he found it necessary to break Kathryn's trust in this way? What had it gotten him?

Stop it, she told herself, stomping her foot. You're doing it again. You're blowing everything out of proportion. There are any number of ways Kathryn's suicide attempt could have come up in conversation. Philip probably mentioned it quite innocently as a way of illustrating a point. She had to stop all these suspicions. Stop behaving like a prosecuting attorney, she told herself. Leave the lawyer at the office.

Renee looked around the room, her eyes focusing on the patio doorway. Philip was even now out there with Kathryn. He had been wonderful to her all night, staying close beside her, making sure that she was comfortable, that she had been introduced to everyone, that she was never alone and that her plate was always full. He had been doing his concerted best all evening to make Kathryn feel as if she were not some third wheel he was stuck with, but someone he genuinely wanted in his company, someone he cared about and wanted to have a good time. He was a determined escort, never allowing Kathryn the opportunity to sulk in a corner or to drift off by herself. Renee felt grateful to him for the kindness and sensitivity he was showing her sister. How could she subject him to her infantile ravings, even if they were all unspoken? She did him a disservice even with her thoughts.

". . . Speak of the devil," she heard her hostess exclaim,

and Renee looked over to see Alicia Henderson approaching at a determined, if leisurely, pace.

"Alicia Henderson," the tall redhead said, extending her hand and introducing herself to Renee as if this were their first encounter.

"Hello, Ali," Renee replied, taking the woman up on her earlier offer. "We've met before," she reminded her. Alicia Henderson looked surprised, then amused.

"Oh, that's right. At Judy's surprise party. I almost didn't recognize you. Have you put on a little weight?"

"I was just remarking to Renee that her sister is so thin," Melissa Lawless said, obviously delighted that her earlier observation could be worked into the conversation.

"How long is your sister going to be staying with you?" Alicia Henderson asked, adjusting the shoestring strap of her black leather dress.

"I have no idea," Renee answered truthfully, seeing no reason to lie. Aside from the brief exchange she had had with her sister before the party, it was something that had never been discussed.

Alicia Henderson brushed her long red hair away from her face in an exotic sweeping gesture that Renee realized was fueled more by habit than necessity. Renee watched the hair immediately tumble back into place. "You have quite a full house then, what with Debbie there too," Alicia Henderson said, casually dropping the name of Philip's only child into the conversation.

"Debbie's no trouble," Renee lied.

"I would think she's quite a handful. We went for lunch one day last week. Philip asked me if I wouldn't mind taking her out, said that she spends a lot of time alone." Alicia Henderson smiled broadly. "You know how hard it is to refuse Philip anything."

Renee felt her mouth about to drop open and she resolutely held her lips firmly together, gritting her teeth. Why had Philip asked this woman to take his daughter out to lunch? And could she even ask him about it without risking a major confrontation?

"She seemed like quite a handful to me, but then I guess you're used to handfuls," Alicia Henderson continued obliquely.

"I beg your pardon?" Renee asked.

"Well, your sister, for one, what with trying to kill herself that way, and then, of course, there's Philip . . ." Alicia Henderson's voice got dangerously low.

"I beg your pardon?" Renee repeated, as if her voice were a recording, its needle stuck in a familiar groove.

"Excuse me," Melissa Lawless chirped pleasantly, and was suddenly gone.

"Where *is* Philip tonight? I haven't seen him."

For the first time in the conversation, Renee felt her facial muscles relax and her mouth arrange itself into something close to a smile. There was something in Alicia Henderson's last question that betrayed a certain anxiety. It was the voice of a woman who knows she is losing ground. So the affair had run its course, Renee thought, at least on Philip's part. Renee instinctively relaxed her posture. Ali Henderson was no longer a threat to her, just an unpleasant reminder of Philip's occasional lapse in taste. If Alicia Henderson hadn't seen Philip, it was only because Philip hadn't wanted to be seen.

"The last time I saw him he was heading for the patio."

"Not alone, I'm sure." Alicia Henderson's voice was suddenly petulant, as if Renee were now an ally, and not a rival. Renee braced herself for the appalling possibility that this woman was about to confide the details of her affair with Philip.

"Never alone," Renee replied evenly, telling the woman in two short words that she was not the first and probably not the last, but that they were all of the same minor importance, and an indulgence on her part as much as Philip's. Alicia Henderson's well-manicured fingers swept through her long red hair nervously and then she was gone.

A few minutes later, Philip walked back through the balcony doors, Kathryn still at his side. She had obviously been laughing, and looked happier than Renee had seen her since her arrival. Renee's small grin grew wider and more pronounced as Philip hurried past Alicia Henderson with scarcely a nod in her direction. Renee had seen that look before. He was definitely through with her. By the time Philip was at her side, Renee was smiling from ear to ear, her heart full of gratitude and love. Her husband had come home again.

"How's the most beautiful woman at the party?" he asked, his arms encircling Renee's waist, spinning her around playfully. "Having a good time?"

"A terrific time," Renee told him, and realized it was true.

"Would you mind if we made a fairly early exit? I thought we might have a smaller party of our own." He leaned forward, and Renee felt his tongue licking her ear.

"I'm ready anytime," she said, feeling her body start to tingle, eager for him as she always was.

"Then let's go," he said, his arms around both Renee and her sister as he led them toward the front door. "Some guys have all the luck," he said, and both women laughed.

17

The two women sat staring at each other from opposite sides of the desk. "Are you sure I can't get you a cup of coffee?" Lynn Schuster asked the pale blond woman who balanced on the edge of the chair and trembled noticeably.

Patty Foster shook her head. She wore no makeup except for a subtle touch of mascara around her large hazel eyes. Her complexion was dotted with freckles. If this was a woman who spent hours lounging in the sun, as her neighbor Davia Messenger had claimed, she obviously covered herself with plenty of sunblock. Patty Foster smiled briefly, the corners of her mouth flexing up and then back down almost before the smile had time to register. She chewed nervously on her bottom lip.

"Of course, it's not nearly as good as the coffee I had at your house," Lynn said, trying to get the woman to relax. Patty Foster had been in Lynn's office for almost ten minutes, and Lynn could scarcely recall interviewing anyone more obviously uncomfortable. Or frightened. "What's your secret?"

"I add a bit of cocoa to the coffee," Patty Foster answered tentatively, as if she weren't sure Lynn's question had been in reference to her coffee. "It was a trick my grandmother taught me."

"Were you close to your grandmother?"

"She raised me."

"Oh?"

"My parents died when I was very young. I guess that explains my father complex." Patty Foster tried again to smile, but failed. "My grandmother took me in, looked after me like I was her own. She was strict, like Keith is with Ashleigh, but I learned a lot of things from her. It all worked out in the end." The young woman promptly burst into tears. "Everything's all right, isn't it? I mean, you told me that the doctor said that there were no signs of abuse . . ."

"Everything is fine, Mrs. Foster."

Patty Foster pulled a tissue from her pocket and blew her nose loudly. "I love her more than anything in the world, Mrs. Schuster. The thought that you might try to take her away from me scares me so much . . ."

"What else scares you?"

"What?"

"What else scares you?" Lynn repeated quietly.

"I don't understand."

"I think you do." Lynn stared deep into Patty Foster's eyes. The young woman tried to look away, but couldn't. Instead she blinked several times in rapid succession, and blew her nose again, although this time much more quietly.

"Does your husband scare you, Mrs. Foster?" Lynn's voice was gentle, probing quietly, carefully, like a surgeon's knife.

"No, of course not. What do you mean?" Patty Foster answered quickly, too quickly, then stopped. "I don't know what you're talking about."

"Tell me about your husband."

"Keith is a wonderful man. He's gentle and thoughtful and good. Really, a good person. He's a very important man."

"So I understand."

"A very busy man. He works long, hard hours."

"It must be difficult for him some nights when he comes home tired after a hard day at work to have such a young child running around the place, making noise, occasionally misbe-having."

"Ashleigh's the light of his life," Patty Foster told her, and Lynn made a mental note of the fact that she had used the same phrase as her husband. "It was hard for him at first," Patty Foster confided, staring into her lap. "Like you said, he wasn't used to having a small child around. He was a little jealous about all the attention I had to give her. But he got over that." Patty Foster looked up from her lap and stared directly at Lynn, her eyes suddenly brimming over with a second on-slaught of tears. "He never meant to hurt her," she whispered. "You have to believe me. He just doesn't realize his own strength sometimes."

Lynn measured her next words very carefully. "Are you trying to tell me that your husband broke your daughter's arm?"

"Would that mean you'd take Ashleigh away from me?" There was a renewed note of panic in Patty Foster's voice.

"No, of course not," Lynn said quickly, trying to reassure her. "But we have counseling sessions for families like yours . . ."

"Keith would never go."

"I'm sure we could persuade him . . ."

"No, no. He'd never go." Patty Foster jumped off her chair with such suddenness that it nearly toppled over.

"Mrs. Foster . . ."

"You think just because you say something, that's the way it's going to be? What's it like to have such control over other people's lives, Mrs. Schuster? What does it feel like to have people trembling in front of you, knowing that one wrong word could mean the loss of their child? How does it feel to have that kind of power?"

"Believe me, Mrs. Foster, I have no intention of trying to take Ashleigh away from you."

"As long as we do what you say."

"We're trying to help you . . ."

"I made it all up," Patty Foster exclaimed, her voice rising.

"My husband has never touched Ashleigh. He loves her. He would never hurt her."

"Mrs. Foster . . ."

"Ashleigh broke her arm at school. Keith has never been anything but a wonderful father to her . . ."

"There's nothing to be afraid of."

"The doctor examined her. He found no evidence of abuse. Ashleigh is a happy, healthy little girl, and no one is going to take her away from me."

"No one wants to do that . . ."

"If you tell anyone I said any of those things, I'll deny it. I'll say you're lying, that you made the whole thing up. Do you understand me? My husband is a very important man. He can make things very uncomfortable for people when he wants to."

"I'm not afraid of your husband, Mrs. Foster, and you don't have to be either."

"I don't know what you're talking about," Patty Foster said evenly, and fled Lynn's office.

Arlene, Lynn's secretary, stuck her head quickly through the doorway. "Problems?"

"You'd better go after her. See that she's all right. Oh, and close my door, will you? Thanks." The door to Lynn's office closed, surrounding her in welcome silence. "Now what?" she asked out loud, rubbing her eyes, hearing her mother tell her not to. She looked absently around the room, wondering how to deal with Patty Foster's outburst. The woman had all but admitted that her husband had broken their daughter's arm, and yet she had just as quickly denied it. Davia Messenger had been right about the abuse, just wrong about the perpetrator. She had been blinded by her eye for beauty, Lynn thought, and almost laughed, wondering what to do next. If she could locate Ashleigh's teacher and get her to confirm that Ashleigh's arm had not been broken in any playground fall, then that plus Davia Messenger's accusations would probably be sufficient to force Keith Foster into counseling. But so far, Lynn had been unsuccessful in her attempts to locate Ashleigh's teacher. Gulfstream Private School was closed for the summer, as Keith Foster had predicted, and Lynn had already checked out all the

Templetons in Delray and in the greater Palm Beach area. She checked through her file on the Foster case to make sure of the correct spelling of the teacher's name. None of the women she had talked to taught in the exclusive private school. Lynn stared at the telephone as if it could provide her with the right number to call. She still hadn't tried Boca Raton or Pompano Beach, she thought, dialing information. "Boca Raton," she said, after the operator had asked her the city she was seeking. "Templeton. No, I don't have an initial or an address. Just give me all you have."

Luckily, there were only four listings for Templeton in Boca. Lynn dutifully copied them down and was about to begin trying each one in turn when the door to her office burst open. She looked up, startled, and then more startled still when the angry form she saw rushing into the room turned out to be that of her husband. "Gary . . . what are you . . . what's the matter?"

"What the hell's going on, Lynn?" he demanded angrily.

"I don't know what you're talking about," she said, but even as she spoke the words, she knew them to be false.

"You know damn well what I'm talking about. Marc Cameron is what I'm talking about."

Lynn's eyes widened in alarm as Gary slammed his fist down hard on her desk. "I think you'd better calm down," Lynn said, trying to calm herself as she walked to her office door, mindful of the curious stares of other office workers. She caught sight of the concerned look on Arlene's face as her secretary returned to her desk. "It's okay," she whispered to the clearly apprehensive young woman just before closing the door.

"I want to know what the hell is going on," Gary demanded a second time, no quieter than the first.

"There's nothing going on," Lynn told him, determined to keep her own voice down.

"Just what do you think you're trying to do?"

"I'm not trying to do anything. Look, why don't you sit down and we can try to discuss this calmly . . ."

"I don't want to sit down, and I don't want to discuss this calmly. As far as I'm concerned, there's nothing to discuss."

"Then why are you here?"

"Because I didn't think that coming to the house yesterday and sounding off in front of the kids would be a very good idea."

"Then we're agreed on something anyway," Lynn said, thinking that Marc Cameron would probably laugh at this remark, but noting that Gary did not. "Just what are you so upset about, Gary?"

"Do you really have to ask?" He stared at her incredulously.

"Apparently."

"Just what are you trying to prove by dating Marc Cameron?"

Lynn reached the safe side of her desk and lowered herself slowly into her chair. "I'm not trying to prove anything."

"What's gotten into you lately, Lynn? What's going on in your head? First you follow Suzette into a dress store . . ."

"I didn't follow her."

"Then you try to humiliate her by trying on the same dress . . ."

"Believe me, I wasn't trying to humiliate her . . ."

"Then why did you do it? Can you tell me that? What were you doing in that store in that goddamn dress?"

Lynn shrugged. What could she say? That the afternoon had just kind of gotten away from her? That she didn't know what she was doing in that store except indulging her curiosity? That the only person who had been humiliated that afternoon was herself? And how dare he question what was going on in her head? Had she been the one to send flowers on their erstwhile anniversary?

"And then on Saturday, Suzette goes to see her husband to ask him if he can take the boys that night . . . her babysitter canceled . . . and who does she find when she opens the door? The lady in the orange dress—little Miss Schuster herself."

"*Mrs.* Schuster," Lynn said evenly, and for a minute, Gary was speechless.

He bounced his fists against his thighs, pacing back and

forth in front of her desk. Lynn noticed that her own hands were shaking and quickly hid them in her lap. "What were you doing in Marc Cameron's apartment, Lynn?" Gary asked after a long pause.

"I'm not sure that's any of your business," Lynn answered steadily.

"I think it is."

"Why?"

"Because it concerns my children, for one thing."

"What are you talking about? How does it concern your children? *Our* children," she corrected.

"Think about it."

"I *am* thinking about it. You're not making any sense."

"How do you think the kids would feel if they found out their mother was dating . . ." He stumbled, not sure what words to use.

". . . the husband of the woman their father ran off with?" Lynn finished the sentence for him, surprised to find that it gave her a certain satisfaction to see him flinch.

Gary Schuster was shaking his head. "I didn't think you were a vindictive person."

"I'm not being vindictive."

"Dating Marc Cameron isn't your way of getting back at me?"

"Dating Marc Cameron has nothing to do with you."

"Oh, come on, Lynn, stop kidding yourself. Why else would you be seeing him if not to get back at me? It would be funny if it weren't so pathetic," he said, and Lynn felt stung by his words, as if she had been slapped with a ruler by her favorite teacher. "Can't you see what you're doing?"

"No, I can't see what I'm doing," she replied, putting equal emphasis on each word, as he had done.

"You're using this man to try and hold on to me, or at the very least to keep tabs on me. Marc Cameron is an irresponsible bum. He's not your type at all. You wouldn't let yourself get within ten feet of the man if it weren't because of me."

"Marc Cameron is not an irresponsible bum. He's a very talented man in a very insecure profession."

"He's an irresponsible bum. I don't want him anywhere near my children.

"I'd like to keep our children out of this discussion."

"How do you think they're going to feel when they find out about you and Marc Cameron?"

"Are you going to tell them?"

"Of course not." He seemed genuinely angered by the suggestion.

"Well, then, since we've already agreed not to introduce any further complications into our children's lives for at least a few more months," Lynn said pointedly, watching Gary wince at the veiled reference to Suzette, "I don't think you have anything to worry about."

"This is a small town, Lynn. People talk."

"Who are you really concerned about, Gary? Your children or yourself?"

"That kind of remark is really beneath you, Lynn."

"I'm trying to understand why you're so angry."

"I'm angry," he said, spitting the words, "and frankly, I wouldn't have thought it required a master's degree in social work to figure it out, because you are deliberately using Marc Cameron to hound me."

"I'm doing no such thing. My relationship with Marc Cameron doesn't concern you at all. It has nothing to do with you."

"It has everything to do with me. The man wouldn't exist if it weren't for me."

Lynn almost laughed but stopped herself. Marc Cameron might appreciate the irony, but Gary Schuster certainly wouldn't.

"Just what *are* your intentions concerning Marc Cameron?" he asked, almost primly.

"That's none of your business," Lynn said, and realized it was the second time she had said it. The knowledge that things that concerned her were no longer any of her husband's business made her feel empty and more than a little strange.

"I think I have a right to know."

"I think you forfeited any rights you had with regard to me when you walked out."

"Are you going to marry him?"

"Oh, please . . ." Lynn said, the words spilling out of her mouth in a gasp.

"But you are sleeping with him," he stated as if it were fact.

Lynn stared at her husband in astonishment, unable to form the proper words of denial.

"Marc Cameron is a loser, Lynn. The man is forty years old. He's never made more than thirty thousand dollars a year in his life."

"What has that got to do with anything? Since when has a person's income been the sole judge of his worth?"

"Oh, come on, Lynn. Let's not go all teenage idealistic on me, okay? And don't try to put words in my mouth. You know what I'm trying to say. The last thing you need . . ."

"Please don't tell me what I need."

"All right, then, the last thing our children need is a man around the house their mother has to support."

"Our children are *our* responsibility—yours and mine—not Marc Cameron's, and what he does for a living, unless he's breaking the law, is no concern of either theirs or yours." Lynn rose to her feet. "And not that he needs defending, but Marc Cameron happens to be a very gifted writer. If his wife was too stupid to understand that, that's her problem, not mine."

The color drained from Gary's face. "I won't stand here and let you insult Suzette."

"Perhaps, then, you'd better leave."

Gary turned abruptly toward the door, then stopped, whipping back in her direction. "My money's not going to support him, that's for damn sure."

"What are you talking about?"

Gary walked back toward her desk, waving his arms. "I'm not going to work like a dog in order to give you money every month so that you can throw it away on bums like Marc Cameron."

Lynn felt her body lift out of her chair. She leaned forward, balancing her fists on the top of her desk. "May I remind you that the money you give me every month is for your children. You're not paying me any alimony."

"I'm not going to keep paying the mortgage so you can move some other guy into my house a few months after I'm gone."

"I don't believe I'm hearing this."

"Can't you see what a fool you're making of yourself, Lynn? Can't you see how pathetic this makes you look?"

It was the second time he had used that word, and it had lost none of its power to sting. Lynn felt wounded. She felt her eyes fill with tears and quickly turned her head toward the window. She didn't want Gary to see her cry. Dammit, she didn't want to cry at all. She was too angry to cry. Why did women always have to cry? Tears rendered them useless, branded them emotional cripples, rendered them mere children in the battle of the sexes. Children were always the first casualties in any war. She was a grown-up, dammit. Why did she have to cry?

"I'm not trying to hurt you, Lynn," he said, and a sound escaped Lynn's mouth that was halfway between a laugh and a howl. "Well, you can believe me or not, but it really wasn't my intention to hurt you."

Lynn swallowed the large lump in her throat and turned back to her husband, her eyes glistening. "Just what *was* your intention?" she asked, almost the same prim question he had asked earlier.

"I was angry, I admit that. I was shocked. I mean, how would you feel?"

"I imagine it's a bit like the way you feel when you find out your husband is leaving you for another woman."

There was a pause. "All right. I guess I deserved that. But the point is . . ."

"Yes, what is the point?"

"The point is that you and I both know that you're using this man as a way of getting back at me, and I can't let you do that. Not to me, not to yourself, not to our children."

"I don't understand how you're . . ."

"Let me explain, then," he interrupted, his voice carrying an unpleasant undertone which threatened to overtake it completely. "If you don't agree to stop this affair with Cameron . . ."

"We are *not* having an affair!"

"If you don't agree to stop this affair with Cameron," he continued as if she hadn't spoken, "then you can forget all about our generous settlement agreement. Not only will I not pay the mortgage, but I'll fight you for half the house. You won't see a dime from me."

Lynn could hardly hear what he was saying over the loud thumping of her heart. "But why, for God's sake? Is your ego so bruised . . ."

"My ego has nothing to do with this. If you aren't thinking clearly enough to see how your actions could hurt our children . . ."

"Isn't it a little late to be worrying about hurting our children? You didn't worry about that when you left. Isn't walking out on them enough without forcing them out of their house as well?"

"My children will always have a place to live," Gary said steadily. "I'm their father. I have as much right to them as you do. If you can't look after them properly . . ."

Lynn felt her blood turn to ice. "Are you saying you'd try to take them away from me?" she heard herself ask, hearing Patty Foster's voice.

"They're my children too."

"But we agreed they would live with me. It was never an issue."

"It's an issue now."

Lynn lifted one hand to her forehead. "Are you saying that if I don't stop seeing Marc Cameron you'll fight me for custody?"

"I don't want to have to go that route, Lynn."

"I can't believe you would do that to me."

"Don't force my hand."

"Why would you want to hurt me like that?"

"I'm not trying to hurt you. I'm trying to protect you."

"I don't need your protection!"

"That was always our problem," he said quietly. "You never needed me at all."

Lynn sank back into her chair. "I guess I don't know you very well," she said, a wondrous quality to her voice. She stared into her husband's eyes and was surprised to find them the same deep brown they had always been. "I can't believe you'd do this."

"I have to protect myself, Lynn. I have to protect what's mine."

Lynn said nothing, too stunned even to cry.

"Think about it," Gary told her. "It doesn't have to be this way. You can have your lawyer call mine by the end of the week. I'm sure we'll be able to work something out." He walked to the door and stopped. "I'm sorry if what I've said sounds harsh . . ."

"No, you're not."

("No, I'm not," Marc Cameron would have answered.)

"Have it your way," Gary said, and was gone.

18

"I've been paying for my mistakes long enough, thank you," the elderly woman was saying, her face flushing pink with anger under her soft gray hair, "and I have no intention of paying you to make more for me."

Renee Bower leaned across her desk, her hands reaching out to the woman in a placating gesture. "I'm sorry, Mrs. Reinking. Maybe I was out of line . . ."

"No maybes about it," the woman responded, her watery blue eyes not ready to let go of her indignation. "I understand your intentions are good, but may I remind you that *I* am the client and that you are being paid to represent my wishes . . ."

"You're paying me to represent your best interests."

"In this case, they are one and the same thing. And I will not be bullied into doing something I don't want to do. Now, I have already instructed you to accept the settlement offer . . ."

"But it's not a good one, Mrs. Reinking. Your husband is a very wealthy man and what he's offering you is almost laughable after all the years you've been married, and what you've put up with during that time. We can do much better."

"I just want to be free of him."

"I understand that, but you have to think of your future . . ."

"I have no future," the woman told her directly. "I am dying, Mrs. Bower." She delivered this last statement in so matter-of-fact a fashion that Renee's mouth fell open before she had time to temper her response. "I have perhaps another year to live, and what my husband is offering will be more than enough to see me through it comfortably. My children are grown-up and well provided for. All I want from you is my divorce decree. I'm not interested in what you think is fair, or what you might think about anything, for that matter. I have taken orders throughout forty-six years of marriage and I am sick, quite literally to death, of doing what other people tell me to do. I am not about to start taking orders from you. Now, either accept the settlement offer or I'll find myself another attorney. Am I making myself very clear?"

Renee picked up her phone and buzzed her secretary. "Marilyn, get Mitchell Weir on the phone and tell him we accept his client's offer of settlement."

"Thank you," Gemma Reinking said, a touch of the aristocrat in her New England accent. "Now I know why Fred liked to give orders. It feels good."

Renee stood up and extended her hand across the top of her desk. "I'll call you as soon as we get the papers. You can come in and sign them at your convenience."

"Are you happily married, Mrs. Bower?" the woman asked suddenly.

Renee's eyes opened wide, her smile freezing on her lips as she struggled to find a suitable response. What was the matter with her? she thought, wondering why the words refused to form. Of course she was happily married. She enjoyed a lifestyle most people could only imagine, and she was married to the man of her dreams. What was the matter with her? Why didn't she simply open her mouth and tell this woman she was happy?

"Never mind, dear," Gemma Reinking said softly. "Maybe one day you'll understand why I'm doing things this way.

You'll know that sometimes it's worth anything just to be rid of them." She winked, and her face instantly dropped fifty of its almost seventy years. In that minute, Renee caught a glimpse of the young woman Gemma Reinking had been.

"Goodbye, Mrs. Reinking," Renee told her, surprised by the strength of the frail woman's vigorous handshake. "Good luck."

"Good luck to you, dear."

As soon as Gemma Reinking was out of her office, Renee buzzed her secretary. "Marilyn, get me Lynn Schuster on the phone, please." She reached into her bottom drawer and pulled out a Mars bar, which she devoured quickly before realizing that she hadn't really been hungry. Eating had become an unwitting habit, something to do to avoid doing other things. "Like what?" she asked herself, discarding the empty wrapper into the wastepaper basket. Like thinking about your happy marriage, came the immediate reply. Renee quickly reached into the drawer for a second chocolate bar.

"Lynn Schuster on line one," her secretary announced, catching Renee in mid-chew.

"Lynn, just a second, I've got something caught in my throat." Renee swallowed what remained of the candy bar, then cleared her throat directly into the receiver. "How are you?"

"Lousy," she said. "I really screwed up, didn't I?"

"You didn't make things easy. But that's okay. Easy's no fun."

"Have you spoken to Gary's lawyer?"

"We've set up a meeting for next Monday at two o'clock. Why don't you come to my office at one-thirty." It was a statement, not a request.

"Do I have to be there?"

"Oh, I don't think you'll want to miss this." Renee heard Lynn sigh. "Don't worry, Lynn. I'm in my element. This is a piece of cake." Renee grimaced, wondering why all her metaphors were food-related.

"I hope you're right."

"You'll stay well away from Marc Cameron until then?"

"Yes," Lynn promised softly.

"I can't hear you."

"I'll stay away from him."

"One more time. I didn't quite catch it," Renee prodded.

"I said I'll stay away from him," Lynn said loudly as Renee pushed the phone away from her ear.

"Good girl. I used to be a cheerleader in high school, you know."

"I bet you were terrific."

"I was," Renee said out loud after Lynn had hung up. "I *was* terrific." The image of herself in the uniform of her cheerleading days came into her mind. She recalled with a mixture of fondness and dismay the fluffy white sweater and red-and-white pleated short skirt which flew up over her ample bottom when she did cartwheels and jumps. What she had lacked in skill, she had made up for in sheer enthusiasm and her I'm-so-thrilled-to-be-here smile. While she was far from the prettiest girl on the cheerleading team, and had far from the best figure, she was unquestionably the loudest and most persistent. She never missed a practice, never missed a game. She might not have had the greatest legs, but she had the most powerful lungs. And she knew how to use them. Some things never change, she thought.

The intercom on her desk buzzed and Marilyn's voice cut into her reveries. "Mr. DeFlores on line two."

Renee glanced at the phone. Mr. DeFlores had returned home one evening to discover that his wife of five years had left him, taking with her virtually every stick of furniture, including the plastic dishes that had been left over from his bachelor days. Would Mr. DeFlores believe that she had been a cheerleader in high school? "Mr. DeFlores," she said into the receiver, trying not to sound pessimistic as she explained that his estranged wife had again refused to sign the agreement she had already approved, even with the changes she had insisted on. "There's really nothing we can do at this point unless you want to go to court, which, as I've explained, will be a very expensive proposition. Why don't we give her a few more weeks. You're not in any hurry for this divorce, are you?"

Mr. DeFlores agreed he wasn't in a hurry.

"Good, then I'll explain to your wife's attorney that there will be no more changes, and that until your wife is ready to sign the agreement as written, we have nothing further to discuss. We're quite prepared to wait as long as necessary. If she wants this divorce as quickly as she says she does, she'll have to make the next move. . . . Yes, I'll get back to you. In the meantime, Mr. DeFlores, try to stay calm. Time is always kind to the person who's willing to wait." Renee wasn't sure if this was true, but it sounded good, and seemed to make her client happy. She hung up and was about to dial Mrs. DeFlores's lawyer, then changed her mind. Mrs. DeFlores's attorney was a thoroughly unpleasant young man who never failed to give Renee a headache. He talked loud and fast, and Renee could actually see him punching the air with his fingers through the phone wires when they spoke. Every time she talked to him, she was reminded of the joke Philip had told at a party one night. Question: what have you got when you have six lawyers buried up to their necks in sand? Answer: not enough sand. Renee had found the joke painful, but because she didn't want to be accused of lacking a sense of humor, she had laughed along with everyone else.

Renee decided she needed a cup of coffee and headed for the staff room at the far end of the hall. She poured herself a cup from the pot that was kept brewing all day, adding ample amounts of cream and sugar, and sat down in one of several low-lying blue chairs, lifting her feet onto the well-scuffed coffee table in front of her.

It was all a matter of control, Renee understood, her mind back on Mr. DeFlores, though to tell him that would only upset him further. Agreeing to sign separation papers and then refusing to do so at the last minute, finding something unacceptable in what had already been declared quite proper, throwing out old demands, making fresh ones, all at the eleventh hour, that was all part of the game. Divorcing couples did it to each other all the time. It was their way of trying to maintain the upper hand, of calling the shots, pulling the strings. Lisa DeFlores was doing it to her husband; Gary Schuster was doing the same thing to his wife. Renee closed her eyes, stretching her head back across the top of the chair so that her Adam's apple protruded into the air.

At least her clients weren't giving in, giving up, she thought gratefully, especially pleased that Lynn Schuster had decided to fight back. So many women didn't. They collapsed under the pressure, either financial or psychological, sometimes both. Lynn was frightened and hurt, but she had given Renee permission to do whatever she felt necessary to deflate Gary's threats. Renee was looking forward to their meeting next Monday.

Renee realized she liked Lynn Schuster and hoped that when Lynn's divorce was settled, they could be friends. She'd lost touch with all her close female friends over the years, and she was just beginning to realize how much she missed them. Despite everything that was happening to her, Lynn Schuster seemed to be a woman who had her life under control. Well, so what? Don't I? Renee asked herself, suddenly angry and impatient, though she wasn't sure why.

"Hi. Everything all right?"

Renee opened her eyes to see Margaret Bachman, a lawyer who had recently transferred into the firm, standing a few feet away, watching her with a mixture of curiosity and concern. "I'm fine," Renee said.

"Your face was twitching," the woman explained. "You looked like you were in pain."

Renee tried to smile. "Just arguing a case in my mind."

Margaret Bachman laughed. "John says I do that all the time. Now I understand what he was talking about. How's the coffee?"

"Great." Renee watched the woman, who was approximately the same age as herself though her voice made her sound older, help herself to a cup of coffee. Renee also noticed that she took it black.

"We missed you at the party Saturday night."

"Party?"

"At Bob's."

Bob was Bob Frescati, one of the firm's original partners.

"Oh, I'm sorry," Margaret Bachman said immediately, obviously embarrassed. "I just assumed you'd been . . ." She stopped, knowing that whatever she said now would only make matters worse.

"We had another engagement on Saturday night," Renee told her, giving Margaret Bachman her widest, most sincere grin. It was true after all. She and Philip *had* had another engagement on Saturday night, the party they had attended with Kathryn. So they wouldn't have been able to make Bob Frescati's party anyway, even if they had been invited. Just like they had been unable to make any of the other firm get-togethers lately because Philip always had other plans. Bob had undoubtedly sensed this. People had a way of not extending invitations once they had been turned down too many times. Still, she had to admit that it hurt. She had cut herself off from all her friends over the years. Was she starting down the same path with her partners and colleagues as well?

"I'd been looking forward to meeting that handsome husband of yours. He's the buzz of the secretarial staff, you know. They all say he's so gorgeous." Margaret sat down beside her.

"He's a very handsome man," Renee agreed.

"Lucky you."

Renee nodded. She recognized the look. How did you manage to land a man who's the buzz of the secretarial staff? it said.

"I was thinking of having a small dinner party one of these nights. Maybe you and your husband would like to come?"

"I'm sure we'd be delighted," Renee told her, sure of no such thing.

"Well, why don't you tell me when is good for you—I understand you're pretty hard to pin down—then I'll work around that."

Renee took her feet from the coffee table, trying not to show the effort it involved. "I'll call Philip now," she told the startled woman, who obviously had not been expecting such immediate action.

Renee returned to her office, feeling angry and hurt, knowing it was all her own fault. She couldn't expect people to keep inviting her to parties when she made something of a habit of not showing up, sometimes not even calling until she was already late. She wondered if there had been other events from which she had been excluded. Well, that was it. It was time to start fresh. She picked up the phone and dialed Philip's office, bracing herself for the fake friendliness of Philip's would-be English secretary.

"Dr. Bower's office."

"Samantha, can I please speak to Philip?"

"Who's calling, please?"

"It's Mrs. Bower," Renee said, not quite believing her ears. The nerve of that woman!

"Oh, do forgive me, Mrs. Bower. I didn't recognize your voice. Dr. Bower is gone for the day."

Renee checked her watch. It was barely three o'clock. "Gone? When did he leave?"

"About an hour ago."

"Did he say where he was going?"

"I believe he said he was going home."

"Home? Was he feeling all right?"

"He was feeling fine," Philip's secretary said with an unpleasant laugh. Does he have to be feeling sick to want to go home? it asked.

"Thank you." Renee replaced the receiver and immediately buzzed her secretary. "Marilyn, can you try to reschedule my four o'clock meeting? Thanks." Then she dialed her apartment, letting it ring eight times before hanging up. Maybe Philip was out on the balcony and couldn't hear the phone, or maybe he was down at the pool. She wondered again if he was feeling all right. It was very unlike him to go home in the middle of the day. She wondered where Debbie and Kathryn had gone, recalling that Debbie had said something about going to Singer Island with friends. Kathryn had declined Debbie's invitation to join them, saying she just felt like a quiet day around the apartment. Maybe she and Philip had gone for a walk on the beach together. Maybe Renee could get home in time to find them and join them. The hell with work.

"Your meeting's rescheduled for Thursday at four-thirty," Marilyn's voice announced over the intercom.

"I'm at home if there are any emergencies," Renee told her a minute later on her way out.

"Everything all right?"

"Everything's fine," Renee said.

Philip's white Jaguar was in his parking spot when Renee pulled her white Mercedes in beside it. She walked briskly through the lot, then through the lobby, greeting the obviously disinterested doorman with perhaps a touch too much enthusiasm. She rode the elevator up to the sixth floor and found herself almost skipping down the lushly carpeted hall, then she pushed the key into the lock and opened the door. "Philip . . . Kathryn . . . anybody home?"

She heard familiar noises and realized it was the sound of the shower in her bathroom. What the hell, she thought, feeling reckless. Should she take off her clothes and join Philip in his midday ablutions? What was the old saying from the sixties? Save water—shower with a friend?

Philip would be surprised to see her. He had claimed several times that she lacked spontaneity. Perhaps he would be sufficiently stirred by her leaving work early and joining him in the shower that he might find time for a little love in the afternoon. It definitely beat arguing with Mrs. DeFlores's attorney.

"Renee?" A thin voice from another room. "Is that you?"

Renee followed the hollow sound to the guest bedroom. Kathryn was sitting up in bed, her blond hair disheveled, her green eyes clearly frightened, the white sheet pulled up tightly to just beneath her chin. Renee walked quickly to the side of her bed. "Kathryn, what's the matter? Are you all right? You look awful."

"I don't feel very well."

Renee reached for her sister's forehead and was surprised when Kathryn jerked quickly out of her reach, surprised also when she realized that underneath the sheet, Kathryn was nude.

"I don't have a fever."

"Maybe not, but look at you. You're perspiring. Maybe you need a doctor."

"It's just a little touch of flu," Kathryn protested, tears starting to form. "I've been trying to get some sleep."

"Oh, I'm sorry. Did I wake you?"

"No, it's all right."

Renee sat down on the bed beside her sister. Something in the air caught her attention momentarily but it disappeared before she had a chance to identify it. "Have you had anything to eat?"

Kathryn started to respond but froze at the sound of Philip's voice.

"What say we go out and grab an ice-cream cone?" he was saying as he approached the door, his hips wrapped in a familiar white towel, shaking his wet hair dry with a few careless tosses of his head. Renee's eyes shot from her sister, whose skin had turned whiter than the sheet with which she was protecting herself, to Philip, who was as imposing as ever despite the fact he was barely dressed. "Well, what do you say?" he continued without missing a beat. "I heard you come in and thought you might feel like a nice, cold ice cream." He looked toward Kathryn as if seeing her for the first time. "Hi, Kathryn. I didn't know you were home."

"I'm not feeling very well," Kathryn whispered. "I must have fallen asleep. I didn't hear you come in."

"Patient canceled, so I decided to come home early and relax, take a shower. It's hot out there today." He turned his attention back to Renee. "Well, what do you say? Feel like going out with your husband for a giant double-scoop ice cream in a chocolate waffle cone?"

Renee's face relaxed into a wide grin. "Sounds great."

"How about you, Kathryn?"

Kathryn shook her head. She looked like she was about to throw up.

"Kathryn probably shouldn't have any solid foods. I think the best thing you could do, Kathy, would be to just stay in bed and try to get some more sleep. I can make you some tea and toast, if you'd like . . ."

"No, nothing."

"We won't be long."

Kathryn nodded.

Renee stood up, drawing the blanket that lay crumpled around Kathryn's feet up over her shoulders. "You probably should put something on. You don't want to catch a chill." She leaned over to kiss Kathryn on the cheek, but Kathryn turned her head, burying her chin against her shoulder, and Renee's lips brushed against some stray wisps of her sister's hair instead. "You'll be all right," she said, wondering why the words sounded so hollow. Then she put her hand in Philip's and walked from the room.

19

In Lynn's dream, she was in Marc's apartment. They were in the middle bedroom, the one reserved for his sons' visits. The snake slept in its glass tank, and every now and then Lynn cast a wary eye in its direction.

"I know," Marc said, moving toward her. "You like things that jump."

In the next instant, they were on the larger bed in his room and he was removing her clothes. She felt his hands as they moved slowly up and down her body. She felt his beard brushing against the sides of her mouth. She sat up suddenly. "Let's play a game."

"I don't play games," he told her.

"I spy with my little eye," she said anyway, "something that is red."

"There's nothing in this room that's red. Everything's brown."

"I spy something that is red."

"But there's nothing red."

"Do you give up? Give up? Give up?"

The childish refrain turned into the ringing of a telephone. Because it was a dream, Lynn knew who was calling even before she answered it. It was her children announcing that they were alone in the house and that a strange man was trying to get in. "Lock the doors," she told them, running down the street toward her house. But her house wasn't where it was supposed to be. In its place was a small dance studio. Lynn raced to a phone booth which materialized at the corner.

"Mommy, help us," Megan cried. "The man is coming. He's getting in."

"Run," Lynn urged helplessly, not knowing where to find them.

"Where can we go?"

"Go to my half of the house," Lynn instructed, her voice rising. "He can't touch you as long as you're in my half of the house."

"Which half is yours?" the child asked.

Lynn looked up and down the deserted street for answers that refused to come. "I don't know," she said finally, seeing the shadow of the man as he reached for her children. "I don't know which half is mine."

Lynn opened her eyes with a start.

Megan and Nicholas were standing over her bed. "Happy birthday, Mommy," they chimed, almost, but not quite, in unison. Lynn reached up gratefully and encircled both children in her arms.

"Careful," Megan warned, backing gingerly away.

"What have you got there?"

Megan proudly displayed a small round cake covered with white icing and a row of delicate yellow flowers. Lynn scanned the words written across its top. "H.B. Mommy?" she asked.

"The lady in the store said there wasn't enough room to write Happy Birthday. Is this okay? She said you'd like it just the same."

"I love it," Lynn said truthfully, trying not to laugh. "When did you get it?"

"Yesterday. Mrs. Hart took us to the store before you got back from work." Mrs. Hart was the woman who lived a few doors away and who babysat whenever Lynn was going to be late. "She said to keep the cake in the refrigerator overnight but I didn't because I didn't want you to see it. I wanted to surprise you."

"*We* wanted to surprise you," Nicholas interjected testily. "It's not just from you. It's from me too."

"I paid for it," Megan told him haughtily.

"So? It was my idea."

"It was not."

"Children," Lynn said steadily, "it's a lovely cake and it was a lovely idea. It doesn't matter who paid for it or whose idea it was."

"It was mine," said Nicholas.

"Mine," insisted Megan.

"Where *did* you keep the cake?" Lynn asked warily.

"Under my bed."

"All night?"

"Is that okay?" Megan's eyes filled with fear.

"It's fine," Lynn said quickly. "I'm sure it will be delicious."

"Can we have some now?"

"For breakfast?"

"Yea," Nicholas shouted. "Cake for breakfast."

Lynn looked at the faces of her two beautiful children. If she had done nothing else right in forty years—my God, forty years—she had at least managed to produce two beautiful, healthy children. Please, God, she thought, don't let him take them away from me. "Oh, sure. Cake for breakfast. Why not?"

"I'll cut it," Megan exclaimed, running from the room.

"*I'll* cut it," Nicholas shouted after her.

"*I'll* cut it," Lynn told them, though she doubted that either of them heard. She followed them into the kitchen, where Megan had already deposited the cake in the middle of the table and was reaching for a knife. "*I'll* cut it," Lynn repeated.

"Why can't I do it?" Megan asked.

"All right," Lynn said, surprising herself. "You do it. Just be careful."

Megan beamed.

"Daddy's going to have a fit when he hears we had cake for breakfast," Nicholas said, laughing.

Lynn shuddered, feeling the shadowy figure from her dream return to surround the house. "You're cutting too big a piece, Megan."

Nicholas reached across the table and scooped up the enormous piece of cake. "First taste," he cried, stuffing it into his mouth.

"You're such a baby," Megan said.

"Okay, kids, we don't have time to fight. You still have to get dressed for camp and I have to get ready for work."

"You shouldn't have to work on your birthday," Nicholas pronounced, his mouth covered with white cake crumbs. "How old are you, Mommy?"

"She's forty," Megan answered, then looked at her mother with great concern. "How old was your mother when she died?"

"Sixty-two," Lynn told her, feeling strange, as she always did on her birthday, that the woman who had given birth to her was no longer here to help her celebrate. The look on Megan's face went from concern to dismay as she did the appropriate mathematics in her head. "I'll be around for a while yet," Lynn assured her quickly.

"What if something happens to you?"

"Nothing's going to happen to me."

"But what if something does? What if you're in an accident?"

"I won't be."

"But if you are. What happens to us if you get killed in a car crash or something?"

"I'm not going to get killed in any car crash," Lynn said with the certitude of someone who has the power to see into the future. "But if I do," she continued when she saw that Megan was unimpressed by her omniscience, "then you'll still have your father. He'll take care of you." Lynn forced these words out of her mouth with great difficulty, growing desperate for a cup of coffee. "But that's not going to happen." The phone rang. "I want a smaller piece of cake than that, please,"

Lynn told her daughter as she reached for the receiver.
"Hello?"

Lynn thought at first that the woman's voice on the other
end of the line belonged to her father's wife, Barbara, and that
she was calling to assure Lynn that today was the first day of
the rest of her life, so she was surprised when birthday congratulations were not forthcoming.

"You better get over here right now," the voice warned.

"What? Who is this?"

"They're getting away."

"I'm sorry, I think you have the wrong number."

"Lynn Schuster?"

"Yes, this is Lynn Schuster. Who is this?" A blurred picture
was beginning to develop in Lynn's mind.

"The Fosters are leaving town. The moving van is in front
of their place right now."

"What?"

The line went dead. Lynn replaced the receiver slowly. The
blurred photograph snapped into sharp focus, exposing Davia
Messenger, the Fosters' anxious neighbor, her geometric red
hair accentuating the hawklike features of her face.

"Mom, is everything all right?"

Lynn said nothing. Where could the Fosters be going? What
could she do to stop them?

"Are you going to have to leave?" Megan asked anxiously.

"Not till I've had my birthday cake," Lynn told her, watching her daughter's relieved grin spread across her face. "I love
you," Lynn said, hugging her two children close against her,
her thoughts with little Ashleigh Foster. "I can't begin to tell
you how much I love you."

"We love you too," Megan said.

"Can I have another piece of cake?" asked Nicholas.

"As soon as the kids left for camp, I drove out there,"
Lynn was explaining to her supervisor. Carl McVee, a short,
balding man, whose unfashionably long sideburns only accen-
tuated his baldness, sat behind his desk, leaning on his elbows,

his lips in an unattractive pout. "The house was empty. The moving van had already left. The Fosters, of course, were long gone. I called the moving van company. They wouldn't give me any information, but it's a local outfit. They don't travel out of state. So we know that the Fosters are still in Florida. I called Keith Foster's office. They said he'd transferred to another city, but they wouldn't tell me which one. I checked the locations of Data Base International. Their main office is in Sarasota, so that must be where they've gone. I called Stephen Hendrix, the Fosters' attorney . . ."

"I know."

"You know?"

"He called here immediately after he got off the phone with you."

"Then you know he was most uncooperative." Lynn decided she didn't like the way her boss was looking at her.

"On the contrary, I found Mr. Hendrix to be very cooperative indeed. He's agreed not to sue our office for harassment on the condition that . . ."

"What?!"

"On the condition that you leave his client alone."

"His client is a potentially dangerous man."

"His client is a very *important* potentially dangerous man. There's a big difference."

"You're telling me we do nothing?"

"Lynn, be reasonable. We *have* nothing."

"We have plenty. We have the testimony of a next-door neighbor . . ."

"A crazy lady who even you admitted in your report would not make a very impressive witness in court."

"We have Ashleigh's teacher, a Miss Harriet Templeton. I finally managed to get hold of her and she confirmed that Ashleigh didn't break her arm in any schoolyard accident."

"That doesn't prove Keith Foster did it."

"It proves he lied." Lynn paced angrily back and forth in front of McVee's desk. "I also managed to track down Keith Foster's second wife."

"Aren't you the great detective!"

Lynn ignored the sarcasm. "She said that the reason she divorced the great philanthropist was because he was becoming equally generous with his fists."

"Lynn, I admire your sleuthing, but really . . . the word of an ex-wife?"

"What's wrong with the word of an ex-wife?" Lynn caught a sudden, unwelcome glimpse into her future. The dreaded ex-wife! The image of herself as an inflatable doll slowly leaking air appeared before her eyes. She felt herself shrinking, becoming less valid as the conversation progressed.

"One might question her motives," McVee said coldly.

"One might question yours." There was a moment's silence. "I'm sorry. I just don't understand why you're so reluctant . . ."

"Lynn, we had a doctor examine the little girl, didn't we?"

"Yes, we . . ."

"He found no evidence of any abuse, isn't that right?"

"He found no evidence of abuse, that's right. But you know as well as I do how long the Fosters delayed bringing Ashleigh in here. Any bruises she might have had . . ."

"Are pure conjecture."

Lynn forced her gaze to the floor, afraid that her fury would show if she looked at her supervisor's face. Since when did he use phrases like "pure conjecture"? When did he get a law degree? "The Fosters refused permission to let me question their family doctor."

"Perfectly within their rights."

"I know that, but . . ."

"But nothing, Lynn. The case is closed."

Lynn continued as if he hadn't spoken. "But Patty Foster as much as admitted to me that her husband broke her daughter's arm."

"You badgered the poor woman into admitting that her husband has a temper."

"I did no such thing."

"Patty Foster's confession, if you will, tells us nothing except that the woman was distraught. In the next breath, she denies everything. Lynn, face it, we have nothing that we can take to court. Nothing we can use to force these people into counseling."

"We can . . ."

"We can do nothing. We *have* nothing," he repeated for what felt like the umpteenth time.

"We have a ticking time bomb."

"Aren't you being rather melodramatic?"

"I'd like permission to alert the child welfare agency in Sarasota."

"Permission denied." Now he sounded like a Supreme Court judge, Lynn thought, watching him lift and then drop her report on his desk for added emphasis. "I won't risk a lawsuit over evidence as flimsy as this."

"You're not one who normally caves in to outside pressure," Lynn said, trying a different tack, her attempt at flattery sounding as false as the words themselves. Carl McVee was notorious for caving in to pressure from any source.

"I don't call it pressure. I call it common sense." Lynn was about to object further when he added, "Something you seem to be a little short of these days." Whatever Lynn had been about to say froze in her throat. "People love to gossip, Lynn. Word gets around, even all the way up here to the second floor." He paused. "I understand there was quite a scene in your office last week."

"I'm not sure I understand what you're talking about. There are many scenes in my office."

"Involving your husband?"

Lynn said nothing, again directing her gaze to the floor.

"I understand that he was very upset about your recent behavior."

"I don't see where this has any relevance . . ." Lynn began, finding her voice, pushing the reluctant words out of her mouth.

"You've been with the department a long time, Lynn."

"Yes, I have. I still fail to see how my personal life has any bearing on what . . ."

"Sometimes we make errors in judgment. Sometimes these errors can spill over from one area of our lives into another."

"I did not leave my husband, Carl. He left me. The error in judgment was his, not mine."

"And this affair you're having with . . ."

"I'm not having an affair with anybody! How dare you imply . . ."

"All right, all right," McVee said, waving his hands as if he were warding off a physical attack, "perhaps I've overstated my case."

"I'd say you owe me an apology."

"I apologize," McVee said quickly.

Lynn sank into the chair across from his desk, seeing the inflatable doll collapse in a heap, the fight—as well as the air—gone out of her. She said nothing. She had nothing more to say.

Carl McVee came around the side of his desk and balanced his broad backside on the edge. "I really *am* sorry, Lynn. My remarks were uncalled for. You're the best front-line worker I have. But as far as the Foster case is concerned, all we really have are your instincts. A good lawyer—and Stephen Hendrix is a good lawyer—might argue that those instincts have been thrown slightly out of kilter lately."

So he really wasn't apologizing at all, Lynn realized. Just using the words of apology to remake his point.

"We can't save the world, Lynn. Some things are beyond our control."

"And so a little girl forfeits her childhood, maybe even loses her life, because you won't let me pick up a phone."

Carl McVee looked pained, but ignored the latter part of her remark. "We don't know that."

"We know exactly that." Lynn took a deep breath. "Is that all? Can I go?" Lynn was aware she had more than skirted the edge of rudeness, but she felt the overwhelming need to be out of this man's office before she pushed him through his second-story window.

McVee nodded, extricating his bottom from the corner of the desk and moving around behind it, about to sit down again, when he suddenly stopped and smiled at her as if seeing her for the first time today. "By the way," he said, "happy birthday."

20

Renee sat in her white Mercedes and stared at the house in which she had grown up, trying to persuade her body to move, her hand to open the car door. Why was it the same every time she came up here—the shortness of breath, the trembling in her fingers, the constriction in her chest? They were her parents, for God's sake. They loved her, even if they found the words difficult to express. Besides, she had never been one of those people who needed to hear "I love you" every day. They were only words, after all. They weren't that important. Yes, they were, Renee understood, folding her hands in her lap. Words were that important.

She sat behind the wheel of her car, directing her gaze to the front window of her parents' living room. The curtains were closed, as they always were, to the midday sun. Were her parents even at home? She should have called first. She knew her mother hated being caught off guard, that she was wary of surprises because they made her father uncomfortable. Renee looked at the small box wrapped in silver paper that sat on the seat beside her. It was her mother's birthday this week. It had been years since she'd bought her a present. Her father had decided when his daughters were still quite young that gift giving was an unnecessary expense. Renee couldn't remember the last time she had received anything from either of her parents on her birthday, although they had given her a generous check when she and Philip were married.

Renee checked her watch. It was half past one. Would her parents be home? Would they be on the golf course? She remembered that they played golf every Saturday. She just couldn't remember what time. If they were at home, would she be interrupting their lunch? She couldn't remember what time they ate. She should have called first to make sure they would be home. She should have called to make sure she wouldn't be disturbing their lunch. She shouldn't have come at all. Why was she here? "What am I doing here?" she asked out loud. "Why do I put myself through this?"

"Because you're still trying to please them," she heard Philip's voice reply with calm logic. "You're still trying to be Daddy's perfect little angel."

"But I never was. I was never his perfect little anything."

"But that's what you always wanted to be."

Was he right? Was that why she was here? Was that what she was doing wasting half a Saturday afternoon, one of the few times she had to herself, sitting in front of a house that had never been a real home to her, shivering with fear despite the intense heat, knowing that no matter what she said once she got inside that house, it was bound to be wrong? Why did she always seem to find herself in places she didn't want to be?

Philip rarely put himself in that position. "My time's too precious," he would say. "Life is too short." And he was right. Why should he spend his Saturday visiting people he had no use for? She didn't blame him for not wanting to come with her. Debbie would be returning to Boston at the end of next week—not soon enough, Renee thought guiltily—and it was only right that he chose to spend the day with her. She even understood the fact that he hadn't included her in their plans. It was important for a father to spend some time alone with the daughter he too seldom saw. Renee looked back toward her parents' house. It had never been very important to her own father.

She had hoped she could persuade Kathryn to join her. But Kathryn had simply shaken her head no and crawled back inside her bed, lifting the sheet over her head, refusing to discuss it.

Since the afternoon Renee had come home from work early to find her sister in bed, Kathryn had spent the better part of the week in her room. She had no fever, no outward symptoms of flu, but she ate little and said less. Any progress she had made in the almost eight weeks of her visit seemed to be rapidly disappearing. She was retreating into herself again, becoming silent and withdrawn. Renee had mentioned her concern to Philip, who said he'd try to talk to Kathryn again, do whatever he could to help.

He was a good man, Renee thought, understanding for the first time that her family must be as big a trial for him as his was for her.

The image of her sister, pale and frightened, appeared in the reflection of Renee's car window. She saw Kathryn sitting in her bed, pulling the white sheet up around her chin. She saw Philip in the doorway, the white towel draped expertly around his hips. "What say we go out for an ice-cream cone?" he had asked.

A small black-and-brown dog ran by Renee's car and barked, scaring the image away. Good, Renee thought, though she wasn't sure why. She watched the dog bark indignantly at her unwarranted intrusion onto his territory, and then make a hasty retreat. Renee could tell he was an old dog by the way his backside waddled as he ran, as if it couldn't quite catch up to where the rest of him was headed. Just like me, she thought, except I don't even *know* where I'm headed. "Yes, I do," she said out loud, full of sudden, fresh resolve. "I'm headed inside that house. I'm going in there and I'm going to confront those two people who claim to be my parents and I'm going to tell them that I love them. And I'm not going to leave that house until I hear them tell me the same thing."

Renee didn't move. She sat behind the wheel of her white Mercedes. "See that car out there?" she heard herself say to them. "That's *my* car. My husband, Philip, bought it for me. He's handsome and successful and every woman who sees him wants to get her hands on him, but he's mine. He loves *me*. And he bought me that car because he's like you, not very good at telling other people how he feels." Renee fingered the small gift-wrapped parcel on the seat beside her. I love you, Mommy, she thought. Do you love me? Do you love me, Daddy? What can I give you that will make you love me?

She remembered that when she was a little girl they were always taking things away from her. First it was her thumb that they prodded from her mouth, initially with cruel taunts, then with strong fingers, and finally, when those tactics failed to dissuade her, with the aid of some foul-tasting liquid. Next to go was her favorite blanket, a blanket she had cradled since infancy, little more than a flannel rag by the time it entered its fifth year. "You're too old for blankey now," they told her, using the baby word she had discarded years ago, and even though she hid the blanket from them each morning when she left for school, sometimes under the mattress, sometimes folded inside her underwear, always in a different place, she had come home one day to find it gone. "You're too old for blankey now," they told her again when she howled her protest, and then left her to cry in her room with neither her thumb nor her blanket for solace.

"This is ridiculous. What is the point of rehashing this now? I'm being stupid," Renee said, pushing open her car door and stepping out onto the street. A few roadside pebbles immediately found their way into her sandals. "Great," she said, reaching over to dislodge them, almost losing her balance, and barely managing to rescue the gift before it fell to the ground. "Off to a good start." She looked both ways, the way she had been taught as a child—were they watching her?—and then crossed the street, deliberately sidestepping the concrete path that led to the front door of her parents' house in favor of the freshly manicured grass. She kicked off her sandals, shaking free a pebble that had stubbornly wedged between her toes, and dug the soles of her feet into the temperamental Florida grass.

The lawn was kept green—so green it seemed to vibrate—by an underground sprinkler system, something that was more necessity than luxury in the Florida heat. Without constant care and nurturing, the grass simply turned to hay. Just like the rest of us, Renee thought, her hands brushing up against the small bushes that clustered in the middle of the front lawn. The bushes were neatly trimmed into the shapes of pelicans and small horses. "It's called a topiary," her mother had explained to her when she was a child, "and you're not to touch the bushes or sit on them," she warned. Of course, only minutes later, Renee had tried to mount one of the delicate horse's backs and had received a sound spanking for her misdeeds.

Renee now patted the top of the green pelican's head, then crossed in a diagonal to the front door. She thought of the bedroom she had shared with Kathryn, decorated in traditional Florida yellows and greens. Her parents favored large furniture and small objects of art, or so her mother had always referred to her ever-increasing collection of china dolls.

Renee reached the front door and brought her unsteady fingers to the bell. She wondered if her parents were home, what part of the house they were in, what room she would be bringing them from. She remembered that no matter where she had been as a child, her parents always seemed to be somewhere else, and she always managed to disturb them.

She pressed the front doorbell, heard the gentle musical chimes waft through the cool interior of the house. She heard a voice—"I'm coming"—the sound of high heels (her mother never wore less than three-inch heels, even around the house) clicking against the tile of the living-room floor as they approached the front door.

Renee slipped her sandals back on as the front door opened. "Renee." There was no element of surprise in the woman's voice. The name was pronounced plainly, as if she were a teacher checking her attendance sheet at school. And yet there was a slight flicker in the older woman's eyes, an almost imperceptible widening that told Renee that her mother was not altogether indifferent to her visit.

"Are you going to invite me in?" Renee asked her mother, who had changed remarkably little over the years. She was still the beautiful woman Renee conjured up in childhood memories, with the high cheekbones and cool green eyes she had passed on to her older daughter, features that could have made her a successful model had she been taller and so inclined. Renee's mother stepped aside and allowed her into the living room, which opened off the front door.

Helen Metcalfe wore a pale pink jersey over a pair of uncreased white linen pants. She was as trim as when Renee had last seen her, and her hair had been attractively shaped to complement her delicate face. Not someone guaranteed to strike fear into a person's heart, Renee thought. And yet that's exactly what she does to me. Renee stood in the middle of the predominantly yellow room, feeling as if she were standing in the middle of a cold bright sun, and wondered if her mother would ask her to sit down. Hesitantly, she handed her mother the small package. "For your collection," Renee told her, extending the silver-wrapped parcel for her mother to take.

"This was unnecessary," Helen Metcalfe said evenly, looking warily over her shoulder, her hands neatly unfolding the silver paper even as she spoke.

"Well, I remembered it's your birthday this week, and I saw it in a store window on the way over. I hope you don't already have one like it."

Helen Metcalfe removed the delicate figurine from its tissue paper, turning it around in her fingers and examining it from all angles.

"It's Pan," Renee told her.

"It's lovely."

"Do you already have a Pan?"

"One can never have too many Pans," her mother told her with a timid smile, walking across the room to the yellow-tinted upright piano in the far corner, and depositing the fragile figurine in the middle of the others, so that it could not be seen without effort. "Thank you. That was really very sweet of you."

"You can take it back if you'd prefer something else. I have the bill."

"It's fine," her mother said, but she took the bill from Renee's trembling hand.

"How are you?" Renee asked awkwardly, wishing her mother would ask her to sit down, not because she wanted to stay longer than was absolutely necessary, but because she was afraid that her knees might give way.

"We've been fine," her mother said, answering in the plural so as to include Renee's father, who walked into the room from the back garden as she was speaking.

"Hello, Daddy," Renee whispered.

Ian Metcalfe looked toward the front door. "I thought I heard someone come in." He looked toward his wife. "To what do we owe the honor of this visit?"

"I wanted to see you," Renee said simply. "It's Mother's birthday this week . . ."

"That's never meant much to you before," her father pointed out, still not looking at her, his body sinking into one of two yellow tub chairs, his eyes staring straight ahead at the closed curtains.

Renee felt her breathing stall. Her father was an imposing figure, even sitting down. She forced herself into the second tub chair, hoping to will his eyes toward hers, and realizing with a shudder that neither her mother nor her father had tried to embrace her. That's all it would take to make me happy, to make us a family, she tried to tell them silently with her eyes. Just put your arms around me and tell me that you love me.

It's so little. It's too much.

"I don't want to fight with you, Daddy," Renee said patiently. "I thought we could have a nice visit."

"Renee brought me a birthday present, a little figurine of Pan," she heard her mother say, and felt an immediate rush of gratitude. She smiled at her mother, but her mother was looking only at her father.

"So, all of a sudden you want to visit," her father said. "You live ten minutes away but you're usually too busy to drop by, too busy to pick up the phone."

"I *do* call, but you're always on your way out the door and I didn't think you liked me to just drop by."

"You dropped by now."

"Well, I remembered that it's Mother's birthday this week, so I thought I'd take a chance. I wasn't even sure you'd be here."

"Normally, we wouldn't be," her mother agreed. Was she coming to her rescue again? "We'd be playing golf. But your father's back has been acting up lately."

"Helen, I'm sure our daughter isn't interested in my health."

"That's not true, Daddy. Of course I'm interested. What's the matter with your back?"

Her father waved away her concern. "You get old, you get pains in your back. So," he continued, looking at his daughter with a critical eye, "I see you're healthy. Eating well," he added.

"I've put on a few pounds." Renee tugged at her blouse self-consciously.

Her father laughed. "Did they teach you understatement at that fancy law school you went to?"

"You *should* go on a diet," her mother warned with genuine concern. "Philip's a very handsome man. I'm sure you want to hold on to him."

"Philip likes the way I look," Renee told them, trying to underline her words with a smile.

"I could never tolerate obesity in a woman," Ian Metcalfe stated flatly, unmindful of his own increased girth. "Your mother is the same weight now as when we got married. Getting fat is just being lazy and lacking self-control. So," he said again as Renee braced herself for what might follow, "you decided to pay us a visit. I guess we're supposed to be glad to see you."

"I hoped you would be." How could they be? She was fat and lazy and lacking in self-control.

"And grateful too, I suppose."

"No, not grateful . . ."

"We would be grateful to receive an occasional invitation to dinner at your beautiful apartment."

"I *have* invited you. You're always busy." People stop extending invitations when they get repeatedly turned down, she thought, wondering again how many firm get-togethers she had missed lately. "Actually, I was thinking of having a small dinner party next week. Kathryn is in town," she said slowly, not sure this was the right path to follow, but stuck now, "and I thought it would be nice if we could all get together." Could they tell she was lying?

"I didn't know Kathy was in Florida," her mother said. "She should have called . . ."

"Kathryn can call us if she wants to see us," her father said, interrupting his wife and ignoring Renee's invitation.

Renee tried to laugh but the result was more like a harsh cough. "The phone works both ways," she reminded them.

"What's that supposed to mean?"

"Just what I said." Renee was suddenly on her feet despite her best efforts to remain calm. "Why does it always have to be me or Kathryn who calls? You're perfectly capable of picking up a phone and dialing. Why don't you ever call *me?* Why don't you ever ask Philip and me over *here* for dinner? Why can't you just call every now and then and ask how I'm feeling, ask me what's new. You know where I am. You know where to reach me. You know Kathryn's number in New York. You can afford the long-distance charges. How can you be surprised she didn't phone you? Her husband died a few months ago, and you couldn't even break away from your golf game long enough to offer your condolences!"

"Kathryn is a big girl now. She doesn't need to come running to her father and mother whenever things don't work out."

"A husband's death is a little more than things just not working out. Do you really think that because she's grown up she doesn't need you?"

"She knows where we are," her father reiterated.

"She tried to kill herself!" Renee exclaimed in sheer frustration, waiting for them to respond. They said nothing, although Helen Metcalfe's face was momentarily drained of color. "Where have you been all her life?" Where have you been all *my* life? she had to bite her tongue to keep from adding, knowing she had already gone too far.

"How long has she been in town?" her mother asked, her voice a thin sliver.

"Not long," Renee lied again. Had her mother even heard what she had said? Had she heard Renee tell her Kathryn had tried to end her life? *How long has she been in town?* Renee repeated silently, wondrously. "Why don't you phone her? She's staying with me, and I know she'd like to hear from you."

"It's not our place to call," Ian Metcalfe said, staring straight ahead, again refusing to look at his daughter.

"What are you talking about? What do you mean, it isn't your place?"

"Kathryn is visiting you from out of town," her mother said patiently, explaining her husband's position as if she were conducting a class on etiquette. "It's up to her to call."

"I don't believe what I'm hearing." Renee kicked at the base of the small chair on which she had been sitting so that it spun around aimlessly. "Have you no feelings for her at all? Can't you forget about your wounded pride for a few minutes and try to imagine what she's been going through? She tried to kill herself and you're worried about what Miss Manners might say if you were to call Kathryn first?!"

Her father rose to his feet. "It's always the same thing, isn't it, Renee? We're supposed to drop everything and think about what you and your sister might be going through. It doesn't matter to *you* what your mother and I might be going through, what you might have *put* us through all these years. No, none of that counts. Only your feelings are important. You were always selfish children. I had hoped with marriage you'd outgrow it. I thought there was a chance for you when you married Philip . . ."

"You really must lose some weight, Renee," her mother cautioned, and Renee thought for an instant that she was trapped in the middle of another one of her peculiar dreams. Surely they weren't really talking about her weight after she had just informed them of Kathryn's suicide attempt! "You managed to get a man like Philip Bower to marry you. You don't want to lose him, do you? You're not beautiful like Kathryn, but you used to have such a pretty smile." Helen Metcalfe's voice drifted off, faded away, as if she had said the unspeakable.

Renee stared at her mother in disbelief, not because she continued to ignore the news of what Kathryn had done, which was the way her mother had always dealt with unpleasantness of any sort, not even because of her old-fashioned, long-held belief that marriage was the one essential ingredient of a woman's life, but because it was the first time in thirty-four years that her mother had ever told her to her face that she found anything about her pretty. It stunned her now to hear her mother say it. "You think I have a pretty smile?" Renee asked, forgetting the woman's earlier insensitivity, wanting only to rush into her arms. She felt her body gravitate toward her.

"Pretty is as pretty does," Helen Metcalfe said, and Renee's body swayed to a halt.

"She said you *used* to have a pretty smile," Ian Metcalfe continued for his wife. "Now, of course, nobody would notice. It's not just your weight. It's everything. Look at your clothes. Look at your hair. We'll have to start calling you Hairless Joe again, the way we did when you were little and wouldn't sit still long enough for your mother to brush your hair properly."

Renee recalled the long-forgotten nickname, based, if she remembered correctly, on a comic-strip character who had so much hair falling into his face that he could barely see to walk. She had thought she remembered every aspect of her childhood. How could she have forgotten that?

"You expect the world to revolve around you," her father continued. "You expect everybody to drop everything and jump to attention when you snap your fingers."

"I expect a little common decency," Renee said, as angry now as he was.

"Then have some," her father shot back. "And don't raise your voice to me again, young lady."

"Please, Daddy, I don't want to fight with you. That's not why I came over."

"Why did you?" her father demanded.

"I told you. It's Mother's birthday. I just wanted to see you."

"Why?"

"You're my parents. I love you!" Renee cried, and felt the room spin.

"You have a very strange way of showing it," her father said, his anger turning to rage. Renee thought for a moment that he might actually strike her.

"Why do you get so angry when I mention love?" Renee asked, astounded.

"I'm not angry."

"Yes, you are."

"That's always been your problem, Renee. You think you know everything."

"I just told you that I love you, dammit."

"You will not swear in this house," her father warned.

"What is the matter with you?"

"We will not be talked to in that manner, Renee," her father stated, his anger now a cold fury as he walked to the front door. "I'm afraid you'll have to leave before you upset your mother further."

"No!" Renee screamed, and watched them both jump. "No. I'm not leaving this house until you listen to me." She walked toward them, noticing a look of fear creep into her mother's eyes. "I have just told you that I love you. That is probably the first time the word 'love' has ever been spoken in this room, maybe even in this house, and you can ignore what you want to ignore, you can pretend that Kathryn didn't try to kill herself, that I'm making all this up for my own cruel purposes, but I won't let you ignore that I just stood in front of you and told you that I love you. And I am not leaving until I hear you say that *you* love *me!* Do you understand? I am not going anywhere until I hear you say it. I am thirty-four years old but I am still your child. And I have never heard you tell me that you love me."

Her parents said nothing. Were they too stunned to speak or were the words so impossible to say?

"Don't you think it's time you told me you love me? Don't you think I've waited long enough?"

"Renee . . ." her mother began wearily, her voice cracking. "Where is this getting us?"

"I want to hear you say it. I want to hear you tell me you love me. What's the matter? Can't you say it? *Don't* you love me? Not even a little bit?"

"Renee . . ." her mother pleaded, glancing toward her father. "This is so unnecessary."

"It's not unnecessary. It's everything! Please, I'm begging you. I need to hear you say it."

"But why? Why is it so important?"

"I don't know why."

"This is nonsense, Renee."

"I'm not leaving until you say it."

Again, there was silence. Renee studied the faces of her mother and father, watched their mouths open only to close, saw the confusion in their eyes, the tremor in their lips. Slowly, she approached her mother, stopping only when she was within inches of the older woman's still lovely face. "Do you love me, Mommy?" she asked, hearing the voice of the little girl who was still locked inside her.

"You make it very difficult, Renee."

"Does that mean that you love me?" Renee persisted stubbornly.

"You're my daughter. A mother has to love her child." She looked toward her husband.

"No, don't look at him," Renee admonished. "Look at me. Tell me that you love me." Please.

Her mother's response was a few silent tears. Renee waited for the woman to speak, understanding that it was not her mother who had failed but herself. She was unloved because she was unlovable. She was fat and lazy and lacking in self-control.

"Daddy?" she cried, staggering toward her father. "Can't

you say it? Is it really so hard for you to tell me that you love me?"

For the first time since Ian Metcalfe had walked into the living room and confronted his daughter, he looked directly into her eyes. Renee found herself holding her breath as he opened his mouth to speak.

"Of course we love you, Renee," he said, and then looked down at the floor.

Renee stood absolutely still in the middle of the room. It hadn't been the way she'd expected it at all. All these years waiting to hear her father say these words, and then when she finally forced him to read from her script, she discovered that the words had no meaning. There'd been no release, no great meeting of souls, nothing but the words themselves. "Of course we love you, Renee," she heard him repeat in her mind, not the way she had been expecting the words to sound at all.

She looked from her father to her mother, who turned away, unable to meet her gaze. What had she accomplished? What had she hoped to achieve? She had forced two people into reluctantly confronting their emotions. She had finally gotten her father to speak the words she had been so desperate all these years to hear, and yet her victory was a hollow one, at best. "Of course we love you," her father had said, speaking for himself and his wife in that way they both had of speaking for one another, thereby not individually admitting to anything at all.

What had she hoped to gain? A long-lost mother and father? The heartfelt embrace at the end of the story? The final, fade-out kiss? The happy ending?

What difference did it make to her life whether or not her father loved her? Or her mother? "Why is it so important?" her mother had asked. Why are words so important? she asked herself as she fled the house, then answered through her tears, "Because they just are."

21

Lynn sat at her desk, trying to force her thoughts into words. She had been working on the same report for over an hour, trying to organize sentences that refused to take shape, to record observations she was no longer sure of, put forth recommendations that probably wouldn't be of any help to anyone. What was the point? she thought, closing the file. She'd lived long enough to know that people, unlike the words that represented them on paper, could rarely be corralled into neat phrases.

She glanced nervously at the photographs of her two children. Goddamn you, Gary Schuster, she thought angrily. How can you put us through this? She looked at her watch. It was eleven o'clock. In three hours she and Renee would be meeting with Gary and his attorney to decide the future of her family. "How could you do this to me?" Lynn banged her fist on her desk, watching the photographs of her children jump in seeming surprise. "What about the flowers you sent me on our anniversary? What about that dumb card? All those wonderful years you alluded to, your desire to remain friends for many

more? What was all that?" Just a bunch of words, Lynn
thought angrily, reorganizing the papers her fist had disturbed.
"You don't want to be friends now, do you? You want something else. Isn't that right? You want our house sold so you can
claim your half of the profits. You want our children, or at least
you say you do. Renee says you don't really want them at all.
She says it's a common trick husbands use to get their wives to
reduce their settlement demands. She says to let her handle it,
to let the professionals do their jobs. The same thing I'm always telling everybody around here. Words, more words."

The door to Lynn's office opened. Arlene stood in the doorway, a worried look on her face. "Is everything all right in
here? I thought I heard you yelling." The young woman looked
to either side, her ponytail bobbing along behind her.

"Everything's fine. I was just rehearsing a speech."

"A speech?"

Lynn said nothing. The problem with lying was that you
always had to tell more lies to cover up for the first one. Lynn
decided one was enough. Arlene lingered in the doorway for
another few seconds and then retreated, closing the door behind her. "Get a grip," Lynn whispered to herself. "Trust your
lawyer." Trust. Lynn winced. She had trusted her husband.
Where had that gotten her? She was forty years old and facing
life again as if she were twenty. Gary hadn't even acknowledged her fortieth birthday. He'd relayed no messages through
either his lawyer or his children. That she had turned forty was
no longer any concern of his. She was of concern to him only
so far as she was an inconvenience. She existed now as something to be gotten rid of, to be excised from his life. The ex-
wife, she thought, feeling instantly diminished.

The phone rang, then stopped almost immediately. Arlene's
voice came over the intercom. "A man on line one. He
wouldn't give his name."

Lynn picked up the phone. "Lynn Schuster," she said
clearly, glad for the diversion.

"Happy birthday," Marc Cameron told her, without identifying himself. "I know I'm a few days late and I know you

asked me not to call, but I wanted to wish you good luck this afternoon."

"Thank you." Lynn was afraid to say more. She felt her body tense and understood she was angry though she couldn't say why. What had happened wasn't Marc's fault. It wasn't fair for her to blame him for what Gary was doing. Still, she recognized it was easier, more comfortable, to blame Marc—to blame Gary—than to put the blame where it really belonged— on herself.

"Please call me later and let me know what happens."

"If I can." She was about to hang up.

"Lynn . . . ?"

"Yes?"

"Would it upset you very much if I told you I think I'm falling in love with you?"

Lynn felt the breath catch in her lungs. "I'm not sure," she said quietly. "Maybe you better not tell me now."

"Call me later," he said. "I'll tell you then."

Lynn sat in the waiting room of Renee's office trying not to think about what Marc had said or what Gary would say. Everything will be all right, she repeated inside her head, like a mantra. Everything will be all right. Would it?

She thought of an earlier visit to Renee's office. "Why would you want to see this man again?" Renee had asked her after learning of Marc's initial visit. "Do you want to see how far you can go to really mess up your life?"

Well, she had certainly seen. Had she gone too far?

The door to Renee's office opened and Renee emerged looking ready for action, if a little tired around the edges. "Sorry I kept you waiting. Come on in."

Lynn followed Renee into the now familiar room, taking her usual seat on the wrong side of the hopelessly cluttered desk, watching as Renee walked over to the window to look down at the central courtyard. "Pretty day," Renee said.

"I hadn't noticed."

"Nervous?"

"Why should I be nervous? It's just my life that's on the line."

Renee laughed. "I have a story for you. It's supposed to be true, but I have my doubts."

Lynn fidgeted nervously in her chair. She really wasn't in the mood for any stories.

"Supposedly this old couple, both around ninety-five years old, walked into their lawyer's office and told him that they wanted a divorce after over seventy years of marriage. The lawyer looked at these two old coots and couldn't believe his ears. He couldn't help but ask why after all these years, and at their ages, they'd bother getting a divorce. They told him that they'd wanted a divorce for decades, but that they'd been waiting for their children to die."

Lynn stared at Renee dumbfounded.

"It's supposed to be funny. It's a joke. It's supposed to relax you and make you laugh."

Lynn managed a weak smile. "I guess I'm too nervous to laugh." She twisted her hands inside the folds of her beige skirt.

"Don't worry. This is going to be like taking candy from a baby. And speaking of candy, are you hungry?" Lynn shook her head. "Coffee?" Lynn nodded. Renee pressed the button on her intercom. "Marilyn, can you bring us two cups of coffee. How do you take it?"

"Black."

"One black, one with double cream and sugar. Don't be nervous, Lynn. It'll all work out, I promise you."

Marilyn arrived a few minutes later with the coffee. Lynn noticed a number of empty chocolate bar wrappers in the wastepaper basket beside Renee's desk.

"I can't say you didn't warn me," Lynn said, afraid to meet her attorney's eyes.

"Thank God for that," Renee joked, obviously hoping to elicit a smile. Lynn obliged her by lifting her mouth slightly at the edges.

"Everything that you predicted is happening."

"Such as?"

"Such as I've screwed up a perfectly decent separation agreement, for one thing. For another, my boss knows, or thinks he knows, about my relationship with Marc Cameron. He questioned my professional judgment. A little girl's life may have been jeopardized because I lost my credibility. Gary is threatening to take my children away from me because he thinks Marc and I are having an affair. He questions my competence as a parent. Apparently, the whole town is talking. Everyone is convinced I'm having an affair with Marc. And part of me is screaming, 'Why didn't you?' I'm being blamed for it anyway. If I'm going to have to go to jail regardless, I might as well be guilty."

"Nobody is going to take your children away. Trust me. I won't let him."

"I wish I had your self-confidence."

"I wish I had your waistline."

The buzzer sounded. Lynn jumped as Marilyn's voice came over the speaker phone. "Mr. Emerson and Mr. Schuster are here. I sent them to the conference room."

"Thank you," Renee told her, looking over at Lynn. "Ready?"

"Ready or not."

"You have to understand," Renee Bower was saying as she circled the round conference table, forcing all eyes to follow her, "that this most recent offer of settlement is entirely unacceptable. In fact, this whole sudden turn of events strikes me as little more than a scare tactic to get Mrs. Schuster to accept less than her due."

"My client has a right to half the matrimonial home."

"May I remind you that your client is the one who walked out of that home when he left his wife and two children for another woman? I'd say he forfeited any rights he had in that department." Renee looked at the copy of the original settlement offer in her hands. "Your client as much as admitted this and accepted his culpability when he made the original offer of

settlement. We see no reason to alter the terms that were originally stipulated."

"Circumstances have changed."

"Have they? Perhaps you could tell me how."

"My wife is aware of how," Gary Schuster answered, instead of his lawyer, and Lynn winced.

"Perhaps you should tell me anyway," Lynn heard Renee
say, then watched her sit down in one of the large leather arm-
chairs to wait for his response.

Lynn found her eyes drifting toward the face of the handsome man on the other side of the table, wondering if this was
really the same man who had shared her life for so many years.
He seemed the same physically, tall and blond, with a year-
round tan and a pleasant speaking voice not generally given to
anger. But his normally soft brown eyes were, if not quite hard
and cold, then detached, indifferent to her pain. He was wearing a light blue suit, almost identical in cut and color to the one
worn by his attorney, who was dark-haired and pale by com-
parison, and, judging by the thin line of black hairs struggling
to life along his upper lip, trying to add years to his youthful
appearance by growing a mustache.

Paul Emerson had the unfortunate affliction, at least for
members of the legal profession, of looking scarcely older than
a boy, although Renee had told her he was several years her
senior. Renee had faced him before and told Lynn he was a
good lawyer and a reasonable man. He had been married for
close to eighteen years to his high school sweetheart and they
had six children. Renee had told Lynn she felt he had been
pressured to adopt this tough stance by his client.

Lynn coughed nervously into her hands and Renee smiled
in her direction, telling her without the necessity of words to
straighten her shoulders and stare her husband firmly in the
eye. Refuse to be intimidated, she commanded silently, watching as Lynn subtly assumed control of her body, shifting her
weight, turning her head back toward the man whose bed she
had shared for fourteen years.

"At the time I made this offer, I wasn't aware of my wife's
involvement with another man."

"What man is that, Mr. Schuster?"

"She knows." Gary Schuster looked accusingly at his wife. Lynn stared right back, her eyes growing angry.

"Suppose you tell us anyway."

"Marc Cameron," came the terse reply.

"Cameron . . . Cameron," Renee muttered, her eyes scanning the high ceiling. "Sounds like a familiar name. I wonder where I've heard it . . ."

"All right, counselor," Paul Emerson interrupted, as Renee had obviously known he would, "we concede the connection."

"Marc Cameron is the husband of the woman your client ran off with?"

"I didn't run anywhere," Gary Schuster said adamantly. "I'm right here."

"So you are." Renee smiled, adjusting the collar of her navy suit. "And you're still involved with Marc Cameron's wife, is that correct?"

Gary Schuster nodded, and looked to his lawyer impatiently.

"My client's circumstances have not altered," Paul Emerson said.

"Neither have those of mine."

"Are you saying that your client is not seeing Marc Cameron?"

"My client may have had meetings with Mr. Cameron to discuss their mutual interests in this complicated matter."

"You're saying that the relationship is not a romantic one?" Gary's lawyer said.

"Suzette saw them together at his apartment, for God's sake," Gary interjected.

"And when was that?"

Gary sat back in his chair. "A couple of weeks ago."

"Can you be more specific?"

"Saturday, August the third. Around one o'clock. Is that specific enough?"

"One o'clock in the afternoon?" Renee asked quickly, almost innocently. "She saw them together at one o'clock in the afternoon?" Gary said nothing. "Not in the evening? But one o'clock in the afternoon? I'm sorry. Is that what you said?"

"Yes, that's what I said." Gary's voice rose, then lowered, his eyes darting back and forth between the two women. "Look, are you trying to tell me that there's nothing going on?"

"I'm not trying to tell you anything, Mr. Schuster. I'm merely trying to point out to you that, owing to the fact that you ran off with his wife, Marc Cameron's meeting with *your* wife is not altogether unheard of, and that if you insist on holding up the settlement agreement you yourself originally proposed because of it, or trying to intimidate your wife into signing something that is clearly not in her best interests, then you will have a well-earned fight on your hands." She picked up Gary's latest offer of settlement. "This offer is garbage, gentlemen, and you know it. Frankly, Paul, I'm surprised you're not embarrassed to be involved with this. At any rate, we have no intention of giving in to what I consider little more than emotional blackmail." She continued speaking over Paul Emerson's loud objections. "If you want to go to court, well then, go right ahead. We're quite prepared to go to court. But just what is it exactly that you hope to accomplish once we get there? What is a judge looking at this divorce action going to see? Will he see a bad wife and mother, one who willfully neglected her husband and children, who played around with other men, who gambled, cheated, or otherwise abused her marriage vows? No, he'll see a woman whose husband walked out on her and their two children after fourteen relatively strife-free years of marriage.

"And what did the wife do then? Was she bitter? Was she spiteful? Did she try to take her husband for everything he had? No. She instructed her lawyer that she wasn't out for blood. She wanted only to be fair. She even consented to her husband's desire to get their marriage over with as quickly as possible, despite the obvious pain it caused her. She was preparing to agree to the settlement he had offered. As far as she was concerned, there were only a few minor points that her lawyer felt needed ironing out. And then one evening, the husband of the woman her husband abandoned her for called and suggested they meet, that there were some things he felt they should discuss, and the husband found out about it and his nose got all out of joint, for reasons that are known only to him. He made threats. He decided he wanted what he suddenly thought of as his half of the house, though he'd been quite willing to leave it, and he wanted his children, though he'd walked out on them easily enough. He hadn't even thought enough about their welfare to take care of their day camp expenses. He let his wife worry about things like that, the way she always had."

Lynn watched the pained look that crossed Gary's face, invaded the formerly neutral territory of his eyes. "I don't think that even you, Mr. Schuster, would try to argue that your wife is a bad mother. In fact, she's a pretty terrific mother. Isn't that so? Her training as a social worker gives her a particular insight into the needs of her children, and she's always there for them when they get home from school and from camp. Unlike their father, who often has to work late hours, and now finds himself busy with his new family."

Renee paused just long enough for her words to sink in. "Suzette Cameron, I believe, is the mother of two boys." Lynn found herself holding her breath, afraid of what might follow. "I wonder how she'd feel were her husband to make similar threats for custody of his children?" Both Gary and Lynn Schuster's eyes shot to her attorney. "Probably as distraught as my client, if not more so, considering the evidence that could be used against her, the fact that she has committed adultery, not just with Gary Schuster, but, from what I understand, with several other gentlemen as well."

Despite his tan, Gary Schuster turned ghostly pale. "What the hell are you talking about?" He was on his feet. "Is this some sort of threat?"

Renee stared at him with resolute calm. Lynn felt the room spinning. She dug her fingers into the gentle curve of the table. "I never make idle threats, Mr. Schuster. In truth, I have absolutely no idea what plans Marc Cameron may or may not have with regard to his children, but I can assure you that Mrs. Schuster will fight you with everything in her power to hold on to hers, even if it means some unfortunate disclosures with regard to Suzette Cameron's past indiscretions. I can't believe that you are really serious in your intention to sue for custody, nor do I think you really want a lengthy court battle which would prove not only costly but futile. It will delay your eagerly sought-after divorce and ultimately put you no further ahead. No judge in his right mind would award you custody of your children given the evidence, and you know it. You're a lawyer. I don't have to tell you that judges deal in facts. You have only jealous suspicions, for which a judge is likely to tell you to mind your own business." She paused, and Lynn understood it was as much for effect as to catch her breath. "Also, you should know that in the event that you do file this petition, I intend to counterfile. My client has been very generous up to this point in forgoing her right to alimony. Considering her husband's vastly superior income, and his intention to fight her for half the house, she will no longer be in a position to be so generous, especially with an expensive court battle looming on the horizon." Renee handed Gary's attorney a copy of the counterpetition she had drafted. "Much as I love a good fight, I hope we'll be able to settle this matter out of court, and as quickly as I'm sure we'd all like. Why don't you take a while and look this over. We'll be in my office if there are any further questions."

"We hurt Gary," Lynn said sadly after her husband and his lawyer had left the building. She was standing by Renee's window, watching as Gary walked angrily across the center courtyard toward the street. "I think he saw himself as Suzette Cameron's knight in shining armor. I don't think he considered that there might have been others before him." She paused, struggling for the correct way to phrase her next question. "Do you think it was right to use what Marc told me about Suzette's other affairs the way we did?" Lynn thought it only proper to assume at least partial responsibility for her lawyer's actions. She had told her to use whatever she could, do whatever was necessary.

"Isn't that why Marc Cameron contacted you in the first

place? To tell you some things he thought you should know? Well, it turns out he did just that."

"I don't think that when he told me those things about Suzette, he thought I would use them to hurt her."

"Didn't he?"

The question hung in the air like the scent of an unpleasant perfume.

"You were very impressive in there. Awesome," Lynn said, and Renee laughed. "I mean it. I owe you."

"Don't worry. You'll get my bill."

"You know what I mean. If there's ever anything I can do . . ."

"How about lunch one day next week?"

"I'd like that." Lynn looked back out the window at the now empty center courtyard. "What now?"

Renee smiled, holding up a copy of the signed agreement. "Well, I have to admit that even I was surprised that they signed so quickly. We kind of took the wind out of their sails, I guess. Anyway, we have our agreement; the children stay with their mother; the house is yours. We lost out on some of the fine print I was trying to nail down, but that was just the icing on the cake anyway. We'll proceed with the divorce." Her smile widened. "We have the agreement, Lynn. You're free to do whatever you please."

"And Marc Cameron?"

"That's entirely up to you."

22

As soon as Lynn left her office, Renee reached into her desk drawer for a chocolate bar and was dismayed to find the bag empty. She quickly checked two other drawers, feeling vaguely like an alcoholic in search of a bottle, but found nothing. "Damn." Sitting back in her chair, she fought the urge to put her feet up on her desk. The desk top was a mess. Papers seemed to grow out of it as if they were weeds in a garden. There was no room to put her feet. "Hah," she laughed out loud, "who am I kidding? I couldn't get my feet all the way up there if I tried." And if I did, she continued silently, I'd never be able to get them down again. They'd have to use a forklift to get me off. The image of her legs being pried from the top of her desk with a forklift dampened her spirits considerably. She'd been feeling happy, almost giddy, over her triumph. And it *had* been a triumph, she told herself, trying to pump herself up again. She had run roughshod over Gary Schuster and his lawyer. She had called his bluff and then some. She had won. "Did he have any balls when he walked out?" she heard Philip ask, accusingly. "Oh, I let him keep those," she heard herself reply. Had she?

"Oh, Philip, why can't you be proud of me," she wailed, desperately wishing for something sweet to put in her mouth. "Awesome" was the word Lynn had used. She'd been "awesome." "Vicious," Philip corrected. Would she even tell him about her victory today? Would he consider it a triumph or a travesty? She thought of calling him, then decided against it. He'd be with a patient. Besides, he had better things to do than listen to her crow. "What say we go out and grab an ice-cream cone?" she suddenly heard him say, seeing him wrapped in a towel in the doorway of her sister's room. She dismissed the image as quickly as she always did, along with the picture of her sister, pale and frightened, on the bed. "Cheer up," she told herself. "You were great. You were 'awesome.'"

Her sister's large green eyes refused to fade into memory. Renee reached for the phone and dialed her home number. Philip was taking Debbie to a rock concert in West Palm Beach tonight. Maybe she'd be able to persuade Kathryn to join her for a night out, just the two of them. Something was obviously bothering Kathryn. She'd been doing so well and then bingo, back to square one. Perhaps she felt guilty about starting to enjoy life again so soon after Arnie's death. The gnawing feeling still persisted that Kathryn hadn't told her everything about the night he died, that she was leaving something out. Maybe she could persuade Kathryn to tell her what it was.

Renee listened as the phone rang five, six, seven times. She was about to hang up after the eighth ring when her call was suddenly answered. "Kathryn?" Renee asked, the hello on the other end so breathless as to be indistinct.

"Debbie," the voice informed her. "Can't you recognize your loving stepdaughter by now?"

"You sound out of breath."

"I was coming down the hall when I heard the phone. It was a race against time to see whether I could get in the apartment to answer it before you hung up. That's what usually happens, you know. The person hangs up just when you finally get to the phone."

"Good thing I'm the type who holds on."

"Good for who?" Debbie asked, throwing down the challenge.

"Is my sister there?" Renee asked, refusing to pick it up, wondering where else Kathryn would be. She hadn't left the apartment in weeks.

"I don't know. I just got in, remember? Just a minute, I'll check." The phone banged roughly against the kitchen counter, reverberating in Renee's ear, quickly followed by a second, even louder bang. Renee realized the phone had been carelessly tossed against the counter, where it had easily tumbled off, and was currently dangling upside down from its cord, swaying back and forth a mere few inches off the floor. "There's nobody home but us abandoned stepchildren," Debbie announced a few seconds later.

"Kathryn's not there?"

"Not unless she's hiding under her bed. Maybe she went out to get her ticket."

"What ticket? What are you talking about?" For a minute, Renee thought Kathryn might have decided to accompany Debbie and Philip to the rock concert in West Palm.

"Her ticket to New York. I told her I was leaving Friday and she said she might as well fly back with me. Did you know that my mom's treating me to a few days in the wicked city before school starts?"

Renee ignored the question. "Kathryn didn't say anything to me about leaving."

"Kathryn hasn't said anything to you about a lot of things."

"What's that supposed to mean?"

"Come on, Renée. You're supposed to be so smart. You figure it out."

"I don't have time for these games, Debbie."

"No? Too bad. I like games. Anyway, she's not here."

"You're sure she's not out on the balcony?"

"Not unless she's dangling over the side."

Renee was about to hang up when the sound of Debbie's voice froze her hand. "Sorry, did you say something?"

There was a nervous giggle on the other end of the line. "I said maybe she's hiding under *your* bed."

The line went dead. "Now what the hell was that all about?" Renee replaced the receiver and stared across her desk at where Lynn Schuster had been sitting earlier, thoughts of her "awesome" victory all but gone. What was Debbie talking about? And why this sudden decision on Kathryn's part to return to New York? What was going on? She buzzed her secretary. "Marilyn, I'm going home now."

"You have a meeting in ten minutes."

"Cancel it."

"Cancel it?"

"Cancel it."

Renee walked through her apartment door and headed straight for the kitchen. "Kathryn?" she called out, opening the refrigerator and reaching for the plastic bag of miniature 3 Musketeers chocolate bars at the back.

"She's not home yet," Debbie told her, coming up behind her stepmother and startling her. "Having a little snack, are we?"

"*I* am." Renee turned around and displayed two small chocolate bars in her open palm. "Want one?"

"No, thanks. Dad's taking me to dinner before the concert, and I don't want to ruin my appetite. He's taking me to the Troubadour. You remember the Troubadour, don't you, Renée? We went there for lunch."

Renee shut the fridge door, saying nothing.

"I've got to hand it to you, Renée, you sure know how to eat."

Renee ate the first of the two bars, then started on the second.

"How can you eat that stuff? My mother always says that sugar rots your brain."

Renee smiled, and finished the second bar, knowing Debbie was trying to get a rise out of her and getting perverse enjoyment from the fact that she was spoiling the young girl's fun by not snapping up the bait.

"How come you're home so early?" Debbie asked.

"I missed you."

"You'll miss me when I'm gone," she said. "I'm the only fun you have around here."

It was Renee's turn to laugh. "I'll try to cope."

"How? By eating yourself into oblivion?"

Renee felt her cheeks grow red, as if someone had slapped them. She walked out of the kitchen into the living room and sat down on the white sofa, staring out toward the ocean. She pictured herself in a boat, drifting farther and farther away from shore.

"My dad says you didn't always have a weight problem," Debbie said, joining Renee, uninvited, in the living room. "That's how he puts it, a 'weight problem.' He says you were actually quite slim when he met you. Of course, I don't really remember that far back. I was just a kid."

For the second time in as many minutes, Renee laughed out loud. "You were never a kid." It was strange that people in so much pain could still laugh, she thought, wishing she had another chocolate bar. She debated getting up and getting one, before deciding against it. Why give Debbie more ammunition? Philip was taking her out to dinner soon—she'd be gone by the weekend, hooray! hooray!—and what was the point in getting into a shouting match at this late date? What is your objective, after all? she asked herself, deciding on a different approach. "So, have you enjoyed your summer?"

"Not bad."

"You made some new friends."

Debbie shrugged. "I guess. You remember Alicia Henderson, don't you?"

Renee felt her body tense, her throat constrict. "Yes, of course."

"She took me out to lunch one afternoon. Did you know that?"

"Yes, I think she mentioned it."

"I wonder why she did that. It was really nice of her, don't you think?"

Renee forced a smile in her stepdaughter's direction. Debbie was standing beside the Clarence Maesele painting, which hung on the north wall. "Very nice."

"Is this a conversation?" Debbie asked playfully. "Are we actually having a conversation?"

"Let's try not to get too excited."

Debbie walked to the window, Renee following her with her eyes. "No, we wouldn't want to do that. Not with all those extra pounds you're carrying around. It could put too much of a strain on your heart."

Renee got quickly to her feet. Enough was enough. "That's it for me."

"Wait," Debbie called out, and Renee felt her feet stop, though she knew she should keep walking. "I'm sorry," Debbie mumbled. "It was just a joke. I didn't realize you were so sensitive. Come on, Renée, sit down. Where's your sense of humor?"

Renee smiled. Debbie apologized the same way her father did. They both said they were sorry while making sure you realized it was all your fault. She was too sensitive; she had no sense of humor. Renee sat back down. She couldn't win. Where did she think she was going?

"My name is Renee, rhymes with beanie," she said for what felt like the thousandth time. And perhaps it was.

"You don't like me very much, do you?" There was a touch of ingenuousness to Debbie's voice that surprised Renee. Could there really be any doubt?

Renee wondered how to best answer the question. "No," she said finally, opting for the truth.

"Why not?"

"Come on, Debbie," Renee told her, throwing the girl's earlier remarks on the telephone back at her. "You're supposed to be so smart. You figure it out."

Debbie shrugged, turning her profile to Renee, staring at the wide expanse of ocean. "So, Kathryn didn't tell you she was planning to leave?"

"No, she didn't." What was the point in hedging?

"That's strange, don't you think? I mean, I thought you were supposed to be so close."

"I guess it was something she decided on the spur of the moment. She's probably concerned she's overstayed her welcome, and when she found out you were leaving, I guess it seemed like the right time for her to go too."

"Are you going to try to talk her out of it?"

"If I can."

"Why?"

Renee was caught off guard by the question. "Why?"

"If she wants to go, why don't you just let her go?"

"I don't think Kathryn is really functioning all that well right now. I'm not sure she's equipped to make any major decisions."

"She seemed to be doing fine for a while."

"Yes, I know, but . . ."

"What do you suppose happened that made her change?"

"I think she's just tired," Renee said, her tone indicating her desire not to continue with this topic. It was a question she had asked herself repeatedly over the last couple of weeks, and one she had no wish to discuss with Debbie. "I think *I'm* tired. I think I'll lie down for a while."

"Maybe my father should talk to her."

"What?"

"I said that maybe my father should talk to her. I bet he could get her to change her mind. Persuade her to stay."

"Maybe."

"Maybe not."

Renee felt as if she were taking part in a conversation in which all the important pieces of information were being withheld. She was losing patience, losing control. "Is there something you're trying to tell me?"

"What would I be trying to tell you?"

"Beats the shit out of me," Renee said, underlying the profanity and heading for her bedroom.

"You still haven't told me why you don't like me," Debbie continued before Renee could get very far.

"Come on, Debbie, I don't see the point of this."

"I'm leaving in a couple of days. You may never see me again. Now's your chance to set the record straight."

Renee told herself to keep walking, to say nothing and simply make a dignified exit while she still could. Instead, she stopped at the entrance to the living room and turned slowly around. Stop now, her mind shouted. Don't say anything. But it was already too late. "I've tried to like you, Debbie. I really have."

"But . . . ?"

"But you don't give a person much of a chance."

"How's that?"

"I think you know."

"Tell me anyway."

Renee stared across the room at her husband's daughter. Was this the girl's peculiar way of trying to make amends? Was she attempting to wipe the slate clean so that they could begin again fresh next summer? Had Philip talked to her, warned her she'd better change her ways? Was the girl actually reaching out to her? Would this mess of a conversation actually conclude with a tearful, heartfelt embrace? "I've tried to get close to you, Debbie," Renee began. "I've tried to be your friend. I know that I'm not around as often as I should be, but I've suggested that we set time aside to do things together. You always decline my invitations. You always make me feel that you don't want very much to do with me."

"Maybe that's your own paranoia."

"Maybe. Am I wrong?"

Debbie said nothing. She puffed her cheeks full of air and then released them with a thin, popping sound. "What else?"

"Well, since I've said this much, I might as well go all the way," Renee continued, coming back into the room, approaching her stepdaughter.

"Might as well," Debbie concurred.

"I think that . . ."

"Feel," Debbie corrected.

"What?"

"You should say 'feel.' The word 'think' can be inflammatory. That's what Dad always says anyway."

"Oh." Renee heard a warning bell sound somewhere in the distance, but ignored it. "Okay, then, I *feel*," she stressed, "that you resent me, the fact that I'm married to your father, and that you do everything you can during your visits to cause friction between us. Am I wrong?"

Debbie brought her lips together in a wiggly line that admitted nothing but the possibility Renee might be correct. It was the visual equivalent of "I don't know."

"Debbie, nothing would make me happier than for us to be friends. I've always wanted a daughter . . ."

"Why didn't you have one?"

"I don't know. It just didn't work out. Your dad didn't think the timing was right, so . . ."

"So you thought you'd be *my* mother. I already have a mother."

"I know that. It was never my intention to try to take her place."

"You never could. You could try as hard as you want."

"I don't want to take her place." Renee threw her hands in the air. "Look, this discussion was your idea. If it's going to create even more problems, why don't we drop the whole thing right now before we end up saying things we'll both be sorry for later."

"That's the way you deal with everything, isn't it, Renée? If you don't want to deal with something, you just pretend the problem doesn't exist."

"This is getting us nowhere."

"Just ignore the problems and they'll go away," Debbie persisted. "Ignore me long enough and maybe I'll leave. Ignore the women and maybe they'll go away."

Renee stood very still. "What are you talking about? What women?"

"You know what women," Debbie said, then enunciated slowly and carefully, "Philip's women."

"Excuse me. I'm going to my room to lie down . . ."

"Alicia Henderson, for one," Debbie taunted, following her stepmother around the living room.

"Shut up, Debbie," Renee said, not stopping, not turning around, racing to get away from her husband's child.

"Your sister, for another."

Renee stopped as abruptly as if she had just run into a brick wall. She reeled with the impact, feeling her head start to spin. "What are you talking about?"

"About my father and your sister," Debbie said simply, her voice a shrug, as Renee slowly turned around. "They've been sleeping together when you weren't around. Right here, in this apartment. Oh, come on," she continued, forcing a laugh. "Don't look so stunned. You had to know . . ."

Renee saw her husband standing in the doorway to her sister's bedroom, a towel wrapped carelessly around his hips. "What say we go out and grab an ice-cream cone?" he said. No!

"You're lying."

"I saw them together."

"I don't believe you."

"They were in Kathryn's room. I came home earlier than I planned one afternoon. They didn't even hear me. They were really busy."

"I'm getting out of here."

"I bet they've been doing it at the office too. That might even be where she is now. Yeah, that's probably where she is—on that nice comfortable couch, screwing my father!"

Renee's hand reached out and slapped Debbie hard across the face. The girl gasped, large tears immediately springing to her eyes and falling down her cheeks. Renee felt her whole body vibrate, like a tuning fork, and then go numb.

"Can you blame him?" the girl screamed. "Look at you! I'm amazed he can even bear the sight of you. No wonder he turns to other women. No wonder he stays out late and has cozy little lunches with women like Alicia Henderson."

Renee listened in silence, too stunned by her action to stop the angry torrent of words her hand had unleashed.

"I can understand my father," Debbie continued, unable at this point to stop. "The person I can't understand is you. You're supposed to be so damn smart! How can you let my father do this to you? Don't you have any self-respect? How can you let him have affairs with one woman after another? Don't you know you're the laughingstock of this whole town? The famous divorce lawyer whose own husband cheats on her left, right, and center! Why do you put up with it? What are you hanging around for? My father slept with your sister! And you've known about it all along, haven't you? As much as you tried to pretend it wasn't true. You knew!"

Renee saw her sister sitting up in bed, pulling the white sheet around her neck, hiding her nakedness, turning her face away from Renee's concern. She saw Philip in the doorway, fresh out of the shower, nude except for a towel. "What say we go out and grab an ice-cream cone?" he asked. "Hi, Kathryn. I didn't know you were home." And something in the air, a slight musky odor that disappeared on command. The subtle scent of recent lovemaking she had refused to acknowledge, the smell Debbie was rubbing her face in now.

She thought she heard the sound of a door opening and closing, but it sounded so far away, and Debbie's voice was so near and so relentless.

"How much more are you going to stand for?" Debbie was yelling as a figure emerged from the front hallway. "Why don't you just tell him to go to hell?" She paused, sucking in a deep breath of air as the figure moved closer. "Why don't you tell *me* to go to hell?"

Kathryn stepped out of the shadow.

"What's going on?" she asked quietly.

Renee stared at her sister's puzzled face, still praying she was wrong, knowing she wasn't. She felt empty, eviscerated, as if someone had reached down and scooped out her insides.

"Suppose you tell me."

"I don't understand . . ." Kathryn began, then stopped.

"Neither do I," Renee said simply, then: "Is it true?"

Kathryn said nothing, her eyes darting back and forth between her sister and Debbie, who stood transfixed, afraid to move.

"Is it true?" Renee asked again, not elaborating.

Kathryn walked past them into the living room and sank

down into the white sofa, looking out at the ocean exactly as Renee had done earlier.

"Is it true?" Renee said for the third time. "Is it? Have you been sleeping with Philip?"

Kathryn looked confused and helpless, as if she had stumbled onto the scene of a murder and now found herself face to face with the killer, understanding there was no escape.

"I already know the answer," Renee said when it became obvious that Kathryn would not, or could not, speak. "I just want to hear you say it."

"Why?" Kathryn asked, her voice achingly low.

"Because I guess I won't really believe it until I hear it from your mouth."

There was an endless silence before Kathryn finally spoke.

"I didn't mean for it to happen," she whispered, and Renee felt her composure start to crumble. An audible cry escaped her mouth, and she grabbed her stomach as if she had been punched. Debbie backed up against the wall. Nobody seemed to breathe. "I can't tell you why it happened," Kathryn went on, her voice a frightened plea. "I don't even know *how* it happened. I love you. You're my sister. You're all I've got. I'd never do anything to hurt you."

"Then why did you?" The question was painful in its simplicity. Renee reached for the arm of the white chair, her body collapsing into the soft cushion. Why was she still here? Why didn't she just leave? Isn't that what Debbie had asked her?

"I was so unhappy, so confused," Kathryn was saying, obviously trying to sort out the answer in her mind as she spoke. "So frightened. I felt so guilty about Arnie's death. I didn't know whether I wanted to live or die. I thought Philip was my friend." She lowered her head, and when she raised it, she looked even more confused. "He'd been so kind to me. He seemed to understand what I was going through . . ."

"He's a psychiatrist, for God's sake! That's his job."

"Maybe. And maybe in the beginning, he was just trying to help me. But then it changed. Or maybe it was there right from the start. I don't know. I don't know how he felt. I know that *I* felt better when he was around. He made me feel safe."

Renee felt her sense of betrayal turning to anger, then to rage.

"And so you took advantage . . . ?"

"No!" Kathryn's voice was suddenly strong. "I didn't. It wasn't me!"

"What are you trying to tell me? That my husband seduced you? That he would be stupid and insensitive enough to make a play for my own sister?"

"I'm not saying it was all his doing." Kathryn stumbled to her feet. "I know I could have said no. I know I could have stopped him. But I didn't know how. I didn't know what to do. He came home from work early one afternoon and I was there. Debbie was gone for the day. We started to talk. He started to rub my back. He said I needed to relax, that he knew how to make me feel better. I was so confused. He'd been so kind to me. He was so understanding . . ."

"You already said that."

"I'm not trying to say it was all his fault. I know I'm as guilty as he is . . ."

"You seduced him! You saw something you wanted and you went after it. You were lonely and unhappy and probably more than a little bit jealous. And it didn't matter who got hurt or what damage you caused, as long as it made you feel better. As long as you got what you wanted."

"No, that's not true. It wasn't what I wanted."

"How many times didn't you want it, Kathryn? Once? Twice? Five times? Ten times? Did you know that Debbie came home one day and saw you together?"

"Oh God." Kathryn closed her eyes, her body swaying. She looked as though she was about to faint.

"And that memorable afternoon I got the ice cream that was meant for you!"

"Oh God, oh God, I'm so sorry. Please tell me what you want me to say," Kathryn cried, her features looking as though they might dissolve. "Tell me, please. What is it you want me to say?"

"I just want to hear the truth! I want you to admit that you deliberately seduced my husband. That you took advantage of his kindness and concern, and twisted it around . . ."

"No. You're the one who's twisting. I never wanted it to happen. I felt sick about it. Whenever he touched me, I wanted to die."

"But you didn't die, did you?" Renee jumped to her feet, grabbing her sister's damaged wrists and holding them angrily up in the air. "You never do." She flung Kathryn's hands back to her sides. "Goddamn you," she cried, bursting into tears. "Goddamn you." Then, catching only a brief glimpse of Debbie's startled face, she rushed to the apartment door and raced out into the hall. It was only when she was behind the wheel of her car, wiping at her tears with the back of her hand, that she realized she had seen Debbie smile.

23

"Where are we going?" he asked, climbing into the front seat of her car.

Lynn looked over at Marc and gave him her best Mona Lisa smile, saying nothing. She didn't feel like talking.

"I take it everything went well this afternoon," he continued.

"Gary signed the agreement," Lynn told him, feeling she owed him something of an explanation. All she had said to him on the phone earlier in the evening was that she had arranged for a sitter and would pick him up in an hour.

"Speaking of signing things," he was saying, "I relinquished my power-of-attorney over my father's funds today." Lynn regarded him quizzically but said nothing. "It's *his* money. Why should I have any control over how he chooses to spend it? If he wants to send his nurses to Greece, that's his business. If he wants to buy a fleet of baby-blue Lincoln convertibles, what right do I have to rain on his parade? I don't know. It just never felt right, my taking over that way. Besides, if I'm a good boy, maybe he'll let me borrow his car one day.

What do you say? Do you want to go with me on Saturday and see if he'll let us take it for a spin?"

Lynn said nothing, her eyes back on the road. She didn't want to talk about his father. She didn't want to talk about anything.

"Are you going to tell me where we're going?" he asked after several minutes.

"I thought we'd celebrate my victory." There was an edge to her voice she couldn't quite disguise.

"Is something the matter?"

"Why do you ask?"

"Well, you obviously weren't interested in hearing about my father, and you sound almost . . . I don't know . . . angry."

"Why would I be angry?"

"I don't know. Are you?"

"Of course not. I got what I wanted, didn't I?"

"I don't know. Did you?"

"Can we just drop all this cute repartee?" Lynn asked, her voice tense. "I'm sorry. I guess I just don't feel much like talking."

"Are we there yet?" he asked. She knew he was hoping for a smile, so she tried to oblige, forcing the corners of her mouth into something between a grin and a grimace. Marc leaned his head back against the seat and closed his eyes.

Lynn tried to concentrate on the road ahead, her hands gripping the steering wheel tightly. Why had he said she sounded angry? What was he talking about? She didn't sound angry at all. Why on earth would she be angry? She'd won, hadn't she? She got to keep her children and her house. She'd used Gary's threats and turned them against him. And hadn't that been wonderfully satisfying? The look on his face when he learned he wasn't the first of Suzette's infidelities! That alone was almost enough to make up for the anguish he had put her through. Why shouldn't she feel satisfaction at his humiliation?

She reminded herself of what Gary had put her through these last few weeks. How could he have been prepared to use their children so cruelly against her? How much anger he must have been hoarding through all those seemingly happy years of marriage that he had tried to hurt her in this way! How could he have been so spiteful? Wasn't leaving her for another woman hurtful enough? Had it really been necessary to put her through—put *both* of them through—this afternoon's ordeal? How long would it be before she could look at him with anything other than contempt? How much time would have to pass before she could greet her children's father at the door to *her* house with something other than forced conviviality? And how much did her anger at Gary have to do with her rendezvous with Marc tonight? Goddamn him, she thought, looking over at Marc, wondering which man she was damning. How dare he suggest she was angry!

"We're here," she said, pulling her car into a narrow parking lot and coming to a sudden halt between a new sports car and an old sedan.

Marc opened his eyes and looked around. "Lynn . . ."

"Come on." She was out of the car before he could say another word.

"Lynn, what are you doing?"

"This was your idea, remember?" Lynn took a deep breath and walked past him into the office of the Starlight Motel, trying to savor the look of surprise in Marc's eyes as she requested a room and plunked forty dollars on the desk. "It may not be the same room they had," she explained, walking briskly down the outside corridor, "but it'll do." She inserted the large, unwieldy key into the lock and pushed open the door.

Marc flicked on the light switch as she closed the door behind them. The lamp over each of the two double beds, as well as one perched on top of a chest of drawers, came on, illuminating a standard beige-and-brown room. A large television set sat in the far corner beside a small circular table. The dark drapes were pulled shut. "It looks like my apartment," he said with a wry smile.

"Turn out the light," she told him.

"Whatever the lady says." The room went suddenly dark.

"Don't talk."

She was suddenly in his arms, her body pushing against his,

her hands on his face, her fingers at the sides of his beard. She pressed her lips hard on his, her tongue forcing his lips apart. Clearly, she had taken him by surprise, she thought, feeling him stumble slightly as she pulled at his jacket, pushing it off his shoulders, trapping his arms at his sides.

"Easy," he said, trying to return her kisses, match her ardor, but unable to find her rhythm or anticipate what she wanted to do next.

"Easy's no fun," she said, using Renee's words. "I don't want to go easy." Again she covered his lips with hers as he struggled to free his arms of his jacket. Her hands moved to the buttons of his shirt, but her fingers were too impatient and she had little success. She felt him reach down and pull his shirt free of his pants, then push her fumbling fingers aside so that he could do the job himself. That accomplished, his hands slid effortlessly around her, wrapping themselves across her back, holding her still, trying to slow her down. She pushed herself free and backed just out of his reach, not waiting for him to make the next move, pulling her blue jersey over her head, unsnapping her brassiere, and placing his hands on her bare breasts.

He needed no further encouragement. Marc picked her up and deposited her on the first of the two beds, kicking off his shoes and pulling her sandals free. Then he was on the bed beside her, his lips tenderly on hers, his hands soft and gentle as they traced the curves of her body. Lynn quickly rolled over on top of him. She didn't want soft and gentle and slow and easy. She wanted hard and fast and over and done.

She wanted to be taken roughly, violently, with no time to think, no time to feel. Her hand moved to the buckle of his belt and she tugged at it impatiently until she felt it loosen, her fingers quickly moving to the button of his pants, pulling down on the zipper. She reached inside, her hand wrapping firmly around his penis.

"Hey, take it easy," he said, flinching at her touch.

She ignored him, manipulating him in her hand as if she were rolling a piece of Plasticine, feeling him grow soft as her efforts increased. What was happening? She realized he was trying to push her away, to slow her down, but she would have none of it. Didn't he realize there wasn't time for soft caresses? That that wasn't what she wanted? What was the matter with him? Why wasn't he responding?

She pulled at her own slacks, unzipping them and twisting them down over her hips, kicking them free before guiding his hand between her legs. What was the matter with him? Why wasn't he getting aroused? She was doing everything she was supposed to. Gary had always liked it when she was the aggressor. She moved down on Marc with her lips, trying to take him in her mouth.

"Lynn, you're hurting me," he whispered, his hand on her shoulder, pushing her mouth away.

"What's the matter?" she asked angrily, trying to force him into an erection.

"I'm not a punching bag, Lynn," he said, evading her grasp and pushing his body into a sitting position, covering—protecting?—himself with his hands.

"I thought you wanted to make love to me."

"I do."

"That's not the message I'm getting."

"You're not giving me much of a chance."

"How much of a chance do you need?" Lynn buried her face in her hands, fighting back the tears. "What's going on, Marc?"

"Suppose you tell me."

"I thought this was what you wanted. You said as much the first time we met. You said you wanted to go to a motel room, preferably the same motel room, preferably the same bed . . ."

"I know what I said."

"Well, here we are. Or close enough."

"What else did I say?"

Lynn looked helplessly through the darkness. What was the matter with him? Why this insistence on dialogue? She didn't want to talk. She had already told him that.

"What else did I say?" he repeated stubbornly.

"Is this some sort of quiz? Do I get a prize if I get the right answer?"

"I also told you I think I'm falling in love with you. Doesn't that mean anything to you?"

"I don't want to talk about love."

"You want to *make* love but you don't want to talk about it?"

"That's right. That's what I want."

"You don't want to waste time talking." It was a statement, not a question.

Lynn nodded, aware of the growing anger in his voice.

"You want it angry and mean and over with fast?"

"Just do it. Stop talking about it."

"Tell me exactly what you want me to do."

"Whatever you want. Just do it."

"No. You're calling the shots here. You tell me."

Lynn realized they were yelling and wondered if their voices could be heard in the next room. "I want you to make love to me," she whispered, her voice tight.

"No, that's not what you want." He took her hand and returned it to the front of his pants. "I'll show you what you want," he said angrily, "and it has nothing to do with making love."

He pushed her back against the pillow, pulling her bikini panties roughly down over her hips, straddling her. "Is this what you want? Is it? Because if it is, I'll be happy to oblige. I'm no saint, Lynn. If this is the only way to have you, then I'll take it. You don't want to talk about love? Fine. Then let's get the terms straight. You don't want to make love. You want to fuck! Isn't that what you want? Well, answer me. Is that what you want? Because if that's what you want, you're going to have to tell me. You want me to fuck you? Is that what you really want? Tell me. Is that what you want?"

"Yes! No! God, I don't know," she cried, rolling away from him, bringing her knees to her chest, curling in on herself as if she were a baby in the womb. "Oh God, I don't know. I don't know." She started to sob, and he took her in his arms, covering her shaking shoulders with the mass of his body.

"It's all right, Lynn. It's all right. I'm sorry. It's all right."

"It's not all right. I don't know what I'm doing anymore. I don't even know who I am. I don't recognize myself when I look in the mirror."

He was kissing the back of her neck. "It's all right. It'll be all right."

After what felt like a long time, Lynn sat up, pulling the bedspread free of its pillows and trying to hide herself inside it. "I want to tell you about this afternoon."

Marc reached over and yanked the bedspread off the second bed, wrapping it around her shoulders, watching her disappear inside it. Then he leaned his bare back against the wall. "I'm listening."

Another long pause before she spoke again. "I did something that I'm not very proud of." She twisted around to face him. Marc said nothing, sitting very still, his eyes never leaving hers, waiting for her to continue. "I told my lawyer what you told me about Suzette's other affairs." She waited, but Marc said nothing. "She used the information to get Gary to back down from his custody threat. The implication was that if he didn't back down we might be tempted to use that information in court. Or that you might." Again Lynn paused, expecting him to speak, but Marc remained silent, his face impassive, impossible to read.

"You should have seen Gary's face. I don't think I'll ever forget it, and I feel guilty not only because I hurt him but because I *wanted* to hurt him. I enjoyed hurting him. And I used the things you told me to do it."

"You use what you can," Marc told her, breaking his silence, staring straight ahead.

"Is that why you told me those things? So that I'd use them?"

Another silence. A long sigh. "I don't know."

"What about me? Are you using me?"

Marc smiled, his eyes shadowed in the darkness of their motel room. "Tonight was your idea," he reminded her.

"Am I using you?"

"I don't know. You're angry. Confused. Scared. You've just

signed away almost fifteen years of marriage. You're in a motel room with the husband of the woman your husband is planning to marry. Is that why we're here? I don't know. I honestly don't know how much Gary and Suzette have to do with our being in this room together, and at this precise moment, I don't know whether to curse them or thank them. I do know that I'm falling in love with you, that I'd like to spend as much time as I can getting to know you, getting to know your kids. I know that I'd like to do all the things grown-ups do together in a relationship, including making love to you. I know I'll kick myself forever for blowing what might have been my only chance. Am I using you? In the beginning, maybe. Now, I don't think so. But how do I know for sure? Are you using me? Maybe. *Probably.* I don't know. I don't care. Sometimes you just have to take a chance."

"I've never been very good at taking chances."

"You don't always have to be in total control, Lynn. Sometimes it doesn't hurt to just let yourself go."

"And sometimes it does."

"I guess the trick is finding the balance." He stood up, zipping up his pants and scooping his shirt off the floor.

"You're a nice man," Lynn said, as she had said once before, realizing only now how true it was.

"Yeah, well, we better get out of here before I get tired of being such a nice guy. You look awfully cute sitting there shivering under that tatty bedspread, and I've just about used up my quota of good intentions for one night."

"What now?" she asked.

His answer was slow in coming, obviously difficult for him to say. "I think you need more time to sort things out, to catch your breath, decide what it is you really want." He smiled, his voice wavering. "I'm not going anywhere. You know where to find me. I have faith in your instincts, even if you don't."

"And if my instincts lead me in another direction?"

He shrugged, and though his words were casual, the tone of his voice was not. "Sometimes you just have to take a chance," he repeated.

.   .   .

There was a white Mercedes parked outside Lynn's house when she pulled into her driveway at just after ten o'clock that evening. Lynn sat for a moment, recalling the image of Marc as he climbed out of her car and headed toward his apartment. So she needed time to sort things out, she thought, barely glancing in the other car's direction as she walked toward her front door. The babysitter would be surprised. She had told her not to expect her until late.

"Lynn . . ."

Lynn spun around in the darkness, frightened by the sound of her own name.

"It's Renee," the woman emerging from behind the wheel of the white car said, her voice breaking. "I'm sorry. I didn't mean to scare you. I just didn't know where to go. I have no one to turn to. I have no friends . . ." She broke off. Lynn could hear the amazement in Renee's voice as she spoke. She walked quickly toward her.

"What's the matter? What's happened?"

"Kathryn's gone."

It took a minute for Lynn to digest that Kathryn was Renee's sister and that she had not merely returned to New York. "What do you mean, she's gone?"

"We had a fight. A terrible fight. About Philip," she whispered, then returned to her normal voice. "I ran out of the apartment. I wasn't thinking clearly. I wasn't thinking at all. I just needed to get away. I drove around for hours. I don't even know where I went. I just drove. I forgot all about the gun."

"The gun? What gun?"

"Philip keeps a gun. I was afraid to get rid of it because he might get angry. I kept telling myself to find a better place to hide it but I didn't know where. It doesn't matter. She would have found it anyway."

"What are you talking about? I don't understand."

"I raced back to the apartment as soon as I remembered about the gun, but Kathryn had already gone. Nobody was home. Philip was taking Debbie to dinner and to a rock concert in West Palm. He wasn't home when we had our fight. I'm sure that Debbie didn't say anything to him about it, or he never would have gone."

Lynn could tell by the look on Renee's face that she wasn't sure of any such thing. "When you got back to the apartment, Kathryn wasn't there," she repeated, guiding Renee back on track, trying to make sense out of what she was saying.

"I knew the gun was gone even before I started looking for it." Renee was shaking as Lynn took the trembling woman in her arms. It didn't seem possible that this could be the same woman she had seen in action this afternoon.

"Did you look everywhere? Maybe Philip moved it . . ."

"I tore the place apart. It's gone."

"Did you call the police?"

Renee shook her head. "I know I should have called them. I'm a lawyer, for heaven's sake. I know I'm supposed to call the police. But I didn't know what to tell them. I don't know where to tell them to look, and I didn't want to get Kathryn in trouble. Oh God, Lynn, listen to me. I'm not making any sense. I'm worrying about not getting her in trouble and she's probably dead. Oh God, oh God, it's all my fault."

"Okay, hold on. Come on, Renee. We don't have time for this. Feel sorry for yourself later, after we've found her."

"I said terrible things to her. I practically told her to kill herself. I almost dared her to do it."

"Okay, listen, get in the car." Lynn directed Renee to the passenger side of the white Mercedes, then got behind the wheel. "Now think," she said, pulling the car away from the curb. "Where would she go?"

Renee burst into tears. "I don't know."

"What about your parents'?"

"No. That's the last place she'd go."

"Does she have any friends?"

Renee shook her head. "There was only me. Oh God, what have I done?"

"Take it easy, Renee. We'll find her."

"Where are we going?"

"Back to your apartment. Maybe she said something to the doorman."

"I already asked him. But he'd just come on duty. He wasn't there when she left."

"Who was on duty before him?"

"I don't know. I didn't think to ask. I've done everything wrong."

"Renee, calm down. This isn't helping you or Kathryn. Now tell me how to get to your place."

A few minutes later, they pulled into the circular driveway that led to the entrance of Renee's condominium and stopped directly in front of the door.

"You know you can't park there, Mrs. Bower." The gray-haired doorman, whose uniform identified him as Stan, scolded before either woman could get out of the car.

"We need the phone number of the guard who was on duty before you," Lynn instructed him sharply. "It's urgent." The startled doorman, whose officiousness collapsed with the sound of Lynn's voice, glanced warily at Renee, no doubt wondering how his fine tenant came to be associated with so rude an acquaintance, and returned to his desk, immediately riffling through his records. The two women followed him. He wrote out George Fine's name and home phone number on a piece of paper and handed it to Lynn.

"He's probably asleep," the elderly doorman grumbled, not used to changes in his routine.

Lynn usurped his position behind the front desk and dialed the number he had given her. "Mr. Fine?" she asked as soon as the phone was picked up on the other end by a man who, as his successor had predicted, had been asleep. Lynn quickly explained who she was and what she wanted. "He says Kathryn took a taxi," she said, handing the phone back to the doorman. "Diamond Cab Company."

"I know the number for Diamond Cab," the doorman said, suddenly warming to the urgency of the situation, reclaiming his place behind the desk and dialing the number for them.

Lynn repeated the information to the dispatcher, and listened as the youngish-sounding woman told her she'd phone her back as soon as she managed to locate the driver who had picked Kathryn up. "In the meantime, we have to call the police." Lynn got on the second line and spoke to first one officer, and then another, stressing that Kathryn was a danger to no one but herself. "They'll be here in a few minutes." She patted Renee's hand and led her to the burgundy-and-white sofa in the center of the front lobby.

"Thank you so much. I don't know what I would have done without you." She laughed, the tears falling down her cheeks. "When you told me to call if I ever needed you, I don't think you expected to hear from me so soon."

"I'm glad I could be here for you," Lynn told her, wondering how long Renee had been parked outside her house, what Renee might have done had she not come home. She refused to let herself think of where she had been, of what she might have been doing right at this moment had she not come home. In truth, she had been glad for Renee's sudden appearance at her doorstep. Concentrating on someone else's problems had always been easier than thinking about her own.

The phone rang. "Lynn Schuster?" the doorman asked, holding the phone in her direction. "Diamond Cab," he whispered loudly, almost eagerly, his dormant sense of adventure having been fully roused.

Lynn took the receiver from his outstretched hand. "This is Lynn Schuster," she said, surprised to discover she was talking to the driver of the taxi, not the dispatcher. "I understand you picked up a woman from the lobby of the Oasis on South Ocean Boulevard sometime between five and nine o'clock tonight. . . . Yes, blond hair, very slim." She looked to Renee for confirmation. "Yes, kind of sad-looking. That would be her. Can you tell me where you took her?" Lynn felt her hand start to shake as he gave her his answer. Slowly, she returned the receiver to the doorman's waiting hand. She watched Renee rise cautiously to her feet. "He says he drove her to the cemetery," Lynn said.

24

Renee could barely sit still as Lynn sped down South Swinton Avenue. Unconsciously she mimicked Lynn's every move, braking when Lynn did, pressing her foot to the floor whenever Lynn pressed down on the gas, propelling the car forward with her shoulders, growing increasingly impatient with each stoplight.

South Swinton Avenue had once been *the* street of Delray Beach, but time and a changing population had transformed it —reduced it—to one of the town's main arteries, although it was relatively quiet now. Renee looked out of the side window, absently absorbing the large ficus trees that lined the once fashionable street. "Why on earth would she go to the cemetery?" Renee rubbed her forehead as if she were trying to reach inside her brain for an answer. Her body rocked back and forth. "For inspiration?"

Lynn laughed softly and again Renee felt grateful for her presence. "Relax, Renee," Lynn told her, sounding very much in control of the situation. "We know where she is and the police are on their way."

"What if she's already . . . ?"

"She isn't." They stopped at another stoplight and Lynn turned in her seat, taking Renee's hands in her own. "Renee, if Kathryn really wanted to kill herself, you would have found her dead when you first returned to your apartment. People with access to a weapon and an empty apartment don't go searching for exotic locales if they really want to die. They don't have the doorman call them a taxi and leave a trail even Hansel and Gretel could follow. She doesn't want to kill herself, although she probably thinks she does. What she really wants is for you to find her." The light changed. "And you will."

They continued west to SW 8th Avenue. Lynn hadn't quite pulled to a halt in front of the Delray Municipal Cemetery before Renee was out of the car. Standing alone at the side of the road, Renee peered through the moonlit darkness across the rows of graves, marked by plants or flowers only, that made up the newer section of the cemetery. This section was clearly differentiated from the old section, whose tombstones, long since rusted a deep orangy brown, spoke more of decay than tribute. "I don't see her," Renee whispered as Lynn came up behind her.

"She's probably over that way." Lynn pointed to a group of heavy cement vaults, also completely rusted over, which resembled large caskets and which sat aboveground, as if still awaiting burial.

"This is not my idea of a good time," Renee muttered, using humor to mask her fear, proceeding slowly forward. "Kathryn," she called out, hesitantly at first, and then louder. "Kathryn, where are you? You know I've never liked cemeteries." She laughed at her choice of words, feeling foolish and useless and inadequate, hearing Kathryn, as a child, tell her that cemeteries were very popular places: people were just dying to get in! "Come on, Kathryn. I'm allergic to all these plastic flowers." She turned to Lynn, her casual façade cracking. "Oh God, what if she can't hear me? What if she's already dead?"

"Keep walking," Lynn told her.

Renee continued slowly stepping around the rows of rusted vaults, terrified as she inched her way around each one that she would find her sister sprawled on the ground, bleeding her life away into the dull earth. How could she have said those things to her? And what was she going to say to her now?

"Renee . . ." Lynn's hand on Renee's elbow stopped her where she stood. Renee looked over at Lynn, then followed the direction of her gaze.

Kathryn was sitting beneath a giant gumbo-limbo tree, her head down, her back pressed against the tree's smooth silver bark, her legs splayed haphazardly out in front of her. For a minute, it was impossible to tell whether the still figure was alive or dead. Renee clutched Lynn's hand. The two women inched forward. The figure under the tree moved. Kathryn raised her head.

"Please go away," she said, her words clearly audible despite the lowness of her voice.

"Kathryn . . ."

"No!" Kathryn lifted the gun, which had been resting in her lap, and pressed it against her temple. "Go away."

"Please don't do this, Kathy."

Kathryn's eyes moved suspiciously from her sister to the woman standing beside her, clearly nonplussed by the appearance of this stranger. "Who are you?"

Lynn stepped forward, the moon catching the side of her face, highlighting her soft brown hair. "It's Lynn Schuster," she said, then: "Actually it was Lynn Keaton. We went to school together. I don't know if you remember."

"I remember. Hell of place for a high school reunion."

"Why don't we go someplace else."

"This is the end of the line."

"I think we could find somewhere better, somewhere we can talk."

"I don't want to talk."

"Please, Kathy," Renee urged, finding her voice. "Let us help you."

"I don't want your help. I don't deserve your help." Kathryn looked back at Lynn. "Did she tell you what I did?"

"It doesn't matter," Renee said. Oh, please God, don't say it, she was thinking. Not out loud. Don't say it.

"What do you mean, it doesn't matter? I slept with your husband. How can you say that doesn't matter?"

Renee found herself looking to Lynn for her reaction, but if Lynn felt anything—disgust, alarm, surprise—none of it showed in her face. "Honestly, Kathy," Renee cried, "it doesn't matter. It's not important."

"What are you talking about? How can you say it's not important? Philip is your whole life."

"No!" Why was she denying it? Philip *was* her whole life. Hadn't she spent the past six years *making* him her whole life?

"Yes, he is. Just like Arnie was my whole life. I deserve to die," she said, waving the gun recklessly, as if she were unaware of its existence.

"You don't," Lynn told her steadily.

"You never knew my husband, did you, Lynn?"

Lynn shook her head.

"No, I didn't think so. I met him just after we graduated from high school. He was a lot older than I was. He was down here on vacation. What can I say? He swept me off my feet." She laughed, temporarily lost in the memory. "We got married, moved to New York. We were married over twenty years. He took care of me. He did everything for me. We were always together. Just like our mother and father," she said, glancing back at Renee. "And then one night, he got up from the dinner table—I'd made this spicy meat loaf; I shouldn't have—and he keeled over, dead."

"Kathryn," Renee started, "how many times can you go over the same thing? It wasn't your fault."

Kathryn continued as if no one had spoken. "He got up from the dinner table and he keeled over, and he was dead. Just like that. And I looked at him lying there on the floor and I saw my whole world collapse. He'd looked after me for twenty years and suddenly I was alone. I felt frightened and desperate and angry."

"That's only natural."

"And I felt"—she looked around as if searching for a specific word—"relief." She said it, then gasped for air, her eyes darting between her sister and her former high school classmate, her hands lifting to the sides of her head, the gun simply another appendage, like an extra finger. Her voice became a dull monotone. "I saw him lying there and I felt . . . free. All those years of being slowly smothered to death . . . Oh God! Arnie loved me. He spent his life taking care of me. And I loved him. I really did."

"I know you did," Renee assured her, creeping closer.

"Then why did I feel that way? Why, when Arnie died, did I suddenly feel as if I'd gotten my own life back? As if I'd been given a second chance?"

"It's not unnatural to feel those things," Renee heard Lynn say as she crept still closer. "You were in a state of shock. All kinds of things go through your mind. Things you can't control."

"Not things like that."

"Exactly that," Lynn told her. "When my mother died, I felt the same anger, the same desperation and isolation. And relief. And not just relief because her suffering was over, because she hadn't really suffered, or at least she hadn't known she was suffering. It was my father and I who suffered the most during those last few years. I watched my beautiful mother turn into a virtual stranger. She became a willful child, and then not even a child. Something barely human. She didn't know who I was. She didn't know who *she* was. She kept asking the same pointless, dumb questions. I spent those last few years answering those same stupid questions over and over again, repeating the same things until I wanted to scream."

Renee heard the pain in Lynn's voice, saw her eyes fill with tears. "I was ashamed of her. I knew she couldn't help it. I knew it was something beyond her control. But I was still ashamed of her. I couldn't wait for her to die so it would be over and I could get on with my life. And I loved her! I loved her, but I was glad she was dead. Does that make me a bad person?"

"But you were strong," Kathryn protested. "Stronger than

I am. You made something of your life. You didn't destroy anyone else's."

"Neither did you." Lynn took a deep breath, not sure whether or not she should continue, then plunged ahead. "If Renee has problems in her marriage, then they were there long before you came along." Both women looked to Renee for confirmation.

Renee nodded. "Let me help you, Kathy," she pleaded gently. "Please let me help you. Don't block me out. You need me. *I* need *you.*"

"Why? So I can hurt you some more?" Kathryn looked from her sister to Lynn, her voice remarkably steady in light of what she was saying. "I slept with her husband, you know."

Lynn shrugged. "I just got out of bed with the husband of the woman my husband left me for." She watched Kathryn's eyes widen.

"Say that again," Kathryn said, and almost smiled.

"If you want the sordid details, you'll have to put down that gun and come with us. We make quite a pair. I'd say we have a lot to talk about."

The gun wavered in Kathryn's hand. "I never meant to hurt you," she cried, looking at her sister. "Please believe me. I never meant for it to happen. I wouldn't hurt you for the world. I love you."

Renee rushed to her sister's side and took her in her arms, feeling the gun drop to the ground with a sickening thud. She sensed Lynn at their side, pulling the weapon out of reach. She heard the sound of sirens, the dull echo of doors slamming, voices approaching, people running. Renee hugged her sister tighter to her chest and rocked her in her arms as she had when they were children. "I love you too," she whispered.

"Well? She's all right, I take it," Philip said as Renee walked through the front door of their apartment.

"She will be," Renee said flatly, brushing past him into the kitchen and pouring herself a tall glass of cold water. She drank it in one noisy gulp, then poured herself another. "The police questioned her, took her to the hospital. They checked her over pretty thoroughly there."

"Is that where she is now?"

"No. She's at Lynn's." He looked puzzled. "Lynn is a friend of mine." The word "friend" seemed to confuse him, so she clarified it further, put it into a word she thought he could understand. "A client." Renee stared at her husband with something approaching disbelief. "Did you really expect me to bring her back here?"

"I never know what to expect with you, Renee." His voice was ice cold, colder than the water she was drinking. Renee put the glass in the sink and walked into the living room, Philip right behind her. "First, Debbie and I come home to find out we're the talk of the building. The doorman can't wait to give us the news. 'Frantic phone calls,' he says. 'The police. Your sister is missing. She has a gun. She's going to kill herself.' We come upstairs. The place looks like it's been ransacked. Then Debbie tells me the two of you had a terrible fight earlier in the afternoon."

Renee approached the window and stared at the black ocean below. "How could you do it, Philip?" she asked quietly, all emotions drained. "How could you sleep with my sister? Not even rats foul their own nests."

"What are you talking about?"

"My sister tried to kill herself tonight. She put a loaded gun to her temple and almost pulled the trigger."

"And you blame me?"

"Why on earth would I blame you?"

"I guess it's only natural," he said, as if he were being generous. "It's been one hell of a night for you. You're angry. You're confused. You're upset. You're very tired. You look awful. It's only natural for you to take it out on the person closest to you."

"And who would that be?"

"Look, it's almost two o'clock in the morning. I suggest we get some sleep. You'll see things clearer in the morning."

"I doubt that."

"Renee, you know what happens when you're tired. You

say things you end up regretting. I'm urging you not to put our relationship in jeopardy because of a few ill-chosen words."

Renee stared at the man to whom she had been married for the past six years. As he always did when backed into a corner, he was putting their relationship on the line. Their whole marriage, he was telling her, could be jeopardized by what she said next.

Renee played back the six years of her marriage from the beginning, as if they had been recorded on videotape, fast-forwarding her life, trying to find the good spots, except that when she tried to stop the tape, to slow down for the good times, she found they had been too fleeting. There was nothing to slow down for. She stared at Philip. This was the man she had built her life around, the man she had convinced herself she couldn't live without.

Even now, after everything he had done, the thought that he might walk out on her sent her arm reaching for the side of the sofa. Why had she come back? Did she really think there might be something he could say that would change the way things were? She steadied herself and stared deep into his eyes. "You bastard," she said calmly.

"All right, Renee," he said, "if this is going to degenerate into name calling . . ." He started to leave the room.

"Don't you dare walk out on me."

"I certainly won't stay here and be abused."

"You'll stay in this room until I'm finished."

"I'd say you're finished now."

"Oh no, I'm just starting."

"Renee, as far as I'm concerned, this discussion is over. You're tired; you're upset. With good reason. I'm not trying to pretend that you don't have reasons . . ."

"That's very kind of you."

"But you'll escalate what's happened out of all proportion. You'll say things you'll regret in the morning. I know you, Renee. I know your pattern. You'll say things you'll wish you hadn't come daylight when it'll be too late to take them back, when the damage will have already been done. I don't want that to happen. I won't stand here and let you destroy our relationship."

"Me? You won't stand here and let *me* destroy our relationship?"

"I won't let you erase the memory of the past six years, of what we've meant to each other . . ."

She almost laughed. "I didn't know I had that kind of power."

"You have that kind of *anger*."

"And I shouldn't?"

"It's not healthy."

"So what you're saying is that whatever happens tonight is my responsibility."

"Yes, it will be, if you go any farther."

"Good," Renee said evenly. "It's about time I assumed some responsibility for my life, wouldn't you say?"

"I'd say it's time you got some sleep. See how you feel in the morning." Again he turned, about to leave.

"Don't you take another step," she called after him, her voice rising.

"Lower your voice." He indicated Debbie's room with his eyes.

"You'll stay here in this room until I've finished what I have to say. I warn you, if you try to leave, I'll follow you. I'll follow you from room to room, and if you leave this apartment, I'll follow you down the hall and into the lobby. Past the doorman. That'll give him something else to talk about. I'll even follow you into the street. I'll chase your car, if I have to. *Naked*, if I have to." The reference to his first wife was deliberate and could not be missed. For the first time, Renee understood the utter desperation that could drive a woman to such an act.

Philip turned to her and smiled derisively. "That would be a sight," he said cruelly, walking slowly back into the center of the room. "Go ahead, Renee. The thought of you running naked into the night screaming is enough to daunt any man. Say what you have to say. Wipe out all that stands in your way. To hell with the consequences."

"To hell with you!" Renee shot back. "It wasn't bad enough

that you had to sleep with every Alicia Henderson who crossed your path. That wasn't enough for you. You had to sleep with my sister!"

"All right, so I slept with your sister! It was nothing. It didn't mean anything."

"Oh God."

"Happy now that I said it? Make you feel better?"

Renee collapsed onto the sofa. "How could you? How could you do that to me? To her? You knew how fragile she was."

"Your sister was not the innocent victim you make her out to be."

"My sister turned to you for help. Her husband was dead. She felt guilty and lonely and confused. She didn't know which end was up."

"You underestimate her. She knew exactly which end was up. She knew exactly what she was doing."

"My sister almost killed herself tonight, and you have the nerve to tell me that she knew what she was doing. Do you feel no responsibility at all for what happened?"

"I won't accept the blame for your sister's actions."

"I don't care whether you accept it or not," Renee shouted. "What kind of doctor are you? What kind of person are you?"

"What's going on?" Debbie asked, appearing in the doorway, wiping the sleep out of her eyes. "What's all the yelling about? Did you find Kathryn?"

Renee stared at the innocent-looking face of the stepdaughter she had tried for six years to befriend, recalling Debbie's earlier questions. "How much more are you going to stand for?" she had demanded. "Why don't you just tell him to go to hell? Why don't you tell *me* to go to hell?"

Suddenly Renee smiled. "Go to hell," she said.

"Renee, for Christ's sake," Philip started.

"Get back into your room, Debbie, and stay there," Renee told the surprised girl.

Debbie automatically took several steps back. Philip's eyes moved from his wife to his daughter, slowly, carefully, as if he was afraid to make any sudden moves. "Go back to your room,

Debbie," Philip told her. "Kathryn is all right. Renee's just a bit upset."

"A bit . . ." Debbie's voice was incredulous.

"Go to your room, Debbie," Philip instructed forcefully.

"What'd *I* do?" Debbie asked, closing her bedroom door behind her.

"Don't ever talk to my daughter that way again," Philip warned.

"Don't tell me what to do."

"You want to talk to me that way, that's between us, but I won't tolerate your talking to Debbie that way."

"You won't have to."

"What's that supposed to mean?"

"It means I'm leaving." Renee heard the words escape her mouth before she realized she had even been thinking them. Surely they were too awful to think about. Surely she hadn't said them.

"You don't mean that."

"You sleep with half the women in this town, including my sister, and I'm just supposed to ignore it because it doesn't mean anything. You have spent six years undermining my success and my self-confidence and I'm supposed to sit here like a good little girl and thank you for it. I have no friends and no relationship with my partners, and I'm supposed to be thankful because you've chosen to stay with me. I've eaten myself into emotional oblivion, as your darling daughter would say, and I'm supposed to keep eating my chocolates and grow fat and actually feel grateful for my own demise." Renee looked at her husband, clearly astonished at what she was saying. Then she ran from the room.

"Renee, where are you going? You know none of that is true. You just acknowledged that those affairs meant nothing to me."

"What *does* mean anything to you?" Renee asked, running into the kitchen. "Does *anything*?"

"You do," he said simply.

"Bullshit!"

Renee tore open the refrigerator door, rummaging through

the bottom shelf. She quickly located the two large bags of miniature chocolate bars at the back of the fridge, and carried them to the sink, tearing open the first bag and watching the chocolate bars tumble one by one into the garburator. Then she turned on the water and flicked on the switch, listening as the machine ground the bars into mush.

"Renee, you'll break the damn thing . . ."

"Look at me!" she screamed, emptying the bag and running her hands down the length of her dark green shirt and pants. "I'm a mess!"

"And I suppose I'm responsible for that too?"

"No, you're not responsible. I'm the one. I did it," Renee shouted, pouring the contents of the second bag into the garburator. "I did it all by myself. I tried for six years to get you to love me, the same way I've tried all my life with my father, and this is where it got me."

"Don't compare me to your father."

"Why not? You're just like him. I've been a damn fool. What makes him so great that I have to beg him to love me? Am I so awful? Is he so wonderful? Are you?"

"Renee, I love you. I know you're too angry to see that now . . ."

"No, you don't love me. What you love is your power over me! You love it that you can turn a smart, capable woman into a quivering bowl of jelly every time she sees you. Listen to me! Everything I say is food-related."

Renee stared at her husband helplessly, even now hoping that he would somehow be able to reach into his magic bag of tricks and find the correct combination of words to release them all from this horrible spell, that he could somehow come up with the words that would make everything all right again.

Had they ever been all right? Did he really have this kind of power over her that even now she was waiting for him to make things right again simply because that's the way he said it should be?

"I think I've heard enough," he said instead. "I've told you how I feel. It obviously isn't enough for you. You said you were leaving; you made a decision. Now stick to it. It's what you want, isn't it?"

She recognized the tactic. He was calling her bluff, telling her that if she wanted him back now, she would have to back-track, to apologize, to admit she was wrong. Was she prepared to go that far? Could she really walk out? If only she were prepared to try harder, maybe she could still make it work. She was unloved because she was unlovable. She was nothing without him. Hadn't he just told her he loved her? What more did she want?

"Is it what *you* want?" she asked. Even now. Even now!

"What *I* want isn't important. It never has been."

"That's not true. It's been everything." Convince me I'm wrong. Convince me I can make it right. Don't let me leave. I take it back. I take everything back.

"By your own confession, you turned yourself into a choco-late-guzzling mess," he continued, seizing control of the con-versation. "Was that designed to make me happy? How do you think I felt going places with you? How do you think I felt knowing that everyone was snickering at me because my wife, the psychiatrist's wife, couldn't control as simple a thing as her appetite? Can you really blame me for looking elsewhere?" he asked, knowing instinctively that she had asked herself that question many times in the past. Not content with her capitu-lation, he was seeking no less than her total humiliation. He wanted her to beg. Would she? she wondered. "The woman I married wasn't a fat slob. She was slim and pretty and took care of her appearance. She had some pride, some self-respect. She didn't blame everyone else for her inadequacies. Well, what do you think of that assessment?"

"I think . . ." she began, then faltered under the threat of tears. "I think . . ."

"Face it, Renee, you haven't had a coherent thought in years."

"I think . . ."

"You *feel* . . ." he corrected, interrupting her again.

"I *think*," she said again, "that it gives you some sort of twisted pleasure to see me brought to my knees."

"Where you've always done your best work, I'll give you that." His face narrowed, as if he were a reflection in a fun-house mirror.

"I think that . . ."

"You *feel*," he insisted again.

Renee felt the threat of tears suddenly vanish. The image in the fun-house mirror disappeared. Her husband stood before her, tall and dark and handsome, just the way the storybooks had promised. "What I *feel* is anger," she said succinctly. "What I *think* is that you are a coldhearted, manipulative son of a bitch."

There was a moment's stunned silence before he spoke. "That's very good, Renee. I never realized before what advanced vocabularies you lawyers have. Is there anything else you want to say? Because if you're quite through, then I'd like to go to bed."

"There's something else," Renee said steadily.

He cocked his head, waiting.

"Go to hell," she said triumphantly, and walked out of their life together.

25

Gary arrived at the house on Saturday morning at nine o'clock sharp to pick up his children for the weekend. Lynn ushered him inside the front door, looking at her husband as if he were a pleasant acquaintance of fairly long-standing, but someone she didn't really know. She was surprised to discover that her primary feeling toward him wasn't anger, but rather indifference, and perhaps a mild curiosity, of the sort one might feel toward a stranger. Still, he was the father of her children, even though she understood he was no longer a part of her daily life.

"The kids aren't packed yet," she told him, knowing they were waiting anxiously behind their bedroom doors. "They wanted to make sure they were really going this time." Lynn broke off, seeing him flinch. She hadn't meant to reproach him. Obviously, she would still have to be very careful about choosing her words around Gary. She had no desire to hurt him any further. They had hurt each other enough.

"I thought we'd go to Disney World," Gary called out loudly, smiling broadly when he heard his children's joyful hoots. Nicholas ran into the room, grabbed his father around the waist, and squeezed tightly before running back to his room to pack. Gary laughed, his eyes drifting back toward Lynn's. "So, how are things?" he asked, tentatively, and Lynn could see he was still wrestling with his demons, not sure whether to be friends or foes.

"Things are fine." She motioned toward the living room. "Do you want to sit down?" He nodded, and she followed him into the green-and-white room, thinking that perhaps it was time to redecorate. Maybe she would redo the room in soft shades of peach and gray, the colors she had seen in Renee's office. She wondered briefly how Renee and Kathryn were doing. Renee had accompanied her sister back to New York the day before, after announcing that she had left Philip—left everything, including her white Mercedes—and was giving serious consideration to transferring her practice up North, a move she had always wanted to make. "You could take him for every cent he's got," Lynn had told her. "At least take what's rightfully yours." But Renee had smiled an enigmatic little half-grin and told her that sometimes it was worth anything just to be rid of them.

Renee's announcement had propelled Lynn into a few surprise moves of her own. After twelve years of front-line work for the Department of Social Services in Delray Beach, Lynn decided it was high time for a change. She submitted her resignation to an astonished Carl McVee, gave one month's notice, and accepted the job she had been offered with the Palm Beach County Board of Education. That done, she notified the child welfare agency in Sarasota and apprised them of her concerns regarding one of Sarasota's newest residents, one Keith Foster, vice president of Data Base International.

"I want to apologize," Gary was saying, staring into his lap. "It was a rotten thing I did, hauling you into your lawyer's office, threatening you with custody, reneging on our agreement."

"I'm not too proud of myself either," Lynn told him truthfully.

"Divorce brings out the best in people, I guess." He laughed bitterly. "I'm really sorry I hurt you, Lynn."

"I'm sorry I hurt you too."

They sat for several moments in silence, two well-meaning people who for a time had meant only to hurt each other.

"Are you still seeing Marc Cameron?" he asked.

"Does it matter?"

He shook his head. "Just curious." Lynn smiled at the word. "It would be ironic, wouldn't it? If things worked out between you and Marc while they fell apart between me and Suzette?"

Lynn studied his face, trying to remember the way she used to feel when she looked into his eyes. But the face, while handsome, almost kind, held no further allure for her. There was nothing behind it she wanted to see. "I'm sure things will work out between you and Suzette," she said.

Again he shook his head. "Maybe. At any rate, we've decided to cool it for a while. Take a break. Sort things out." He looked toward the picture window, at the silver-framed photograph of the family he had left. "She lied to me," he whispered, almost to himself. "I guess that's what hurts the most."

Nicholas raced into the room, his overnight bag banging against his side. "I'm ready."

"Where's your sister?"

"Getting her toothbrush. I already have mine."

"Good for you."

Megan walked slowly into the room, as if she were afraid it was filled with dangerous land mines. And maybe it was. "I'm all packed."

Gary got to his feet. "Great. Then we're ready to go."

"What are you going to do, Mom?" Megan asked, as if she were afraid to leave Lynn alone, sensing that her eagerness to spend the weekend with her father was somehow a betrayal of her mother.

"I'll be fine," Lynn told her.

"But what are you going to do?"

"I'm sure your mother has plans," Gary said.

"You want to come with us?" Nicholas persisted.

"No, sweetheart," Lynn said gently. "This is your weekend

with your father. You go and have a good time. Don't worry about me." She hugged her children close before releasing them, then watched them run down the front walk to Gary's car.

"I'll have them back tomorrow night around eight o'clock. Is that all right with you?"

"Fine. Drive carefully."

He nodded, a sad smile creeping onto his face. "Have a good weekend."

"You too."

"Come on, Daddy," Nicholas shouted from the car.

Lynn stood in the doorway to her house. If today was really the first day of the rest of her life, she thought, what was she going to do with it? The security of her old job was gone; she didn't have a husband; she didn't even have anything in the house for lunch. What the hell, she shrugged, feeling better than she had in years. Sometimes you just have to take a chance.

Lynn pulled her car into the driveway of Marc Cameron's apartment building. "Could you buzz Marc Cameron for me, please?" she asked the young doorman, who smiled at her as if she were speaking a foreign language. "Marc Cameron," Lynn repeated. "He's in apartment 403."

"No Cameron in apartment 403," the doorman, who was obviously new, said, checking his list of tenants.

"He's renting from the regular tenant."

The doorman, who was tall and slim and sandy-haired and not more than twenty, flipped through the pages of his register slowly. "Oh yeah, here it is. He's subletting from Joel Sanders. Apartment 403. You're right."

"Can you buzz him for me, please."

"Sure thing." His hand lifted languorously to buzz the apartment. Nobody answered. "You want me to phone him?" Lynn nodded quickly, hoping to spur him on, but his fingers pressed the buttons of the telephone as if he had arthritis. Lynn fought the urge to wrest the phone from his hands. Could he possibly be any slower? "No one home," came the lazy drawl after at least half a dozen rings. Lynn thanked him, about to leave. "Is he a tall guy, reddish-blond hair, beard?"

"Yes."

The doorman nodded, pleased to have put a face to the name. "He went out a couple of hours ago."

"Did he say where he was going?"

"Didn't say nothin'," the doorman told her. "You want to leave a message?"

Lynn thought for several seconds, deciding it would take too long. "No. No message."

She got back in her car and turned it toward the beach. It was just as well Marc hadn't been home. His absence had saved her from making a complete fool of herself. What did she want to get involved with someone like Marc Cameron for anyway? A soon-to-be-divorced writer with two sons and an ailing father. Just because he made her laugh? Because he challenged her, dared her to be things she hadn't been in years? Because he was caring and intelligent and just looking at him filled her with joy? What kind of reasons were those? Where was the security in loving a man just because he made her feel good?

She stopped the car. What was the matter with feeling good! Since when was security a substitute for love?

She executed an abrupt U-turn in the middle of the crowded street, the cars around her erupting in angry horn blasts. Instantly she knew where to find Marc. Hadn't he invited her along?

She drove north on Dixie, then west on Lake Drive, hoping Marc would still be there by the time she arrived. The streets were filled with Saturday-afternoon traffic, signaling that the summer was almost at an end. Soon "the season" would be upon them. The "snowbirds" would flock down, followed in predictable holiday bursts by the "snowflakes," fleeing the colder climes. Traffic would be impossible. The beaches would be filled to overflowing and she would hear the usual grumbles from dissatisfied couples as she passed them at the water's edge, complaining about the lack of sunshine, the undependability of the Florida weather, the amount of tar that regularly marred the miles of sand. She laughed. They should come down in the summer she thought. Summer in Delray Beach. There was nothing quite like it.

She passed Military Trail, looking for the cutoff to the road leading to Halcyon Days. Marc had said he'd be visiting his father. He'd invited her along. Yes, but that was then, and a lot could happen in five days. A lot *had* happened.

Gary had said he and Suzette had decided to cool things for awhile. It was possible that Suzette had called Marc and begged his forgiveness, pleaded for him to come back. Would he? Would she burst into Marc's father's room only to find Suzette at his side?

She recognized the car before she saw the driver. The baby blue Lincoln convertible turned off the private road onto Lake Drive and into the traffic going east, the opposite direction. The white top of the car was in place and Lynn watched from a distance of half a block as the driver fiddled with the buttons, the top of the car suddenly lifting and pulling back, folding in on itself like a giant accordion. The driver of the car, license plate PEACHES, smiled broadly, his teeth flashing from behind his beard, his hands tapping out the tune his radio was blasting into the early afternoon sunshine. He looked casually at the cars headed in the opposite direction, his eyes not fixing on any of them, his mind obviously focused on something only he could see.

Lynn's car inched slowly forward. What was she going to do? She couldn't make another U-turn in the middle of all this traffic. She could open her window and scream, hope he'd hear her above the noise of his radio. Look at me, she willed, as their cars drew closer together. Look at me. I'm over here.

Marc lifted his hands into the air and stretched, closing his eyes.

"No, damn it, open them," Lynn said out loud. "I'm over here."

He rolled his head back, then slowly lifted it up again, turning lazily, without thought, in her direction.

"I'm over here," she said again, as his eyes came to rest on hers.

The car behind her honked loudly. She looked ahead. The cars were moving. She was being urged, none too gently, to follow.

In one smooth, continuing flow, Lynn threw her car into park, pulled the key from the lock, and opened her car door. The cars behind her honked furiously. "What's going on?" somebody yelled. "Where the hell are you going?"

She watched Marc's smile grow wide as she approached his car, until it filled his entire face. He reached over quickly and pushed open the door on the passenger side of the blue Lincoln. Savoring the moment, Lynn slowly slid into the seat beside him and closed her eyes.